Vengeful

by

Rosemary Kubli

The Femme Fatale Series

Cover Art by *Teddi Black*

The Wild Rose Press, Inc.
PO Box 708
Adams Basin, NY 14410-0708
Visit us at www.thewildrosepress.com

Publishing History
First Edition, 2026
Trade Paperback Print ISBN 978-1-5092-6335-6
Digital ISBN 978-1-5092-6336-3

The Femme Fatale Series
Published in the United States of America

Dedication

To all the book club friends I've made throughout this incredible journey. Your literary insights have been invaluable.

Prologue

Siena
Mid-October 2023

The last time she stood this close to Matthew Kramer, he'd been lying on his back, naked and unconscious, with one wrist handcuffed to his bed.

Although six years had passed, she remembered that afternoon as though it were yesterday. How she'd staged the scene, then wiped the bedroom clean of her fingerprints. The scornful good-bye kiss she'd blown to Matthew as she exited his bedroom. The way her gaze lingered on the portrait of Matthew's wife as she sauntered through their living room. The finality of the lock clicking into place as she yanked the apartment door closed behind her.

While riding the elevator down to the building's lobby, she'd second-guessed the sanity of leaving Matthew in such a precarious situation. Then again, he hadn't been the first man she'd drugged and abandoned. Matthew would be fine, she assured herself.

Well, physically, anyway.

The mild sedative she'd slipped into his wine would wear off in a few hours. Besides, he'd said his wife was expected home by early evening. She wasn't, after all, completely heartless; she'd just wanted to do Matthew's wife a favor. If Alva Kramer wasn't already aware she was married to a weasel, it was high time someone brought that ugly fact to her attention.

She only wished she could have been in the room to witness firsthand the expression on Matthew's face when his wife entered their bedroom and found the bastard grunting and stretching in a desperate attempt to grab the handcuff keys she had the courtesy to leave on the nightstand…although just out of his reach. What bullshit story had he fed his dear wife when she questioned his state of undress, the handcuffs, the red lipstick stain on the rim of the half-empty wine glass, the woman's lacey black bra and panties strewn across their bedsheets? And why, *oh why*, were the $300,000 diamond earrings her father had given her to wear on their wedding day out of the safe and sitting atop her dresser?

For months afterward, she'd followed online news of their messy separation and subsequent divorce, searching for the slightest mention of Alva's gratitude to the mysterious woman who opened her eyes to the fact that her marriage to Matthew Kramer was a sham.

If only Mrs. Kramer hadn't gotten around to writing Matthew out of her will before she succumbed to her chronic illness the following year.

If only she, the woman who'd portrayed herself as a tax accountant from Virginia named Ellen Randall, had noticed the hidden camera lens that was recording every detail of the vile deed she performed in the Kramers' bedroom that momentous afternoon.

If only she and Matthew Kramer hadn't by chance crossed paths last evening for a second time.

But all those events *had* happened. And so, here Matthew was, standing before her, threatening to ruin her cushy life just as she'd destroyed his. He'd waited six long years to use that incriminating video footage against her. Today he was prepared to launch his plan for revenge.

Chapter 1

Siena
Six weeks earlier

"And the winner is...elevator number four!" announced the guy wearing the pork pie hat. He slung his arm around his friend's shoulders and made a half-hearted attempt to stifle a laugh. "Oh, man, Scotty. That's rough," he said, fist-bumping the third man in their group with his free hand. "Three nights in a row. Ouch!"

"Stop rubbing it in," Scotty grumbled. As the loser, according to the three friends' agreement, he was stuck picking up their bar tabs for the remainder of the evening.

"Seriously, you guys," Scotty's wife said as the three couples sauntered toward the elevator farthest to their right. "This is the last time you're playing that stupid Elevator Roulette game. Our bill for this cruise is ridiculous enough as it is."

Another of the wives, the one with the wiry red hair, spoke her mind. "I agree with Beth. No more games. And each couple is paying for their own drinks tonight."

"Ah, come on," the third man chimed in. "A bet is a bet."

Elevator four's doors opened to reveal a chic couple standing closely together, as if the car were filled with passengers and they'd needed to squeeze their two bodies into a space large enough to accommodate only one. The woman was saying in a matter-of-fact tone, "I just wanted to enjoy the sunset from our balcony one last time."

The couple exchanged good evenings with the group of friends as they stepped out onto Deck 5. Still within earshot, the man was heard saying, "I get that, sweetheart. But let me remind you, there's a fine line between being fashionably late and being downright rude." His response could have been construed as a reprimand, but his playful smile and his hand sliding down the back of her right hip suggested otherwise.

While entering the elevator, Pork Pie Hat exclaimed *Yowzah!* under his breath at the same time Scotty let out a slow, sultry whistle. The women in the group traded wide-eyed glances and mouthed silent *Wows*.

Beth punched the button for Deck 17. "Did you see the size of those diamonds on her finger?"

"Lucky girl," the redhead commented. She glanced at her husband. "I sure hope you look that good when you're his age."

Pork Pie Hat snickered. "Are you kidding? PJ wishes he looked that good now."

Had the man overheard the redhead's comment, he would have been flattered that in his mid-60s he was still charming twenty-somethings with his classic good looks. Tall and debonair in his custom-tailored navy-blue suit, he was a self-assured man of wealth and prominence. His firm, athletic physique gave him a youthful appearance despite the speckles of gray winding through his dark brown hair. While an undergrad at Harvard, his fraternity brothers had often described him as movie-star handsome. The label rang true to this day.

In her heels, the stylish woman wearing the 4-carat cluster of diamonds on her ring finger, was nearly the same height as the man. Her above-the-knee, spaghetti-strapped cocktail dress accentuated her seductive figure and showcased her long, toned legs. The loose waves of her shoulder-length blonde hair framed a face of incomparable beauty, as though her features had been chiseled by a master sculptor. No stranger to turning heads, she had learned at a young age to use her beauty to her advantage—even when her intentions were oftentimes less than honorable.

Navigating their way through the crowd of passengers clogging the hallways, the couple ignored the lingering stares and whispered comments that buzzed around them. Their 30-year age difference was an endless source of controversy to which they'd grown accustomed. While touring Europe over the summer, they'd heard every speculation imaginable. Occasionally, to spice things up—and usually after consuming a liberal quantity of wine—they'd role play different characters: a renowned artist and his model; a film producer and the star of his latest movie; a call girl and her john. They got a kick out of giving the tongues an extra something to wag about.

After three months abroad, they had boarded the Majestic Queen in Denmark and begun their journey home. Having sailed the Scandinavian waters throughout the spring and summer months, the luxury ocean liner departed from the Port of Copenhagen at the end of August and set out on an itinerary known in the industry as a repositioning cruise. Her voyage included stops in

Norway, Ireland, and the Azores before setting off for North America. During the vibrantly colorful fall season, she would journey along the New England coastline and to the islands of eastern Canada, then head south to spend the winter months in the warm waters of the Caribbean Sea. Next April, the ship would sail off to Denmark and begin the cycle again.

The couple entered the Tudor Dining Room where Maître d' Carlos Rivas, imposing in his black tie and dinner jacket, greeted them. "Good evening, Dr. Woodward, Mrs. Woodward," he said with a cordial smile. "The captain is expecting you. Right this way, please."

As they followed Rivas to the Captain's Table, Jonathan whispered into Siena's ear, "I love hearing you referred to as *Mrs. Woodward.*"

Clutching Jonathan's hand, Siena intertwined her fingers with his. "Not half as much as I do," she whispered back.

The ship's captain, Giovanni Camposano, interrupted the table's dinner conversation. "Ah, here is our happy couple now. *Buonasera!* Welcome!" He rose and air-kissed Siena first on her right cheek, then her left.

The Maître d' assisted Siena into the chair to the captain's right as Jonathan claimed the empty seat next to her. "*Bon appetit,*" Rivas wished the entire table before taking his leave.

The head waiter opened a leather-bound menu and handed it to Siena, then repeated the courtesy with Jonathan. He next removed a bottle of champagne from the ice bucket placed at the side of the table and, after popping the cork, proceeded to fill each of the guests' flutes.

Rosemary Kubli

"I hope we didn't keep you waiting," Jonathan said to the captain. He glanced around the table and extended his and Siena's apology to their dinner companions.

"A few moments, at most," Camposano replied, speaking for the group. "But we understand. You are, after all, newlyweds." He grinned and winked knowingly at Siena.

Siena replied with a brazen smile. "Think what you may, but we were simply enjoying the gorgeous sunset from our balcony."

"The perfect setting for romance, yes?" The captain raised his champagne flute. "A toast," he proclaimed in his powerful tenor voice laced with his native Italian accent. "To the newlyweds! *Viva l'amore!*"

"*Viva l'amore!*" echoed the guests seated around the table.

The newlyweds clinked their glasses together and sipped in celebration. Jonathan leaned close to Siena, and whispered, "*Viva l'amore, Bellissima,*" as his lips brushed against hers. How did he always make her arms erupt with goosebumps, as though every kiss were their first?

"Ah, such love, it warms the heart," Camposano said. He signaled for the head waiter and opened his menu. "We are all hungry, yes? Later, we will make more toasts, but for now let us order our food."

While the wait staff served their appetizers, the captain extended his hand and lightly touched Siena's arm. "Mrs. Woodward—"

"Please, call me Siena."

Camposano smiled. "Siena, our other guests met each other before you and your husband arrived, so let us catch you both up on who is who."

The captain first introduced the couple to his left, the distinguished and reserved Heinrich and Elsa Werner who appeared to be in their early-50s. Elsa, Siena had observed, preferred to take a back seat, allowing Heinrich to do most of the talking. Heinrich informed Siena and Jonathan that he was CEO of his family-owned, world-renowned brewery in Germany, a business his ancestors had begun more than five hundred years ago. He also explained that he and his wife had been invited to dine at the Captain's Table that evening because they were booked in the Presidential Suite, the most exclusive accommodation on the ship. Siena, while pretending to be duly impressed, took an instinctive dislike to the couple. Heinrich's arrogance annoyed her. Elsa's penetrating stare set her nerves on end.

Next to Elsa Werner were the 70-ish Frank and Marion Bryson, originally from Alabama, currently residing in Ft. Lauderdale. Frankie and Mare, as they called each other, were being honored for the number of days they'd spent cruising—a whopping 4,018—making them the passengers onboard with the most days spent at sea. And, as the braggy Mare Bryson reminded everyone, those were just the number of days they'd sailed with the cruise line that operated the Majestic Queen. Siena responded with amazed congratulations while pondering how they handled the practical side of their lives while on a seemingly endless vacation.

Wedged between Frankie Bryson and Jonathan was the middle-aged couple from Canada, Eleanor and T.J. Gladstone. A few nights earlier, Eleanor explained with much bravado, she'd screamed with excitement when the casino manager drew her ticket from a barrel, making her the lucky winner of a free 7-day Caribbean cruise for two. "Of course," Eleanor complained, her mouth twisted into a grimace, "I'm not actually getting anything for free since I've gambled away enough money during *this* trip to pay for my 'free' cruise twice over." Winning the prize and gambling were the only topics of discussion that seemed to spark Eleanor's interest. Siena made a mental note to avoid conversing with her.

Heinrich Werner spoke up. "I'm curious, Captain Camposano. What does your future hold? Is there a rank higher than captain, or have you peaked?"

Camposano washed down his last bite of food with a drink from his water goblet. "At the top of the ladder, Herr Werner, is the rank of commodore, and that is the position I seek to achieve."

"Ooh…*Commodore* Campasano," Mare Bryson said, drawing out each syllable slowly in her melodic Southern drawl. "A sexy title for an even sexier man," she added with a titter that raised several eyebrows.

"Well," Camposano replied politely, "let us hope my wife thinks so."

The conversation screeched to an uncomfortable halt. *I guess I'm not the only one*, Siena thought, *who needs a moment to recover from Mare's inappropriate comment*. Conveniently, the assistant waiters arrived at just the right moment to clear away the empty appetizer plates and serve the entrees. As they all dug into their food, Frankie Bryson turned his attention to Siena and Jonathan.

"I'm curious about our newlyweds," Frankie said. "Jonathan, if you don't mind me being nosy, I'd like to hear about how you and your lovely wife met."

Jonathan wiped his mouth with his napkin and cleared his throat. "Now, that is an interesting story." He glanced at Siena, his lips curling into a roguish grin as he covered her hand with his own. Siena gave him a hesitant smile and lowered her gaze. While she trusted her husband of six hours to be discreet, portions of their history—the parts she trusted Jonathan to tactfully avoid sharing—were still fresh enough to sting her with guilt.

"Until my retirement a few years ago," Jonathan explained to the group, "I taught English Literature at a university near Boston and Siena was working at Willow's Auction House in Manhattan. Being in such vastly different fields and with so much distance between us, you'd assume our paths would never cross, but Siena and I believe fate brought us together.

"You see, I am an avid collector of antiques, and a few years ago Willow's was auctioning an item I was interested in acquiring. Siena was assigned to be my liaison and assisted me in bidding by phone during the live auction. She called me to have an introductory, get-to-know-the-client conversation, and we immediately clicked. After that, our phone calls became increasingly longer and more frequent until we finally arranged to meet in person." He gazed lovingly into Siena's eyes. "The second Siena stepped out of the taxi she took my breath away. The rest, as they say, is history."

Mare Bryson sighed. "My goodness. That's a tale right out of a romance novel."

"Well, Jonathan," T.J. Gladstone chuckled, "sounds like you've got some bucks. No wonder such a beautiful young woman was attracted to you."

Eleanor jabbed her husband's arm with her elbow. "T.J., really!"

Gladstone shrugged his shoulders. "Well, I mean, he is a hell of a lot older than her."

Eleanor tsked and rolled her eyes, obviously embarrassed by her husband's frankness.

Siena leaned forward and, glancing past Jonathan, spoke directly to the couple. "Don't worry, Eleanor," she said. "We're not offended."

"Truthfully, T.J.," Jonathan explained, "I'm a few years older than Siena's father and she is younger than both of my children. Age, we've come to realize, is irrelevant when two people are as happy together as we are."

"A beautiful sentiment," the captain commented. "My wife will be boarding the ship tomorrow when we dock in Boston. You remind me of how much I have been looking forward to being with her during our next sailing."

The dinner conversation paused while everyone went back to enjoying their entrees. Then, out of the blue, Elsa Werner mysteriously blurted out, "You have told us only half the story." Her eyes bore into Jonathan.

Frowning, Jonathan glanced up at Elsa. "Pardon me?"

Heinrich Werner stepped in to explain. "My wife is of Romanian ancestry. Gypsies. She is known to have a sixth sense."

"The eyes are the windows to the soul," Elsa said. "Your eyes shine with happiness, but your soul is not at peace."

Elsa Werner had the table's rapt attention. Jonathan set his fork down and leaned back in his chair. His mouth tightened as he glared at Elsa with narrowed eyes. "Go on," he said.

"Someone close to you has been dishonest," Elsa continued. "You have a forgiving heart, but you must be careful. The person who you trust will betray you again."

Siena's left eye twitched. Elsa's fortune-telling powers were eerily accurate, and they'd hit too close to home. When Jonathan was asked how he and Siena became a couple, he'd shared only what they both wanted people to know: the sweet side of their story. The other half was, and would always remain, her and Jonathan's closely guarded secret.

The captain jumped in and tactfully redirected the conversation. "So, what has each of you enjoyed most during your voyage on our magnificent ship?"

****

Siena and Jonathan sauntered into the piano bar for a nightcap. While Jonathan made idle chatter with their cocktail server, Siena gazed pensively at her wedding ring. For three months, she'd been living a glorious dream. She'd had Jonathan all to herself and each new day had been as magical as the day before. Tomorrow, they would return to reality. She couldn't help but worry over the issues that awaited her.

Jonathan raised his martini glass in a mock toast. "Penny for your thoughts."

Siena lifted her own drink. "Sorry. It's been a long day."

"You've been awfully quiet since dinner. Did the Werner woman upset you?"

"Maybe." *Yes.*

"Please don't tell me you believed her." Siena responded with a half-hearted shrug. "Well, I considered what she said to be nonsense. I've already erased Elsa Werner from my mind, and I think you should do the same."

Siena sipped her martini. She wanted to believe

Jonathan, but she had always possessed a keen intuition and easily read his body language. Although he was good at offering soothing reassurances in a calm voice, his bouncing knee and tense muscles betrayed the fact that he paid more credence to Elsa Werner's ominous warning than he was willing to admit. The woman with centuries of Romani blood coursing through her veins had spoken accurately. Someone *had* recently deceived Jonathan, had played tricks on him, attempted to rob him of assets valued in the millions. And who was to say that same person, under dire circumstances, wouldn't deceive him a second time?

What worried Siena the most was that she and Jonathan both knew the dishonest person in Jonathan's life was her.

Chapter 2

Jonathan

Jonathan drummed his fingers against the top of the antique mahogany desk in his library. Three minutes into a video call with his children and Veronica had already launched herself into a full-blown, melodramatic frenzy. He stared at her image on the screen of his laptop and waited for her hissy fit to fizzle out. History had taught him to play the waiting game, but this evening she was wearing out his patience. He glanced at the window on the right side of his laptop screen and caught his son Patrick rolling his eyes.

"Daddy, this was a life-changing event for all of us. You knew that! Why would you—"

"Veronica, please. You're making a mountain out of a molehill."

"A molehill? That's what you call getting married to a woman you barely know? *A molehill?*"

"I didn't mean—"

"Ohmygod!" Veronica slapped her hand against her chest. "Was this a shotgun wedding?" She leaned closer to her computer screen, a distraught expression coloring her face. "Please don't tell me Marie is pregnant."

"Her name is Siena," Jonathan reminded his daughter with thinning patience. Speaking of Siena…Jonathan craned his neck to check if she was still in the library's hallway. If Siena were smart, she'd have escaped to a part of the house where Veronica's voice couldn't be heard. Assuming there was one.

Veronica huffed and fluttered her eyelids. "Marie. Siena. Whatever she calls herself these days." She glared at Jonathan through the computer's camera lens. "Well, is she?"

"Is she what?"

"Pregnant! You know, like Mommy was."

Jonathan heaved a short, exasperated sigh. "No, she is not pregnant, although I'd be delighted if she were. Believe it or not, Veronica, I married Siena because I love her. And I'd appreciate you not dragging your dear mother into the conversation."

Sighing, Veronica sat back and gazed up at the ceiling. "How am I going to explain to my girls that you got married without one single person from your family being present? They'll be crushed, especially Phoebe. She spent the entire summer jotting down ideas to make her grandfather's wedding a big, spectacular event, and now it's all water under the bridge."

"Would you like me to call Gwen and Phoebe? I'd love to personally share my good news with them. As a matter of fact, Siena and I could call them together—"

"No! I'll make sure Brian is with me when I tell them. He's much better at dealing with their histrionics than I am."

Poor Brian. Is it any wonder he works seven days a week?

"Maybe you should let Brian do all the talking," Jonathan suggested. "I've told you repeatedly, your emotional outbursts aren't a healthy example for the girls."

Veronica pouted. At long last, she'd run out of steam. Jonathan's eyes wandered across the screen and studied his son's solemn face. Jonathan's bigger concern, more than Veronica's theatrics, was the lack of response he'd received from Patrick.

"Patrick, you haven't had much to say. Dare I ask—are you happy for us?"

"Sorry, Dad, but I can't stay on the call any longer. It's past Oliver's bedtime and, since I have surgeries scheduled for early tomorrow morning, I need to get to bed soon myself. I'll talk to you another time. Good night, Veronica." With that, Patrick's video feed vanished from the screen.

Veronica smirked. "Well, Daddy, that was as blatant a response as I've ever heard." She glanced down at her cell phone. "I need to go, too. Brian's calling. I can't wait to hear his reaction to this news. But don't for one second think this conversation is over. I'll talk with you tomorrow."

Jonathan's laptop screen went blank. He logged out, sat back in his desk chair, and swiveled to the side. Crossing his legs, he admired his flower garden through the bank of windows on the far side of the library. His gardener, Javier, who was blessed with a God-given talent and a remarkable green thumb, kept the plants healthy and the flowers blooming even this late into the summer. Although Jonathan would never turn down a compliment on the beauty of his landscaping, Javier was the person who was due all the credit.

Jonathan and his late wife, Patricia, had enjoyed an extensive garden on the estate they'd received as a wedding gift from Jonathan's parents, the home he'd later gifted to Veronica and Brian when they married.

Back then, Patricia did much of the gardening herself and insisted that Veronica and Patrick be right beside her. She'd taught their children the names of the plants and flowers, and about the care and attention each required. They'd chased butterflies during the day and caught fireflies at night. Patricia, being the art professor that she was, would oftentimes set up easels and give their children lessons in landscape painting. Veronica pouted over not being as talented an artist as her mother. Patrick quickly lost interest and ran off in search of frogs.

Jonathan, being the literature professor that he was, would sit on a garden bench and read to their son and daughter. A person was never too young, he'd insisted, to be introduced to the American classics. Veronica's attention span was usually short-lived, and she'd be off to phone her friends and catch up on the latest gossip. Patrick, however, had soaked up every word Jonathan uttered. Patrick's interest in literature was just one of the many traits he shared with his father. Veronica's personality, on the other hand, was nothing like her brother's nor either of her parents'. Jonathan speculated that she'd inherited a latent gene from a black sheep ancestor who had intentionally been omitted from either his or Patricia's family tree.

Following Patricia's sudden death, Jonathan was left on his own to finish molding their children into young adults. At the time, Patrick was away at boarding school and Veronica was about to enter college. Becoming a single parent was a challenge, but their new circumstances made Jonathan's close bond with his children even tighter. Nothing, they'd all agreed, would ever come between them.

Then, Jonathan met Siena Ricci.

As the fading sunlight deepened the shadows, a gloominess permeated Jonathan's library. He gazed out at the garden, lines of worry creasing his forehead. In the twenty-three years since Patricia's death, he'd discussed with Veronica and Patrick his desire to remarry numerous times, and they always had his back. He couldn't help the fact that the one woman he'd at last fallen head-over-heels in love with was a reformed thief and con artist.

High heels clicked against the hardwood floor of the hallway outside the library door. Jonathan glanced to his left as Siena entered the room. The faint scent of her perfume, her confident stride, her beauty—hell, her mere presence—filled him with a mixture of pleasure and desire he'd never experienced with any other woman, including Patricia. Was forgiving Siena's past indiscretions and asking her to marry him foolish, reckless, even crazy? Probably. But Jonathan was a man who had never let anything stand in the way of getting what he wanted, and he was willing to sacrifice just about anything to satisfy his craving for Siena.

If only he could make his children understand his obsession with her.

Jonathan extended his hand as Siena sauntered toward him.

"So," she asked, concerned brows raised over her curious brown eyes, "how'd it go?"

****

Siena

"You did what?"

Of all the drama queens Siena had ever met, Veronica deserved top billing. Siena could understand how the news of her and Jonathan's impulsive decision to marry on a cruise ship while crossing the Atlantic Ocean would come as a shock, especially since Jonathan's family was still getting used to the announcement of their engagement, but did Veronica need to respond with such an ear-piercing screech? The rant that followed was classic Veronica—loud, long, and entirely self-centered.

Dear God, how could anyone talk that long without taking a breath?

Jonathan must have been pondering the same question. He'd interrupted and accused Veronica of making a mountain out of a molehill, which only served to fuel the fire.

Nice try, Jonathan.

How was it possible that a calm, introspective man like Jonathan could produce such an egotistical, combative busybody? Patrick, on the other hand, hadn't spoken a word other than to say *Hello* and *Welcome back* at the onset of the call. True, Veronica wasn't giving anyone else much room to wedge in even one word, but Patrick's reticence worried Siena more than Veronica's non-stop blathering.

While Siena's rapport with Veronica was as rocky as a toddler taking his first steps, her history with Patrick was tenuous at best. In the scam Siena attempted to pull against the Woodward family last year, Veronica had merely been an intrusive bystander. Jonathan had fed her a sweetened version of Siena's background, so she was oblivious to the truth about the unsavory extracurricular activities that comprised much of Siena's history.

Patrick on the other hand had been used as a pawn in the scheme, and Siena—or, more accurately, her identical twin Jacqueline—had hurt him deeply. His lack of congratulations and stone-cold silence spoke volumes. Unlike his father, Patrick was not yet ready to forgive and forget. Hell, he might never put last year's events behind him. In all honesty, Siena couldn't blame him for carrying a grudge. She wasn't all that certain she would ever be able to forgive herself for the harm she and Jacqueline had caused, especially if they'd created a permanent fissure in Patrick and Jonathan's relationship.

Coming between the man you love and his family doesn't speak well of your marriage, does it, Siena?

Caught up in her musings, Siena hadn't noticed Jonathan's call with Veronica and Patrick had ended. She glanced down the hallway. Jonathan was gazing out the library windows, seemingly lost in thought. She wandered toward the library, the click-clacking of her heels against the wood floor exaggerated by the stillness of the evening. Jonathan turned and gazed into her eyes, his loving smile and outstretched hand beckoning her.

"So, how'd it go?" she asked as Jonathan drew her onto his lap.

****

Veronica

"So, how'd it go?" Brian asked his wife after she explained that her father had called to say he was back from his extended tour of Europe.

"How did what go?" Veronica sniped. "His ridiculously long vacation, or the phone call?"

"Well, both, I guess."

"The vacation, I'm told, was fabulous." Veronica rose from her chair and stomped out of their home office with Bailey, the family's calico, scurrying behind. "Who wouldn't have a grand time living in a Tuscan villa for the entire month of June, and then hopscotching across

Europe for the rest of the summer? Are you on your way home?"

"Yes." The two restaurants Brian and Veronica Lambert owned and operated, one in Boston and one in their hometown of Burgess just west of the city, were closed for business on Sunday evenings, making Sunday Brian's short day. "I'm bringing home pork tenderloin with a side of grilled veggies, and lobster ravioli. I also have a Caesar salad that we can share."

Veronica entered the kitchen and flipped on the pendant lights over the island. Owning two restaurants while getting a third one up and running out on the Cape was a pain in the ass most of the time, but having a well-known chef prepare dinner for you every night sure beat the hell out of cooking for yourself. However, this evening she was considering a liquid dinner over pork and ravioli. "As yummy as that all sounds, my stomach is too queasy to even think about food right now." She opened the wine cooler and selected a bottle of Reisling.

"What did your father say that has you so upset?"

Veronica switched the phone to speaker mode and set it on the countertop. As she peeled away the foil from the neck of the wine bottle, she vented her grievance. "It's more what he's done than what he said."

"Why? What's he done?"

"Oh, Brian, I just can't believe it. He went and married that blonde gold digger on the last day of their cruise. I'm…I'm still in shock. It makes me sick to talk about it." Several seconds passed without a response. "Brian? Did I lose you?"

"No, I'm still here. I don't see what the big deal is. Your father's been in love with Siena for over a year now, and he'd already asked her to marry him before they left for Italy. At his age, he probably thinks he doesn't have a whole lot of time to waste, so why wait?"

Veronica selected a corkscrew from the ceramic crock sitting atop the island. "Isn't it just like you to side with Daddy over me." Clenching her jaw, she twisted the screw into the cork with the ferociousness of a wild animal attacking its prey.

Brian sighed. "Oh, come off it, Veronica! What's upsetting you more—that Jon married a woman who punches all your jealousy buttons, or that you weren't there to control every aspect of their wedding? Did I just hear a cork pop?"

Veronica ignored Brian's questions. She opened the cupboard behind her and grabbed a wine goblet. "When will you be home?"

"In about fifteen minutes. Please go easy on the wine. After a hectic day, I don't feel like spending the night cleaning wine vomit out of the carpet."

"I'm not making any promises," she told him before disconnecting the call. She absolutely hated it when Brian lectured her. He knew damned well she wasn't inclined to lose herself in a bottle of wine, or any liquor for that matter, when she was upset. The chances she'd even finish the glass she was pouring were slim to none. She was merely using the alcohol to emphasize how upset her father had made her. And Brian knew that, damn him!

She raised the glass to her lips and took a sip. Fifteen minutes, huh? Just enough time to squeeze in a call to Patrick.

****

Patrick

He'd lied. Patrick had used the urgency of putting

his five-year-old son, Oliver, to bed as an excuse to end the call with his father and Veronica. He'd simply had enough. Enough of Veronica's need to be the center of attention. Enough of his father's unconscionable actions. Enough of his own anger and resentment.

His father's marriage to Siena came as no surprise. When he received the invitation to join the family video call, Patrick assumed Dad wasn't calling just to say *Hi! We're back!* Still, that didn't change the fact that he'd spent the entire summer convincing himself that his father would come to his senses and call off their engagement. Apparently, Siena had a much stronger hold on Dad's heart than Patrick imagined.

He should be happy for his father—and for Siena as well, he supposed—but he wasn't. So, now he could add guilt to his growing list of emotional responses to the day's events. First came his anger over the realization that his father had married such a devious and conniving woman. Then came the resentment that his father wanted to spend the rest of his life with a woman who had, along with her twin sister, plotted a scheme to swindle Patrick out of millions of dollars. And let's not forget the fact that he'd come pretty darn close to falling in love with Siena's sister. Her identical twin sister. Now, every time he was around Siena, he'd be reminded of how he'd briefly considered replacing his deceased wife, Catherine, the perfect woman who didn't have a dishonest bone in her body, with a deceitful thief who'd pretended to be his friend and, worse, had toyed with his heartstrings.

Yeah, that was a lot to handle.

Any minute now, he'd be getting a call from Veronica. She'd rage on and on about how their father's marriage would impact *her* life and how *her* girls were going to react. Because, like everything else, their father's marriage was somehow all about Veronica.

Patrick's thoughts were interrupted by rushing footsteps on the staircase. He swiveled his chair away from the window as Oliver burst into the room and ran to Patrick with outstretched arms.

"I came downstairs to say good night, Daddy," Oliver said. Patrick lifted his young son onto his lap as Oliver wrapped his arms around Patrick's neck. "Louise said it was okay."

"And Louise was right." Patrick hugged his son and kissed his forehead. "I was just on my way upstairs to tuck you in."

A moment later, an out of breath Louise entered the room. "Oliver," she said, "you're getting too fast for me. I can barely keep up with you these days." A retired Kindergarten teacher who served as Oliver's nanny in addition to managing Patrick's household, Louise had the option of spending the night when Patrick was on call or, as in this case, he had surgeries scheduled early the next morning. She'd arrived at the house shortly before Patrick joined the family call and had taken over the duty of preparing Oliver for bed. Breathing deeply to catch her breath, she gazed at Patrick, and asked, "So, how'd it go?"

Patrick snickered. "Exactly as I had expected." When he received his father's invitation to join the video call earlier that evening, he had shared his misgivings with Louise. All summer long, Patrick had been haunted by a premonition that his father had married Siena while in Italy or in one of the other European countries they'd visited. He told Louise he anticipated his father would break the news during the family call.

"Oh," Louise replied. When Patrick didn't respond, she said, "You don't seem happy about this news."

Never one to be left out of an adult conversation, Oliver raised his head off Patrick's shoulder. "Daddy, are you and Louise talking about Granddad?"

Patrick gazed into his innocent son's eyes and decided now was as good a time to tell him as any. He tickled Oliver's stomach. "Yes, Mr. Curious," he replied as Oliver let out a sharp giggle. "Granddad called just now with exciting news. He's home from his vacation, and he's gotten married."

Oliver took a moment to mull over Patrick's announcement. "Does that mean I have a new grandmother?"

Patrick glanced at Louise who responded by raising one eyebrow and a shoulder. "Yes, Oliver, I suppose you do." He imagined the young, sultry Siena would not take kindly to Oliver calling her *Granny*. And that notion made him grin.

Just then, Patrick's cell phone rang. He checked the Caller ID. *Veronica.* Shaking his head, Patrick returned his attention to Oliver and let the call go to voicemail.

Chapter 3

Siena

"This washing machine will not get the better of me," Siena grumbled. Her eyes darted back and forth across a control panel that required a degree in aeronautics to operate. How she longed for the low-end machines of her Manhattan apartment building and their two simplistic choices—temperature setting and wash cycle. "I graduated summa cum laude from a prestigious east coast university. I *can* figure this out." She opened the overhead cupboard and rummaged through the various laundry detergents and cleaning aids. "Where the hell is the operating manual?"

"You need help, Mrs. Woodward?" Anita asked from the doorway. Her mildly accented voice was edgy, as though she'd walked in on Siena attempting to stash a pouch of illegal drugs into the cupboard.

Siena yelped and spun around, knocking over a bottle of fabric softener in the process. The hard plastic bottle toppled out of the cupboard, bounced off the edge of the dryer, and splatted onto the tile floor. "Anita! You startled me. I didn't know you were standing there." She bent down to pick up the displaced bottle, but Anita beat her to it.

"I'm sorry to scare you." Anita edged past Siena and replaced the bottle in the overhead cupboard. "Do you need my help?"

"Yes, thank you, I do need help. While Jonathan is golfing this morning, I thought I'd take care of some chores. Can you please teach me how to use this overly complicated washing machine?"

Anita crossed her arms. "*You* want to do laundry?" Siena noticed not only the confusion on Anita's face, but she also detected a hint of hostility in her eyes.

"Yes, I do. I've already loaded in this morning's towels. While they're washing, I'll unpack our suitcases so I can get started on cleaning those clothes as well. If you could please tell me which of these buttons—"

"No, no, no!" Anita stepped past Siena and removed the bottle of laundry detergent from the cupboard. "The laundry is *my* job." She all but shoved Siena aside as she poured in the detergent and punched a few buttons. The washing machine hummed to life.

Great! The first morning in my new home and I've already managed to insult the housekeeper.

"Thank you, Anita. Now, if you could just explain the different settings so I can—"

"No, Mrs. Woodward," Anita insisted. "I always unpack Dr. Woodward's suitcase and wash his clothes. Now, I do the same for you. And I will send special clothes to the dry cleaner."

Siena took a moment to absorb this news flash. Jonathan hadn't bothered to explain Anita's duties other than to say she was his housekeeper, and a housekeeper's sole responsibility, Siena assumed, was keeping the house clean. While not needing to worry about the tidiness of their enormous home was just fine with Siena, she did not relish the thought of someone else laundering her clothes, especially her personal items. Was this one of those aspects Jonathan had informed her would require a *period of adjustment*?

"Okay. Can you tell me, then, how to get to the nearest market? I want to pick up a few items to add to the pantry."

Anita faced Siena, her hand on her hip. "Mrs. Woodward, I buy the groceries. You make the list, and I do the shopping."

Siena got the message. As the housekeeper, Anita did *all* the chores and ran *all* the errands. As the lady of the house, Siena did…nothing? If so, she and Jonathan needed to have a discussion.

"Thank you, Anita," Siena said, grinning and bearing it lest she ruffle any more feathers. "I'll go through the pantry right now and make a list of items I'd like you to buy."

That will be right after I tear apart the linens on our bed that I've already made. Heaven forbid I get called out for committing yet another faux pas. Also, before Anita drags the empty laundry basket upstairs, I need to remove certain items from my suitcase. Anita can do what she wants with the rest of the clothing, but she doesn't need to be privy to the types of intimate apparel I own. Jonathan might not care if she speculates about what goes on behind our closed bedroom door, but I do!

****

While Siena was struggling to fit into a new role in unfamiliar surroundings, Jonathan seemed eager to return to his comfortable routine. Earlier that morning, after introducing Siena to the staff and gulping down a quick breakfast, he'd rushed off to play a round of golf at his club. Siena kept checking the time, anticipating his return home by noon as promised, only to receive an apologetic phone call. His friends, Jonathan explained, had pressured him into joining them for their customary lunch in the clubhouse. "I hope you don't mind, sweetheart," he'd said. "We've been out of the country for three months. The guys and I have a lot of catching up to do." He had just enough time to bop home for a shower and a change of clothes before rushing off to attend a board meeting for one of the non-profits his family facilitated.

When she lived in Manhattan, relaxation had been a luxury Siena rarely enjoyed. During their summer in Europe, she and Jonathan were constantly on the go. She was accustomed to being busy from morning until night, but those days apparently were over. Today, she entered a new phase of her life and, like it or not, the dilemma of how to occupy her time was as real as it was frustrating. Siena, however, was never one to shy away from a good challenge.

So, she poured herself a fresh cup of coffee and set her mind to giving this new lifestyle her best shot. She carried her mug into the den, curled up in a chair, and finished reading the novel she'd purchased on the cruise ship. She strolled through the house making mental notes of updates to the decor she might like to make. She even planned their dinner menus for the entire week, a miraculous accomplishment considering she had never cooked a full meal in her life. After a brief call with her family in Santa Martina—*they* were all too busy to chat at length—Siena faced an afternoon filled with plenty of time to do…what? Hell if she knew.

"And this," she groused, tossing her phone onto the bed and flopping down next to it, "is only Monday."

When she and Jonathan first met, she'd fantasized

about exchanging her chaotic life in the big city for the peacefulness and serenity this home afforded. Now that her dream had come true, she found herself missing Manhattan. The irony made her laugh out loud.

She dragged herself off the bed and moseyed down the staircase, tapping her fingers against the handrail as she descended to the first floor.

So, what to do next?

Well…she still faced the arduous task of cleaning out the apartment she'd abandoned in a New York minute as soon as Jonathan asked her to marry him. *Maybe planning a trip to Manhattan will brighten my spirits. It's not like I have anything else on my agenda this week.*

Clasping her laptop to her chest, Sienna plodded down the first-floor hallway that led to Jonathan's library—correction, *their* library—to make the arrangements. The reality that everything in this house now also belonged to her was taking a while to sink in. But, oh, how she loved the tingle of excitement that coursed through her body each time she reminded herself that her last name was now Woodward.

The door to the library was partially closed. When Siena opened the door farther, she found Brenda, Jonathan's assistant, seated behind the desk with her cell phone in hand. Several manila folders and notepads were spread out on either side of her laptop. Brenda nonchalantly glanced up from her phone.

"I'm sorry for intruding," Siena said. "I didn't realize you were in here."

"Oh, you're fine," Brenda replied with a smile. "Just give me a moment to finish this text."

Siena drummed her fingers against her laptop while

she gazed out the window and waited for Brenda to be free. Javier, their gardener and general handyman who was also Anita's husband, was right outside the window. What was he doing? Pruning the late summer blooms? Siena recalled the term *deadheading* being used in the book she'd been reading earlier. Personally, she knew zero about caring for flowers and vegetables. *Well, I now have all the time in the world to learn.*

After a few moments, Brenda leaned forward and set her phone on the desktop. "There, all done. Sorry. I guess Jonathan didn't tell you that I work from this room when he isn't using it. The window in my little office faces the driveway, and I much prefer this view of the garden."

"I can't say that I blame you." What a sharp contrast between Brenda's picturesque setting and the cramped workspace in the center of a bank of cubicles Siena had occupied at Willow's Auction House.

"Siena, is there something I can help you with?"

Brenda's tone hinted of impatience, which unnerved Siena. After starting off on the wrong foot with Anita, she dared not make an enemy of Brenda as well. At the same time, Siena grew irritated with herself. Anita and Brenda were Jonathan's and, therefore, her employees. Why was she allowing them to intimidate her? She squared her shoulders and regained her self-assuredness.

"I need to take a trip to Manhattan and empty out the apartment I still have there. You know, book a flight, order shipping containers, that sort of thing. I thought I'd use this desk to make the arrangements, but you're obviously in the middle of something. I'll find another space."

"You don't need to do that," Brenda said, her grin never faltering.

"No, it's fine. You're already set up here and—"

Brenda's grin widened. "I mean you don't need to bother booking a flight and arranging to ship your belongings yourself. That's what I'm here to do."

Siena shook her head. "I'd prefer to take care of it myself." How insulting! Did Brenda think she couldn't manage such a mundane task on her own?

With a notepad and pen in hand, Brenda rose from her chair and stepped around the desk. "Siena," she said in a firm voice while shooting Siena a look of determination that would bring a high-speed locomotive to a screeching halt, "it's my job. Jonathan told me this morning that I'm to begin assuming the same duties for you that I handle for him." Now face-to-face with Siena, she rested her backside on the edge of the desk, crossed her legs at the ankle, and jotted down notes. "I'll contract a moving company, then I'll book you a flight to New York and a driver to take you around town while you're there. All you'll need to do is to supervise the movers while they're packing up your apartment." She glanced up from writing, her *you'll-wonder-how-you-ever-lived-without-me* smirk scraping against Siena's last nerve. "Oh, and while I'm thinking of it, is there a specific charity you'd like me to contact about donating your furniture? If not, I'll choose one myself."

Tonight, Jonathan and I will have a talk. In the meantime, I'll take my newfound authority for a test drive and see how I like it.

"Thank you, Brenda. I appreciate your help, but I've changed my mind. I'm still recovering from jetlag, and suddenly the thought of traveling to New York and tackling such a huge chore seems exhausting. However, my hair and nails need some attention. I liked *Alive!*

when I went there last year with Veronica. Could you make an appointment for me? Any time this afternoon is good if they can fit me in on such short notice." Sauntering from the room, she called out over her shoulder, "Thanks much!"

****

"I'm thinking about changing the color of my hair," Siena announced during dinner that evening. Jonathan lifted his chin. His left eye wrinkled with scrutiny. "Shall I take that glaring look as an expression of your disapproval?"

"Depends on which color you're considering. If it's green, then no. But if you want to become a redheaded vixen, I'm all for it." He popped a forkful of steamed broccoli into his mouth and painted a naughty grin on his face.

"Keep wishing," Siena teased. "What I want is to stop dying my hair altogether."

"Oh." Siena glimpsed that *you-can't-be-serious* expression in Jonathan's eyes before he lowered his gaze and went about slicing into his lamb chop. Regardless, she pressed on.

"I discussed my idea with the colorist at the salon today. She'll want to do a gradual change, start with a light brown and go darker in stages as my roots grow out." Silence. "I'm not doing a good job of convincing you, am I?"

Jonathan leaned against the back of his chair and dabbed the corners of his mouth with his napkin. "Siena, I love you, and I wouldn't care if you shaved your head bald. My concern is for Patrick and Oliver."

A flush of guilt rooted itself in Siena's chest and crept up her neck. She got it. Jonathan's issue wasn't about the color of her hair. He was worried about the effect her appearance would have on his son and grandson. Even with her hair dyed blonde, a change she'd made solely to coincide with the Marie Lacroix persona she'd lived under for the past twelve years, Siena could still be mistaken for her twin. Restoring her hair to its natural dark brown would make her resemblance to Jacqueline even stronger. Patrick didn't need any reminders of Jacqueline and the way she, under the alias of Kelsey Adams, had stolen his heart and then played him for a fool. Nor did Oliver need to be confused by Siena's resemblance to "Kelsey," the woman with whom Oliver had begun to form a maternal bond.

Siena placed her hand on Jonathan's forearm. "Jonathan, I'm so sorry. Patrick and Oliver are my family now, too. I should have taken their feelings into consideration without you needing to remind me. My only excuse is that I'm so used to being on my own—"

"Sweetheart, you don't need to apologize." He raised her hand to his lips. "You'll get used to fitting in with the rest of the family soon enough."

Siena sat back and freed her conscience. "Well, any further talk of me making a change to my hair color is officially off the table."

"Not forever," Jonathan said as he lifted his wine glass. "Just for the time being."

Siena sucked in a deep breath before broaching the next topic she'd been waiting for an appropriate time to mention. "Speaking of fitting in, there's another matter we need to discuss."

"Does it have anything to do with the reason Brenda pounced on me the second I returned from my board meeting this afternoon?"

"Huh." Siena straightened her back. "So, in addition to being devoted, reliable, and extremely efficient," she said, the sarcasm dripping off her words, "Brenda is also a tattletale."

Jonathan chuckled. "Siena, you don't need to get defensive. Brenda and I debrief at the end of every day, although today her feathers were ruffled. She wasn't being a snitch. She simply asked me to review her and Anita's roles in our household with you."

Siena shook her head. "Jonathan, you don't need to outline their job descriptions for me. By the end of the day, they'd made me keenly aware of who is responsible for doing what and for whom."

"Good. Then, enough said. Now, before I forget, we received an invitation to—"

"*However.*" Siena leaned forward and rested her elbows on the table. She hadn't yet finished what she had to say about her run-in with the staff. "What I made clear to Brenda and Anita is that I have always managed my own affairs and, while I welcome their assistance, there are certain aspects I will continue to take care of myself."

"So, that's the reason Brenda asked me to speak with you."

"Well…that and the fact that I purposely didn't converse with Anita in Spanish until late in the afternoon. And, yes, that was wrong of me, but I took a sadistic kind of pleasure in watching her flinch when she realized I understood every word she'd been muttering about me under her breath."

"Siena, you didn't." Although Jonathan's demeanor remained serious, Siena detected that familiar twinkle in his eye.

"Oh, I sure did."

Jonathan shook his head. "Poor Anita. Please be nicer to her, Siena," he said as he drained the remainder of the wine from his glass. "She's been excellent help, and I would hate for her last few months to be unpleasant."

"Her last few months? Where is she going?"

"Didn't I tell you? Javier wants to start his own landscaping company. He's been working on a business plan and Anita has been taking night classes to earn her degree in accounting. They want to have the business up and running by next spring."

"That's wonderful news!" Siena remarked as she refilled their glasses. "Can we do anything to help them get started?"

"Actually, I've already committed to making an investment."

"An interest-free loan?"

Jonathan shrugged his shoulder. "Something like that."

Siena grasped Jonathan's hand. "I love you for helping them. First thing tomorrow, I'll congratulate them both and wish them the best of luck."

"Thank you. I'm sure they'll appreciate your support. Now, tell me why Anita was muttering about you under her breath."

Siena rolled her eyes. "When she caught me separating my intimate apparel from the rest of the dirty laundry, she took offense." Siena dabbed her mouth before tossing her napkin onto the table. "We had…words."

"Siena, seriously." Jonathan winced and shook his head. "Why make such a big deal about the laundry?" He stood and gathered their dirty dishes together. "Maybe if

Anita got an eyeful of that skimpy lingerie you brought back from Europe, she'd be inspired to go shopping for herself." He leaned down and kissed her. "I know Javi would thank you."

Siena helped Jonathan carry the dishes to the kitchen sink. "You're used to having people on staff who know everything about your private affairs. I'm not. My personal life is my own, and I prefer to keep it that way."

"Suit yourself."

"Anyway, in case you haven't picked up on my frustration, I was bored out of my mind today. Until a few months ago, I had a demanding job and in my little bit of free time I took care of all the chores Anita and Brenda are now expected to do for me. You're busy most days with board meetings and charity commitments, and it's obvious Veronica and I will never become lunch buddies. So, what is there for me to do? Jonathan, honestly, if I spend another day like I had today, I will go out of my mind."

"You're right, and I'm sorry for being so inconsiderate. Tell you what—for starters, why don't you go with me to the soup kitchen tomorrow? The coordinators never turn away extra help."

"I would enjoy that."

"Then, later this week, I'll introduce you to the ladies at the club. They're always enlisting warm bodies to serve on their committees. And now that I think of it, Veronica serves on the board at the art museum. I'm sure they could use a woman with your knowledge and experience in some capacity."

"I would love to be involved with the museum. Thank you."

"You're welcome. Speaking of Veronica, she called

this afternoon." He scraped the remnants of their dinners into the trash, then rinsed the dishes and handed them to Siena.

Siena braced herself for another of Veronica's daily intrusions in their lives. During the infrequent weekends she had spent with Jonathan before they married, Siena found Veronica palatable in small doses. Now that she lived but a few miles away, Siena was growing weary of Veronica's constant need to secure her dominance in the family hierarchy. Were her nature more like her cerebral, amiable brother Patrick's, Siena believed she and Veronica could have formed a close friendship. Siena questioned for the umpteenth time why Patrick couldn't be the sibling who resided in Burgess and Veronica be the one who lived three hours away in Connecticut.

"And?" Siena stole a glance at Jonathan as she loaded the soiled plates into the dishwasher. "The fact that you're hesitating means this news can't be good."

Jonathan drew in a deep breath. "She's still miffed that we got married without the family—namely, her—being there. So, she wants to host a reception for us. She's already chosen the date and the venue and insists on handling all the arrangements. All she needs from us is a guest list."

Siena closed the door to the dishwasher and glowered at Jonathan. "You're joking, right?"

"Sorry, sweetheart." Jonathan dried his hands and tossed the towel onto the counter. "You know Veronica well enough by now. She's made up her mind and nothing I said was going to change it."

Siena bit her tongue. As much as succumbing to Veronica's overbearing personality grated against her nature, settling into a comfortable niche in the

Woodward family meant keeping her opinions to herself and going with the flow. Still, the prospect of having her photo and name broadcast on every social media platform was unnerving. In New York, her co-workers and clients had known her as Marie Lacroix, a woman whose French accent was as phony as her blonde hair and blue eyes. What were the chances that no one she'd met over the past twelve years would recognize her from an internet post and start asking questions?

"Please don't get me wrong. A reception would be a lovely way for me to meet your family and friends. But, Jonathan, being the center of attention at a large party doesn't help to protect my anonymity."

Jonathan drew Siena into his arms. "Sweetheart, as much as you want to stay out of the limelight, you can't live in a cave for the rest of your life." He pecked a kiss on her lips. "We'll keep the evening intimate, I promise. Only our closest family and friends. What harm can come from that?"

Siena studied Jonathan's face with bewildered eyes, searching for but not finding even the subtlest indication—a raised eyebrow, an impish grin—that he was joking. She shuddered over the notion that her astute, intuitive, preposterously sensible husband could be that naïve.

Chapter 4

Siena

From her chair near the library windows, Siena overheard Veronica say, "Arianna's only seats one hundred comfortably. Let me think about who I can eliminate."

Siena glanced across the room at Veronica and Brenda. The official party planners were seated on either side of Jonathan's antique desk, thick as two anarchists plotting the overthrow of their government. Based on their near-whispered conversation, Siena understood they were finalizing the guest list. Which consisted entirely of Jonathan's family and friends. Therefore, Siena could provide little input. But still.

By necessity, Siena had walled herself off over the past decade to all relationships other than those useful to her illicit sideline ventures. She'd severed ties with childhood friends, rarely socialized with her colleagues at Willow's Auction House, and had turned down more dinner invitations than she could remember. The number of people in her family could be counted on one hand, and most of them were unable or unwilling to join the festivities. Dominic Ricci, her father, used the difficulty of traveling with his physical limitations as an excuse. Her Nonna Ricci whined about being too old to travel, her way of covering up the fact that she was terrified of flying. Gus Ferguson, Siena's godfather, declined for personal reasons. In the aftermath of his involvement last year in their thwarted plan to steal Jonathan and Patrick's Singing Bird Pistols, Gus thought it best to keep his distance from the Woodward family.

That left Jacqueline who wanted more than anything to be part of the celebration of Siena and Jonathan's marriage. Likewise, Siena desperately wanted to share the festivities with her twin. A few evenings ago, Siena had been about to purchase Jacqueline's airline ticket from the Caribbean Island of Santa Martina to Boston when Jonathan intervened.

"Think about it, sweetheart," he'd reasoned. "With all that happened last year, how can we expect Patrick to be in the same room with your sister? I'm sorry, but it's one or the other, and I personally don't care to spend the entire evening explaining to our guests why my son refused to attend such an important family event."

She hated it when Jonathan threw logic in her face. Reminding herself that she needed to pick her battles wisely, Siena had given in and rescinded Jacqueline's invitation. Then she'd locked herself in the bathroom and had a good cry.

Siena eyed Brenda as she stood and assured Veronica, "I'll check into it," before scurrying from the room, notebook and pen in hand.

Draining the remainder of the coffee from her mug, Siena returned her attention to her computer screen and the one detail over which she had complete authority: the design of her dress for the event. Veronica, in her typical control freak fashion, had made a vain attempt to solicit her own couturier for the job, but after considering the unimaginative and unflattering gowns he'd designed for

Veronica, Siena had taken a hard pass. Besides, she'd already enlisted the services of an up-and-coming designer in Boston named Saundra Brandt whom she'd discovered through a featured article in the local business journal. Impressed by what she'd read, Siena contacted Saundra to set up a consultation and had liked her ideas. At Saundra's suggestion, Siena was scanning the internet for inspiration.

"Excuse me, Ma—" Veronica stopped short before the whole of *Marie* slipped from her mouth. Siena's jaw clenched. She gazed up from the couture designer website she'd been reviewing and glared at Veronica over the edge of her laptop. *"Siena,"* Veronica said, shooting Siena a dismissive smile, as if to say she was sorry (but not really) for almost calling her by the wrong name. *Again.* "I have a question."

"I'm listening."

"This afternoon, I'll be meeting with the florist to discuss table centerpieces. What's your favorite color?"

"Red," Siena replied without hesitation.

Veronica wrinkled her nose. "How garish," she muttered to herself yet loud enough to reach Siena's ears. She heaved a dramatic sigh. "Well, I'll see what the florist thinks."

Siena's blood boiled. *No, you won't. You've already decided on the floral arrangements—just as you chose the date, the time, the venue, the menu, and the entertainment—but Jonathan has reminded you repeatedly to ask for my input. Now, should he inquire, you can answer truthfully that you were the perfect daughter and conducted yourself precisely as Daddy asked. Well, Veronica, I've had enough of your charade.*

Siena snapped her laptop closed. "Now it's my turn

to ask you a question. Why do you insist on turning every conversation we have into a battle of wills?"

Veronica's jaw dropped. She scowled at Siena with an expression that screamed *How dare you!* "Excuse me?"

During their previous face-offs, Siena had noted the excitement in Veronica's eye and the gratification in her sneer. Veronica was a person who relished confrontation. Armed with that knowledge, Siena refused to give her the pleasure.

"You know, Veronica," Siena said, filling her voice with empathy as she crossed the room, "you and I aren't all that different. We're both strong-willed. We both lost our mothers at a young age. We value our families above all else, and we both love your father unconditionally. Regardless, we can't seem to get beyond the animosity that's been wedged between us since the day we met. So, let's be candid and say it out loud—we're never going to be friends. Still, like it or not, we're stuck with each other. What I'd like to propose is that we call a truce and at least pretend to get along."

Veronica raised her eyebrows. "Seriously? After you seduced my father away from us and tricked him into marrying you, you honestly expect me to welcome you into my family with open arms?"

So much for the tender, compassionate approach.

That familiar heat of anger ignited in Siena's chest. *Be the better person, Siena. Remain calm. Do it for Jonathan.* "For starters," she said, the redness creeping up her neck, "that would be nice."

"Well, here's my advice to you, *Siena*: don't hold your breath."

And that was Siena's breaking point. She was about

to lash back with a response she was bound to regret when her phone rang. "We'll finish this conversation later," she said through gritted teeth. She swung around on her heels and stomped out of the library. After taking a deep breath and dispelling her temper, she answered the call. "Hi, Saundra."

"Good morning, Siena. I'm calling to confirm our 2:00 appointment this afternoon."

"Yes, I'll be there. I'm looking forward to it."

"Great! I've sketched out some designs to pass by you. I ran the gamut of conservative to sexy, so you'll have a wide range of styles to choose from. Of course, any of them will look fabulous draped on your figure. But, as I said before, I'm open to any ideas you might have. Oh, one more thing. I want to bring out some samples of material for you to consider. Do you have a preference regarding fabrics and colors?"

Inside the library, Veronica tsked and heaved a sigh that was loud and showy enough to reach Siena's ears. "Why is Brenda never around when I need her?" Veronica grumbled. She stormed out of the library and rushed past Siena, shouting *Brenda!* with increasing intensity each time she called out the name.

Siena rolled her eyes. Was there no end to the melodrama? "I'd be most comfortable in something lightweight," she said into the phone, "silk or chiffon maybe. But, Saundra, I was thinking…" She gnawed on her lower lip. *Go ahead, Siena. Do it. You deserve this guilty pleasure.* "Regardless of the fabric we decide to go with, I definitely want the color of my dress to be red."

Chapter 5

Siena

The invitations had been mailed, the RSVPs had been received and counted, the food was being prepared, and the champagne was on ice. Veronica had seen to every detail. The party was scheduled to start in less than an hour and Jonathan had proclaimed the evening would be nothing less than perfect. Siena had given him an endearing smile. At times, he could be such a romantic optimist.

Decked out in his tux and keen to head off to the venue, Jonathan was pacing the foyer as he waited for their driver to arrive. Siena had promised she'd be downstairs shortly. That had been fifteen vexing minutes ago. She wasn't by nature a dawdler, but psyching herself up for this soiree was proving to be an unwelcome challenge.

On a day when she should have been bubbling over with excitement, Siena's thoughts were preoccupied by Elsa Werner, the woman who had been seated across from Jonathan at the captain's table on the last night of their trans-Atlantic cruise. Elsa had been haunting Siena's sleep of late. Siena would like to believe that her dreams of the Romani fortune teller were a random coincidence, but her intuition told her otherwise. She believed the dreams to be a premonition, and she worried that the ominous warning Elsa had issued to Jonathan was destined to play a decisive part in this evening's outcome.

Over breakfast, Siena was tempted to share her misgivings with Jonathan. She needed his level-headed assurance that the Werner woman was a rude attention-seeker who didn't deserve the time of day. But Jonathan had been so animated the past few days, so eager to show her off to his family and friends, that she didn't have the heart to dampen his mood. Instead, she had smiled and convinced Jonathan that she shared in his enthusiasm.

Masking her true emotions and pretending everything was fine was a habit Siena had fallen into since moving into her new home. In truth, her daily routine was nothing like the fairy tale she had envisioned when Jonathan whisked her away from Manhattan. She'd imagined their life in Burgess, Massachusetts would be an extension of their summer in Europe, those magical days of sharing new experiences with the man of her dreams. Instead, Jonathan had returned home to his board meetings and golf outings and his multitude of other commitments while Siena was left floundering to find meaningful endeavors to fill the empty hours.

Seemingly in an instant, Siena's life had gone from one extreme to the other. She'd exchanged a demanding position as an antiques expert at a renowned auction house in one of the largest cities in the world for the quiet existence of an unemployed housewife in a sleepy college town in suburban New England. While she'd willingly sacrifice anything and move anywhere to be with Jonathan, she oftentimes longed for her old life. She missed the sense of self-worth and prestige she had derived from her professional career. What's more, she really missed the buzz she'd gotten from running a dangerous con game.

Siena plopped onto the tufted bench at the foot of their bed and buckled into her heels. She'd had enough of self-pity and her senseless preoccupation with Elsa Werner's dour prediction. As of that moment, she was placing her trust in Jonathan's belief that the evening would prove to be spectacular. Tonight, she would enjoy herself if for no other reason than to make Jonathan happy. Besides, she was honestly excited to meet more of his family members as well as the beloved frat brothers Jonathan spoke of so often.

The satin material of her voluminous skirt rustled as Siena stepped over to the cheval mirror and checked her appearance, both the front view and an over-shoulder inspection of her backside, one last time. Her strapless bustier top with its sweetheart neckline was cropped just above her waistline, exposing an alluring portion of Siena's midriff, and was complimented by a sheer, long-sleeved detachable jacket embroidered in a multi-colored floral design. The same design was repeated in a single diagonal band across the front of her skirt. She loved this ensemble! Siena was so pleased with Saundra's creative vision, in fact, that she'd made Saundra a promise to not only enlist her services for future special events, but also to be her most ardent advocate.

Staring at her reflection, Siena squinted her left eye and pursed her lips. The diamond drop earrings Jonathan had surprised her with as they lazed in bed that morning were perfect, but her bare neckline cried out for a touch of bling. Acting on impulse, Siena strolled into their dressing room and punched in the code that unlocked her jewelry drawer. Her fingers went straight to the piece she had in mind—a silver chain on which was attached a row of diamonds swirled in a unique geometrical pattern and in which a larger solitary ruby was inserted along the upper left curve. Rushing back to the cheval mirror, she blindly hooked the clasp and adjusted the pendant to align at just the right spot above her cleavage. Simple and elegant, the necklace was the perfect complement to her look. She gave her reflection a final approval and exited the bedroom.

As she crossed the upstairs hallway, Siena heard Jonathan say, "Thanks, Bill. We'll be out in a few minutes," then the click of the front door closing. "Siena!" Jonathan called from the foyer. "The limo is here."

"Perfect timing." Lifting the hem of her skirt with one hand while holding the handrail with the other, she gingerly negotiated the steps. Jonathan stood at the foot of the wide staircase, his gaze gliding from the top of Siena's head to the toes of her shoes as though his eyes were hands intimately caressing her body. Siena's stomach fluttered. She grasped the handrail tighter lest her knees buckle out from under her.

When she reached the landing where the staircase turned, Jonathan offered his hand and assisted her with the final few steps. "You are ravishing beyond belief," he said, his lips brushing against the tops of her fingers.

"You're pretty dashing yourself," Siena bantered back.

"Dashing, eh?" He raised an eyebrow. "I like it."

Siena couldn't help but smile when Jonathan's gaze lingered on her necklace. She wanted Jonathan to say he loved the design as much as she did, and that it flattered her appearance. Instead, his brow knitted as he peered at her with questioning eyes. Was he wondering why she hadn't chosen to wear one of the many necklaces he had purchased for her? Without uttering a word, Jonathan stepped around Siena and grabbed her wrap from the foyer bench. The smile faded from Siena's lips.

"I should forewarn you," Jonathan said as he draped Siena's wrap over her shoulders, "although you're bound to receive many compliments on your attire tonight, don't expect to get one from Veronica. She hates the color red."

I know.

Siena cocked her head. "Hm…I wonder why?"

Jonathan shrugged. "Your guess is as good as mine. Just another one of her quirks." He retrieved Siena's evening bag from the bench along with a legal-sized envelope. "Before we leave, I have a gift for you."

"Another gift?" Siena's eyes filled with curiosity. "Jonathan, these earrings are enough."

"This one is different." He enfolded Siena's hand in his. "Sweetheart, I couldn't stand the thought of you going through this evening wearing a happy face when I know how sad you are that your own family isn't here to share this special occasion with us. So, I wanted to do something to brighten your spirits." He handed Siena the envelope.

"What is this?" Frowning, Siena lifted the flap and peeked inside. "Jonathan, is this what I think it is?" She removed a sheet of paper and read the details of their round-trip flights. "We're going to Santa Martina?" she choked out over the lump in her throat.

Jonathan's face beamed with delight. "We most certainly are." Siena screeched and threw her arms around his neck. "Call your family from the limo and tell them they have one day to prepare for our visit. We fly out on Tuesday morning."

Chapter 6

Siena

The party was held at Arianna's, one of the restaurants owned by Veronica and her husband, Brian. As the guests arrived on that crisp evening, the third Sunday of October, Jonathan eagerly introduced Siena to his relatives and friends. During all the conversations, the cocktails and hors d'oeuvres, the dinner and the champagne toasts, Siena had no idea Jonathan was preparing to spring yet another surprise on her.

While the servers were clearing the tables, Jonathan and Siena joined a group of his fraternity brothers and their wives who had gathered near the bar. The portly, balding frat brother, Harry, was in the middle of a long-winded recount of his most recent business acquisition when Jonathan whispered into Siena's ear. "Excuse me. I need to attend to something."

As he hurried away, Joanie Osgood, the wife of another of the frat brothers, slinked into the space Jonathan had vacated.

"Harry does so love being the center of attention," Joanie said, cocking her head so that only Siena was within earshot.

Siena chuckled, amused by the way Joanie's English accent colored her refreshingly candid comment with a touch of sophisticated cheekiness. "Since I've only just met him," she said, "I can't pass judgment."

"Trust me, I've known these boys since our Harvard days. Harry's nice enough, but even during sex he can't refrain from talking about spread sheets and profit margins." She shot Siena a sideways glance. "Or so I've been told. Is it any wonder he's been married and divorced four times?"

Siena raised her eyebrows. Four ex-wives must be taxing on one's private life. "When Jonathan gave me a rundown on his friends, I don't recall him mentioning that."

"Of course not. Jonathan spread gossip about his frat brothers? My dear, we're more likely to see the moon fall out of the sky." Joanie punctuated her sentence with a sip of wine.

Siena glanced around the room. "I don't remember. Is Harry with anyone tonight?"

"No. The coals haven't cooled off yet after his split with wife number four. Oh, dear, I can't now recall her name. How awful of me. Well, anyway, don't worry about Harry. His fortune is still considerable. The next time you see him, he'll have another pretty young airhead attached to his arm. That is, if his combative children don't give him a heart attack first. By the way, you should know I don't often remark on appearances, but I've been meaning to tell you how stunning you look this evening. Not everyone can carry off a crimson red, but that color is perfect on you."

"Thank you. I appreciate the compliment."

Joanie focused on Siena's neckline. "And your necklace is lovely. So unusual."

Siena ran her fingers across the necklace. "This is one of my favorites. Deciding to wear it was a last-minute decision."

"Hm…the design is so awfully unique." Joanie frowned and tilted her head. "It's rather like a necklace a dear friend of mine owned once upon a time. If I'm not mistaken, my friend's necklace was—" Siena's breath caught. *Please don't say* stolen—"one of a kind."

Siena bit the inside of her lip. Joanie's comment had skirted a little too close to the truth. Siena had obtained the necklace in an unconventional manner and the original owner, now deceased, had been a prominent figure. The chance Joanie had known her was improbable, but not entirely impossible. And if Joanie had been friends with the original owner, might Jonathan also have been part of their inner circle?

Siena was fighting the urge to ask Joanie the name of her friend when the lights in the room dimmed. Out of the corner of her eye, she noticed Jonathan returning to her side. As Jonathan placed his arm around her back, Siena settled her curious eyes on him.

"Why are you grinning at me like that?" she asked.

"You'll see."

Siena's brow furrowed. What lavish treat did Jonathan have in store for her this time? She was staring at Jonathan, attempting to read his mind when a spotlight clicked on, illuminating the makeshift dance floor on the opposite side of the dining room. Veronica stepped out of the shadows, plucked the microphone from the baby grand piano, and strolled to the center of the spotlit area.

"May I have everyone's attention?" She tapped the head of the microphone. "Everyone, please. If you could all be quiet." She waited a moment more for the chatter to die down. "Thank you. Most of us here have waited a good many years for this event to happen. At long last, my father has taken the plunge—even though he chose to do so without inviting any of his children to attend the ceremony."

I've got to give Veronica credit. She never misses an opportunity to twist the knife.

Veronica cleared her throat, as though insulted that her stab at sarcasm had garnered only a few snickers from her audience. Undaunted, she continued. "Regardless, please join my brother, Patrick, and me in welcoming our guests of honor, Jonathan and Siena Woodward, to the floor as they dance to the music of Cassidy, performed live for us tonight by—hold onto your hats, everyone—the artist herself!"

The room exploded with applause as Cassidy, a superstar in the music industry, emerged from the shadows wearing a dark green sequined evening gown, her famous waist-length purple-tinted hair swept into an updo. She waved to the guests as Veronica handed off the microphone.

Cassidy seated herself at the piano and attached the mic to its stand. The room grew silent. "Thank you, everyone, for that warm welcome. I'm honored to be here. When I found out my pal, Jonathan, had gotten married and he wanted me to share in this celebration, I simply couldn't refuse the invitation. Then, when I was told his wife is a fan of mine, I insisted on serenading the happy couple during their traditional first dance. I hope you don't mind that I'm kind of taking over your party." She chuckled as the guests met her comments with more applause and shouts of approval. "Okay. Well, I'll take that as an invitation to proceed." Her fingers hit the keys, and she launched into the instrumental opening of her most famous love ballad, *Without You.* "Siena, this one is for you."

Jonathan clasped his hand around Siena's and led her onto the dance floor. Siena, too stunned to speak, couldn't take her eyes off Cassidy. Jonathan twirled Siena around, then drew her close as they slow-danced to one of Siena's favorite tunes.

"Surprised?" Jonathan asked, his smile wide, his eyes twinkling with delight.

Siena tore her attention away from Cassidy and gazed at Jonathan. "Surprised doesn't even begin to cover it. Give me a moment to wrap my head around the fact that Cassidy, the most popular recording artist in the world the last time I checked, is performing *live* just ten feet away from us. *For* us." Jonathan hugged her closer and rested his cheek against her temple as they swayed to the hauntingly sensual melody. "Jonathan, we promised not to keep secrets from each other. So far tonight, I've discovered that Senator Chalmers was one of your fraternity brothers, that former Secretary of Education Wallace Brookmeyer was your mentor at Harvard, and that Leo Summerfield, CEO of the largest cable news network on television, is an old family friend. So, tell me, how is Cassidy part of your social sphere?"

"Do you remember meeting my cousin JoJo, the one whose perfume is so strong you said it made your eyes water?"

Siena grinned and rolled her eyes. "How could I forget her?"

"Yes, well, her husband, Russell, is Cassidy's business manager."

"You're kidding." Siena was still new enough in the Woodward clan to be amazed by the family's sweeping connection to the world of fame and wealth.

"No, I'm not. Russell has been Cassidy's manager since the days she was taking any bar gig she could get in and around New York City. On Russell's recommendation, I went to New York to hear her a few times when she was starting out, and we became acquaintances."

"Wait a minute," Siena interrupted. "Knowing she's one of my favorite artists, and knowing how often I listen to her music, you never bothered to tell me this until now?"

Jonathan shrugged his shoulders. "You know I don't like to brag. Anyway, I wanted to make this an evening you'll never forget. So, I did some research and discovered that Cassidy is on a break from her touring schedule. I called Russell and asked for a favor. He contacted Cassidy and she immediately said yes. She's a sucker for romance."

"Apparently, so are you." Siena traced her fingers along the side of Jonathan's neck as her lips curled into a tender grin. "Do you know what I'm a sucker for? Those adorable dimples of yours."

"So, you're telling me I didn't need to arrange for a private performance by Cassidy to lock in a night of passion? A simple smile would have done the trick?"

Siena wrapped her arms around Jonathan's neck. "Pretty much, although Cassidy has definitely earned you several bonus points."

"Mm…" he moaned, tightening his hold on her. "And I plan to cash in every one of those points as soon as I get you alone."

Cassidy's fingers caressed the piano keys, playing the final notes of the song and bringing her performance to a close. Swept up by the evocative ambience, Siena's lips met Jonathan's. For several seconds, she was deaf to the roar of whistles and applause, to Jonathan's frat brothers shouting out *Woodward, you dawg!* and *Get a room!* Nor did she care.

Cassidy chuckled into the microphone. "Now, this is the type of romance I had in mind when I wrote that song. Ladies and gentlemen, let's hear it for Jonathan and Siena."

****

Wedged between her husband, Brian, and her brother, Patrick, Veronica folded her arms across her chest and glared at the amorous scene playing out on the dance floor.

"Oh. My. God."

Patrick placed his hands on his hips. "I can't believe Dad is behaving this way in public."

"Get used to it," Veronica snapped.

Sneering, Patrick glanced sideways at his older sister. "Are you serious?"

Veronica raised an eyebrow as she gazed into Patrick's eyes. "Are you blind? Haven't you noticed the way Daddy can't keep his hands off her?"

Patrick's eyes followed Veronica as she spun away from him and stomped off toward the bar. "So," he asked Brian, "what's your opinion of my father acting like a teenager in heat?"

Keeping his gaze glued on Jonathan and Siena, Brian placed his hand on Patrick's shoulder and spoke in confidence. "Promise me you won't tell Veronica, but I'm insanely jealous."

****

What is happening? Am I truly standing here listening to a conversation between my husband and a global superstar? Who are chatting as though they're old neighbors catching up with each other in the produce aisle of the grocery store? Wow!

Okay, so, it isn't like I've never met a celebrity before. My position at Willow's connected me with plenty of well-known people. Hell, I even ran cons on a few noteworthy politicians and business moguls. But well-known isn't famous. Cassidy is famous. *A musical phenom who sells out venues within minutes. A singer who's performed before kings and sultans. At the White House for the President and the First Lady, for God's sake! And she flew across the country from LA to perform just one song as a favor to my husband. Wow!!*

Years later, when Siena would reminisce about this event, she'd remember it as the night her eyes were opened wide to the extent of the Woodward family's far-reaching influence. Still, although the perks of being married to a multi-millionaire could be spectacular, they weren't what mattered. Siena wouldn't bat an eyelash if Jonathan gave away every penny of his wealth tomorrow and they moved into her tiny Manhattan apartment and scrimped by on meager salaries earned from mediocre jobs. She'd willingly give away every material possession she owned to be with him.

Siena inched closer and squeezed Jonathan's hand. Without missing a beat, he continued chatting with Cassidy while at the same time wrapping his arm around Siena's back. Siena's heart fluttered. Jonathan's touch always had that effect on her.

One of the guests bumped into Siena. She glanced over her shoulder to except the woman's apology and discovered that, while she'd been caught up in her reveries, a crowd had formed around Cassidy. Their guests were clamoring to meet the music star and take selfies with her. At the behest of his granddaughters, Jonathan was holding the girls' phones and snapping photos as they posed with Cassidy, using Gwen's phone first and then switching to Phoebe's. Siena was tickled by the typically reserved Gwen behaving with as much unabashed exuberance as her naturally bubbly younger sister.

Siena was advising Phoebe to toss her hair behind her shoulder and suggesting that Gwen lower her chin when the nerves in the back of her neck unexpectedly prickled. The kind of sensation you experience when someone untoward is staring at you. She sucked in a breath, hoping to shake off the menace that was creeping into her bones.

She glanced around the restaurant and noticed a man standing alone near the front entrance. He appeared out of place as his attire—an open-collared shirt and leather jacket—was far too casual for such a formal event. Neither was he part of the catering staff. When she pivoted around to catch a better look at him, he raised his cell phone and aimed it at Siena as though he were taking a photo of her. When he lowered the phone, she caught a brief glimpse of his face before Burt, Jonathan's brother, stepped in front of him. When Burt sauntered away a few seconds later, the man was gone.

Siena's heart was pounding. *Please let me be mistaken.* She fought her way through the horde, searching for the face of a man she'd known for a brief time under dubious circumstances. When at last she reached the front entrance, Siena examined the area, even rushed outside and surveyed the parking lot, but to no avail. Shivering, she wrapped her arms across her chest. He may have vanished, but there was no way in hell that man's appearance at a party being thrown in her honor was a mere coincidence.

So…what if it were?

The chances were next to nil that she would ever be recognized by any of the men she'd targeted for her con jobs. Siena had been a chameleon with her disguises. She'd taken every precaution to protect her identity, and she'd prided herself on never having made even the tiniest slip-up.

On the other hand, the names and faces of the men she'd scammed were forever inscribed in her mind. Great remorse, she'd discovered, works in strange ways. At the forefront of that list was Matthew Kramer, the target of the most heinous and vengeful scheme she'd ever devised. And his, Siena was convinced, was the face of the man she'd caught spying on her from the restaurant's shadows.

The question was, what was Matthew Kramer doing at her wedding celebration?

Chapter 7

Siena

Siena returned to the throng inside Arianna's and located Jonathan standing amid the abandoned, linen-covered tables, hands on hips, his face a giant question mark as his eyes surveyed the dimly lit room. When he noticed Siena sauntering toward him, his frown lifted. He aimed an adoring smile her way and coiled his arm around her waist, tugging her close for a light kiss.

"Where did you disappear to?" he asked.

Siena didn't dare admit the truth. "All of a sudden, I got claustrophobic. I stepped outside for some fresh air."

"Too many bodies in too close quarters." Jonathan snatched a champagne flute off the tray of a passing server and handed it to Siena. "Here. Quench your thirst."

"I'm not sure I should have any more, but thanks." While sipping her drink, Siena pondered how to lead into the question she needed more than wanted to ask. "Jonathan, while I was outside, I was thinking—wasn't there a Matthew somebody on the guest list? The last name escapes me right now, but I don't recall being introduced to anyone named Matthew."

Had Siena not been so intent on his reaction, she wouldn't have noticed the mild knit in Jonathan's brow and the way the corner of his eye wrinkled for a split second. "You're thinking of Matthew Burton, one of my frat brothers. Unfortunately, Matt couldn't join us tonight. He's in India on business."

"No," Siena replied, shaking her head. "Not Burton. Maybe the last name started with an *N*," she squinted her eyes as if doing so would bring the puzzling name into focus, "or a *K*?"

Jonathan's expression hardened. He stared straight ahead, avoiding eye contact with her. "I can assure you, no one named Matthew whose last name starts with and *N* or a *K* was on our guest list."

Hm...Exactly what are you saying, Jonathan? That you don't know anyone named Matthew N- or K-something? Or are you admitting you do indeed know a person by that name, but this person for some reason was cut from the guest list? My intuition tells me you're hiding something. But, what? And why?

One awkward moment turned into another when Jonathan's gaze fell to Siena's neckline. "You know, I've been meaning to ask all evening where you got that necklace."

Siena swallowed her mouthful of champagne in a hard gulp. On the heels of Joanie Osgood's interest in the necklace and the appearance of the mystery man who may or may not have been Matthew Kramer, Jonathan's pointed question made her chest tighten. Her last-minute decision to wear this necklace may not have been such a good idea after all.

"Oh, this?" she asked, her fingers caressing the jewels. "I came by it when I worked at Willow's. I think it was part of an estate sale."

"Huh." Jonathan seemed as though he couldn't take his eyes off the sparkling jewels. "I thought it might be something you obtained during one of your…" He hesitated, as if searching for the proper word and at last settling on, "…jobs."

Siena needed a hasty diversion. As the music cranked up, she swigged down the remainder of her champagne and set the empty flute on the nearest table. "Come on," she said, leading Jonathan onto the dance floor. "Let's have some fun!"

When Cassidy noticed Jonathan and Siena had rejoined the crowd, she grasped their hands and drew them into her circle. For the remainder of the event, Siena sang to the lyrics, smiled into the camera lens that seemed to always be in her face, had two more glasses of champagne—maybe three—and danced until she and Jonathan were obliged to bid their guests goodnight. By the time they settled into their limo for the ride home, Matthew Kramer was a distant memory.

As their driver closed the limousine door, Jonathan removed his tuxedo jacket. "Ahh…it feels good to take this jacket off and relax."

Siena lifted the filled champagne flutes from the service bar and handed one to Jonathan. "Bill was kind enough to open a fresh bottle for us."

"Here's to Bill, then." Jonathan clinked his flute against Siena's and gazed into her eyes as he downed a mouthful. "So, on a scale of one to ten," he asked, shooting her a wicked grin, "how do you rate tonight's party?"

"A twenty, maybe higher." Siena's eyes were glued to Jonathan as she drained the champagne from her flute. She'd been biding her time all evening, eager for the party to end so she could be alone with him.

Jonathan raised an eyebrow. "That good, huh?

Based on any one thing in particular?"

Siena giggled. She was riding high from the music and the dancing and meeting Cassidy and Jonathan's dimples. Not to mention, she hadn't consumed this much champagne in a long time. Maneuvering herself on the leather seat, she placed her hand on the back of Jonathan's neck and drew him closer. "Based on how we're about to spend the rest of the evening." She kissed Jonathan as the limo rolled into motion.

When the kiss ended, Jonathan swilled down the remainder of his champagne. "How much have you had to drink tonight?" he asked, raising one eyebrow as he placed their empty flutes on the service bar.

"Remember our first night in Rome?"

Jonathan's eyes twinkled. "In vivid detail."

"Mm…" She pressed her body against his. "About that much," she said before kissing him again.

Jonathan gripped a fistful of red satin and tugged up the hem of her skirt. "Time to get the answer to the question that's been on my mind this entire evening." He whispered into her ear. "What are you wearing tonight? A silky thong? Lace panties? Are they black, or red to match your dress?" His lips trailed kisses down her neck as his fingers took their time slinking upward along her thigh.

Siena's giggle was as sultry as her reply. "Check the righthand pocket of your jacket and you'll find out."

Jonathan raised his head and gazed at her with mystified eyes. Sliding his tuxedo jacket closer, he reached into the right pocket and withdrew a pair of red lace panties. "Is this some sort of magic trick?"

"Hardly," she teased. Tugging on the end of Jonathan's bowtie, she undid the knot and opened the top three buttons of his shirt. "Remember when I excused myself to use the restroom just before we left Arianna's? Well, you started something while we were dancing to Cassidy's serenade..." She leaned in to kiss the side of his neck as her finger traced the dimple in his cheek. "And the ride home isn't that long..."

Jonathan lifted the phone receiver and punched the intercom button. "Bill?" he asked.

"Yes, sir?"

"Do you have any plans for the rest of the evening?"

"Just going home after I drop you and Mrs. Woodward off."

"In that case, I'd be happy to double your tip—" Siena raised her head and made a face that said *You know I'm worth more than that.* "Correction—I'll quadruple your tip if you find a longer route back to our house." Siena grinned her approval. She leaned back and, raising her arms, stretched out along the cushioned seat. Jonathan lifted her legs and draped them across his thighs. Starting with her left foot, he set about unbuckling her shoes.

"How long of a drive would you like me to take?" Bill asked.

"Um...why don't you hop onto 90 West? Drive out to Framingham and back."

"You got it."

"Thanks, Bill."

"My pleasure, sir."

Jonathan was about to hang up the receiver when he had another thought. "Bill, one more thing—"

Suddenly, loud music from an oldies station blasted through the earpiece. "Sorry, Dr. Woodward," Bill said. "I can't hear anything when I have the radio turned up this loud."

Jonathan chuckled. "Thank you, Bill."

"You're quite welcome."

"How long is the drive to Framingham and back?" Siena asked as Jonathan replaced the receiver in its cradle.

Jonathan slipped off her shoes and massaged her feet. "About an hour."

"Mm…" she moaned. "Is that enough time?"

Jonathan leaned over her. "To finish what I started on the dance floor? Maybe. I do have one request though."

Siena wound her fingers through his hair. What titillating pleasure did Jonathan have in mind? "Anything," she purred.

"Take off your necklace. It's distracting me."

Chapter 8

Veronica

Veronica found Brenda perched behind the desk, fingers flying across her laptop's keyboard. Honestly, the woman was a workhorse. Did she never take a few minutes to lounge on the terrace with a glass of iced tea? Gossip on her phone behind a locked bathroom door?

"Good morning, Brenda," she said as she strolled into Jonathan's library and dropped her oversized handbag onto the desk. "Did you enjoy yourself at the reception last night?"

"Hi, Veronica. Yes, my wife, Lily, and I had a wonderful time. My compliments again on organizing the perfect party. I still can't believe you managed to get Cassidy to attend."

"I'd like to take the credit, but Cassidy was all Daddy's doing."

"You know, I'd noticed Jonathan having a few phone conversations behind closed doors last week. I wondered who he was talking with."

Veronica shot Brenda a condescending grin. "Well, now you know."

"Have you seen Cassidy's social media pages this morning?" Brenda asked while typing and clicking on the keyboard. "They're covered with photos from last night's party."

"Seriously?"

"They sure are." Brenda waved Veronica over to join her at the computer screen. "Here. I've pulled up one of her pages." She scrolled the screen upward as Veronica viewed the photos over her shoulder. "Look, you're with Cassidy in this one."

"Oh. I think that's the one Phoebe took with her phone. She must have sent it to Cassidy." *How dare Phoebe!* Cassidy was gorgeous in the photo, but Veronica had been captured with her mouth open and an unbecoming scowl on her face. Both Phoebe and her older sister, Gwendolyn, had returned to boarding school that morning. Tonight, Phoebe could count on receiving a phone call—along with a firm reprimand—from her mother. Rest assured.

"Here's a great photo of Jonathan and Siena with Cassidy. Wait. Is that..." Brenda gave the laptop's mouse a couple of taps. "It is! Look, Veronica. When I enlarge the picture, you can see Lily and me in the background."

"Huh," Veronica grunted, giving the screen a cursory glance. Siena looked beautiful, *of course*. She'd probably never taken a bad photo in her entire life. "So you can."

"Anyway," Brenda said, gazing up at Veronica, "your father isn't home right now, but if you want to say hi to Siena while you're here, she's upstairs packing for their trip."

"A nice thought," Veronica said with a dismissive grin. "Too bad I'm short on time this morning." She rounded the corner of the desk, removed a large brown envelope from her handbag, and placed it on the desktop. "I just stopped by to drop off these quotes I gathered for the Improvements Committee I'm co-chairing at the club with Daddy."

"Oh, great! Jonathan's been waiting for these." Brenda placed the envelope inside the top right-hand desk drawer. "I'll make sure he knows they're here."

"Thank you." Veronica lifted her handbag onto her shoulder. "And, uh, I'd appreciate you not mentioning to Siena that I stopped by."

"My lips are sealed," Brenda promised. "Have a nice day, Veronica."

"You, too," Veronica replied as she sauntered out of the room.

****

Siena

"No way!" Jacqueline shouted at Siena through their cell phones. "Cassidy?"

"Cassidy!" Siena confirmed. Holding the phone in front of her face with one hand, she opened one of the drawers to the unit built into the center of her and Jonathan's dressing room and rifled through her lingerie, searching for matching bras and panties. "I'll text you the photos Jonathan's granddaughters took."

"I wish I could have been there." Jacqueline scrunched up her face showing her disappointment.

Siena closed the drawer and tossed the garments into her open suitcase. "As do I. But guess what? Cassidy is going on tour in a couple of months. Jonathan and I want to treat you to a concert when she performs in Miami in February."

"I'm in! Just tell me when and where and I'll be there."

Siena leaned her back against the dresser and gazed lovingly at her twin's image on the cell phone screen. "I

70

am so happy we can openly be together again after all these years."

Jacqueline blinked several times while fanning her eyes with her hand. "Stop. You're making me cry."

"Save your tears for when we get there." Siena opened another dresser drawer and selected swimsuit tops and bottoms. "What's the weather like in Santa Martina this time of year?"

"Warm and sunny, same as the rest of the year."

"Good. I need some sunshine. I've been spending too much time indoors since moving to Massachusetts."

Jacqueline gave a sympathetic groan. "Tell Jonathan he needs to take you on long, romantic walks through the woods, or ice skating or something."

"Ice skating?" Siena chuckled. "Jac, it's the middle of October. We don't live in the Yukon."

"You know I'm only kidding. But speaking of Jonathan reminds me—Nonna hasn't left the kitchen since you called us last night. I hope you've forewarned your husband about the enormous amounts of food she'll expect him to eat."

Siena laughed out loud. "Yes, I have. As a matter of fact, Jonathan is quite the chef himself. He's looking forward to picking up some of Nonna's culinary techniques. I'm sure she'll be thrilled." Siena placed her bikinis in the suitcase and closed the dresser drawer.

"Well, the new man in *my* life certainly enjoys Nonna's cooking," Jacqueline said in that way she had of throwing out a teaser instead of spilling the entire story all at once.

Siena took the bait. "The new man in your life? This is intriguing. Come on, cough up the info—Who? How long? Is it serious?"

Jacqueline laughed. "I was going to tell you when you got here, but I couldn't wait a second longer. Oh, Siena, this guy has me all tied up in knots. We've only known each other for a few months, but—"

"Hold on a second, Jac. I think someone knocked on my bedroom door."

"Mrs. Woodward?" Anita called from the open doorway. "You in here?"

Siena emerged from the dressing room with her cell phone in hand. "Yes, Anita. Do you need something?"

"Sorry to bother you. A man is downstairs. He asked to see you."

Siena frowned. "A man? Did he give his name?"

"No, ma'am," Anita replied. "I asked, but he just grinned and said he wanted to surprise you."

Last night's shadowy image of Matthew Kramer flashed before Siena's eyes. A cold shiver ran up her spine. "Please offer him something to drink and tell him I'll be downstairs in a few minutes."

"Yes, ma'am." Anita stepped closer to Siena and lowered her voice. "Javier is in the garden. You want me to ask him to come inside?"

Anita's concern brought a smile to Siena's lips. This was the first genuine act of kindness the woman had shown her. "Thank you, Anita, but that won't be necessary. As I said, I'll be downstairs shortly."

"Yes, ma'am."

Siena's eyes followed Anita as she exited the bedroom, crossed the upstairs hall, and disappeared down the staircase. "Jac, I'm guessing you heard that conversation."

"I did. Any idea who your mysterious caller is?"

"I think he might be one of Jonathan's friends I met

at the party last night. He mentioned stopping by while he was still in town." Although Siena would like for her concocted story to be the case, she doubted any of Jonathan's friends would drop in unannounced.

"So, he's there to see you but not Jonathan? That's kind of weird."

"Well, he's odd to begin with." The deeper Siena dug herself into this lie, the more she was convinced of exactly who awaited her downstairs. Her anxiety was rising by the second. "Anyway, I'd better not keep him waiting."

"See you tomorrow then. I'll meet you at the airport in baggage claim."

"I can't wait. Love you." Siena gave her sister an air-kiss and disconnected the call.

As she slid the cell phone into the back pocket of her jeans and started toward the bedroom door, Siena caught a glimpse of herself in the mirror. She hadn't showered yet, her hair was tied up in a ponytail, and she was dressed in a pair of ratty jeans and an old T-shirt. Good enough for suitcase packing, but unsuitable for greeting a guest. Nonna Ricci's voice, as it had so often since her adolescence, spoke to Siena from the recesses of her mind. *Siena,* Nonna had scolded many times, *we do not go out in public dressed that way.*

"Yes, Nonna, I know," Siena mumbled to herself. She entered the dressing room and changed into slacks and a sweater and slipped on a pair of shoes. Dashing into the bathroom, she let down her hair and applied a touch of makeup. *Is this much preparation necessary, or am I stalling for time?*

As she stared at her reflection, she recalled the rush she'd gotten when confronted with a dangerous situation in her previous life. The memory caused her pulse to quicken. Whoever awaited her downstairs, she was suddenly quite eager to meet him.

****

The man was gazing out the terrace doors with his back to Siena when she entered the great room. His sandy brown hair and average build were a match to Matthew Kramer's, but then any number of men would fit that description. As she approached him, the man's head turned toward her before the rest of his body swung around, leaving no doubt in Siena's mind. The face of Matthew Kramer was not one she would soon forget.

"Hello," she said, extending her hand and pretending they were complete strangers. "I'm Siena Woodward. Sorry I kept you waiting."

Matthew grinned back, although his was more of a smirk than a happy-to-meet-you smile. "That's all right," he said as he accepted her hand. "I've waited six years to come face-to-face with you again, *Siena Woodward*. Five more minutes wasn't too much to ask."

Playing dumb, Siena cocked her head and frowned. "I'm sorry. Have we met before?"

Matthew's eyes cruised down her body then up again, as though he wanted to check his familiarity with her every feature and curve to ensure she was indeed the sordid woman from his past. "You know damned well we have. Although back then you were a green-eyed accountant with short dark hair who called herself Ellen Randall. Maybe that little tidbit will jar your memory."

Siena's ears perked up to the sound of footsteps coming down the hallway that led to the library, a reminder that others were in the house. Needing to stop Matthew before he said anything more, she smiled and strolled toward the French doors. "It's such a nice afternoon. Let's chat outside on the patio."

****

Veronica

As Veronica stepped out of Jonathan's library and ambled down the hall toward the center of the house, she detected a man and a woman conversing in the great room. One of the voices was Siena's, the other was a man's that sounded familiar but which Veronica couldn't quite place. She tiptoed into the foyer and hid alongside the landing of the stairway.

"It's such a nice afternoon," she overheard Siena say. "Let's chat outside on the patio."

Curiosity may have killed the cat, but nothing stopped Veronica from gathering useful intel—especially that which included dirt on her new stepmother. She scurried into the first-floor bedroom, then into the attached en suite which faced the back patio. Cranking the bathroom window open an inch, she eavesdropped on the conversation Siena was holding with the mysterious man on the outside terrace.

Chapter 9

Siena

Voices carried outside the house as well as inside. When Siena stepped onto the terrace, she scanned the yard beyond the low fieldstone wall that separated the paved patio from the flower and vegetable gardens and spotted Javier trimming back the rose bushes, well beyond hearing range. Besides, with his head bobbing and his voice filling the air with Latino lyrics, Siena was certain he was wearing his earbuds.

The smile fell off Siena's face as she closed the terrace doors. After all, what was the point of continuing her clueless act? "So, that *was* you I noticed at Arianna's last night."

"Indeed, it was. Sorry about crashing your party." He gave an insolent shrug of his shoulder. "My invitation must have gotten lost in the mail."

Siena ignored his sarcastic innuendo. "I'd ask you to have a seat, but something tells me this isn't a social visit."

Matthew's upper lip curled into a sneer. "Oh, I think you put an end to any friendly relationship we might have had the day you drugged me and left me handcuffed to my bed."

Siena grimaced and turned her back to Matthew. The cool autumn air chilled right through her light sweater. She folded her arms across her chest and sauntered over to a sunny spot near the back corner of the house. With her head lowered out of respect, she said, "I was sorry to read about your wife's death."

"Yes, well, she was my *ex*-wife by then, which I'm sure you already know. Alva's death was no great revelation. Right after our divorce, her illness advanced rapidly, as her doctors had predicted." He let out a sardonic grunt. "I don't know why I'm telling you this. As I recall, I'd shared her deteriorating condition with you while we were groping each other under the sheets."

Siena glanced at Matthew over her shoulders, her eyes filled with contempt. "And you're showing about as much compassion for her now as you did then."

Matthew strolled past Siena. He sat on the fieldstone wall and faced her as he spoke. "You know, all through my marriage to Alva, I considered myself a real pro when it came to bamboozling people. I had everyone convinced I was her loving, doating husband. But you...well, I've got to hand it to you. You put on an act that made my charade look like amateur hour. Hell, to this day I still get excited when I think about how delicious you looked sitting on that bar stool, how you lured me over with just a glance and a smile. Then you turned on the charm, inviting me to have a drink with you, hanging on my every word, making me believe you actually had the hots for me. Before I knew what was happening, you had me confiding my deepest, darkest secrets."

Siena snickered. "You flatter yourself. As I recall, I was minding my own business that evening when you accosted me."

"Well," Matthew said with a snort, "I imagine your

memory would get foggy when you've made a career out of picking up men in bars." He glared at Siena with narrowed eyes. "I'm curious. How many other men did you con before you targeted me?"

"About as many women as you had affairs with behind your unsuspecting wife's back." Siena immediately regretted her words. Her biggest fault had always been not being able to control her temper.

Matthew nodded his head. "I figured as much. Nobody's that good right out of the gate."

Siena needed the answer to her most burning question. "I'm curious as well. How did you find me?"

"Oh, I'm a hound dog. I've been searching for you in the face of every woman I've even taken a glance at over the last six years. It took a while." He lowered his chin, giving his countenance a sinister appearance. "Then, one day, I just got lucky."

"You're lying. I might believe the element of chance, but…" Siena's brows knitted with confusion. "How could you possibly have recognized me?"

"Babe, I have every inch of your body committed to memory." *Babe.* Siena had forgotten how often Matthew loved to use that term of endearment when speaking to her. She abhorred its connotation today even more than she'd hated it back then. "The first time I was shown a photo of Jonathan with his new wife, I knew my patience had paid off."

"That's impossible," she spat out. "I went to great lengths to make sure Ellen Randall looked nothing like me."

As a con artist, Siena was second to none when it came to altering her appearance. She'd owned an array of wigs and colored contact lenses and, as a skilled makeup artist, she could tweak her facial features as well as any plastic surgeon with a few well-placed brush strokes. She was an expert at mimicking accents. Creating a false identity was a major component of each scheme she devised, and she'd never used the same persona twice. As Ellen Randall, the short chestnut wig Siena used had given her a lower hairline. She'd worn green contact lenses and had fashioned her makeup to give herself the appearance of having higher cheekbones and a wider nose. She'd worn low-heeled shoes to avoid calling attention to her five-feet-nine-inch stature.

Matthew nodded in agreement. "That you did. But, you see, you made the mistake of removing your disguise before you left my apartment that afternoon—leaving me, I might add, splayed out on the bed in a rather compromising position." He heaved a sigh. "As you can guess, Alva was not too pleased with me when she returned home that evening."

With a slight shake of her head, Siena stared down Matthew's smug expression with disbelieving eyes. "But you couldn't have seen my face, unless..." Her breath caught. In slow motion, Siena's gaze drifted upward as the shock of her own stupidity slowly drained from her lungs. How could she have been so damned careless?

Matthew rose from the stone ledge, slid his hand into his coat pocket, and retrieved a handheld camera no larger than the size of his palm. "When she redecorated our bedroom, Alva had wanted a simple frame for the mirror above her dresser, but I talked her into getting the more ornate one. Truthfully, I couldn't have given a rat's ass about the mirror, but those scrolly designs were the perfect place to imbed a camera lens." He paused, as if enjoying Siena's reaction. She was certain her complexion had gone sallow from the bile churning in her stomach. "You're not alone, you know. None of the women I entertained in our bedroom knew the camera was rolling. And, in your case, I was fortunate enough to capture a lot more than your bare ass on film." He flipped open the cover of the camera's screen and pressed the play button. "Care to take a stroll down memory lane with me?"

Chapter 10

Siena
Spring 2017

The evening was young, but Kudos was already hopping with activity. Siena located an open seat midway down the bar and ordered a glass of white wine. While sipping her drink, she searched the faces in the crowd for Arthur Campbell, the man she'd chosen as the mark of her next scheme. He had to be in the lounge somewhere. During the elevator ride she'd shared with him that afternoon, Arthur had been on his cell agreeing to meet for drinks at seven o'clock. She'd followed him down Park Avenue for three city blocks from his office building to this location. Not more than five minutes ago, she'd spied him entering the lounge from her vantage point across the street.

So, where the hell is he?

As the couple next to her got up to leave, she noticed Arthur emerging through an archway to her left above which the word *Restrooms* was printed in bold letters. Siena's brow unfurled. Silly of her not to consider that his first order of business might have been to use the facilities. Her eyes followed Arthur to a table in the far corner where he joined two other men also dressed in business suits. She'd observe the group for a while, assess the situation, before deciding on the best way to make her approach.

She became aware of the man and woman standing in front of the table where Arthur was seated. They were holding a conversation, the woman's back to Siena, the man facing her. The man—fifty-something, well-dressed, handsome in a "pretty boy" sort of way—was leering at Siena with one eyebrow raised.

What is his *problem?*

He said something to his companion and headed in Siena's direction. At once, she understood what was happening. While she'd been staring at Arthur Campbell and imagining the nice profit she would soon be making off him, an avaricious grin had inadvertently crept onto her face. The man making a beeline toward her had intercepted her smile and misinterpreted it as an invitation to join her.

Shit.

"Hi," the stranger said as he slid onto the empty seat beside her.

Siena grinned politely. She swiveled around on her chair, placed her elbow on the bar, and sipped her wine.

"You know," he continued, "when you smile at a man from across a crowded bar, he's obligated to buy you a drink."

Gosh, that's quite the come-on line—not that I was smiling at you *in the first place.*

"Sorry about that," she said in the light Southern drawl which, along with her physical disguise, was part of the persona she'd created specifically for Arthur Campbell. "Without my glasses and in this dim lighting, I mistook you for someone I work with."

"So, it was kismet that brought us together. Now we're required to spend time getting to know one another. What are you drinking? Chardonnay? Riesling?"

Please go away. I'm trying to attract Arthur Campbell's attention, and your interference is not helping.

"Thanks, but no thanks," she said. "I'll be leaving soon."

He leaned closer. "Ah, come on. Have some pity on me. I've had a crappy afternoon."

You can have a crappy night, too, for all I care.

Siena glanced over her shoulder, keeping tabs on Arthur, just as three middle-aged women entered the lounge and strolled over to his table. The men rose and greeted the ladies with hugs and kisses. Their wives, no doubt.

Damn.

"Yeah," the wannabe Casanova rambled on, as though she cared. "My bank asked me for an updated personal financial statement, so I had my wife's jewelry re-appraised this afternoon. The idiot low-balled me on a pair of her diamond earrings. Said they're not worth the $300,000 we have them insured for."

Excuse me? Did you say $300,000 diamond earrings? Well, now, when one door closes…

Shifting her focus from Arthur Campbell to the brag-complainer sitting next to her, Siena filled her eyes with concern. "I imagine that sort of news would put a damper on your day." She angled her body toward him. "I'm sorry. I didn't catch your name."

"It's Matthew," he replied, the smile on his face broadening. "Matthew Kramer."

"Nice to meet you, Matthew. I'm Ellen Randall." She clinked her goblet against his whiskey glass. "Here's to kismet bringing us together."

****

"So, you're a tax accountant from Richmond," Matthew said. He and Siena's Ellen Randall were sitting sideways on their bar chairs facing each other, Siena ensuring their knees made contact every now and then. "Interesting. How did you end up in New York?"

"A job transfer. Three years ago, I was offered a position in our Manhattan office and, well, here I am."

Matthew raised one eyebrow. "Here you are indeed."

Siena held his gaze. Let the flirting begin. "So, what do you do for a living?"

"Take a wild guess."

She lifted her chin in pretended interest. "Hm, let's see…I think you're a corporate attorney." Matthew grinned and shook his head. "No? All right then…you're the police commissioner. No?" She tsked and sighed. "I missed again?"

"One more strike and you're out," Matthew teased, his eyes filled with infatuation.

"Oh, the pressure's on now." She frowned and squinted her eyes, continuing the farce. "I know! You're a brain surgeon by day and a vampire slayer at night."

"You saw the silver bullets in my pocket, didn't you?" he joked.

Siena chuckled with delight. "Okay, okay, I give. What do you honestly do for a living, Matthew Kramer, man of mystery? And please don't tell me you're a tax accountant." She downed the remainder of her wine.

"You can relax. I'm not an accountant." He signaled the bartender for a refill on her drink. "I'm a portfolio manager. My offices are in the Stambaugh Building

84

around the corner on Fifth."

"Your offices?" she asked, sounding duly impressed. "As in, you're the company owner?"

"That I am," Matthew admitted with a proud smile. "We're a small firm that caters to a select group of savvy investors."

"It's a competitive field, but I've no doubt you're quite successful."

"Well, I like to think so." Just then, the bartender delivered Siena's wine. Matthew thanked him and slid the glass toward her. "Speaking of portfolios, I wouldn't mind taking a look at your assets before the night is over."

Siena had to stop herself from laughing in Matthew's face. She'd seen that cheesy double entendre coming a mile away. Instead, she pasted on a grin that said she found him to be alluring and desirable. "If you're talking about my finances, thank you for the offer but I manage my own investments." True. Siena refused to let her high-priced B.S. degree in Finance go to waste, especially when paying for her education had nearly cost her father his life. "However, if you're suggesting we go somewhere that's more intimate...why don't we take it slow? Get to know each other first."

"Fair enough." Matthew's eyes bore into her as he sipped his scotch. "You're not bothered by the fact that I'm married?"

"Why should I be? We're merely having a friendly conversation in a public bar."

"For now, that is." He raised an eyebrow. "And you? Is there anyone special in your life?"

Siena crossed her legs, the movement inching her skirt farther up her thighs. "Not at the moment." Also true, for now and most likely always. Siena had resigned herself to the fact that no man of the caliber she desired would want anything to do with her once she came clean about the numerous acts of grand larceny she'd committed.

Matthew scrunched his chin. "Good." His mouth formed a devilish grin as his hand found its way to her knee, his fingers caressing her bare thigh.

One corner of Siena's mouth curled in self-satisfaction. She'd seduced Matthew in what? Less than fifteen minutes? Not a record, but close. However, she was approaching this potential con game ass backward. Normally, she would have already done her homework (case in point, Arthur Campbell) and filled a notebook with the information she'd gathered on her mark. To make sure she wasn't wasting her time on Matthew Kramer, she needed to conduct some fast research. Leaning forward, she placed her hand on Matthew's shoulder and whispered into his ear. "I need to use the little girls' room. Don't you dare give away my seat."

Once she was around the corner and out of sight, Siena typed Matthew's name into the browser on her cell phone. With such a common name, she expected the process of eliminating all irrelevant hits to take a while, but the Matthew Kramer she was investigating surfaced right away largely due to the esteemed reputation of his wife, Alva Kramer, nee Paulson, sole heiress to Paulson Industries. Alva, a wealthy socialite and active benefactor to a varied list of charities and organizations, had lived her entire life in the spotlight. Siena's thumb touched the screen of her cell phone repeatedly as she skimmed through article after article searching for as much useful information as she could gather within a five-minute span of time.

She learned that Matthew, in his mid-fifties, was four years younger than Alva. He'd had a brief marriage twenty-some years ago that had produced no children. He was Alva's third husband, her first having been a British race car driver with whom she'd had her only child, a daughter, and her second husband having been a New York fashion designer. A news article written about Matthew and Alva's wedding, which took place eight years ago, mentioned the $300,000 diamond earrings the bride had received as a gift from her father, the late Sanford Paulson. Siena enlarged the accompanying photo. Well, surprise, surprise. Siena half-suspected the earrings to have been a contrived part of Matthew's come-on line, but here was proof they truly did exist. And that was as much as Siena needed to know.

Siena was about to close her browser window when the headlines of a more recent article caught her attention: *Alva Paulson Kramer's Health Deteriorating.* She skimmed the article and learned that Alva had been diagnosed last year with a rare neurological disorder. According to the medical experts providing her treatment, her prognosis was grim.

So, instead of being home attending to his wife's needs, Matthew is in a bar picking up women. Gee, what a sweetheart. A real shoo-in for the Husband of the Year Award.

Siena had a sneaking suspicion that Matthew hadn't been faithful to his wife from day one. Her intuition also warned her that he wasn't the successful businessman he made himself out to be, that he lived mainly off his wife's fortune. From the articles Siena had breezed through, Alva Kramer was no pushover. She'd taken the necessary steps to protect her finances in her previous two marriages, and she probably kept a tight hold on her purse strings where Matthew was concerned. If that were the case, Siena doubted Matthew had the funds to pay for a separate love nest, so to speak, and frequent splurges on hotel suites most likely weren't in his budget either. That left him with few options other than to lure his paramours to the couple's Manhattan apartment while his wife was away on one of her frequent charitable sojourns. At least, that was what Siena was banking on.

Assuming that getting into Matthew's apartment would be easy enough, her challenge would be convincing him to take those $300,000 diamond earrings out of safekeeping. Fortunately, Siena's devious mind had never been short on crafty ideas. The plan she had in mind, however, was a two-person job. She made a call to Gus, her godfather and partner in crime, explained the situation and asked if he'd be willing to play a role in the long con that was taking root in her mind. They had a brief discussion after which Gus gave her the green light to proceed.

Strolling back to her seat at the bar, she noticed that Matthew was scanning the room as though he were pondering who to pounce on next just in case Siena had used the excuse of the ladies' room to give him the slip. She rolled her eyes.

Seriously?

"Sorry I was gone so long," she told him while sliding onto her chair. "There was a long line in the ladies' room." She crossed her legs and allowed Matthew's eager hand to reclaim possession of her thigh. "You know, I was thinking about the low-balled appraisal of your wife's jewelry that you said ruined your afternoon. I might be able to help."

Matthew lifted his whiskey glass and swirled what was left of his scotch around the melting ice cubes. "How's that?" He drained the glass and signaled the bartender to pour him another.

"One of my clients is a jewelry appraiser. I could give him a call, if you'd like, and ask if he'd be willing to give you his own valuation."

"You'd do that for me?" Matthew's reaction was one of genuine amazement, as though it had been ages since anyone had offered to do him a favor.

Siena rested her arm on his shoulder and gently massaging the nape of his neck with her fingertips. "Oh, darlin', in a heartbeat."

Chapter 11

Siena
October 2023

Matthew Kramer may as well have yanked the cap off a marking pen and written *BLACKMAILER* across his forehead. Why else would he be standing before Siena with that shit-eating grin on his face? Was he waiting for her to collapse into a puddle of tears and promise to give in to his demands if he would *please* make this despicable video disappear? If so, Matthew was in for a rude awakening. He wasn't the first man who'd attempted to extort Siena, and things hadn't turned out so well for the other guy.

Siena pressed the camera's fast forward button. Why waste time watching a recording of what she and Matthew had said and done to each other when every second of that stormy afternoon was permanently embedded in her memory? As the tape neared the end, she reset the speed back to normal. She needed to view the last few minutes—the truly important, personally incriminating portion of the video—in full detail.

Jesus! This is bad. This is really bad.

With the timer on the video winding down to zero, Siena had mere seconds to decide how to handle this situation. Aside from the con she'd played on him six years ago, what other incriminating information did

Matthew have on her? Siena's guess was—nothing. How could he? She'd lived under the guise of Marie Lacroix for most of the last twelve years. Internet searches on both Siena Ricci and Siena Woodward produced little information. Siena knew this. She'd performed the research herself. While Matthew may have assumed he'd struck gold when he discovered Siena's real name, he'd probably come away from his computer scratching his head, puzzled as to why her online presence led him to a cavernous void.

Siena had been raised among con men and forgery artists, and she'd been groomed by two of the best: her father, Dominic Ricci, and her godfather, Wendell "Gus" Ferguson. She'd prided herself on having completed dozens of successful cons. Fearing she was pressing her luck, she was considering getting out of the game when Gus approached her with a plan to obtain the legendary Somerset Necklace from Jonathan Woodward who, at the time, was nothing more than one of the many wealthy clients Siena assisted at the auction house. She'd intended for the Somerset Necklace job to be her swansong, but she'd gotten greedy. And sloppy. The scheme had blown up in her face, bringing her criminal escapades to an untimely end. Had Jonathan not fallen in love with her and forgiven her sins, she would be serving jail time right now instead of being the adored wife of one of Boston's most revered citizens.

Which raised the question of what Matthew intended to do with this video. Siena's gut told her that he was planning to use it to out her to Jonathan just as she'd betrayed him to Alva. But, again, Matthew was missing pieces of the puzzle. He wasn't aware that Siena had already shared her tainted history with Jonathan—at least in generalities. All Jonathan had cared to know was why Siena had worked as a con artist, not the intricacies of how she'd committed the crimes.

Still, the idea of Jonathan viewing this video made the remnants of Siena's breakfast curdle in her stomach. Jonathan worshipped her, so much so that he'd been willing to sweep her sordid past under the rug, had hidden the truth about her from his family and friends, and had even allowed their marriage to create a rift between him and his son Patrick. But Siena knew as sure as she was standing there that this recording of what had taken place inside Matthew's bedroom that day would be Jonathan's tipping point.

I don't care how low I need to sink; there is no way this camera will ever find its way into Jonathan's hands.

Matthew had obviously come here seeking revenge and money. He'd shown up on her doorstep full of arrogance and swagger, assuming he held the upper hand. Little did he realize who he was dealing with, and that he was about to pit himself against a master manipulator who had wormed her way out of stickier predicaments than this.

Lace up your gloves, Matthew. Round One is about to begin.

At last, the video footage ended with the sound of an air-kiss followed by Siena's voice off-camera saying *So long, Matty. Have fun weaseling your way out of this one.* Siena raised her head and glared at Matthew. "Let's cut to the chase. What do you want?"

"In exchange for not handing this camera over to your husband? And not providing the police with evidence of the robbery you committed?"

Siena's eyes narrowed. "You wouldn't dare," she

growled through clenched teeth. Her gaze drifted beyond Matthew to the boat dock where their property butted up against Lake Burgess. The idea of racing across the backyard and hurling the evidence into the lake occurred to her a split second too late.

Matthew snagged the camera from her hand and slid it into the inside pocket of his jacket. "Don't push me," he warned. "I'd like nothing better than to knock Jonathan Woodward off that pedestal he's been perched on since the day he walked through the front door of our fraternity house." Siena's eyes widened. "Oh! You didn't know that I'm one of your husband's fraternity brothers, did you?" He tossed his head back in a burst of laughter.

"It would have been nice for you to have shared that detail with me before now."

Matthew snorted. "It would have been nice for Jonathan to have mentioned *me* to *you* before now." He strolled to the edge of the terrace and removed an e-cigarette from his pocket. Without asking Siena if she minded, he began to vape. "But I'm not surprised," he said, exhaling a puff of smoke. "Most of the guys, your husband included, are a few years older than me. Even though Jonathan was assigned as my Big Brother when I joined the fraternity, I'm not as close to him as I am to most of the other guys. His doing more so than mine." Taking a drag off the cigarette, he swiveled around and faced Siena.

"When Alva filed for divorce, all the guys rallied around me. They asked why our marriage had failed and I was painfully honest. I told them I'd been having a fling with this gorgeous young tax accountant from Virginia, and she'd taken me for a ride. I shared every wretched detail with them. How you'd seduced me into my bedroom, then drugged and handcuffed me to the bed. How Alva went batshit crazy when she found me like that and made a beeline to her attorney's office."

He drew another hit off the e-cig. "The guys were indignant. *What a bitch!* they'd shouted...and don't think your illustrious husband wasn't right in there with them. *If we ever get our hands on that tramp,* they'd said, *we'll destroy her!* They're still mad as hell about it. Matter of fact, when we got together for dinner last month, they asked if I was any closer to tracking down the woman who'd caused Alva to disown me." He smiled broadly. "God, I can't wait to get their reactions when I send this video out in a mass text, and they recognize Jonny Woodward's new wife as the woman they've been champing at the bit to tar and feather."

Without warning, the implications of Matthew's threat struck Siena like a punch in the gut. As if the fallout from Jonathan and the NYPD viewing the footage wasn't enough to cripple her with fear, her ruination took a backseat to the damage that would be done to Jonathan's reputation.

"You're disgusting." Siena snarled as she stepped toward him. "You were disgusting when I met you six years ago, and you're even more disgusting today."

Matthew grunted. "Says the con artist from the video."

"I was merely doing your wife a favor."

Matthew's face filled with confusion. "What are you talking about?"

"I never believed for one second that I was the first woman you'd picked up in a bar. You hadn't been faithful to Alva from the day you married her, and she had a right to know her husband was a cheating louse."

"Ah…so you volunteered to step up to the plate and knock the comfortable life I had with Alva right out of the ballpark. How kind of you. Did you even consider a less drastic way of informing her? A phone call? An anonymous letter in the mail? Or was drugging and leaving me naked on the bed just an add-on to your scheme to steal her earrings?"

Siena pursed her lips. Her temper was getting the better of her and she dared not provide him with an admission of guilt.

"Alva not only divorced me right after that incident, but she also wrote me out of her will altogether. I was damned lucky that our pre-nup granted me ownership of the apartment." He chuckled as if to himself. "When her attorney asked me to stop by and collect a piece of jewelry she'd bequeathed me, I foolishly assumed Alva had a change of heart as she neared the end of her life. I almost choked right there in the attorney's office when I opened the jewelry case and found the fake earrings you'd left in place of the original pair. You know, the earrings you helped yourself to while I was lying unconscious on the bed. Alva couldn't pass up the opportunity to drive another screw into me, even if it was from the grave."

"How do you know that was her intention?"

"Because she left a note in the box that said *My father warned me never to trust you.*"

Siena nodded. "Smart man, her father." She took cruel pleasure in making Matthew snarl. "Again, I ask— What do you want?"

"For this video to go away permanently? Five million dollars. And I want it, in cash, by the end of the month."

Siena cocked her head and stared at Matthew. Did she hear him correctly? She exhaled a sharp, disbelieving snort. "I'm sorry. Did you say five *million* dollars?"

"Yes."

"By the end of this month? That's only two weeks from now."

"Your point being?"

Siena's left eye twitched. "That it's impossible. Jonathan and I are going out of town for a week beginning tomorrow. The trip can't be cancelled without drawing suspicion, so now we're down to one week. You cannot expect me to accumulate five million dollars in seven days."

Nor does that give me sufficient time to steal that camera from you and destroy the evidence, which is the real plan I have in mind.

"You managed to screw up my life in only seven days. I think you'll figure out a way to come up with five million bucks in that amount of time."

"It wouldn't matter if I had seven months or seven years." Siena crossed her arms and stepped away from him. "I don't have access to that kind of money."

"Siphon it out of one of Jonathan's accounts. Hell, he wouldn't even miss it."

She swung around and confronted Matthew head-on. "Let's say I do give you what you're asking, and you turn that camera over to me. What guarantee do I have that you didn't create several duplicates? That you won't keep coming back demanding even more money?"

Matthew shrugged his shoulders. "I guess you'll just have to trust me."

Siena derided him with a cold, hard stare. "You

mean, like your wife did?"

Matthew glared at her, contempt in his eyes. "And to think I was once in love with you."

The scowl melted off Siena's face. Her remembrance of their fleeting relationship was that Matthew had been using her for short-term pleasure just as she'd been using him for financial gain. The notion that she'd truly captured his heart came as a gut-wrenching revelation. All his moon-eyed musings, all his plans for their future hadn't been a lame way of enticing her into his bed after all.

"Yeah," Matthew continued, "I mean *completely* in love with you, not just keeping you around until I got tired of you and found someone better. Hell, since I'm making confessions, you may as well know that you broke my heart. So, just imagine how furious I was when I recognized you in those photos Jonathan sent out. I felt like we were back in college and Playboy Jonny had once again taken home the party girl I'd been making the moves on. Well, this time I've got the upper hand, haven't I? Jonathan has no idea that his foxy new wife was in my bed before she fell into his. Until he sees this video, that is."

At that moment, Siena would have happily agreed to pay five million dollars for the pleasure of scratching Matthew's eyes out. Instead, she mustered every ounce of willpower she possessed to prevent herself from physically attacking him. Fighting Matthew on his playing field, she deduced, was the better approach. She'd back down and make him believe he was in control while she set about undermining his scheme.

"Fine," she spat out. "You win."

Proud as a peacock fanning his feathers, Matthew

shot her a lop-sided grin and stepped closer. He slid his hand into his pocket, withdrew a cell phone, and handed it to Siena. "Take this burner phone and use it to communicate with me. My number is already programmed into it."

"You should know, this won't end well."

Matthew snickered. "For me or for you?" They stared into each other's eyes as though playing a game of chicken. Who would be the first to blink? "Have a nice trip. If I don't hear from you in the next eight days, I'll be stopping by for another visit as soon as you get home. Don't bother seeing me out."

Siena's eyes followed Matthew as he sauntered through the backyard and disappeared around the corner of the house. She crossed her arms, fending off a shiver that was brought on more by the sharp finger of dread coursing down her back than the cool autumn breeze. Had she seriously been so naïve as to think that moving away from New York was a guarantee that her past wouldn't follow her?

The seed of an idea planted itself in her brain. She re-entered the house and dashed upstairs to her bedroom. As she showered and dressed to go out, she worked out the details. As much as she regretted going against the vow she and Jonathan had made to always be open and honest with each other, she needed to brush the dust off her old con artist techniques—that cunning, deceitful side of her personality—for a short while. Just long enough to wrench that hateful video away from Matthew and reset her life back to normal.

Without making Jonathan aware of what she was doing.

****

Veronica

Well, well, well! My father's sainted wife has secrets to hide after all.

Once again, Veronica's instincts had paid off. The first time she encountered Siena lounging by the pool at the family's Nantucket compound in a bikini made from *at most* six inches of material, she sensed something sinister lurking beneath that all-too-perfect exterior of hers. She now had hearsay evidence that Daddy did indeed sugarcoat Siena's background to make her an easier pill for his children to swallow, but Veronica had been convinced all along that she'd uncover the truth eventually. Thank God she wasn't above eavesdropping when the opportunity presented itself.

And the fact that Siena has a history with, of all people, Matthew Kramer. Oh, this was too good to be true!

Veronica leaned her back against the bathroom vanity and pursed her lips. Truth be told, she was intrigued by Siena's dubious past. That sweet as pie, coddled beauty queen persona had always grated on her nerves. And the way Siena handled Matthew just now? Something told Veronica he wasn't the first man Siena had needed to strong-arm.

So, what should I do with this newfound knowledge?

The responsible thing would be to drive home, close the door behind her, and erase the last twenty minutes from her memory. Never again think of the conversation that took place on the terrace just now or speak about it to anyone. Ever. Especially not Daddy. As much as she hated to admit it, Daddy truly was madly in love with Siena. And, based on what she'd observed during last night's party, Siena's love for Daddy was genuine.

Siena's affectionate touches, the way her face lit up each time she glanced Daddy's way, how she regarded him with that sparkle of adoration and desire in her eyes. How many times had Veronica admired her dear late mother when she gazed at Daddy in that same fashion? She dabbed away a tear from the corner of her eye before it spilled onto her cheek.

Her conscience advised her to keep her nose out of Daddy and Siena's affairs.

Still…

How could she *un*hear such an intriguing conversation? The urge to take matters into her own hands was too tempting. Which was a bone of contention in her marriage. Brian was always accusing her of being a buttinski, a trait he claimed was getting worse as she got older. Well, seriously. Was it her fault the men in her life needed so much supervision? Brian refused to acknowledge her point of view. Of course, he couldn't. He was one of the men she was constantly keeping tabs on.

Screw it! Her gut instincts had served her well in the past and, in her opinion, this situation was no different. She eased the bathroom window closed, bolted through the first-floor suite, burst out of the bedroom, and collided full force into Brenda.

"Ohmygod! Sorry, Brenda. I didn't see you coming down the hall."

"Veronica, what are you doing here? I thought you left a while ago."

"I…uh…I was on my way out when nature called. I couldn't wait."

"Oh," Brenda said with concern. "Are you okay?"

"Yes, I'm fine" Veronica backed her way down the

hall. "Too much rich food last night. I've got to go. Have a good day." She spun around, rushing toward the foyer and out the front door. As she steered her car to the end of the circular driveway, she accessed the phone feature on the car's control screen and commanded Bluetooth to place a call. She tapped her fingers against the steering wheel, impatient for the call to connect and be answered.

"Cancel all your appointments for the rest of the day," Veronica said, barely giving the person on the other end of the line the chance to say hello. "We need to have a conversation right now that is much more important than anything else that's going on in your life."

Chapter 12

Siena

Brenda glanced up from her laptop and gave Siena the once-over. "Looks like you're heading out."

From the library's doorway, Siena piled yet another fib onto her *mensonges du jour*. "Yes, I'm going shopping for some gifts to bring to my family in Santa Martina."

"Thanks for letting me know. I'll tell Jonathan when he returns."

"No need. I already texted him. Besides, he'll be home late. He's having dinner tonight with Veronica."

Brenda frowned. "You're not joining them?"

"No," Siena replied with a grin and a quick shake of her head. "I think it's good for them to continue their tradition." The truth was, since their return from Europe Jonathan had attempted to discontinue this weekly father-daughter get together, but Veronica had thrown a tantrum and Jonathan had, as usual, given in. *She just needs more time to adjust to us being married,* Jonathan had told Siena. *What she needs,* Siena had wanted to reply, *is for everyone in this family to stop enabling her childish behavior.* But, once again, Siena had held her tongue. Her relationship with Veronica was contentious enough without making herself more of an enemy than she already was.

"Well, then, do you need me to suggest some stores? Or do you need directions?"

"No, I've got it covered. Thanks, anyway."

"Sure. I doubt I'll see you again before you leave, so let me wish you safe travels to the Caribbean and back. Have a wonderful visit with your family."

"Thank you," Siena said as she hurried away. "I'll see you next week."

In the garage, Siena tossed her purse into the SUV Jonathan purchased for her and had delivered to the house a few days after they returned from Europe. Although Siena loved Jonathan for surprising her with her own vehicle to tool around town in, part of her resented him for making this important decision without consulting her first. While Jonathan thrived on the element of surprise, he oftentimes forgot he'd married a fiercely independent woman who was accustomed to making her own decisions. While she'd learned to graciously accept his extravagant gifts, she understood that training Jonathan to occasionally let her take the reins was going to be an ongoing challenge.

She buckled into the driver's seat and entered the Watertown address she'd gotten off the internet into the navigation system. The estimated drive time was thirty-four minutes. Plenty of time to review the details of her plan to foil Matthew Kramer. Plenty of time to stop herself from setting into motion what might be one of the worst ideas she'd ever had. She shifted the car into *Drive* and hit the accelerator.

Think, think, think, Siena! Yes, the conniving, manipulative side of your brain has gone rusty with disuse over the past year, but that's no excuse. Just grease up those wheels and get your mind back into the game. You can do this. You must do this! What other options do you have?

Well...there's always the alternative.

You could take your chances and come clean with Jonathan. As the expression goes, honesty is the best policy. At that notion, Siena laughed out loud. *Don't kid yourself. You viewed the video. You were issued the threat. Matthew Kramer has thrown down the gauntlet. You have no choice but to beat him at his own game.*

Siena steered her car into a visitor spot in the parking lot next to the McGraw Business Center. She turned off the ignition and tapped her index finger against the steering wheel as she stared at the brick building before her. The drive to Watertown had given her sufficient time to develop a workable plan of action. However, convincing the man who operated his business inside Suite 310 of that building to be her co-conspirator was an entirely different matter. She'd double-crossed him during their previous business arrangement. What were the chances he'd be willing to work with her a second time?

Regardless, she couldn't stall any longer. Slinging her purse over her shoulder, Siena dashed across the parking lot and entered the building lobby. She was directed to the third floor where, following the hall to the left as she stepped off the elevator, she located the door on which was affixed a metal placard reading *LB and Associates, LLC*. She took a deep breath and placed her hand on the doorknob.

Well, here goes nothing.

Siena opened the door and stepped into a dingy, oppressive reception area. The space was just large enough to cram in a small desk for the receptionist to squeeze behind, and four well-worn chairs notably devoid of potential clients awaiting their scheduled appointments with the business owner. In one corner, a two-drawer metal filing cabinet supported a printer that doubled as a copier. In the opposite corner was an identical cabinet atop which sat a coffee maker and related accoutrements. Adding a touch of greenery to the décor was a potted schefflera, its droopy leaves making a desperate cry for either more water or more sunlight. Probably both.

Straight ahead was an archway through which Siena eyed two doors, the left one slightly ajar and labeled *Restroom*, the other closed and unmarked. She stood in the center of the room and waited for the receptionist to tear her attention away from the gossipy tabloid that lay open atop her desk. The periodical, Siena noted, was the only item occupying the desktop save for a computer monitor, a corded phone console, and the woman's elbows.

The receptionist—middle-aged, overweight, and about as animated as a boiled potato—lifted her head and gazed up at Siena. "You got an appointment?"

So much for Lou's hiring skills. Did he not understand the importance of making a good first impression? Which was exactly what his receptionist was *not* doing. Siena wanted so badly to take the woman aside and kindly inform her that she could no longer get away with referring to the gray streaking through her mousy brown hair as "highlights", and that she needed to admit her expanding body no longer fit comfortably into the size small, candy pink knit top she was wearing. Maybe mention that a smidgeon of concealer would do wonders to camouflage those dark circles under her eyes.

Please let her be a relative Lou was coerced into hiring.

"Yes. I called earlier. Siena Ricci."

"Oh, yeah," the receptionist said in her thick Boston accent. "Have a seat. I'll tell Lou you're here."

Siena sneered at the grimy upholstered chairs. "I don't mind standing."

The woman shrugged her shoulders. "Whatever." She lifted the receiver and punched a button. "Hey. Your next appointment is here…Okey-dokey." Replacing the receiver in its cradle, she told Siena, "You can go on in. Lou's office is the door on the right."

As opposed to the door labeled "Restroom" on the left?

Siena smiled politely. "Thank you." She stepped through the archway, rapped lightly on Lou's door and waited for an invitation to enter. Instead, without warning, the door was thrust open and there she was, after nearly fifteen months, standing face-to-face once again with Lou Biondi. His face was creased with a few more wrinkles and his hair was thinner than the last time she'd had the displeasure to share his company, but he was still in good shape for a man in his mid-50s. He was all smiles and warm welcomes—until recognition set in.

"Jesus Christ!" Lou stumbled backward as if careening away from a den of venomous snakes. "What the hell are you doing here?"

Siena greeted him with a rueful smile as she entered his office and closed the door behind her. "Nice to see you, too, Lou."

Lou's sarcasm was blatant when he asked, "Are you alone, or did you bring the police with you?"

"Come on, Lou. I came here on friendly terms. Can't

we forget the past and start over?"

Lou maneuvered himself behind the desk as if concerned about keeping a safe distance between them. "Forget?" He placed his hands in the center of his desk and leaned toward her, the veins in his forehead bulging. "Forget how you used me? Came close to getting me arrested on a breaking and entering charge? Oh, sure, Marie. No problem. Water under the bridge."

"Uh…first of all, my name isn't Marie Lacroix," Siena informed him with a sly grin. She checked the cleanliness of the chairs facing his desk before taking a seat.

Lou straightened his back and reviewed the calendar on his computer screen. "So, you're the Siena Ricci who called to schedule a last-minute appointment with me this afternoon? Christ! How many aliases do you use?"

Crossing her legs, Siena breathed a heavy sigh. "Believe it or not, Siena Ricci is my real name." Lou stared at her with suspicious eyes. "Actually—legally—it's Siena Woodward."

"Woodward?" Lou's jaw dropped as he lowered himself into his chair. "You're kidding. So, which one of the millionaires did you con into marrying you, the father or the son?"

Siena answered him with stone-cold eyes. "The father. And I didn't con him into anything. He married me despite the scam I—*we*—tried to play on him."

"Yeah? Well, he knows more than I do." Lou leaned forward and placed his forearms on the desk. "Why don't you fill me in? What scam were *we* pulling off the night you tricked me into believing you were helping me steal that Duncan Cordray painting from Patrick Woodward's house?"

Siena pursed her lips and averted Lou's piercing stare. "Look, you were right. I was running a con that summer on both Jonathan and Patrick Woodward. But, halfway through, I was struck with a terrible case of guilty conscience." She lifted her head and gazed directly into Lou's eyes. "I tried to cancel the job, but by then my partners and I were in too deep. The buyer had backed me into a corner and time was running out. Setting you up as the patsy in the scheme was a sneaky tactic, but it was the only way I could save my own ass." The scornful expression on Lou's face sent the clear message that her apology was not well taken. "If it's any consolation, the con ended up backfiring on me."

"Oh, poor you." Lou stuck out his lower lip as if mocking her. "*I* went through hell that night. Envisioned going to jail, having to hire a lawyer, my business going belly-up. All I could think of was how much I wanted to tighten my hands around that gorgeous neck of yours and squeeze the life right out of you. And now, to top it all off, you saunter in here and tell me you came out of it smelling like a rose." He tossed his head back and let out a sarcastic laugh. "Hah! Oh, that's rich."

Siena frowned and shook her head. "Look, I'm sorry. What more can I say?"

Lou glared at her for several seconds. "So, that's it? You came here just to apologize?"

"That," she shrugged her shoulder, "and to ask for your help."

"My help?" Lou snickered. "What's that expression about fooling me twice? You can't seriously think I'd be willing to team up with you again. *Ever!*"

Siena inched forward and placed her hand flat on Lou's desk. "I *am* serious. Dead serious. I'm being blackmailed, Lou, and I need your help to get out of a…" She hesitated, not sure which words would best describe her predicament. "…a messy situation."

Lou's eyes squinted with suspicion. "Now, don't get me wrong. I'm good at what I do, but with the kind of money your husband has, you could hire the best P.I. in the world. Why'd you come to me?"

"Because I'll be paying for your services out of my own pocket, and you're all I can afford." Siena sat back in the chair, crossed her legs, and picked a piece of imaginary lint off her slacks. Anything to avoid making eye contact as she confessed, "And because I owe you one."

"I see." Lou drummed his fingers on the desktop. "You know, normally, I don't ask my clients too many questions, but then they usually don't give me a reason to distrust them. You, on the other hand, make me break out in a cold sweat. So, you're married to this Woodward guy. That doesn't change the fact that you're a con artist. How do I know you're not using me in another one of your schemes right now?"

Siena lifted her eyes and confronted Lou. "Listen, I was only in the game for a few years and only because I needed the extra money to pay for my invalid father's medical needs. That part of my life is behind me. Or at least I believed it was until this morning. I'm not messing around, and I don't have time to waste." She rose from the chair and slung her purse over her shoulder. "If you're not interested in working with me, then I need to find someone who is."

Lou threw up his hands. "Okay, okay. Don't get your panties in a bunch. I believe you. Sit down and give me the particulars. What kind of job are you talking about?"

"I'm going out of town tomorrow for a week." As Siena retook her seat, she responded before Lou had the chance to make a snarky remark. "I know. Bad timing, but it's unavoidable. This man who's blackmailing me— I need you to follow him while I'm away. I want to know where he goes and what he does when he gets there; how he gets around town; who he visits, and who visits him. If he so much as sneezes, I want to know about it."

Lou rocked back in his chair. "Is this guy local?"

"No. He lives in Manhattan."

"Manhattan?" Lou raised an eyebrow. "Was he the target of one of your con games that went bad? He tracked you down and wants payback?"

Siena sighed. "The con I pulled on him ran without a hitch. It's just…" She lowered her eyes. "I didn't know until this morning that he'd captured me on film."

Lou grinned. Siena imagined he was loving this scenario, that someone—*anyone*—had managed to make her squirm. "And now he's blackmailing you with that video tape." Siena didn't respond, merely held Lou's gaze. Lou puckered his lips, his breath exhaling in a slow whistle. "I hope whatever scam you pulled on this guy was worth the price you're paying for it now."

"What I did to him was personal."

"Yeah? You care to fill me in on the details?"

"Not necessarily."

"I didn't think so. I'm also guessing you don't want any of this leaked to your husband."

"You guessed right. Which means you can't let anything slip to either Veronica or Brian Lambert either." Siena was referring to Lou's frequent visits to Benvenuto, the Boston restaurant owned and operated by

Jonathan's daughter and son-in-law.

"Are you on drugs? I wouldn't dream of showing my face to either of the Lamberts again after that debacle over Veronica's brother's painting."

"Still, just in case you do see either of them…"

"Restriction noted." Lou opened the desk drawer to his left and removed a legal document. "Sounds like an easy enough gig, and needing to be in Manhattan for the next week shouldn't interfere with the other jobs I'm working on." He clicked open a pen and filled in the blank spaces on a contract form. "I charge $200 an hour, plus expenses. Since I'll be spending several days out of town, I'll need an advance retainer. Let's say," he gazed up at the ceiling and scrunched his chin while performing, Siena assumed, the math in his head, "fifteen thousand."

Hmm…Lou is awfully eager to take me on as a client. And here I was, expecting him to kick me out of his office. Business must be slow. Which is a sad reflection on his reputation. Thankfully, I only need him to perform surveillance work and, from my previous experience with him, I know Lou's at least good for that.

"Ten," Siena countered. "That pays half your fee up front plus any expenses you incur. I still have my apartment in Manhattan. You can stay there and save me the cost of a paying for a hotel room."

Lou chuckled and shrugged his shoulders. "Sure. Why not?" He slid the contract across the desk, reviewed the terms, and addressed Siena's concerns. "If you don't have any other questions, I need you to sign and date the last page."

Lifting Lou's pen from the desk, Siena added her own clause under the signature line. "First, I'm including a stipulation to say I'm granting you permission to use my apartment only on the specified dates covered by the contract, and that you are obligated to pay for any damages made to the property and/or its contents during that period." She glanced at him. "It's not that I don't trust you…"

Lou's lip curled into a sneer. "But you don't. I get it. No wild parties. I promise."

Siena signed and dated the contract, then passed it back to Lou for his signature.

"I'll be right back." Lou stood and crossed the office. Opening the door, he stepped out into the reception area. Siena overheard him say something to the receptionist about copies and envelopes. Returning to the office and taking his seat, he told Siena, "Gemma will have your copy of the contract on her desk. You can pick it up as you're leaving."

"So, her name's Gemma." Siena smirked. "I must say, she's a real *gem*."

Lou threw up his hands. "Yeah, yeah, I know. She's my sister-in-law and she's only here three days a week. And that's about as much as you need to know about my crazy family."

"Agreed." *More than I care to know,* she wanted to say.

Lou positioned his keyboard in front of him and typed in his password. "Now, I'll need the name, a photo if you have one or a detailed physical description if you don't, the home address and, if it's different, the business address of the man you want me to follow. I'll also need your phone number. And a check for ten thousand dollars."

Siena's heart sank as she opened her purse and

fished out the checkbook for the account she'd opened twelve years ago, the account into which she'd deposited her profits from all the illicit jobs she'd engineered during her run as a con artist. This fund had been her nest egg, earmarked as her financial means when she escaped New York and joined her family in the Caribbean. She'd dreamed of using the money to start her own business or to place a down payment on a house. Her goal had been to make that transition by her fortieth birthday.

Marrying Jonathan had changed all that. Rather than being needed to pay for expenses, the funds in that account were now discretionary. Remorseful over the fact that the money had been obtained through ill-gotten means, Siena had planned to do something honorable— make generous donations to her favorite charities, perhaps open a scholarship fund at the high school she'd attended—in addition to continuing to pay for her father's medical needs. Instead, because of her own recklessness and stupidity, the money was being wasted on a two-bit P.I. The irony that she was relying on one regrettable mistake from her past to help erase another both repulsed and saddened her. She was reverting to the liar, the cheater, and the thief she had grown to resent and had vowed to bury for good.

This is a necessary evil, Siena rationalized as she filled in the blank spaces on the check.

And this, she promised herself, *will be the last time.*

Chapter 13

Siena

Over the din of the rotating luggage carousel and the jets departing on the all-to-close runways and the stop-and-go traffic on the access road behind them, Siena tuned in to the voice calling out to her.

"Sissy! Over here!"

Siena glanced around and spied Jacqueline standing near the curb, waving her arms. She returned the wave as she touched Jonathan's arm. "There she is!"

"Where?" With their suitcases in tow, Jonathan's eyes scanned the crowd as he followed Siena. When his gaze fell on his new sister-in-law, he shook his head. "Geez. How could I have missed her?"

Siena quickened her pace and rushed into Jacqueline's outstretched arms. "I'm so happy to see you!" She pinched back the tears as she and Jacqueline squeezed each other in a loving embrace.

"I can't believe you're finally here," Jacqueline choked out, allowing her tears to flow freely. Wiping her cheeks dry, she glanced at Jonathan. "Does this man who's gawking at us belong to you?"

Stepping back, Siena wrapped her arm around Jonathan. "He sure does. Jac, this is Jonathan. Jonathan, meet my sister, Jacqueline."

Jonathan's eyes widened as they bounced between

Siena's and Jacqueline's faces. "I had to see it to believe it, but you two truly are identical." With a guarded smile, he said, "It's a pleasure to finally meet you, Jacqueline."

"Likewise." Jacqueline flashed him a hesitant grin. "So, we need to get your luggage into the car before that cop comes down on me again for parking illegally."

Siena stood aside and studied Jonathan and Jacqueline's interaction as they loaded the suitcases into the car's trunk. The moment was uncomfortable, a mixture of stilted politeness and forced tolerance, just as she'd anticipated. Siena loved them both for making a sincere effort to be civil to each other, but they were a long way from having a warm brother-slash-sister-in-law relationship.

The part Jacqueline had played last year in Siena's ill-fated attempt to con the Woodward family—befriending Jonathan's recently-widowed son and worming her way into his home for the sole purpose of stealing his most valuable antique treasure—was still too fresh in both their minds. Jonathan may have been willing to forgive Siena for the crimes she'd committed against *him*, but how dare Jacqueline exploit his son's vulnerability while Patrick was still reeling over the loss of his wife. When it came to his children, Jonathan was the protective father through and through. Until Patrick was ready to move on from that stinging experience, neither was Jonathan.

For her part, Jacqueline was dealing with her own demons. More than a year had passed and her regret over the trick she'd played on Patrick was lessening, but she admitted the guilt would always weigh heavily on her heart. And, although she'd only laid into Siena once to, as Siena recalled her saying, *get it off her chest*, Siena sensed Jacqueline's resentment over having been dragged into the con was still smoldering under the surface.

Siena, on the other hand, was an expert at compartmentalizing her emotions. Yes, she'd been the instigator of the con and, if not for her, none of them would be in this situation in the first place. But Siena had a talent for isolating the unpleasant aspects of her life, locking them into a space in the back of her mind, and throwing away the key. If any of these memories found an escape route, she kept her emotions in check and dealt with the situation pragmatically. Sometimes she wished she possessed more of Jacqueline's rosiness and compassion, but that simply wasn't her personality. Besides, when it came to handling problems, like the one Matthew Kramer had dropped on her doorstep yesterday, possessing the skill to fight back was an extremely handy trait.

The slamming of the trunk lid drew Siena out of her musings.

"Come on, you two." Jacqueline rounded the fender and opened the driver's door. "Hop in and let's get out of here."

Jonathan opened the front passenger door for Siena. "You'll have an easier time chatting with your sister if you sit up front. I'll take the back seat."

With everyone buckled in, Jacqueline steered the car into traffic. "I was thinking I'd drive first to the resort so you can check in and drop off your bags, maybe freshen up and change clothes if you want. That will get us home right in time for lunch."

"Is the resort far from the house?" Siena asked.

"Um…" Jacqueline mumbled as she leaned into a

left-hand turn. "It's about a fifteen minute drive, depending on traffic. I wish you could stay at our house, but we're tight enough as it is."

"Don't worry about it," Siena told her. "Is Nonna in the kitchen cooking up a feast?"

"Of course. I'm not sure what she'll be serving, but there were some mouth-watering aromas coming from the kitchen this morning."

"Good. I'm starving." Siena partially turned her head toward the backseat. "Jonathan, are you hungry?"

"I could eat."

Jacqueline aimed a smile at Jonathan through the rearview mirror. "I promise, you won't be disappointed in Nonna's cooking."

Siena grinned as she gazed out the window at the landscape of tall palm trees and cascading bougainvillea. Leave it to Jacqueline to be the first to extend a hand of friendship across the turbulent waters. The question was, how much longer would Jonathan continue to give Jacqueline the cold shoulder?

"Jac," Siena said, glancing over at her sister, "before we get to the resort, I want the details on this man you've been seeing."

As Jacqueline steered the car into a roundabout, her face glowed in a way Siena hadn't seen since the night of their friend Chelsea's sweet sixteen birthday party when Jacqueline drew Siena aside and confessed that, for the last half hour, she'd been in the backyard making out with Sean Munroe. "Oh, Sissy," Jacqueline said, "this guy is The One. I can't wait for you to meet him." As an afterthought, she added, "You *and* Jonathan. You're both going to love him."

Siena delighted in her sister's euphoria. "So, what's

his name? Does he live on the island? How did you meet? Come on, don't hold back."

"His name is Tyler and, no, he isn't a local. He came to Santa Martina two months ago to vacation with his teen-aged sons—he's divorced—and right after they arrived, he slipped on the wet tile around the pool at their rental and broke his leg. He needed surgery to reset the bone, and I treated him in post-op. I'm not kidding when I say it was love at first sight. We've seen each other every day since his discharge and our relationship has gotten serious." She'd driven the car into the resort's parking lot and stopped under the canopy at the front entrance. "He's a celebrity of sorts, so you may already be familiar with him. But that's as much as I'll tell you for now."

Siena drew Jacqueline into a hug. "He sounds wonderful, Jac. We can't wait to meet him."

****

Siena and Jonathan followed Jacqueline around the side of the family's bungalow to the backyard patio. Siena hurried to her father's side as Dominic Ricci shouted out, "Hey, everybody, Sissy's here!"

Siena's heart swelled as she knelt beside her father's wheelchair and enveloped him in her arms. "Dad, I'm so happy to see you. How are you doing?"

"I'm good." Dominic brushed back a lock of Siena's hair and kissed her forehead. "How can I complain now that you're here?"

"Dad, I can't wait one more second to introduce you to my husband." Siena rose and extended her hand, beckoning Jonathan to join them. "Dad, this is Jonathan. Jonathan, meet my father, Dominic."

Jonathan shook Dominic's hand. "It's a pleasure to

meet you."

"Same here," Dominic said. "It's about time Sissy brought you here to meet us."

"Hey," Gus said as he sauntered toward Siena, "don't forget about me."

Siena wrapped her arms around Gus's neck and kissed his cheek. "Gus, I've miss you so much!"

"Not nearly as much as I've missed you." Releasing Siena from his embrace, Gus placed his arm around the woman standing beside him who was so petite that, despite her wedged sandals, the top of her head was still an inch or so shy of Gus's shoulder. "Siena, this is Marielle. I haven't told you this, but Marielle and I have been seeing each other since…" he glanced at Marielle as if needing her to validate the timeline, "…well, almost since the day I moved to the island. Yeah, so, anyway, Marielle, this is Siena, my other goddaughter."

"Welcome to Santa Martina, Siena," Marielle said, her voice carrying the distinctive cadence of the native islanders. "An introduction wasn't necessary. I'm certain you hear this all the time, but you and Jacqueline are identical."

"True," Siena said, nodding in agreement, "although my blonde hair makes it easy for everyone to tell us apart." She grasped Marielle's hand. "I'm delighted to meet you, Marielle."

Siena soaked in Marielle's countenance in a quick glance. The short, tight curls of her shiny black hair. Her amber eyes, the rich mocha-colored tone of her skin. Her bright and friendly smile. No wonder Gus was attracted to her.

"So, tell me," Siena asked, her gaze shifting from Marielle to Gus, "how did you two meet?"

"At a bar," Gus chuckled. "Where else?"

"Actually," Marielle added, "at M's Bar down by the beach. A bar which I own and which, I'm sorry to say, I need to get back to. Gus promised to bring you all down to M's this evening, so we'll talk more then."

"Yes, we will," Siena replied. "But please don't leave without first meeting my husband."

While Siena was introducing Jonathan to Gus and Marielle, Carmella Ricci stepped out of the house carrying a pitcher of iced tea which she set on the cloth-covered table. "Sissy, come give your Nonna a hug!"

Siena rushed into her grandmother's outstretched arms. "Nonna, there you are! Come, let me introduce you to my husband." Placing her arm around Carmella's back, Siena guided her grandmother toward Jonathan. "Jonathan, you have one more person to meet. This beautiful woman is my Nonna Carmella."

Carmella's face beamed with approval. "Oh, Sissy," she exclaimed as she raised her arms and placed her palms against Jonathan's cheeks, "why you not tell me you marry such a handsome man?" Although she'd left Tuscany as a young woman, Carmella's speech was still thick with an Italian accent and her English often lacked polish.

"Neither did Siena tell me she had such a charming grandmother." Jonathan leaned down and accepted a kiss on both cheeks. "It's a pleasure to finally meet you, Nonna."

"*You* call me Carmella," she ordered, wagging an arthritis-gnarled finger at him. "Only Jacqueline and Sissy call me Nonna."

"As you wish, Carmella," Jonathan said with a wink and his most winning smile. "Now, I'm dying to know why everyone calls Siena 'Sissy'?"

"Oh, that started when the girls were toddlers," Dominic explained. "Instead of calling Siena by her name, Jacqueline always referred to her as 'sister'. But 'sister' came out sounding like 'sissa', and before long, we were all calling Siena 'Sissy'."

"Sissy," Jonathan repeated with a knowing grin. "I like it." Siena was all too familiar with that mischievous twinkle in his eye. She imagined him teasingly whispering *Sissy* into her ear as soon as he got her behind the closed door of their suite at the resort that evening.

Just then, Jacqueline stepped out of the house followed by a man hobbling on crutches. His right leg was in a cast that extended from his ankle to his thigh. "Careful of the step, hon," she warned.

"I'm fine," the man replied. Intent on watching his footing, his head remained downcast as he maneuvered on the crutches toward the patio.

Jacqueline dragged a high-backed lawn chair across the grass and held it steady. "Come, sit here, and I'll introduce you."

With Jacqueline's assistance, the man settled into the chair and handed her the crutches. "Thanks, Jackie. Do you promise this cast is coming off tomorrow?"

"That's what Dr. Montas said," Jacqueline assured him, "*if* your x-ray shows the bone has healed properly. But don't forget you'll need a few weeks of rehab."

"Can I request you as my physical therapist?" he asked with raised eyebrows.

"Ty, I'm an RN. My training doesn't cover therapy." The man placed his arm around her. Drawing her close, he whispered into her ear. Jacqueline giggled. "I don't need to be a physical therapist to do *that*," she told him before pecking a kiss on his lips. Straightening her posture, she glanced over at Jonathan and Siena. "Sissy, Jonathan, I'd like you to meet Ty—"

"Tyler Winslow?" Jonathan blurted out. He darted across the patio, his hand extended. "I thought I recognized you! Jacqueline, why didn't you tell us the Tyler you were so eager for us to meet is *the* Tyler Winslow?" He shook Tyler's hand, his face beaming as though he were a little leaguer meeting a baseball Hall of Famer.

"Pardon me for not standing," Tyler said, not seeming at all surprised to be recognized. He cocked his head and knitted his brows. "You are…?"

As Siena stepped beside Jonathan, Jacqueline placed her hands on Tyler's shoulders and completed the introductions. "Ty, this is my sister, Siena, and her husband, Jonathan."

Tyler shook Siena's hand. "So, you're the famous Sissy. Jackie talks about you all the time. I'm happy to finally meet you."

"It's a pleasure and, may I say, an honor to meet you, Tyler," Siena said, her expression nearly as awestruck as Jonathan's. "Jac, you might have given us fair warning that the man in your life is a world-renowned novelist, especially since he's Jonathan's favorite author."

"Sorry," Jacqueline replied. "I wasn't sure if either of you would be that familiar with him."

"Are you kidding? Jonathan's a huge fan. In fact, Tyler, your novels occupy an entire shelf in our library. And, based on Jonathan's recommendation, I've also gotten hooked on your books."

"Thank you," Tyler said. "I'm pleased that you follow my work—as is my publisher." Squinting his eyes, Tyler gazed at Jonathan. "Jonathan Woodward," he said as though thinking out loud. "Your name and face seem so familiar."

Jonathan pulled up a lawn chair and sat beside Tyler. "I doubted you'd remember, but about eight years ago we met at a literary conference in Tampa. We served on a panel together, something about the development of the detective novel—"

"*From Poe to Winslow!*" Tyler broke in. "Oh! You're the, uh, the American Lit professor from Boston. Yes, I remember now. We were having a fascinating conversation afterward which I was forced to cut short for one reason or another."

"You needed to rush off to lead a writers' workshop, if I'm not mistaken."

Tyler grinned. "I'll trust your memory on that one. It may have taken eight years, but we'll have lots of time going forward to continue that discussion." He smiled at Jacqueline and placed his hand over hers. "Right, Jackie?"

Carmella, who'd slipped inside the house while the couples were talking, stepped onto the patio carrying a platter of sliced tomatoes, basil leaves, and fresh mozzarella. "Who's hungry?" she asked. "Such a beautiful day, we eat *al fresco*."

Jacqueline left Tyler's side and stepped toward the house. "Nonna, you sit. Sissy and I will bring out the rest of the food."

While Carmella called out instructions on which bowls and trays were needed from the kitchen and Gus helped Dominic wheel his chair to the outdoor dining table, Tyler asked Jonathan for his help. "Jonathan, do you mind handing me those crutches?"

"Of course." Jonathan held the crutches steady as Tyler rose from his chair. "I hope you don't think I'm overstepping my bounds but, when we have time, I'd like to share an idea I have for a plot you might want to use in one of your upcoming novels."

"Hey," Tyler said, his expression conveying his delight. "I'm always open to fresh ideas. Jonathan, something tells me we're going to be great friends."

Siena observed Jonathan and Tyler's exchange through the open kitchen window while she added olives, cheeses, and crackers to the antipasto tray. Jonathan's affable personality had not only won over Tyler, but he'd also made the effort to connect with Jacqueline when he offered to carry the casserole of eggplant parmesan to the table for her. During lunch, she sat back as Jonathan enthralled everyone with tales of the rare antiques he'd collected during his adventurous travels around the world. Later that afternoon, she was tickled by the belly laughs that emanated from the kitchen as Jonathan helped Nonna prepare dinner. While she couldn't imagine adoring Jonathan more than she already did, by the end of the day her cheeks ached from the smiles his charm and wit had brought to her face.

Separated from Manhattan by thousands of miles and surrounded by the few people she truly loved and who loved her in return, Siena forgot about the troubling situation awaiting her back home. That evening, while she and Jacqueline washed and put away the dinner dishes and Dominic and Gus amused Jonathan and Tyler with stories of their teenaged antics, she couldn't imagine her life being any more perfect.

Then, Jonathan received the first text.

Chapter 14

Siena
Spring 2017

"Mr. Kramer's apartment is on the twelfth floor, number 1201," the security guard behind the lobby desk at the Hudson informed Siena. "When you get off the elevator on twelve, hang a left."

"Thanks so much." Siena said, allowing the slight southern lilt she'd adopted as part of her Ellen Randall guise to color her speech. Gazing sideways at Gus, she said, "Shall we?"

Together they strolled across the historic co-op's elegant lobby, Gus's eyes trained on the embossed tin ceiling. "I always wondered what this building looked like on the inside," he said. In his dark suit and striped tie, briefcase in hand, he appeared every inch the professional jeweler on his way to appraise gemstones for an important new client.

Siena, dressed in a tailored jacket and skirt, the hem hitting just above her knee, pressed the elevator's call button. "Is it as posh as you imagined?"

"And then some," Gus replied, his eyes soaking in the rest of the lobby's décor. "I take it you've been here before." The elevator bell dinged. The doors opened. Gus followed Siena into the cab and pressed the button for the twelfth floor.

Siena leaned her back against the handrail and nodded. "One of my first jobs. My mark lived on the third floor, unit three-oh-four if my memory serves me right."

Gus frowned, his eyes filling with concern. "You're not worried about bumping into him? Being recognized?"

"That won't happen. He died in a traffic accident about a year ago."

Gus raised an eyebrow. "I didn't realize you keep such close tabs on your marks."

Siena glanced at him out of the corner of her eye. "You know I'm all about risk management." The elevator slowed to a stop. As the doors slid open, Siena straightened her stance and sucked in a deep breath. "Are we ready?"

Gus flashed her a shrewd smile. "Absolutely." He extended his arm. "Ladies first."

The hallway, long and wide, was illuminated by art deco sconces affixed to walls painted a soft beige. The mosaic tiled floors were original to the building's construction. Double wooden doors at either end of the hall confirmed this level held only two apartments, each being of substantial square footage. Following the security guard's instruction, Siena and Gus headed left toward the door at the far end of the hall. Siena rang the bell. Within seconds, they were greeted by a short, middle-aged woman clad in a plain black dress.

"Good evening." The woman's demeanor was at once formal and welcoming. Siena detected the slightest hint of an Eastern European accent. "Please, come in. Mr. Kramer is expecting you."

Siena barely had the words *Thank you* out of her

mouth when Matthew rushed into the foyer. "I've got it, Margaret," he said as the woman, whom Siena assumed was his housekeeper, closed the door behind them. "Matter of fact, I won't be needing you this evening. You can have the rest of the night off."

"Thank you, Mr. Kramer," Margaret said. "I set a tray of hors d'oeuvres on the cocktail table in the living room."

"That's perfect. Thanks." As Margaret bid them a good night and disappeared around a corner, Matthew eyed Siena from head to foot, his gaze lingering on her legs before traveling back up to her face. "Ellen, it's good to see you again." He brushed a cordial kiss against her cheek. "And you brought with you...?"

"Matthew," Siena said in her Ellen Randall voice, "this is Stanley Bartlemay, the jeweler who's offered to help you. Stanley, this is Matthew Kramer."

To polish off his performance, Gus had adopted the persona of an urbane gentleman from the UK. Shaking hands with Matthew, he said, "It's a pleasure to meet you, Mr. Kramer."

"Please, call me Matthew. Do you go by Stan?"

Gus shrugged his shoulders. "Stan or Stanley. I answer to both."

Matthew placed an arm around Gus's shoulders. "Well, Stan, how about we start off the evening with a drink?"

Gus grinned. "Matthew, you've read my mind."

Wrapping his other arm around Siena, Matthew guided them through an archway and into the room to their left. "Let's get comfortable then. Have a seat and help yourselves to the food Margaret set out for us." He sauntered over to the wet bar. "Ellen, as I recall, you drink white wine. I opened a bottle of Pinot Grigio, a '57 San Remy, especially for you."

Siena smoothed the back of her skirt as she seated herself on the sofa. "Pinot Grigio is my favorite. Thank you, Matthew."

"Stan, you strike me as a man who enjoys a good scotch."

Gus, his back to Matthew as he lowered himself into one of the adjacent easy chairs, glanced at Siena and rolled his eyes. "Matthew," he replied in his most congenial voice, "you've got me pegged. I'll have mine straight up, please."

"Straight up, it is." Matthew kept the conversation going while he prepared their drinks. "So, Stan, you're a Brit. What part of England are you from?"

"A small village north of London." Siena had roughed out a background for Gus's character but hadn't concocted many details. From what little time Siena had spent with Matthew, she'd determined he was a man who preferred to keep the attention focus on himself. "One I'm sure you've never heard of. To be honest, I schooled in London and moved to the States so long ago, I remember little about it."

"I can relate," Matthew said as he served the drinks. "I grew up in a small town on Long Island. The only reason I go back there these days is to visit my mother."

And that, as Siena had predicted, was the extent of Matthew's interest in Stanley Bartlemay.

Matthew plopped himself down on the sofa beside Siena. "Anyway, I appreciate you meeting with me here tonight. I'm barely comfortable taking my wife's jewelry out of the safe, let alone the apartment."

"Don't think you're alone," Gus replied with an

understanding grin. "You'd be surprised by the number of appraisals I've conducted in my clients' residences."

Siena draped a linen napkin over her knee and placed a cluster of red grapes and one of the mini-quiches Margaret had prepared onto a white plate trimmed in gold. "Will your wife be joining us tonight?" she asked Matthew.

"No. She's vacationing in Europe with her daughter until the end of the month." Matthew reclined and rested his elbow on the back of the sofa, a subtle move which allowed him, Siena construed, to caress her back without Gus noticing. "Until then, I have the place all to myself." Slurping his scotch, he stared into Siena's eyes and raised a suggestive eyebrow over the rim of his glass.

Not even ten minutes into their meeting and Siena was already wishing she could bolt out the front door. Leaning forward to lift her wine glass from the cocktail table, she fired a desperate glance at Gus. For most of her adult life, Gus had been her surrogate father and business partner. Aside from her twin sister, he understood Siena better than anyone. He read her SOS message and was quick to respond.

"Matthew, I'd love to chat the night away, but I do have another engagement this evening. Might we get down to business?"

"Not a problem. I'll get the earrings from the safe and be right back." Setting his drink on the table, Matthew sauntered out of the room.

"Try the quiche, Stanley," Siena said, pretending to converse with Gus as she rose from the sofa. "It's delicious." She glimpsed Matthew through the doorway as he approached the far end of the hall where she presumed the main bedroom and his wife's jewelry safe were located. A handy bit of information she filed away for future reference, if needed. With Matthew out of earshot, she was free to share an observation with Gus.

"Gus," she whispered, "this room is a treasure trove." Lifting a twelve-inch glazed ceramic figurine of an Asian cat, one of a pair displayed on the built-in bookshelves, she elaborated. "These statues appear to be eighteenth century Persian. The coloring is remarkable. Last year, I helped a client bid on a similar set that went for one point four million."

At the mention of the high dollar figure, Gus sat up straighter. "Christ!" he muttered, his eyes perusing the other treasures displayed on the shelves. "What are you thinking?"

"That I may need to get cozier with this jerk than I'd intended." Siena replaced the Persian cat next to its mate. "Look around. Does anything pop out at you? Something you could easily duplicate?" If Gus could create a replica of any one of the items, her short-term relationship with Matthew Kramer could end up being exceedingly profitable.

Gus threw up his hands. "Take your pick. I could make a forgery of just about anything in this room."

Siena detected Matthew's footsteps thudding against the carpet runner in the hallway. She rushed over to the wet bar and, grabbing the bottle of Pinot Grigio, appeared to be inspecting the label as he entered the living room.

"Ready for a refill?" Matthew asked.

Siena chuckled. "Not yet. I was just curious about the vineyard. A '57 you said?"

"Yes. That bottle was part of a shipment Alva received last month from a private vintner she deals with." He stepped closer and whispered into her ear. "And I'm not letting you go home tonight until you've downed every last drop."

"Then I'll make sure to sip slowly," Siena whispered back with an enticing smile that made Matthew lick his lips.

Gus cleared his throat. "Let's get on with the appraisal, shall we?"

Matthew jerked his attention back to the matter at hand. "Sorry, Stan." He pried open the case he'd carried in and presented the jewels to Gus. "These are the earrings my wife's father gave her to wear on our wedding day. They've got to be worth more than the value my regular jeweler recently placed on them."

"May I?" Gus asked, taking the case from Matthew. "Oh, I must say, they're a stunning set. However, is there somewhere else in the apartment where we might relocate? I will need to examine the diamonds under better lighting."

"Oh, yeah, sure. Uh...how about under the chandelier in the dining room?"

"That should do." With his briefcase in hand, Gus rose from his seat. "Lead the way."

"Ellen, are you joining us?" Matthew asked.

"You two go on." Siena slid her cell phone from her jacket pocket. "This being tax season, I need to make a brief call to the office."

Matthew turned his back on Gus. Inching closer to Siena, he faked a pout. "I'm sorry. Did I steal you away from your work?"

"Darlin'," she said, her grin alluring, "I'd happily trade hours of combing through tax forms for the pleasure of spending an evening in your company.

However, I'm afraid we're both stealing too much of Stanley's time."

Matthew jerked his head around and eyed Gus who was standing in the doorway, his lips seemingly pursed with impatience. "Sorry, Stan." Returning his attention to Siena, he leaned closer and whispered into her ear. "After I take care of this business, we'll have the rest of the evening to ourselves."

Siena forced a giggle. *Poor, deluded man. If he weren't so arrogant, I might feel sorry for him.*

Matthew hurried past Gus. "Okay, Stan. Follow me. The dining room is this way."

Gus gazed at Siena with a raised eyebrow as though asking if she were pleased with the way the scheme was unfolding. Siena grinned and nodded her head in response, indicating the job was running according to plan. Gus returned the nod and strolled into the foyer. A moment later, Siena heard him exclaim, "Why, this lighting is much better. Much better indeed."

In the off-chance Matthew would pop back into the room, Siena faked a conversation with an imaginary colleague from her office. Speaking to her phone as though she were on speaker, she murmured questions and responses about capital gains and allowable expenses while snapping photos of the Kramers' treasures. The pair of Persian ceramic cats. The 19th century solid gold candlesticks sitting on the fireplace mantle. The etched crystal Wilton-Smythe egg cradled in a silver stand and nestled between stacks of leather-bound books, many of which she verified as first editions. She would text the photos to Gus and let him choose from the lot. Her mission accomplished, she carried her wine glass into the dining room and rejoined

Matthew and Gus.

"Here she is now," Matthew said as Siena sauntered through the doorway. "Ellen, Stan needs to take photos of the earrings on a live model to accompany his appraisal."

"Oh?" Siena responded, feigning confusion.

"For perspective, you see," Gus's Stanley explained. Siena studied Matthew's reaction to ensure he was buying into their engineered ploy. Stanley's appraisal didn't require such validation. Gus, however, needed the photos to craft his replica of the earrings. "Would you be a dear?"

Siena rounded the table and positioned herself between Gus and Matthew. "Absolutely. Anything I can do to help."

A phone rang in another part of the house. "Damn," Matthew grumbled. "Listen, Stan, I know you're in a hurry, but I need to check who's calling." He snatched the earring case off the table. "And I don't feel comfortable leaving—"

"You're not serious!" Straightening his back, Gus glared at Matthew and tossed his pen onto the table. "I don't recall the last time I was so insulted." He bolted from his chair. "If you have such little faith in my credibility—"

Matthew was hasty to apologize as the phone continued to ring. "Ah, shit! I'm so sorry. I don't know what I was thinking. Of course, I trust you. Please, stay. Again, I'm sorry. Please," he said, placing the jewelry box on the table, "continue with your appraisal. I'll be right back."

Siena's eyes followed Matthew as he rushed from the room. "Well done, *Stanley*," she whispered into

Gus's ear. Carrying the jewelry box to the mirror affixed above the sideboard, she replaced her own faux diamond studs with Alva Kramer's sparkling gems and stood back to admire her reflection.

A cluster of eight diamonds formed the base for each earring. Seven of the stones, some marquise and some pear-shaped, fanned around a central round-cut diamond, giving the grouping the appearance of a flower in bloom. Dangling from the "petal" stones were three strands of diamonds, all two inches in length, with the center strand extending one diamond lower than those on either side. Each strand contained six stones of varied designs so that an emerald-cut might hang from a heart-shaped stone, a princess-cut from a baguette. Siena estimated each of the stones to be around a quarter carat.

Keeping her eyes fixed on the mirror, Siena swiveled her head from side to side. "Just in case you're stuck for ideas on what to get me for Christmas this year, I wouldn't mind having a pair of earrings like this."

Gus snorted. "Yes, your majesty. Would you also like the matching tiara?" He grabbed his cell phone and tapped the camera icon. "When you're done drooling over yourself in the mirror, I need you to come here and stand under the chandelier so I can get some good shots."

"Don't be such a downer, Gus." Siena posed for the camera, tilting her head as Gus directed. "Someday I might actually own jewelry like this."

"Sure, doll. You keep dreaming that dream." Gus flipped through the photos he'd taken, enlarging and examining each in detail.

"Do you have what you need?"

"Sure do. Plus, Matthew offered to give me a copy of the designer's paperwork, so I have all the specifications—the dimensions, the carat weight and cut of each diamond. I rarely have this much detail to work with." Gus glanced up from his phone. "You can take the earrings off now. That is, unless you want to keep imagining you're the heiress to a massive fortune."

Siena wrinkled her nose. "Like Alva Kramer? No, thanks. You know what they say—money doesn't buy happiness." She removed the diamond earrings and returned the jewelry box to the dining room table. Taking the seat next to Gus, she spoke in a confidential tone. "I need your help. When we're done with this appraisal business, Matthew is going to insist on me staying. He believes he's got a night of wild sex in store, but that's simply not happening. After you leave, wait a few minutes and then call my cell and act like you're one of my underlings from the office. You're having a breakdown because you're convinced you totally messed up a client's balance sheet and you need me to come into the office to fix it before our client meeting tomorrow morning."

"Got it."

Matthew rushed back into the room. "Sorry," he said, "but I needed to take that call."

"I'm surprised you still have a house phone," Siena commented.

"I keep it mainly for my mother. She has early onset dementia. As often as I tell her to call my cell, she can only remember that we have a house phone."

This was a side of Matthew that Siena hadn't yet seen. Concerned, thoughtful, caring. Too bad he didn't speak as tenderly about his wife.

"Is your mother all right?" Siena asked.

"Oh, she's fine. She'd gone out with some friends

and couldn't find her house key when they brought her home. She wanted me to drive all the way out to Long Island to unlock the door, but I reminded her that we keep a spare key in one of those fake rocks in the flowerbed next to the back patio. Her friend helped her find it and she's now safely inside her house."

"You're a good son, Matthew," Gus said.

Matthew shrugged. "I try." He glanced at Gus's paraphernalia strewn across the dining room table. "Did you get the photos you'll need?"

"Yes, I did." Gus inserted his phony forms along with his loupe and the copy of the jewelry designer's documentation into his briefcase and clicked the flap closed. "I'll complete my appraisal within the week and have it delivered to you. In the meantime, please don't fret. Just by eyeballing the earrings, I can assure you they're worth close to half a million."

Matthew's smile couldn't have been wider. "That's great news, Stan! Hey, listen, I'd love for you to stay but since you said you're in a hurry to get to your next appointment, let me show you to the door." As they strolled toward the foyer, he brushed against Siena's side. "You're staying, aren't you?" he asked in a low voice.

Siena gazed into his eyes and grinned. "If you'd like." Matthew responded by sliding his hand down her back and giving her ass a gentle squeeze.

"Thanks again, Stan," Matthew said when they'd reached the front door. "I can't tell you how much I appreciate your help. I assume you'll invoice me for your services?"

Gus chuckled. "No, Matthew. Consider this one on the house."

Matthew placed his hand on Gus's shoulder. "Oh, now, come on, Stan. Tell me how much I owe you. I'll be glad to pay."

"No, no." Gus shook hands with Matthew. "Ellen always gives me good tax advice, so I'm happy to do a friend of hers a favor. It's been a pleasure doing business with you." He winked at Siena. "Ellen, I'll be talking with you soon. Have a good rest of the evening, you two."

"Good night, Stan," Matthew said, opening the door. "It was nice meeting you."

"'Night, Stan," Siena said. As Matthew was closing the door, she scurried into the living room and headed straight for the wet bar. To get through the next several minutes, she needed an immediate infusion of alcohol. She drained her wine glass, poured a refill, and downed another hefty swig. The glass had barely left her lips before Matthew was at her back.

"Mm...I'm glad Stan was in a rush to leave." He slipped his arms around her waist and planted wet kisses along the side of her neck. "I finally have you all to myself."

"Stanley is a great guy, isn't he?" An idle comment, yes, but Siena needed to keep the conversation going without being too obvious that she was attempting to stall his advances.

"I'll wait to get his appraisal in writing before agreeing with you." He spun Siena around to face him.

"He's a fountain of know—" Before Siena could complete her comment, Matthew tightened his hold on her and pressed his open mouth hard against hers. She pretended she was enjoying the sudden intimacy while at the same time keeping her ears perked for the phone call from Gus. As Matthew's kisses became more ardent, she pushed away. "Matthew, you're moving too fast for this old-fashioned Southern girl. I like to be romanced. You know—flowers, wine, a nice dinner."

"I can do that," Matthew assured her while continuing to peck kisses on her lips. "But we're here now, and the bedroom is right down the hall." His lips moved to her neck as he slid Siena's jacket off her shoulders.

Come on, Gus! Make the call!

Fixing her arms on Matthew's shoulders, Siena took advantage of the situation to determine if she truly held Matthew under her spell. She began by stroking the nape of his neck with her fingertips. When he didn't resist her touch, she snaked her fingers upwards and playfully twirled his sandy brown hair. This was a tried-and-true technique she used on all the men who fell victim to her schemes. Her theory was, if her target didn't resist being touched in such a tender spot, she'd earned his trust and had free rein to manipulate him any way she pleased. Matthew, not surprisingly, passed her test with flying colors.

Matthew's eager hands moved onward to Siena's blouse. "But, what about your wife?" she asked as he tugged the material loose from the waistband of her skirt.

He smirked and shrugged his shoulders. "Out of sight, out of mind. Besides, she won't be with us much longer." He breathed heavily into her ear while she allowed his hand to roam freely underneath the ivory silk.

Siena played ignorant. "Whatever do you mean?"

"She has a degenerative illness." He planted kisses on her neck as his right hand traveled south down her backside. "She won't make it another year."

Siena wanted to scream. How could he have such little compassion for his own wife? "That's awful," she said, maintaining her cool. "You must be devastated."

Matthew grunted, as though not ashamed to admit his attitude was just the opposite. "Far as I'm concerned, our relationship is one of convenience. She enjoys my companionship, and I enjoy her lifestyle."

Siena squeezed her eyes shut and bit the inside of her lip, anything to stop herself from exploding into a tirade. She wanted nothing more than to tell Matthew her candid opinion of him—that he was a selfish, heartless monster. Did his wife have the slightest clue about the true nature of the man she'd sworn an oath to love and cherish the rest of her life?

Jesus, Gus! Why are you taking so long to call?

"We would have gotten divorced eventually," he continued, as if he hadn't been heartless enough already. "It's pure luck on my part that she'll be kicking the bucket before our marriage starts to deteriorate."

At long last, Siena's phone chimed. She wiggled out of Matthew's grasp. "Sorry, but I need to see if this is my office." Pivoting away from Matthew, she retrieved her jacket from the floor and slid her phone from its pocket. After a brief conversation during which she faked reacting to an assistant who had botched a major client's account, she said, "No, don't do anything until I get there. I'm on my way now." She swiveled around and apologized. "Matthew, I'm sorry to cut the evening short, but I need to go into the office. There's a huge mistake that needs to be corrected before we meet with the client early tomorrow morning." Shrugging on her jacket and retrieving her handbag, she headed toward the foyer.

"But we were just getting started," Matthew whined. "Can't someone else fix the problem?"

"Oh, sure. If you don't mind the office calling me with questions every two minutes."

As she neared the front door, Matthew grabbed her arm and spun her toward him. "Then, get the mess straightened out and come right back." He attempted to draw her into his arms again, but Siena resisted.

"From the sound of things, I may be there all night." As she grasped the doorknob, she reminded herself not to burn her bridges. Taking a deep breath, she forced a smile. "I'm truly sorry, Matthew. Let's plan to have dinner tomorrow night and pick up from where we left off." Siena kissed him with as much passion as she could muster before rushing from the apartment.

She had less than twenty-four hours to convince herself this job was worth dealing with the most despicable man she'd ever met.

Chapter 15

Siena
October 2023

"How dare you!" Siena growled into the burner phone Matthew Kramer had given her.

From the other end of the line, Matthew snickered. "Well, hello, Mrs. Woodward. I thought I might be hearing from you."

"What kind of game are you playing?"

"Game? Well, now, a game would suggest an element of fun," Matthew taunted. "Are you having fun, Siena?"

Siena took a deep breath, although it did little to calm her. "We have an agreement, and according to my calendar this isn't the last day of the month."

"True, but surely you remember how impatient I can be."

Siena's temper ignited when a vision from six years ago of Matthew pinning her against the wall in his co-op's elevator and hiking up her skirt flashed into her mind. The prudent response would be to keep her lips tight, but the words shot from her mouth before she could stop them. "Surely you remember how *vicious* I can be."

"Are you threatening me, Siena?"

"I'm *warning* you." Silence hung between them as Siena waited for Matthew's reply.

"Get me my money, Siena, or every day I'll text another piece of that video until my frat brothers have a clear view of the depraved woman our pal Jonathan married." With those words, Matthew ended the call.

"Damn you!" Siena slammed the phone against the wooden patio table. Crossing her arms, she stood with her back to the house and gazed at the calm Caribbean Sea as the last remnants of daylight fell below the horizon.

Gus emerged from the shadows. "You want to tell me what that conversation was about?"

Siena's hand flew to her chest as she spun around to face him. "Jesus, Gus! You nearly gave me a heart attack."

"On top of the stroke whoever was on the other end of that call was about to give you?" He handed her a glass of chilled wine. "Have a drink. I noticed the defiant look on your face when you stormed out of the house and figured you could use one."

"Thanks." Siena gulped down a healthy swallow as she glanced into the house through the kitchen window. "Is Jonathan back yet?"

"No, he and Tyler are still off on their secret mission. Why? What don't you want him to overhear?"

Siena treaded farther into the yard and away from the house. Gus followed. "I'm not so good at this, Gus."

Gus frowned. "Not so good at what?"

"This relationship thing. I'm afraid I'm failing miserably at my marriage." She choked back a sob.

Gus wrapped his sympathetic arms around Siena. "Listen, nobody said marriage was easy but since when have you ever backed down from a challenge? You just need to give it some time."

She rested her cheek on Gus's shoulder, comforted by his familiarity. "You make it sound so simple." She stepped back and wiped away the moisture from the corners of her eyes. "It's not only my marriage, Gus. The truth is, I miss my old life. I'm used to working, interacting with people from all over the world, being respected for my knowledge and expertise."

And, dare she admit it, she missed most of all the thrill of working with Gus on their sideline ventures.

"The days used to fly by. Now the hours drag on as I wander around the house searching for something, *anything,* to occupy my time. I could open a used bookstore with the number of novels I've read in the past two months."

Gus thrust his hands into the pockets of his shorts. "And here I imagined you and Jonathan taking one day trip after another, him introducing you to all his favorite New England haunts."

Siena scoffed. "That was my dream, too. Unfortunately, Jonathan is committed to so many organizations, he's gone most days from morning to night. While my life has been turned inside out, his routine hasn't changed at all."

"So, talk to him about it," Gus said, taking a drink of scotch.

Siena sighed. "I have. His solution was to get me involved in the community. Which is fine. I enjoy helping at the soup kitchen." She pictured the faces of a few of the regulars with whom she'd become familiar during her six-week stint as a volunteer. One woman had especially touched Siena's heart, a young mother with a son in kindergarten and a preschool-aged daughter. The family lived out of their car. One day, Siena got up the courage to ask why. The mother explained that most of the money she earned from her minimum-wage job was eaten up by daycare expenses. She fell behind on the rent and had been evicted. She never mentioned, and Siena did not ask, if she received any support from the father of her children. On her next volunteer day at the soup kitchen, Siena slipped two gift cards into the woman's pocket, one for a clothing store and one for a gas station. A kind gesture, but merely a band-aid. The situation had prompted Siena to start a discussion with Jonathan about more impactful ways to help single parents in similar situations.

"But then," she grunted, "there are the women at his club. Excuse me, I need to get used to saying *our* club. Jonathan approached a few of his friends and asked that I be added to their committees. From the first meeting I attended, I've had the impression these women resent me for being forced on them. They assigned me to the most mundane tasks—you know, the stuff no one else volunteers to do—as though I'm an airhead who can't navigate her way out of a box. Not one of them has asked what talents or professional experience I can bring to the table. I'm so frustrated, having to take a back seat when I know I could run those committees ten times better than the women who are currently in charge."

"These things don't happen overnight, Siena. They'll notice your worth soon enough."

"Maybe." Siena sipped her wine and gazed into the darkening sky. "I never imagined I'd ever be so utterly bored. I can't so much as make the bed without angering our housekeeper. And can you believe I have a personal assistant?"

Gus chuckled. "Who helps you to do what?"

144

Siena shot Gus a sly grin. "She takes care of all those mundane tasks the ladies at the club dump on me."

Gus clinked his glass against hers. "Now that's my girl."

Siena's grin was melancholy. "At least the gardener welcomes my company. I've learned a hell of a lot about how far apart vegetables need to be grown, and the best months to plant flower bulbs."

Gus chuckled. "At least you've got *that* going for you." He stared at Siena as though waiting for a continuation of her rant. Instead, she lowered her head, her mood growing somber. "But the snooty ladies at the club and the over-zealous house staff aren't what made you swear and throw your phone down just now, are they?"

"No, they're not."

"You want to tell me what's really bothering you?"

Siena lowered her eyes and her voice. "Gus, I'm being blackmailed."

Gus's brow furrowed with concern. "Christ," he muttered. "Who?"

"Do you remember the con we pulled about six years ago on a guy named Matthew Kramer?"

He frowned and shook his head. "No, although the name sounds familiar."

"Kramer was married to Alva Paulson." The light bulb in Gus's head remained dull. "The heiress to Paulson Industries. They lived on the twelfth floor of the Hudson."

"Oh, right." Gus nodded his head in acknowledgment. "I pretended to be a jewelry appraiser from London. Stanley something, wasn't it? We acquired a pricey pair of diamond earrings on that job."

"Yes, quite pricey. And it didn't take Alva Paulson long to figure out that her diamond earrings had been replaced with a pair of worthless fakes."

"So, how did that lead to you being blackmailed?"

"A few days ago, I had a chance encounter with Matthew Kramer." Siena breathed a heavy sigh. "Turns out he's one of Jonathan's fraternity brothers."

Gus's mouth dropped open. "You're kidding."

"If only I were." Siena shook her head and let out a sardonic chuckle. "You know, I always had a gut feeling my luck would run out one day." Glancing away, she drank the remainder of her wine in one swallow. "Anyway, Alva Paulson divorced Matthew Kramer a few months after we played the con on him. He blames me for ruining his marriage—or I should say the lush lifestyle his wealthy wife afforded him."

Gus shook his head. "Sounds to me like pure supposition on his part. Tell him he's confused you with someone who looks like you. He has no proof that you were the woman who stole his wife's earrings." Unwilling to tell Gus he was wrong, Siena continued gazing into the evening sky. "Oh. I get it." He winced and sipped his scotch. "Kramer has something else on you, doesn't he?"

"I got far too carried away on that job, Gus." Gus barely moved a muscle while Siena let the whole sordid story spill out. She ended by admitting, "My one mistake was not performing a thorough check of the bedroom. I missed the camera lens that was embedded in the frame of the bedroom mirror. Everything I did that afternoon was captured on film."

Gus shrugged his shoulders. "I don't see what the big deal is. Nothing on that video would come as a shock to Jonathan. He already knows about your past."

"Gus, you're not listening. When I said *everything* I did was captured on film, I wasn't referring only to the part where I swapped the real diamond earrings for the fake pair."

Gus's eyebrows shot up. "Oh! You're worried about the part where you and Kramer—"

"Exactly. How would you feel if an old friend of yours handed you what basically amounts to a sex tape of himself with Marielle?"

Gus cleared his throat. "I'd be enraged."

"So, you can understand why I don't want anyone to see what Matthew and I did with *and to* each other that night. Especially not Jonathan. However, that's not the worst part. Kramer gave me until the end of the month to come up with the five million he wants in exchange for the film, but he's gotten impatient. Earlier today, Jonathan and all his fraternity brothers received a text from Kramer in which he told them he'd just recovered a video of the woman who ruined his marriage, and they were going to be amazed to find out who she is. Attached to the text was a ten-second clip of the video. If his frat brothers learn the truth about me, Jonathan will be humiliated. I can't let that happen."

Gus strolled across the yard and leaned against the trunk of a Sabal palmetto. "Was the image clear enough for you to be identified?"

"No, not in the clip Kramer sent out today. But, you see, he's toying with me. Little by little, the mysterious woman in the video will be exposed until my face is fully recognizable. Or until I pay him the five million dollars he's demanding. Even then, I don't trust that he'll hold up to his end of the bargain."

"Was Kramer the person you were speaking with on the phone just now?"

"Yes. I called to remind him of our agreement."

"What did he say?"

"What do you think? He laughed and hung up on me."

"What was Jonathan's reaction to the text?"

"Like everyone else who received it, he was confused. For most of the afternoon, all the frat brothers were texting and calling, asking each other what the hell Matthew is up to. So far, they think it's a joke. Matthew, I'm told, has a reputation for playing silly pranks."

"What guarantee do you have that there aren't multiple copies of the video? That he won't keep asking for more money?"

"None. But neither do I have the five million dollars to satisfy his demand."

Gus shook his head. "I wish I could help you out, but five million—"

Siena laughed. "Gus, I would *never* expect you to hand over five million dollars. This is my problem. I'll deal with it."

"What are you going to do?"

"I'm going to find every version of that video Matthew Kramer owns and destroy them all."

"If I were speaking to anyone else, I'd say good luck. But you?" Gus grinned. "If Kramer thinks he's going to win this battle, he's in for a rude awakening."

"Let's hope you're right. I hired a private investigator to keep an eye on him and dig up whatever information he can find so that I'm prepared to attack this situation the minute we return home."

"Let me know if there's any way I can help. I'll do

whatever you need."

Siena placed her arms around Gus's neck and kissed his cheek. "Thank you. You're always there for me, and I don't tell you often enough how grateful I am."

"You know I love you like you're my own daughter," he said, hugging her in return. "Besides, I kind of miss working with you. Santa Martina is beautiful, but it lacks that element of danger you and I are used to."

Their tender moment abruptly ended when voices high with excitement exploded inside the house. Puzzled, Siena stepped back and gazed into Gus's equally bewildered eyes. "What the…?"

They rushed inside the house to find Jacqueline, home from her shift at the clinic and still dressed in her scrubs, squealing and giggling and wiping tears from her cheeks. Dominic, laughing with delight, was holding her left hand and gawking at the ring adorning her finger. Tyler stood by her side, his face one gigantic smile.

"Jacqueline!" Siena rushed forward and stole her sister's hand from Dominic.

"Sissy, Tyler asked me to marry him!" Jacqueline wiggled her ring finger, the diamonds sparkling under the incandescent lighting. "Will you be my matron of honor?"

Siena squeezed Jacqueline into a hug. "Of course, I will. I'm so happy for you." Keeping one arm around Jacqueline, she extended her other arm to bring Tyler into the embrace. "For both of you. Congratulations!"

Dominic twisted his upper body around in his wheelchair. "What do you think, Gus?" he asked, grinning at his old friend. "Now your *second* goddaughter is getting married."

"I think it's about time!" Gus stepped forward and hugged Jacqueline. "I couldn't be happier for you." Shaking Tyler's hand, he said, "We knew the day Jacqueline brought you home to meet us that you two would tie the knot before long. Congratulations!"

"Thank you," Tyler replied. "I would have asked Jackie sooner, but I was waiting until my cast was removed. It's hard to get down on one knee when your leg is encased in plaster."

"Tyler proposed on the beach—*at sunset!*" Jacqueline wrapped her arms around Tyler's neck. "Isn't he the most romantic man on earth?"

At the mention of romantic men, Siena glanced over at Jonathan. Her heart fluttered at the still fresh memory of the night she'd received her own proposal of marriage. She sauntered toward the sofa where Jonathan had a loving arm around Nonna Carmella. Nonna was whimpering in Italian about marriage and babies and dabbing at her eyes with a tissue.

Siena teased Jonathan with a phony scowl. "You knew this was happening and didn't tell me?" In truth, she was delighted that Jonathan had slipped so easily into her world. Why was she having such a difficult time fitting into his?

Jonathan chuckled and covered her hand with his as she sat beside him. "Sorry, sweetheart. Tyler had this all planned. He asked Jacqueline to meet him on the beach when her shift ended, and he wanted me there to film the proposal with his phone. If he hadn't sworn me to secrecy, you know I would have told you." He gazed intently into her eyes. "After all, we made a promise to always be open and honest with each other. Remember?"

A cold chill crept up Siena's spine. Jonthan had

done this before, given her that three-second stare that spoke volumes. His eyes conveyed a message meant to be more than a simple reminder of their wedding vows— which, in less than two months, she'd already managed to break. She was certain Jonathan knew she was hiding something from him, maybe even knew what her secret was. Or was she blowing out of proportion a casual comment and an innocent sideways glance? Guilt has a way of playing strange tricks on one's mind.

This is the perfect opportunity. I need to take Jonathan aside right now and confess that one of his friends is blackmailing me. He'll understand. He loves me. All I need to do is tell him.

Siena opened her mouth to speak, but the words caught in her throat.

Jonathan cocked his head. "Siena," he said, giving her wide berth to bare her soul, "is there something you want to tell me?"

"I was just going to say…" She stroked the back of his neck with her finger and flashed him a smile to knock his socks off. "…I hope Jacqueline and Tyler's marriage is as wonderful as ours."

Chapter 16

Siena

The second text was sent two days later.

"I received another text," Jonathan announced as he stepped into the bathroom of their suite at the resort and handed his phone to Siena. "Would you like to watch it?"

Tossing her mascara tube into her makeup bag, Siena glanced at Jonathan with anxious eyes. She'd have preferred to take a pass, but she needed to stay on top of this potential crisis. She tapped the play button on the screen of Jonathan's cell and set into motion the image of herself in a lacy red bra and a shirtless Matthew, both in profile from the waist up. Thanks to her wig and Southern accent, Siena was unrecognizable as she teased, *"Oh, no you don't. Nothing else comes off until I adorn myself with another piece of jewelry."*

Siena handed the phone back to Jonathan. "These videos are disgusting. I wish he'd stop sending them."

"Yes." Jonathan slid the phone into the pocket of his chinos. "I'm sure you do."

****

On the morning of their return flight to Boston, Siena and Jonathan were en route to the airport when the third text arrived.

"Yet another video," Jonathan grumbled.

Siena tsked. "I wouldn't even open it if I were you."

She silently begged Jonathan to follow her advice—*Please, please, please don't open that text!*—but to no avail. With her pulse pounding in her ears, she pretended to be disinterested while at the same time angling her head just enough to view the video out of the corner of her eye. What she witnessed made her stomach turn. The image showed her once again facing away from the camera, although this time her back was bare. Her hand itched to wrench the phone from Jonathan's grasp and hurl it out the car window.

Five seconds into the video, Jonathan hit the pause button and closed the text. "I refuse to watch this," he muttered under his breath as he zippered the phone into his carry-on bag. Siena attempted to take his hand, but Jonathan crossed his arm over his lap and angled his body away from her.

The sting of rejection caused tears to well in Siena's eyes. Jonathan had never refused her hand. She crossed her leg and stared out the window on her side of the car as Jonathan continued to stare out his. They rode to the airport in silence.

****

That evening, home from their trip and easing back into their routines, Siena was stunned when Jonathan announced he had a board meeting in the morning and was going to bed early. Her troubled eyes followed him as he climbed the stairs to their bedroom. For the first time since they'd met, he hadn't gathered her into his arms and seduced her into joining him.

****

The surveillance report Lou handed Siena boiled down to a few simple facts: Matthew Kramer had a penchant for poker; Matthew Kramer was unlucky at cards; Matthew Kramer owed money to some notoriously bad people.

Siena tossed the report onto Lou's desk. "At least now we know why he's blackmailing me."

"What do you think he'll do with your money?" Lou asked. "Pay off his gambling debts or skip town?"

"I have no clue." Siena rose and paced the area behind her chair. "Anyway, it doesn't matter. He's not getting one cent from me."

Lou scrunched up his face. "No? What's your plan then?"

"To destroy all copies of that video tape so he has nothing to hold over me."

"Uh…How are you going to do that? Unless you're keeping some vital information from me, you don't know how many copies he has, nor do you know where he keeps them."

"Not true." She stopped pacing and placed her hands on the back of the chair. "I know he has at least two copies. The original is on a handheld camera, and he transferred portions, maybe the entire video, onto his cell phone."

"Obviously, you know where he keeps his phone," Lou said, sliding the report back into its folder. "What about the camera?"

"That's the hurdle we need to overcome, isn't it? But not to worry. I've gotten myself out of worse situations than this."

Lou sat up straighter in his chair. "Hold on a second. The hurdle *we* need to overcome?" He pointed his index finger between himself and Siena. "As in *us*—you and me? Or *we* as in you and somebody else?"

"You and me, of course."

"Oh, no. I finished the job you hired me to do. As far as I'm concerned, *we* are done."

"What's wrong, Lou?" Siena taunted. "Have you gotten cold feet?"

"Hey, I'm no coward but I'm also not a fool. The last thing I need is to be used as the scapegoat in another one of your schemes. I don't need your business that bad."

A rap sounded on the door to Lou's office. Gemma opened the door halfway and poked her head inside. "Hey, Lou, sorry to interrupt but that firm you had an appointment with this afternoon just canceled. The guy said they had a change of heart. Since there's nothing else going on, I thought I'd take off."

Siena caught the abject disappointment in Lou's eyes. He sank back in his chair, his gaze drifting to the side and taking on the dazed stare of an about-to-graduate college senior who's just been told he flunked his final exam. She was tempted to suggest they both escape reality for the afternoon and drown their sorrows in never-ending bowls of ice cream.

"So, is that all right with you?" Gemma asked.

Lou heaved a troubled sigh. "Yeah, go ahead, Gem. Just make sure the coffee pot is turned off."

"Cool. See you Wednesday." As she inched the door closed, Gemma called out a reminder. "Don't forget Little Joey's birthday party is tomorrow night."

"Yeah, yeah. Thanks for the reminder."

"Okey-dokey. Bye, now." With that, the door clicked closed.

Siena glanced around the dingy office before settling her gaze on Lou. The lines on his face seemed to have grown deeper over the last minute. "Sounds like you just lost a pretty big account."

Lou ran his hand across his face as though he were attempting to wipe away his misery. "You could say that."

Siena nodded her head. "Would you like to reconsider my offer?"

Lou leaned his elbows on the desk and stared Siena square in the eye. "What do you need me to do?"

****

"Did you decide on a gift for Patrick's birthday?" Siena asked Jonathan while they were preparing dinner that evening.

"Yes, I came across something interesting this afternoon." Jonathan sampled a spoonful of minestrone and sprinkled in more black pepper. "Willow's has a signed first edition of *The Great Gatsby* listed in their online auction. Would you mind having a look after dinner and determining whether it's worth the price?"

"I'd be happy to." Siena went about removing soup bowls and plates from the cupboard and fishing utensils from the silverware drawer. "What's the asking price?"

"Two hundred thousand."

Siena scrunched her chin. "Seems fair, *if* the book is in excellent condition and comes with the original dust jacket. Let me do some research before you make an offer."

"Thanks." He sauntered over to Siena and, wrapping his arms around her from behind, planted a kiss on her cheek. "What a luxury, being married to my own personal antiques consultant."

"To be honest, I miss working at Willow's."

"Why don't you apply for a position at one of the auction houses in Boston? I'm sure they'd be delighted to add a person with your background to their staff."

"A great idea, except you're forgetting that I worked at Willow's under a false identity. I'll never be able to list all those years of experience on my current resume."

"Sorry. I wasn't thinking."

Siena pivoted around and faced Jonathan. "Speaking of upcoming family events, I spoke with Jacqueline this afternoon. She and Tyler set a date for their wedding."

"That's great. When is it?"

"November seventeenth. I was thinking we could go to Santa Martina a couple of days before and stay through the weekend."

"I don't think I have anything important scheduled in November, but I'll give the dates to Brenda in the morning and have her clear my calendar just in case. Is this going to be a big affair? Casual or formal?"

"Since this is a second marriage for Tyler, and Jac doesn't care for pomp and circumstance, they want to keep it small and casual." Siena rinsed the cherry tomatoes before adding them to their salad. "They're planning a ceremony on the beach followed by a dinner at Marielle's restaurant for immediate family and close friends. Tyler's sons from his first marriage will act as his best men."

"That's a clever idea, to have both his sons stand with him."

"Yes. I'm looking forward to meeting them."

"Tyler told me they wanted to get married as soon as possible, but the seventeenth is only a few weeks away. Why the rush?"

"That's Jacqueline—everything needs to be done yesterday. Personally, my twin sense is giving me a strong vibe that she's pregnant."

Jonathan grunted. "Huh." He placed two goblets on the counter and uncorked the wine bottle.

Siena wanted to kick herself. She should have known better than to bring up the topic of babies. Jonathan loved children, would fill the entire house with them if he could, but the maternal instinct didn't run strong through Siena's veins. Nor did she have the desire to suffer through the discomfort of pregnancy and the pains of childbirth. But more than the physical aspects of becoming a mother was the worry that she would one day leave emotional scars on her child just as her own mother had left on her. This was a fear she shared with no one.

The oven's timer buzzed, breaking the uncomfortable silence festering between them.

Siena removed the pan and breathed in the aroma of the freshly baked bread. "Mm…this smells wonderful," she said, transferring the loaf onto a wooden cutting board. "Anyway, Jac can't find a wedding dress she likes in any of the shops in Santa Martina, so she's flying to New York tomorrow, and she begged me to join her. Do you mind if I spend the rest of the week gown shopping in Manhattan?"

"Not at all. As a matter of fact, I was planning a trip to New York myself."

"Oh?"

"I didn't tell you this, but my friend Mack called the other day. We haven't seen each other for a while, and I promised to pay him a visit when we returned from the Caribbean."

"Mack? I don't recognize the name. Have you mentioned him before?"

Jonathan shrugged his shoulders. "I may have.

Anyway, I'm just going for the day, but you should stay longer and enjoy your time with Jacqueline. Make up for all those years you spent apart."

"Thank you. I may just do that." Siena didn't expect the gown shopping to take up much of her time, but the other business she needed to tend to probably would.

"I was thinking, we've been flying so much lately. Let's drive to New York instead."

"I like that idea," Siena said as she selected a bread knife from the cutting block.

"Good. I'll have Brenda reserve a car for us first thing in the morning. Hopefully, Bill will be available to drive us. Do you want me to have Brenda book a hotel for you as well?"

"Yes, please. A suite with two bedrooms would be nice."

One that I can share with Jacqueline, the other for Gus and Marielle.

Chapter 17

Siena

Jacqueline stood before the open closet door and thrust her hands on her hips. "Sissy, how can you live like this?"

"Live like what?" Having been separated for so many years, Siena had forgotten how annoying Jac's compulsion for neatness could be.

"I mean, look at this." Jacqueline chastised her sister while she rearranged the garments, first by type then by color. "You've got creams mixed with reds, slacks mixed with sweaters. How can you find anything?" She singled out one of Siena's dresses. "No way! You're shopping at Bocciolo now?"

"Could be worse. I normally don't even bother to unpack my bags." After wheeling her empty suitcase into the corner of the bedroom she was sharing with Jacqueline in Manhattan's famed Baldwin Hotel, Siena plopped onto the edge of the bed and kicked off her red heels. "So, now that we finally have a moment alone, I'm curious about something."

Jacqueline seemed hesitant when she asked, "What's that?"

"How honest have you been with Tyler about our family history? Does he know the type of business our father operated with Gus? Is he aware that for most of my adult life I earned a large part of my income illegally, and that you were complicit in some of the scams I ran?"

Jacqueline leaned back against one of the closet's bifold doors and faced Siena. "Let me put it this way. Tyler doesn't know everything, but he knows enough." She drew in her breath. "By our second date, when it was clear we were getting serious, I told Tyler I couldn't let our relationship go any further without him understanding the kind of people he was getting involved with. I mean, if the environment I grew up in and the cons I got pulled into were going to be deal breakers, I'd rather we end things right then. So, I started to tell him about our family background and truthfully, Sissy, I didn't hide anything. But, as I was getting into the details, Tyler told me to stop. He said he didn't want me to give him a reason to walk away." She chuckled. "Then he told me he thinks we're the most curious family he's ever met, and one day he might use my unorthodox upbringing as the basis for a novel."

"No wonder he and Jonathan get along so well." A faraway look glazed over Siena's eyes as she envisioned the many occasions in Santa Martina when she'd observed Tyler and Jonathan, their heads bent toward each other in deep conversation. Had they been trying to sort out why they were attracted to women who'd grown up surrounded by pickpockets and petty thieves?

An upturn in activity, along with an unfamiliar voice and alluring aromas, drew Siena's attention toward the doorway leading to the common area of the suite. "I think our food might have arrived."

Jacqueline slid the closet door closed. "Let's hope so. I'm starving."

"I'll bet you are." Siena rose from the bed, her bare

feet hitting the floral-patterned carpet.

"What's that supposed to mean?" Jacqueline asked over her shoulder.

"The rushed wedding, your increased appetite. When is the baby due?"

Jacqueline swiveled on her heels and faced Siena. "I didn't realize I was being that obvious." The twins stared at each other for a few seconds until Jacqueline broke into a huge grin. "Well, aren't you going to congratulate me?"

"Of course, I am." Siena rushed forward and squeezed her arms around Jacqueline. "I'm thrilled for you, and for Tyler." She patted Jacqueline's abdomen. "How far along are you?"

Jacqueline shrugged. "About six weeks. And listen, we want to wait before telling everyone else, so please keep the news to yourself."

"It will be our little secret, I promise. Now, come on, let's get some lunch into you. Oh, my gosh! I can't believe I'm going to be an auntie!"

As they strolled from the bedroom and crossed through the short hallway leading to the shared quarters of the suite, Siena overheard Gus escorting the server to the door. "Thanks again. Have a good afternoon." The door clicked closed and Gus rejoined them in the living room. "I hope it's okay that I signed your name to the receipt."

"That's fine." Siena stood by as Jacqueline and Marielle loaded their plates with salads and sandwiches. "Did you give him a nice tip?"

Gus grinned. "Sure did." Foregoing the food, Gus dropped a few ice cubes into a crystal glass, cracked open the bottle of scotch he'd ordered, and poured himself a drink. "When I'm spending someone else's money, I can be quite generous."

"That's fine," Siena assured him. "But please let me handle the expenses from now on." As she was dishing salad greens onto her own plate, the doorbell chimed again. "That's probably Lou. I'll let him in." Carrying her plate with her, she entered the foyer and opened the door.

"Hey," Lou said in greeting as he stepped over the threshold. "Sorry I'm late. I walked over instead of taking the subway. Big mistake."

"You haven't missed anything," Siena said, closing the door behind him. "Actually, you're just in time for lunch."

"I was hoping you'd say that." As Lou headed toward the living room, Siena grabbed his arm and stopped him short.

"Uh…before you meet the others, there's something I need to explain."

Lou gazed at her with curious eyes. "What is it?"

"One of the people I'll be introducing you to is my sister. My identical twin sister."

"Yeah? So, you have a twin." Lou shrugged his shoulders. "So, what?"

"Well, you don't know this, but you already have history with her. Fifteen months ago, you knew her as Kelsey Adams." Lou shook his head, obviously confused. "The woman who was seeing Patrick Woodward. Veronica Lambert hired you to follow her in Connecticut." Siena studied Lou's face while the cogs slowly clicked into place.

"No shit! The chick who was conning Veronica's brother?" Siena confirmed with a nod. "But wasn't that you?"

"Well, for part of the time, I *was* pretending to be Kelsey Adams."

"Okay. Now you've got me totally confused."

"I know. It's complicated. For right now, I just wanted to forewarn you so your jaw doesn't drop when I introduce you. Anyway, you can get to know Jacqueline, Gus, and Marielle over lunch. Afterward, I'll explain how I plan to handle my situation with Matthew Kramer."

****

Siena inserted a pod into the coffee maker and brewed herself a fresh cup. She added a splash of skim milk and savored the first sip, allowing the hot java to warm her insides on this brisk autumn day. She could abstain from any other indulgence, but God help the person who deprived her of her daily caffeine intake.

She strolled into the living room, took a seat on one of the room's two sofas, and set her mug on the glass-topped coffee table. Directly across from her, Marielle and Jacqueline sat beside each other on a matching sofa. The sofas were flanked at either end by complementary armchairs, Gus in one, Lou in the other. Siena crossed her legs and glanced around at the others. Expectant eyes stared back at her.

Gus sat forward in his chair. "Now that we're all here, Siena, what do you need us to do? Kramer's deadline is only a few days away. We don't have any time to waste."

"Wait a minute," Jacqueline said, her eyes darting between Siena and Gus. "What deadline are you talking about? And who is Kramer?"

"Sorry, Jac," Siena said. "It's a long story. I'll fill

you in later. All you need to know right now is that I've been recognized by one of my former marks, a man named Matthew Kramer. He wants five million dollars by the end of the month in exchange for a video he has of me that I'd rather the world not see. My mission is to get my hands on that video and destroy it. Gus and Marielle offered to help, along with Lou. Lou is also the private investigator I hired to shadow Kramer while Jonathan and I were in the Caribbean last week."

Jacqueline glanced from Marielle to Gus, her brows raised. "So, you two didn't fly here with me just to spend a few fun days in New York as you claimed." The cynicism in her voice was thick when she said, "Nice. *Real* nice. Marielle, I sure hope you know what you're getting yourself into." She frowned as her attention shifted to Siena. "And you. Don't expect me to play a part in whatever this plan is that you're concocting. I told you after the last time you recruited me that I was done for good, and I meant it."

"Jac," Siena said, "take a breath. I'm not asking anyone in this room to do anything illegal or dangerous. Gus, Marielle, and Lou are simply going to gather information on Kramer for me while you and I are out shopping for wedding dresses."

"So, I'm your cover. Is that it?" Easing back against the cushions of the sofa, Jacqueline's brow knitted. "Tell me one thing. Does Jonathan know about any of this?"

Siena stared at her twin with scornful eyes. "No, and I plan to leave it that way."

Chapter 18

Siena
Spring 2017

Siena's face twisted into a grimace. Staring across the table at Matthew sucking Pasta Bolognese through his puckered lips reminded her of city street workers vacuuming sludge out of a sewage drain. Chalk up *Bad Table Manners* to her growing list of reasons she disliked Matthew Kramer. But then, how was Matthew any different from the other domineering, self-indulgent fools she'd targeted in her previous schemes? *If only my brain were equipped to function like my laptop,* she mused. How she'd love to hover the cursor over her memory bank, drag all the data she'd collected from all the con jobs she'd ever pulled to the Recycle Bin, and click on the *Empty Trash* button. The folder labeled "Matthew Kramer" would be the first file she'd delete.

Then again, retaining all that data—details such as which techniques she'd employed and which personas she'd created for each job—was essential to avoiding pitfalls. In the six years Siena had been living under the guise of Marie Lacroix, respected antiques expert by day and unscrupulous con artist by night, she'd carried out dozens of con jobs and could recite in precise order the details of each beginning with Perry Chaplin, her first, to Thomas McMaster, her most recent, the way some people pride themselves in being able to rattle off the names of their teachers, along with subjects taught, from kindergarten through high school.

Gus argued that her gift of total recall was a blessing. *Would you rather run the risk of keeping written records that could fall into the wrong hands?* he'd asked. Siena, however, considered her inherent trait to be a curse. Ninety-nine percent of the men she'd targeted were afflicted with overplayed egos and wayward horniness. Not necessarily the type of memories she cared to treasure.

A vision from the previous night of Matthew yanking up her skirt and coming damned close to assaulting her in his building's elevator invaded her thoughts. She cringed at the possibility of what might have happened had his wife's timely phone call not interrupted what he referred to as "a taste of what he wanted to do to her." What fortuitous event might grant her a way to fend off Matthew tonight when, at the end of dinner, he suggested—correct that, *insisted*—they head straight uptown to his co-op? Something told her she'd seen the last of fate intervening on her behalf.

Shit.

The waiter passed by their table for a courtesy check. "Can I bring you more bread?" His accent reminded Siena of her Nonna Carmella. She was tempted to strike up a conversation in the waiter's native tongue, but being fluent in Italian didn't jive with her tax accountant from Virginia façade.

"We're fine," Siena replied in her Ellen Randall drawl. "Thank you."

With a smile and a tap of his fingers against the edge of their table, the waiter rushed off to check in with the party of five in the corner booth.

"Your gnocchi looks good," Matthew said, pointing his fork at her plate.

"It's delicious." Siena was about to play into his passive-aggressive ploy and offer to spoon a sampling onto his plate, but Matthew was too impatient. Reaching across the table, he pierced two of the dumplings with his fork, popped them into his mouth, and made yummy sounds while nodding his approval. Siena raised an amazed eyebrow and glared at him. How rude, how arrogant, how *typical* of him to presume he was welcome to help himself, as though whatever was hers automatically belonged to him. Then again, what did she expect? Matthew had been playing with her body like it was his own personal toy since the first night they met.

Having lost her appetite, Siena dropped her fork onto the plate. "So," she said, dismissing the incident from her mind, "you spoke with your wife last night?"

"Yeah." Matthew obviously didn't care to discuss the matter. Siena, not giving a damn, pressed on.

"Did she have good news to report? Is the treatment helping?" The previous evening, after one too many glasses of scotch, he'd confessed that Alva hadn't gone to France with her daughter for pleasure. She was undergoing an experimental treatment for her rare neurological disorder with hopes of slowing its progression. Siena assumed his reluctance to discuss the results Alva had reported during their call last evening stemmed from the stress associated with facing his wife's mortality. She couldn't have been further from the truth.

"Doesn't appear to be," he said with a shrug, as though Alva had informed him the radical medicine the doctors were administering wasn't clearing up her sinus infection as expediently as she'd hoped.

Siena glanced away, needed a moment to process his lack of concern. This was his *wife* they were talking about, not some impersonal subject of a documentary about breakthroughs in medical science. Regardless, she would remain calm. Not be judgmental. Not give in to her Italian temper and ruin a relationship she'd taken such pains to nurture.

"I'm so sorry to hear that," she said. "She, and you, must be devastated."

"Yeah," Matthew replied as he mopped up the remaining Bolognese sauce with the last slice of bread. "Well, she is anyway."

Take a deep breath, Siena. Bite your tongue. Make him believe you're on his side.

"Matthew, I admire the way you're keeping yourself together, I truly do. But please know I'm here for you whenever you need a shoulder to cry on."

With his eyes glued on Siena, Matthew washed his food down with the last swig of scotch. Setting the empty glass on the table, he leaned forward. A sly grin spread across his face. "Trust me, babe." Siena gritted her teeth every time he called her *babe*. "I'd like nothing more than to bury my head in your shoulder, but the moans I make won't be caused by crying."

Siena swallowed hard to keep her food down. Ellen Randall, on the other hand, giggled over the insinuation. "Matthew, you naughty boy!"

"Babe, if you think that's naughty, wait until you find out how hard I can make you—"

"How was everything?" The waiter was back to present the dessert menu and clear their plates from the table.

"Excellent, as usual," Matthew replied. "Give the chef my compliments."

"He'll be happy to hear. Miss, would you like me to put the rest of your dinner in a take-home container?"

After Matthew's fork contaminated the food? "No, thank you," she replied, her stomach still nauseous over Matthew's brash allusion to his prowess in the bedroom.

"I'll give you a moment to look over our dessert selections. Will you be having anything more to drink? Coffee?"

Matthew wiped his mouth and flung his napkin onto the table. His body language implied he was impatient for their evening to progress. "I think we're ready for the check."

"Now, Matthew, don't be so hasty," Siena scolded. To the waiter, she said, "I'd like coffee with cream and, Matthew, I understand their tiramisu is to die for. Let's order one to share."

"Fine," Matthew huffed at the waiter. "Since it appears we're staying a while longer, you may as well bring me another scotch."

Siena grinned. She wanted neither the coffee nor the dessert, but she'd willingly order every item on the menu to delay leaving the restaurant.

"Coffee with cream, a scotch, and one tiramisu to share," the waiter confirmed. "I'll be right back."

Matthew extended his arm across the table and grasped Siena's hand. "You know, babe,"—*Call me* babe *one more time and I swear I'll flip this table onto your lap*—"Margaret, our housekeeper, is on vacation for the next week. It's awfully lonely being in that big apartment all by myself."

"What are you suggesting?" Siena's Ellen Randall curled one side of her mouth into a seductive grin and played along.

"That you stay with me while she's away." He drew her hand to his mouth and brushed his lips across the backs of her fingers. "We've waited long enough. Tonight, I will take you back to my apartment, and nothing is going to interrupt us this time. Not your work, not my sick wife. I want us to spend the entire night together. Tonight," he said as he kissed her fingers one by one, "and tomorrow night, and the next." Siena's jaw clenched when, expecting Matthew to plant one final kiss, he gazed knowingly into her eyes and licked her pinkie with his slimy tongue. "It's a great apartment. You might just want to move in permanently."

What I want is to rush into the ladies' room and scrub my hand under hot water.

Siena intertwined her fingers with his and pouted. "But, Matthew, you're married. Don't you think your wife might object?"

Matthew shook his head and scrunched his chin. "Based on the report Alva gave me last night, I don't expect her to be around much longer. When she passes, not only do I get the apartment but, according to her will, I'll receive a generous inheritance. I'm merely planning my future, and I'm counting on you taking the journey with me."

Siena needed a moment. Was she understanding Matthew correctly? Admittedly, she was no saint. After all, she wouldn't have become a successful con artist if she hadn't willingly lied, stolen, and enticed many of her targets into an extramarital affair. But Matthew had just crossed the line from being a wife-cheater to wishing his wife dead, and she had the distinct impression that he assumed she shared his repugnant dream. As Matthew caressed his thumb across her fingers, Siena's blood ran cold. She may as well have been holding hands with the devil himself.

Keep that grin on your face and the sparkle in your eyes, Siena. Those $300,000 diamond earrings are worth turning a deaf ear to every despicable word that comes out of Matthew's mouth.

"Your *babe* needs to take baby steps, darlin'," she said, flirtatiously cocking her head. "Let's start with tonight and take the future one day at a time."

Chapter 19

Siena
October 2023

Jacqueline threw back the curtain and stepped onto the raised dressing room platform. Facing the mirror, she smoothed her hands over her midriff and crinkled her nose. "What do you think about this one?"

Siena cocked her head and shrugged her shoulders. "Does my opinion even matter? You obviously don't like it."

"It's too tight across my stomach."

"Jac, you're not even two months along. What are you worried about?"

"But my waistline is expanding every day," Jacqueline said as she stepped off the platform. "I just want to be comfortable on the day of the wedding. This one's a definite no," she told Evie, the bridal consultant who was helping her in and out of each of the dresses she'd plucked off the racks.

Siena couldn't sit still any longer. Maybe she'd overdosed on coffee that morning. She rose from her chair and paced the expanse of the viewing room. "Face it, Jac. The first gown you tried on is still the nicest."

"Which one was that?" Jacqueline asked from behind the closed curtain. "I've already forgotten."

"The flowy one with the empire waistline."

From behind the curtain the bridal consultant chimed in. "I agree. You were stunning in every gown you've tried on, but the first was my favorite as well."

"Plus, it coordinates well with my dress," Siena said. Having decided on her attire for the wedding two hours ago, she was growing impatient. Normally, she wouldn't have minded if Jacqueline modeled every gown in the showroom, but she had other pressing matters that required her attention.

"Are you being honest," Jacqueline asked, "or do you want me to make an uninspired decision so you can get on with that *other matter* you came to New York to deal with?"

Siena sighed and rolled her eyes. Did Jacqueline need to go there? "I'm being completely honest, Jac. But if you're still not convinced, I can go through the backroom again with Evie and pick out even more styles for you to try on." A long pause followed. The rustling of satin and tulle gave Siena hope that Jacqueline was about to announce the winner in her search for the perfect wedding gown.

"Just a few more, okay?"

Siena clenched her fists. "Give me a minute," she said. "I need to pee."

****

Siena envied Gus and Marielle. While they'd spent the day enjoying a carriage ride in Central Park and strolling through the exhibits at the Natural History Museum, she was trapped inside a bridal salon stroking Jacqueline's unusually fragile ego. She had not been prepared for the havoc this pregnancy would play on her twin's emotions.

So, as best as she could, Siena endured an afternoon

of paying compliments, forcing smiles, and stealing glances at her watch. She dared not give the wrong impression. Shopping for Jac's wedding dress was a special treat Siena wouldn't have missed for the world, but she couldn't take her mind off the threatening issue looming over her head. When Jacqueline finally slipped back into the first gown, the one Siena and Evie favored, and announced it was *The One*, Siena shouted "Yes!" and jumped out of her chair. She threw her arms around Jacqueline and declared her the most beautiful bride in all of history.

Deciding on the dress, however, didn't mean an immediate exit from the store. Jacqueline still had a few follow-up items to attend to, such as paying for the gown and meeting with the seamstress for minor alterations. By the time they pushed through the revolving door and stepped out onto the sidewalk, Jacqueline was exhausted. Her eyelids fluttered during the short taxi ride back to the Baldwin Hotel. When the twins entered their suite, Jacqueline made a beeline for their room. Dinner, she declared as she collapsed onto the bed, was out of the question.

"I'll call for room service after I take a nap," she said with a yawn. "Please give Marielle and Gus my apologies and tell them not to think me rude, but I'd much rather lounge in bed and have a video call with Tyler than spend the evening sitting in a noisy, crowded restaurant."

Siena was alarmed. Was Jacqueline, her typically vivacious and sociable sister, not feeling well? "Jac, is something wrong? Should I take you to urgent care?"

Jacqueline chuckled. "Sissy, I'm not sick. I'm pregnant."

"So?" Siena asked, panic stricken. Was Jac ill on top of being pregnant? Was the baby in danger?

"Are you seriously that clueless? Tiredness is common during the first trimester."

Siena crinkled her nose. "Really?" *Yet another reason not to have children.*

"Yes, really. Just be thankful I'm not throwing up all over you. Now, go, have a nice dinner and let me sleep."

Leaving Jacqueline curled up under the covers, Siena hastened across Seventh Avenue and up six city blocks where she joined the rest of her group at Maestro for drinks, dinner, and a debrief regarding what more Gus and Marielle had unearthed about Matthew Kramer's secrets.

Chapter 20

Gus

Not much had changed since Gus last set foot inside Eddie Davis's private poker room. The tables were in the same arrangement, the bar was still in the far corner, the heavy brocade drapes were still drawn closed. Come to think of it, Gus couldn't say for certain whether those curtains concealed windows or areas of the establishment in which other, perhaps more clandestine, activities were taking place. As far as Gus was concerned, what other people did in privacy was nobody else's damned business.

"Nice place," Marielle commented. "Quieter than I expected. Did you come here often when you lived in New York?"

Gus shook his head. "Rarely. Twice, maybe three times at the most. I only dropped in when Ed invited me." After climbing the tall staircase of the century-old building in Brooklyn and being buzzed in by security, he and Marielle were standing in the entryway where they'd been instructed to wait. Gus scanned the faces of the players seated around the tables, searching for but not identifying Matthew Kramer. "These are high stakes games, and I don't consider myself a card shark."

"Tell me again how you know the owner."

"Ed Davis was a frequent client of mine. He liked to

impress his girlfriends with expensive gifts he could buy from me at bargain prices. This is him coming toward us now, the big guy with the deep tan and slicked-back hair."

Eddie opened his arms as he approached them. "Gus, my old friend! How the hell have you been?" He clasped Gus's hand with one arm and gave him a manly hug with the other.

"I'm good, Ed. Real good. How've you been?"

"Ach, you know me. I never complain." Eddie clenched Gus's shoulders as he stood back and admired him. "Damn, you look great! What's your secret?"

"Retirement," Gus replied with a cockeyed grin. "You should try it."

Eddie half-turned and extended his arm toward the room behind him. "And walk away from all this? Nah. I'm still having too much fun. Now, hold on a second. Who's this lovely lady standing beside you?"

Gus drew Marielle to his side. "Ed, I'd like you to meet my friend, Marielle Saint-Fleur. Marielle, this is Ed Davis."

Eddie took Marielle's hand in his. "A beautiful woman with a beautiful name to match. Welcome, Marielle."

Marielle rose up on her tiptoes, meeting Eddie halfway as he leaned in and kissed her on each cheek. "Thank you for the compliments. It's a pleasure to meet you, Ed."

Eddie stepped back and shook his index finger at her. "Now, none of this 'Ed' business. Call me Eddie like everybody else. Everybody but Gus, that is. He believes men should be called by their grown-up names. Right, Gus?" He gave Gus a playful punch to his upper arm.

"That's right, Ed." At least that was the reason Gus hid behind, which was easier than admitting that the name *Eddie* brought back painful memories of Gus's younger brother who, in his early twenties, had been killed in a knifing incident. What Eddie Ferguson had been doing in the dicey neighborhood of Bedford-Stuyvesant at four in the morning was a question to which Gus would never know the answer.

"Rocco," Eddie said to the burly man in the dark suit standing behind him, "take our guests' coats. Gus, you remember Rocco, don't you?"

"Sure do." Gus shook hands with Rocco. "Nice to see you again."

"Good to see you, too, Mr. Ferguson." Gus helped Marielle with her coat and, after removing his own, handed both over to Rocco.

"Come," Eddie said. "Let's sit and have a drink." He guided Marielle and Gus to a dimly lit alcove where a plush sectional sofa was fitted against a red brick wall. Marielle took her place next to Eddie while Gus sat on his other side. "Marielle, do you like a dry martini? Jake, my bartender, makes the best in the city."

"I would love one," Marielle said. "Thank you, Eddie."

Eddie addressed the server who magically appeared before them. "Georgene, one dry martini for the lady." Turning his head sideways, he asked, "And you, Gus?"

For the moment, Gus was too busy ogling Georgene to respond. The impossibly tall brunette was clad in a cropped jacket and a pair of low-slung slacks that flaunted her smooth, firm abdomen and slender hips. He glanced up and gazed into eyes that were as blue as the sapphire stud pierced in her navel. "Whiskey," he

179

ordered. "Neat."

"Bring me the same," Eddie said, dismissing the waitress with a grin and a wink.

Marielle placed a cordial hand on Eddie's arm. "Eddie, while you and Gus catch up with each other, would you mind if I sat at the bar and spoke with your staff? You see, I am the owner of a bar back home and I would like to pick up some tips on the way your servers run things."

Eddie patted her hand. "You go right ahead, sweetie. But make sure you tell Jake he has orders not to give away any secrets." His gaze lingered on Marielle as she sashayed across the room. "I have to say, Gus, you always did attract the hot ones."

As Gus recalled, Eddie was notorious for his wandering eye. "This one's a keeper, Ed," Gus said, his glare issuing a warning. "Feel free to look, but don't you dare touch. Which reminds me, how's your wife? I assume you're still married to Carla?"

Eddie chuckled and gave Gus a slap on his knee. "You need to catch up, old friend. Carla was two wives ago. Right now, I'm playing the field."

Gus responded with a nod of his head. What was that, four marriages? He hated to imagine what Eddie paid in alimony support. Gus slid his hand into his pocket and retrieved a jewelry box. "Is there anyone special at the moment who might like to have this draped on her wrist?" He opened the box and revealed a diamond tennis bracelet. Anticipating he'd need to offer Eddie something sweet in exchange for the information he was after, Gus had asked a favor of Christopher, the younger man who'd taken over Gus's operation when he relocated to the Caribbean the previous year. Gus didn't know from whose wrist the bracelet had been pilfered, nor did he care. The deal was purely transactional, the price was right and, most importantly, Siena was footing the bill.

Eddie accepted the box and angled it for better lighting. Gus followed Eddie's drifting gaze as his eyes feasted on a gorgeous thirty-something serving drinks to a table of Texas Hold'em players across the room. "As a matter of fact, there is. Thanks, Gus." He snapped the lid closed and dropped Gus's bribe into the inside pocket of his jacket.

"Happy to oblige."

"On the phone earlier, you said you wanted to talk to me about someone."

"That's right." At that exact moment, Georgene returned with their drinks. When she bent at the waist to set their glasses and a bowl of munchies on the table, her single-buttoned jacket gaped open, satisfying Gus's curiosity about whether undergarments were a required part of the uniform. "I'd appreciate any information you can give me on a guy I understand is one of your regulars. A guy named Matthew Kramer."

Eddie grunted as he leaned back against the sofa and tossed a handful of munchies into his mouth. "Your timing's impeccable."

Gus cocked his head. "Why is that?"

Draping his arm across the back of the sofa, Eddie nudged his chin in the direction of the poker room's entrance. "That's Kramer being escorted in by a couple of my guys right now."

Gus glanced over his shoulder and verified the man being manhandled through the front doors was indeed Matthew Kramer. Although he doubted Kramer would glance their way, Gus was thankful he was tucked into the dark alcove. He couldn't risk being recognized as Stanley Bartlemay, the jewelry appraiser who'd played a part in Kramer's sting operation six years ago.

"What's your interest in him?" Eddie inquired.

Gus was reluctant to share too much. He and Eddie were friendly, but Gus was cautious about where he placed his trust. "It's not me. Kramer's trying to pull off something underhanded on someone I know. You might say I'm asking for a friend."

"Underhanded, huh? Well, that's typical."

When Eddie didn't elaborate, Gus pressed him for more. "Sounds like you've had some unpleasant dealings with him yourself."

Eddie sneered. "The guy was nice enough when he first started coming here, but he's turned into a real douchebag."

"How so?"

"Well," Eddie hedged, "let's just say the animosity between us is both professional *and* personal." Eddie leaned forward and rested his forearms on his knees. He jerked his head to indicate Gus should come closer. "Kramer and I had a brief shall we say *discussion* in my office last night," he said in confidence. "I told him in no uncertain terms that I've extended his line of credit for the last time, and he has until the end of the month to pay his account in full. In the meantime, he's not welcome to play cards here."

Gus waited, but further details were not forthcoming. He was getting tired of prompting Eddie for information. "So, what happens if he doesn't pay his account in full?"

Eddie's attention was drawn to the rising

confrontation taking place near the poker room's entrance. Gus swung his head around and checked out the ruckus. Rocco had his hand clamped around Kramer's arm. The scene was deteriorating quickly.

"Excuse me." Eddie stood abruptly and buttoned his suit coat. "I need to take care of this situation before it gets any uglier."

****

Marielle

"Who's the man talking with Rocco?" Marielle asked the bartender.

Jake strained his neck and got a glimpse of the action taking place on the other side of the poker room. "Oh, that guy." He poured vermouth into the cocktail shaker, attached the lid, and gave the container his signature shake. "Name's Matt Kramer. He's here three, four nights a week."

"Huh." Marielle swiveled sideways and kept a close eye on the heated exchange taking place across the room. So, that was the man she and Gus had flown all the way from Santa Martina to spy on at Siena's behest. "If he's a regular, why isn't Rocco letting him past the front door?"

"Because he's pushed Eddie's patience to the limit," Georgene chimed in.

Marielle befriended strangers faster than ice melted on a summer sidewalk. Her tactic: ask pertinent questions and be a good listener, the same qualities that made her a successful restaurateur. In a mere ten minutes, she had Eddie's busy bartender and sensual server revealing the poker room's private goings-on.

"Why? What's he done?" Marielle punctuated her question by forming a concerned crease in her brow.

"You didn't hear this from me, but he's in debt big time. He's got a gambling addiction which wouldn't be so bad if he were lucky at cards—which he can be but most of the time isn't. It's my understanding he owes money all over town." Georgene rearranged the drinks on her tray, making room for a bourbon on the rocks. "Plus, I know for a fact he's having an affair with one of our servers."

Marielle's eyes darted between Georgene and Jake, expecting one or the other to fling more dirt her way. She noticed the way Jake's eyes flashed up at Georgene, as though cautioning her to keep her lips sealed. *Oh, this story is getting juicy.* "That's not unusual. I've owned a bar long enough to know that sort of thing happens all the time."

Her drink order complete, Georgene lifted the tray to her shoulder. As she stepped away from the bar, she leaned close and whispered into Marielle's ear. "Not when the server's also sleeping with Eddie Davis, it doesn't."

Chapter 21

Siena

Maestro had been a regular meeting place for Siena and Gus during their association as business partners, which now seemed like a lifetime ago. After years of strategizing her exit from Manhattan, Siena had left the city in a rush and never intended to look back. However, being in Maestro again, connecting with the staff, and ordering her standard grilled salmon with roasted asparagus filled Siena with a genial familiarity and solace. Was this what "coming home" was all about?

"So, what did Eddie Davis do?" Siena asked Gus. "Have it out with Kramer in front of the entire poker room?"

Gus swallowed his scotch and, shaking his head, set the highball glass on the table. "No. Rocco strong-armed Kramer up the stairs to, I assume, Ed's office. About fifteen minutes later, Ed came back down—alone."

"And in a foul mood," Marielle added.

A frown of confusion burrowed into Siena's forehead. "Then, where did Kramer go? Did Rocco show him out through a back door?"

Gus shrugged his shoulders. "I have no idea. When he sat down with me again, Ed got real tight-lipped. I asked a few questions about Kramer, but he gave no answers."

"Well, Kramer must have gotten out somehow," Lou added. "I watched him bolt out of a black SUV and practically run into the Hudson about…" he glanced at his wristwatch, "thirty minutes ago."

Siena considered Matthew's predicament while refilling her wine glass. Whatever happened in the poker room's upstairs office couldn't have been good. "Sounds like our boy has gotten himself tangled up with the wrong people." She lifted her glass and swilled down a gulp of Chardonnay.

"I've known Ed Davis for a long time," Gus said, "and I've heard stories about what happens to people who cross him. Stories that would curl your hair."

Siena's gaze bounced from Gus to Marielle. "I owe you two a huge debt of thanks. The information you gathered will give me the upper hand when I meet with Kramer tomorrow morning."

Gus raised a bewildered eyebrow. "I wasn't aware you two had a meeting set up. How are you going to play it?"

"Before Jac and I went dress shopping, I called Kramer and insinuated that I have his money and I'm anxious to hand it over. He invited me to his place, which is exactly the offer I wanted. While I'm in his apartment, I'll create an opportunity to steal both the camera and his cell phone, the two devices on which I'm positive he has the video saved."

"Then, do you still need me to tail him?" Lou asked.

"That depends on how successful I am tomorrow morning. Just be at your usual post at the park entrance across from the Hudson. I'll check in with you after I leave his co-op."

"Yes, ma'am," Lou said with a nod of his head.

Gus sat back and crossed his arms. The worry lines on his face deepened. "What happens if your mission tomorrow isn't successful?"

Siena shot him a sly grin. "You know me better than that, Gus. I always have a Plan B."

****

With Gus and Marielle holed up in their bedroom and Jacqueline fast asleep in the other, Siena took advantage of her alone time to place a video call to Jonathan.

"Hi," Jonathan said with a tender intimacy in his voice. Although his face filled up most of the screen area on her phone, Siena caught enough of his surroundings to determine he was seated in his reading chair in the library.

"Hi, yourself. Sorry to call so late. I wanted to wait until Jac was asleep."

"That's okay. Like I said in my text, make the most of this time with your sister. Honestly, I'm surprised she's already down for the night. I figured you two would be up for hours rehashing the wild days of your youth, talking about your old boyfriends and how they were so much sexier than Tyler and me."

Through the phone's screen, Siena detected the twinkle in Jonathan's eye. "Oh, now, that's not even close to the truth," she bantered back. "As far as you're concerned, that is. I can only speculate about Tyler."

Jonathan chuckled. "Nice save." He gazed at Siena with eyes that expressed his longing for her. "I miss you."

"I miss you, too." She'd give anything to be able to crawl through the phone and curl up in Jonathan's lap, to lose herself in his warm embrace. "So, did you have a nice time today with your friend Mack?"

"Yes." Jonathan's gaze wandered, as if he were recalling the visit in his mind. "We, uh, we had a lot of catching up to do. As a matter of fact, I just got home not too long ago."

"What did you and Mack—"

"How did the dress shopping go?" he asked. Jonathan didn't normally interrupt her in the middle of a sentence, but he seemed more interested in discovering how she'd spent her day than elaborating on his reunion with Mack.

"It went well. I found my dress right away, but Jac took forever. Finally, after hours in the fitting room, she decided to buy the first dress she tried on. By then, I was ready to pull my hair out."

"Patience, sweetheart. This is an important moment for her."

"I know. She was just concerned about finding a style that would conceal her expanding waistline."

"So, your hunch is confirmed. She and Tyler are expecting?"

"They sure are. But they want to wait a while before making the announcement, so please keep the news to yourself."

"Will do. In the meantime, let's think of a gift to send them."

"Good idea. I'll search the internet for something unique."

Jonathan exhaled a heavy sigh. "Any chance the baby bug has rubbed off on you?"

Although Siena should have been prepared for the conversation to steer in that direction, Jonathan's persistence in getting her to commit to starting a family caught her off guard. With heavier matters presently weighing on her shoulders, his question struck the wrong nerve. She sucked in her breath and shifted her gaze away from the phone screen. "Jonathan, can we please not have that discussion right now?"

"All I'm asking is that you give serious consideration to us starting our own family." The annoyance in his voice was unmistakable.

"I will, I promise," Siena replied, although she'd already dismissed the notion from her mind. "Have you gotten any more text messages with those awful videos attached?" She held her breath as she waited for Jonathan's response.

"No, thank goodness."

Siena wasn't certain whether she should take this as good news or be concerned that Matthew had a more sinister plot in the works. She rose from the sofa and strode across the room as she summoned the nerve to roll another fib off her tongue.

"Jonathan...um...Jac needs to stay here for a few more days while her gown is being altered. I thought I'd stay with her. Maybe spend an afternoon cleaning out my apartment. Is that all right with you?"

"Of course. Is there..." Siena detected a hesitancy in Jonathan's voice, as though he'd changed his mind about what he was about to ask. He then cleared his throat and proceeded. "Is there any other business you need to take care of while you're in New York that I should be aware of?"

Siena's mouth went dry. Why would Jonathan ask her such a pointed question? Regardless, he'd opened the door for her to come clean about her real purpose for staying in New York and, for a brief second, she almost convinced herself to admit the truth. Gazing out the window at the lights dotting the Manhattan skyline, she forced a smile. "Well, I am planning to go shoe shopping. In your book, is that business or pleasure?"

Some secrets, Siena rationalized, were too hurtful to share.

Chapter 22

Siena

Holding the phone receiver to his ear, the guard in the lobby of the Hudson stared at Siena and shook his head. "Sorry, ma'am." He returned the receiver to its cradle. "Mr. Kramer still isn't answering. Perhaps he's in the shower...or is otherwise occupied."

"And he didn't provide my name as a guest he was expecting around this time?"

The guard glanced down at his computer screen. "Sorry, ma'am. There are no notes regarding guests for Mr. Kramer."

Siena drummed her fingertips against the countertop that separated her from the guard. *Matthew and I agreed on this time just yesterday and he seemed eager to meet, especially when I indicated that I'd be handing over his $5million ransom. So, where is he?*

"If you'd like to stick around," the guard suggested, "I'll be happy to try him again in a few minutes. You can have a seat on that couch while you wait."

"No, thank you." Gazing through the front windows at the red, orange, and yellow leaves fluttering on a gust of wind as they cascaded from the treetops to the sidewalk below, Siena considered her options. "You're certain you didn't see him leave the building this morning?"

"No, ma'am. I'd remember because Mr. Kramer always stops by my desk to pick up The Times and ask about my family."

What a sweetheart.

"Tell you what," she said, slapping her palm on the countertop with a thud of finality. "If you do manage to get in touch with Mr. Kramer, please relay a message for me. Remind him that he and I had an appointment scheduled for 10:00 this morning. Tell him I was here and that I needed to step away, but I'll be back."

"I'll be sure to do that." He placed his hand on the mouse, made a few clicks, and typed a note into his computer. "Would you like to leave your name?"

A devious grin slithered onto Siena's face. "Tell him Ellen Randall is looking for him."

"Ellen Randall," the guard repeated as he typed the name. "Got it, Ms. Randall."

"Thank you." Siena turned on her heels and sauntered across the lobby. From her crossbody purse, she removed the burner phone Matthew had given her. Still no missed calls. *What the hell?* She stuffed the phone into the pocket of her cape so that when Matthew called, she'd be able to access the phone faster from her pocket than from her purse.

Outside, a light drizzle had begun to fall. Siena raised the hood of her cape and located Lou standing under the arched entrance to the park across the street. Stepping to the curb, she was waiting for traffic to clear when she heard a woman's voice calling out her name.

"Siena? Siena, is that you?"

Siena crooked her head to the right, her eyes scanning the half dozen or so people scurrying along the sidewalk, their heads bent downward against the inclement weather. Only one person had been prepared to venture outside—the woman gazing at Siena from under the cover of her umbrella.

The woman treaded closer. "Yes, I'm sure it's you." Siena's stare was blank. With her short auburn hair and deep blue eyes, the woman's tall stature rivaled Siena's own. Her engaging British accent seemed familiar, but Siena's preoccupied mind wasn't making the connection. The woman placed a reassuring hand on Siena's arm. "Siena, surely you remember me. Joanie Osgood, Gaylor's wife. We met a few weeks ago at your marriage celebration."

All at once, the pieces snapped into place—the chatty woman who'd commented on Siena's necklace, married to Gaylor Osgood, one of Jonathan's frat brothers. "Oh, my goodness, Joanie! I'm so sorry. You know how it is when you see someone out of context."

"Of course! That's happened to me a million times and it's always so embarrassing. In fact, when you rushed past me just now, I said to myself, *I know that woman*, but it took me a moment to remember how. Oh, dear, here comes the real rain." She stepped closer and, linking arms with Siena, drew her under the umbrella and prompted her toward the Hudson's front entrance. "Let's get under the canopy. Tell you what. Are you in a hurry? I've just been to Domani's, which is my absolute favorite bakery. Have you ever been? No? Oh, my dear, you must stop in. Their selection of pastries is extraordinary. Anyway, I had an awful craving for a scone this morning, but I couldn't decide on which flavor and ended up buying half a dozen. I can't eat them all myself and Gaylor needs to watch his cholesterol." She sighed. "Life just isn't as much fun once you hit your sixties. Anyway, would you like to come up to our apartment for tea or coffee or whatever drink you prefer and share these scones with me?"

Siena's eyebrows shot up. "Do you mean to your apartment here? Do you live in the Hudson?"

"Yes, dear, on the seventh floor. I have nothing on my schedule until later this afternoon and Gaylor's gone off to the office, so it will be just us girls. Well, my housekeeper is in today, but Imelda won't bother us. So, what do you say?"

Siena hesitated, torn between what she wanted to say and what she was obligated to say. With Matthew's imposed deadline closing in on her, she had much on her mind and little time to spare. On the other hand, she anticipated that word of Siena Woodward snubbing Joanie Osgood would spread like wildfire through Jonathan's social circle. As the new kid on the block, she couldn't afford the backlash. Besides, of all the people Siena had met in her new role as Jonathan's wife, Joanie was the only one who seemed genuinely interested in getting to know her, and Siena could use a friend right about now—as well as access to the residences inside the Hudson. She gave Joanie a warm smile. "I can't think of a better way to spend my morning."

While Joanie collapsed her umbrella and blathered on about the first snowfall being just around the corner, Siena's attention was focused on the security guard. How would she respond when he referred to her as *Ms. Randall* and updated her on the whereabouts of Matthew Kramer? By a stroke of luck, a courier with a loaded dolly breezed through the doors ahead of them. The security guard was too busy to take notice of the tall blonde strolling through the lobby with the garrulous

Mrs. Osgood.

****

"Let's sit here in the living room," Joanie said. "The chairs in the corner are so awfully cozy, and I love our view of the park from the windows. Can I share a confidence? Most afternoons, I toss off my shoes and curl up in one of these chairs with a glass of Chablis and a sultry romance novel. There now, see what I mean?"

"Oh, I do." Siena relaxed into the chair and gazed out the window. "This corner reminds me of our library, which is my favorite room in the house." A wave of homesickness washed over Siena. She wanted to tell Joanie about her library windows from which she could gaze out at their garden and the lake at the end of their property; about the oversized chair Jonathan bought for her and how he'd positioned it by those windows, across from his own reading chair; about the ottoman they shared and how she and Jonathan played footsie while they talked for hours on end or as they read, each engrossed in their own novel. Siena wanted to share these personal moments with Joanie, but her throat was too tight. If she attempted to speak, she feared the tears welling in her eyes would spill down her cheeks.

"Mm…" Joanie moaned softly, as though she sensed Siena's melancholy. "Isn't it so important to have a home that gives us such comfort and security? Now, are you as much in need of a scone as I am?" Siena grinned and nodded her head. "Which do you prefer—tea or coffee?"

Siena cleared her throat. "Whatever you're having."

"Well, as much as I enjoy a strong cup of coffee, I am English. Are you sure tea is all right? I can make coffee as well."

"No, please. I would enjoy a cup of tea."

"Tea it is, then," Joanie said as she rose from the chair. "It will just take me a moment to prepare a pot."

"Can I help?" Joanie's down-to-earth personality made Siena feel right at home. She honestly wanted to join her in the kitchen.

"Tut-tut. You stay right here and enjoy the view, or as much of it as you can see through this dreadful rain."

"Thanks, although I do need to make a phone call." By now, Lou must be wondering what she was doing.

"Go right ahead, dear. If you need privacy, feel free to step across the foyer and use Gaylor's office. I won't be offended if you close the door."

"That's okay, I'm just going to touch base with my sister," Siena said, offering a plausible explanation. "I can make the call from here."

Joanie spoke over her shoulder as she sauntered from the room. "Well, the office is there if you change your mind."

Siena rummaged through her purse for the burner phone she'd purchased specifically to communicate with Lou. She waited until Joanie had exited the room before placing the call.

"Hey," Lou said. "What's going on?"

Siena swiveled toward the window and spoke just above a whisper. "It appears our boy is MIA. The security guard couldn't get in touch with him, so I wasn't allowed past the front desk."

"Where the hell is he, then?" Lou asked rhetorically. "I've had my eye on the front door since the sun came up and I haven't seen Kramer leave the building."

"His whereabouts is a mystery, but not to worry. I found another way in. Did you notice the woman I entered the building with a few minutes ago?"

"Yeah. Who is she?"

"She's the wife of one of Jonathan's friends. Can you believe they also have an apartment in the Hudson?"

"It's your lucky day."

"Let's hope so." Siena glanced out the window. The drizzle had turned into a steady shower. "She invited me in for tea, so I'll be here for a while. Before I leave the building, I'll go up to Kramer's apartment. If he doesn't answer the door, I'll keep trying his phone."

"Do you think he's avoiding you?"

"I don't know why he would. Maybe he's just confused about what time we agreed to meet. Anyway, I've got things covered here. Go have a coffee and get out of the rain."

"That's precisely what I was thinking. Call me when you're free."

"Will do." Out of the corner of her eye, Siena spotted Joanie entering the room. "Okay, Jac," she said in her normal volume. "I'll catch up with you later. Bye." She ended the call and tossed the phone into her purse.

"Is your sister all right?" Joanie asked while setting a serving tray on the largest of the nesting tables positioned between the windows. She removed the two smaller nesting tables and set one beside each of their chairs.

"She's fine," Siena replied. "She's finalizing some wedding plans this morning. Then, this afternoon, we'll shop for shoes to wear with our gowns."

"Her wedding?" Joanie's eyes grew wide as she lifted the teapot and filled their cups. "How lovely! And right on the heels of your own. Your mother must be delighted. Tell me everything—When? Where? To whom? Oh, here, dear. Here's a plate. Help yourself to the scones. This bowl is strawberry jam; this one's clotted cream. Not knowing your preference, I also brought out butter. I know our waistlines are screaming at us to avoid all these empty calories, but what fun is life if you can't indulge on occasion? Now, unless I'm mistaken, Jonathan mentioned that you and your sister are identical twins. I must ask, how did your parents tell you apart when you were infants?"

Siena never imagined that one day she'd crave female companionship. Not that she'd ever had all that many girlfriends, but since leaving her life in Manhattan behind to be with Jonathan she'd been more isolated than ever before. Sure, she'd met people who were cordial to her, but none of her new acquaintances called with invitations to join them for lunch or drinks by the pool. The only dates on her social calendar were dinner engagements or fundraisers or commitments at the club that had been made by Jonathan. However, Siena had no one to blame for her loneliness but herself. For most of her adult life, she'd devoted her free time to running cons instead of nurturing friendships. Now that she'd gone legit, she was paying the price.

So when Joanie Osgood showed real interest in her, the flood gates opened. Siena spoke at length about her childhood, what it was like growing up with an identical twin, her family's apartment in Manhattan, her education, her job as an antiques expert at a world-renowned auction house, how she met Jonathan, and how they'd fallen in love over the phone, long before they met face-to-face. She even shared her most hurtful memory of the day her mother, a professional runway model, deserted their family to run off and marry another man in Los Angeles. Joanie was curious. Was Siena's mother still with her second husband, still in LA…still alive? Siena was sorry that she didn't have the answers. And even sorrier that she still cared.

In turn, Siena was enthralled by Joanie's stories, particularly those involving the antics of her three children, all close in age to Siena. Over the next hour, the two women became fast friends. In a way, Joanie was the compassionate mother figure Siena had been yearning for her entire life. While Siena would have loved to chat the entire day away, she needed to refocus her attention on Matthew Kramer.

Carrying the tray containing the empty teapot and cups and the plates spattered with pastry crumbs, Siena followed Joanie through the apartment. In the kitchen, they encountered a short, dark-haired woman who was busy dusting the items displayed on a built-in China cabinet.

"Just set the tray here on the island," Joanie told Siena. Speaking louder to be heard across the room, she said, "Imelda, can you clean the items on this tray before you leave?"

"*Sí, Señora* Osgood," the woman replied without interrupting her work.

"Oh, Imelda reminds me," Joanie said, turning to Siena, "are you aware that another of the fraternity brothers, Matthew Kramer, lives in the Hudson as well? Has Jonathan ever mentioned Matthew to you?"

"No," Siena said, injecting a note of bemusement into her response. "He hasn't."

"Well, I'm not surprised." Joanie lowered her voice. "Just between us girls, Matthew and Jonathan were never all that close. The way I see it, Matthew has been jealous of Jonathan from the day they met. Now, don't get me wrong. Matthew is quite good-looking and friendly enough, but he simply doesn't wear charming and debonair well. He tries to imitate Jonathan, but he'll never possessed Jonathan's…" She took in a deep breath as her eyes glazed over with an expression Siena could only describe as dreamy. Joanie hunched one shoulder, and said, "*Je ne sais quoi.* Do you know what I mean?"

Siena smiled. She understood Joanie perfectly. "So, you think Jonathan has a *special something?*"

Joanie's face flushed. She touched Siena's arm and giggled. "Oh, my dear, yes! Why, when we were at university, all the girls wanted to be with Jonathan Woodward—including me—and all the other frat boys knew it. To this day they call Jonathan the Golden Boy. Now, mind you, everything I've said is just between us girls. Don't you dare breathe a word of it to Gaylor." Joanie's eyes suddenly opened wide. "I've just had a thought. What are you doing this evening? Gaylor and I would love for you and your sister to dine with us. We'll invite Matthew. Hopefully, he's free. That way, we'll get to meet your twin, and you'll get to meet Matthew."

Siena wasn't altogether keen on the prospect of being in the same room with Matthew Kramer and Gaylor Osgood. She cringed at the notion of being trapped in a conversation about the strange videos Matthew had texted to his friends. Wouldn't Matthew relish the opportunity to taunt Siena with a few suggestive comments meant to arouse the Osgoods' suspicions.

While Joanie slid her cell phone from her jacket pocket, Siena attempted a polite decline. "I'm not sure, Joanie. I'll need to check with Jacqueline first. She had talked about getting us tickets for a show."

"Well, let me give Matthew a ring anyway. If dinner doesn't work for you, perhaps we can all meet for drinks before you two head off to the theatre." Joanie's call, like the many Siena had placed earlier that day, went unanswered. She left a voice mail message and disconnected the call. "Bollocks. He's not picking up. Perhaps he's with his mother and doesn't want their visit to be disturbed. Matthew recently moved his mum to an assisted living facility. Fortunately, the place is in Hempstead, just a few miles from the home she'd lived in for the past sixty years, so her friends and old neighbors often stop by to visit. Gaylor and I go to see her about once a month. She was such a dear to us all when we were in school, always sending peanut butter cookies or a cake back with Matthew when he'd been home for a weekend or on break. I hate to see her losing her faculties to dementia. Oh!—now here's another possibility—Matthew may be traveling." She swiveled around to speak to her housekeeper. "Imelda, do you still clean Mr. Kramer's apartment?"

"*Sí*," Imelda replied. "I clean for Mr. Kramer."

Siena stood up straighter. She hadn't thought her day could get any luckier, but…

"Are you cleaning his apartment today?" As an aside, Joanie said to Siena, "Matthew usually cancels when he's out of town. His philosophy is if no one's been there to dirty the place, why pay someone to clean it?"

Imelda stepped off her stool. "*Sí*, I clean for Mr. Kramer when I leave here." She carried the collapsed stool and cleaning supplies through a doorway and disappeared around the corner.

Joanie's cell phone rang. "Oh! Maybe this is

Matthew calling back." She glanced at the screen. "No, it's one of the women on my symphony committee. Will you excuse me for a moment, Siena? This is urgent and I need to refer to my notes which are in the office while I speak with her."

"Go right ahead" Siena replied, grateful for the distraction.

As Joanie exited one end of the kitchen, Imelda re-entered at the other end. "*Señora*," she said, smiling politely at Siena as she moved the tray of dirty cups and plates to the sink.

Siena rounded the corner of the island and approached her. "Imelda," she asked in whispered Spanish, "how would you like to make an easy five hundred dollars?"

Chapter 23

Siena
Spring 2017

The most difficult aspect of being a con artist wasn't maintaining a false identity, or earning the mark's trust, or diverting his attention long enough to pilfer the goods. Hell, Siena was experienced enough to pull off any of those feats blindfolded. But when circumstances required her to string the target along, when she needed to use her body as a last resort to get the job done—that was the part of the con Siena dreaded. With a little ingenuity she could most often manipulate the situation and avert this pitfall. Unfortunately, the scam she was pulling on Matthew Kramer wasn't shaping up to be one of the easy ones.

Siena didn't miss a beat of heavy breathing, even threw in an *Oh, yes!* for good measure, as she glanced sideways and checked the time on Matthew's bedside clock. The hour was getting late, and she wanted to get back to her apartment if for no other reason than to contact Gus. The entire day had passed without a word from him, and his silence gave Siena an ache in the pit of her stomach.

Last evening, tired and frustrated, she'd unleashed her temper on Gus. Why, she'd asked, was he taking so goddamned long to make the forgeries of the earrings she needed for the Matthew Kramer job? And if he fed her that lame excuse about how he'd caught a flu bug and couldn't get out of bed for three days one more time, she swore she would scream! Did Gus imagine that handling Kramer during those three extra days was an easy task? Did he understand what *she* was sacrificing? That she'd long ago run out of viable reasons to avoid falling into Kramer's bed? "I need this job to end," she'd growled through gritted teeth. "NOW!"

Matthew nuzzled his face into the crook of Siena's neck and released one last moan of pleasure. As his body relaxed, he kissed her shoulder and whispered into her ear, "*That* was spectacular."

"Mm," Siena responded, the purr being every bit as fake as her responses to his lovemaking over the last— she glanced again at the clock and rounded up—four minutes.

After what seemed like an eternity, Matthew rolled off her and onto his side. He slid one arm under his pillow and draped the other arm across Siena's waist as she tugged up the sheet from the foot of the bed. She stared at the ceiling and contemplated how soon was too soon to offer an excuse that would get her the hell out of his apartment. Tonight, she'd use the pretext of needing to tackle her growing mound of laundry. When Matthew shifted his legs and snuggled even closer, Siena assumed he was preparing to doze off. She gave him a sideways glance and, instead, found him gazing at her with love-struck eyes.

Slipping into her Ellen Randall role, Siena breathed a contented sigh. "What are you thinking?"

"I'm remembering the night we met at Kudos. What a lucky break it was that I caught you sizing me up from your seat at the bar. Otherwise, I would have gone home that night with what's-her-name, and we never would have met."

From what I observed, what's-her-name seemed more interested in slinking away than inviting you back to her place, but if you need to create that fantasy to inflate your ego…

"Well, if you hadn't sauntered over to me," Siena said with a coquettish grin, "I'd have invented some way for us to meet."

Matthew snickered. "And here I imagined you were giving me the brush-off when I took the empty seat next to you."

Siena traced her fingers down his arm. "Oh, Matty," she teased. "A well-bred Southern lady always plays hard-to-get. Don't you know that?"

"I do now." He placed his hand behind Siena's neck and drew her closer for a long kiss. Siena was about to disentangle her body from his and launch into her *I need to be getting home* speech before his body heat began to rise again when Matthew made a comment that Siena found impossible to ignore. Ending the kiss, he gazed at her with lustful eyes. "A year from now, maybe sooner, I'll be single again. Then this apartment will be all mine, and we can spend every night together just like this."

Siena clenched her jaw before it dropped open. How could a husband write off his ailing wife with such callous wishful thinking? She was itching to give Matthew a sample of her temper the same way she'd laid into Gus last night, but she dared not take the risk. Gus promised he'd have the forgeries completed within the next few days. The end was in sight and she had too much invested in this job to blow it now.

Instead, she masked her repulsion with a concerned frown. "Matty, you know I love this apartment, but I can't think about living here while your wife is suffering so."

Matthew smoothed his thumb over Siena's cheek. "Let's not ruin the mood by talking about Alva."

Siena shifted onto her side and faced Matthew. "I guess I just don't understand how you can put her out of your mind so easily. She's your wife and she's combatting a potentially terminal illness."

"Just because Alva's my wife doesn't mean I'm mourning the fact that we won't spend the rest of our lives together."

Just when I was convinced he couldn't get any more contemptible.

"But...don't you love her?"

"Nope. I mean, she's all right, but I can't say what I feel for her is love. That's not to say she doesn't believe that I'm devoted to her."

"What does that mean?"

"Oh, babe, I treat Alva like she's a queen. I do what she wants to do, and I go where she wants to go. I hang on her every word, and I attend to her every need. *And*," he cuddled closer, "I give her the best sex she's ever had in her life."

I sincerely doubt those words ever crossed Alva's lips, but if they did, she has my sympathy.

"If you've never loved her, why did you marry her?" Siena already knew the answer, but she wanted Matthew's admission in his own words.

"Why *wouldn't* I marry her?" Matthew raised himself up on one elbow and gazed down at Siena with incredulous eyes. "Do you know what Alva's personal

206

net worth is? She's one of the wealthiest women in the country." He swung his free arm through the air, encompassing the room. "Hell, this place alone is valued at twenty mill."

"So, what are you saying? You only married Alva for her money?"

"Damn right. When we met, she had just come out of a messy divorce, her daughter was off living with an Italian count in Switzerland, and sweet Alva was lonely and vulnerable. She was in her mid-fifties and simply looking for companionship, but she found out that I could be so much more. Basically, I had what she needed, and she had what I wanted."

Siena's left eyebrow shot up. *Well, Matthew Kramer, when it comes to using people, turns out you and I aren't so different after all.*

"Still…what if she finds out about us? All the plans you're making for our future will go up in smoke."

One side of his mouth curled upward. "Babe, I hate to break this to you, but you're not the first *other woman* I've been with since I married Alva, and I haven't been caught yet."

Siena's brow furrowed with feigned worry. "But still…"

Matthew placed his forefinger against Siena's lips and shushed her. "Don't worry about it. I've always been extremely careful with my liaisons. But, in the off-chance Alva does find out about us and files for divorce, I've got us covered."

Intriguing. "How so?"

"Babe,"—*God, how I hate being called babe!*— "don't forget, I'm a financial planner by profession, and I manage no one's finances better than my own. Plus, I have the best of both worlds: a lucrative income from my business *and* a generous monthly stipend from Alva that pays for all my personal expenses. Now, I'll let you in on a secret." He lowered his voice, as though worried there might be a hidden microphone recording their pillow talk. "I've been siphoning from my allowance from the get-go and Alva doesn't have a clue. Between that and the cash I can get for the pieces of her jewelry I've been helping myself to—a diamond bracelet here, a ruby broach there—I'll have enough money for us to live quite comfortably in Europe or on an island in the South Pacific, anywhere you want to go."

Siena's eyes filled with curiosity. "My goodness, Matty. How much money are we talking about?"

"At last count, it was well into the seven-figure range."

"At last *count*? Are you saying you have that much money in cash?"

Matthew snorted. "Babe, we couldn't make a quick escape if all my funds are tied up in investment accounts. As far as the jewelry is concerned, I figure I can hock each piece as needed."

Poor Matthew, ignorant to the fact that the woman he's confiding this information to is a skilled thief herself.

"Won't your wife notice some of her valuables are missing?"

"Nah," he said, scrunching his chin. "She has so much jewelry in that safe it's ridiculous, and I've been careful to pick pieces she never wears. Besides, dealing with this illness has her totally distracted. Bracelets and earrings are the furthest things from her mind."

"I can see the logic in your reasoning," she replied,

attempting to goad him into revealing the location of the hidey-hole where he stored his treasure, "but aren't you afraid she'll stumble across your stash?"

Matthew chuckled. "Not gonna happen. You see, it's all stored at my mother's house."

And there goes my dream of strolling out of here with my retirement fund in hand.

"Your mother's house? Matthew, if the wrong people know your mother has that much cash and expensive jewelry in her home—"

"Don't worry. Nobody knows it's there, my mother included." He lowered his eyes as if reluctant to continue. "I'll tell you a story from my childhood if you promise to keep it between us."

"My lips are sealed," Siena assured him, her memory primed to catalogue whatever useful tidbit he was about to let slip off his tongue.

"When I was a kid," he confided, "I had two habits that drove my mother batshit crazy. The first one: I used to leave my shoes wherever I felt like taking them off, and she was always tripping over them and screaming about how shoes belonged in the closet. The second one was, I collected rocks, all different kinds, and I would display them around my bedroom—on my bookcase, on my desk, on the dresser. Once a week, when Mom cleaned my room, she'd take them all and pitch them into the woods behind our house, but I'd just go find other rocks and start a new collection. So, my dad, wanting to please both me and my mother, built a shelving unit in my bedroom closet for me to store my shoes. Now, this unit appeared to be attached to the wall, but Dad installed a small latch in the floor. When I pulled up the latch, the unit swung out and there, set into the wall, Dad had built several rows of shelves where I could keep my rock collection. I can tell by the grin on your face that you know where this story is going. My rock collection is long gone, and that space is now filled with Alva's cash and jewelry."

"Does your mother know about this compartment?"

"Nope. Dad died years ago, but I doubt he ever told her and I sure as hell never did. That latch is so well-concealed, even the most expert thief wouldn't notice it."

"Matty, I'm so proud of the way you've planned out your future. You have every contingency covered. Well, all but one."

"What would that be?"

"Let's say Alva finds a treatment that halts the progression of her illness, and she lives for several more years. Would you stay married to her, or divorce her to be with me?"

An avaricious smirk appeared on Matthew's face. "Babe, we could still be together, but I'd have to stay married to Alva. Remember, I signed a pre-nup. Why would I intentionally ruin a perfect arrangement?"

No, I don't imagine you *would do anything to ruin your ideal set up. But I just might.*

Chapter 24

Siena
October 2023

Siena's jittery foot tapped against the worn tiled floor. She was too exposed. Anyone could stroll down the hall and find her lurking in the dimly lit alcove outside the service entrance to Matthew Kramer's apartment. Someone like Matthew himself.

Come on, Imelda. Don't disappoint me.

The elevator door opened at the far end of the hall, giving Siena a start. She folded her arms across her chest and withdrew deeper into the shadows. A bead of sweat trickled down her back. *Good Lord, why did I wear this heavy cape on such a muggy day?* She grabbed the wrap by its collar and yanked it off her shoulders.

At last, the deadbolt unlatched. As the service entrance door creaked open, Siena spotted Imelda's right eye peering at her through the narrow crack. "I'm still here, Imelda," Siena whispered in Spanish. "Is it safe for me to come inside?"

"Sí, señora." Imelda swung the door open wider, giving Siena room to enter. "Sorry to keep you waiting."

Siena closed the door behind her. "Don't worry about it," she said. They continued to speak in Spanish, their voices guarded. From her crossbody purse, Siena retrieved a wad of cash and pressed it into Imelda's hand.

"Here's the remainder of the five hundred dollars I promised you."

Siena hadn't explained why she needed access to Matthew's apartment, but then neither had Imelda asked. Imelda seemed to care only about snagging the easiest five hundred dollars she'd ever made. She lowered her fingers down the neckline of her shirt and stuffed the bills into her bra. "*Muchos gracias, señora.*"

"Thank *you*, Imelda. I can't tell you how much I appreciate your help." As she slung her cape over one of the coat hooks mounted on the wall beside her, Siena noticed the apprehension in Imelda's eyes and the deep furrow that suddenly appeared on her brow. She placed an empathetic hand on Imelda's arm. "Imelda, is something wrong?"

"Please do not tell anyone I did this," Imelda pleaded. "I would not let you into any of the other apartments I clean, but Mr. Kramer," she lowered her gaze, "he is not a good man." When she glanced up, her eyes were filled with concern. "You seem like a nice lady. If he did something to hurt you—"

"Oh, no," Siena interrupted. "He's done nothing harmful." *Yet.* "He has something that belongs to me, and I want it back, that's all." With her most reassuring smile, she whispered, "This will be our little secret. Okay?"

Imelda returned the smile. "Okay."

"Is Mr. Kramer in the apartment now?"

"No," Imelda replied. "His girlfriend let me in."

Siena raised an eyebrow, her curiosity piqued. "His girlfriend? Does she live here?"

Imelda shook her head. "I don't think so. She doesn't keep many clothes in the closet. I think she stays overnight sometimes, but not always."

"Where is she now?"

Imelda shrugged her shoulders. "In Mr. Kramer's bedroom, maybe? At least that's the room she went into after she let me in."

"Okay. Go about your work as you normally would, and I'll make sure to avoid bumping into Mr. Kramer's girlfriend."

Imelda nodded in agreement. She opened the door to a utility closet and removed a vacuum sweeper along with a plastic caddy equipped with cleaning supplies. At the same time, Siena retrieved a pair of thin cotton gloves from her purse. Siena followed Imelda into the kitchen where she remained while Imelda continued into the main hallway. As Imelda switched on the vacuum, Siena slipped on her gloves and got down to business.

Working as quietly as she could, Siena inspected each cupboard and rummaged through every drawer and cubbyhole in search of a hidden camera. She didn't imagine Matthew would carelessly toss an item he was using as blackmail into such an open and unsecured area, but if her years as a con artist had taught Siena anything, she'd learned that people are prone to doing strange things. Even she, in her heyday, had hidden valuable pieces she'd swindled from her targets in an empty oatmeal container until she had the opportunity to hand them off to Gus.

Siena was standing on a kitchen chair and dipping her fingers into a gravy boat when Imelda turned off the vacuum. Through the doorway, she heard Imelda say, "Sorry. I am in your way?"

"No," another woman, whom Siena assumed was Matthew's girlfriend, said with a curtness in her voice.

"You're fine. I just, like, need to get to the kitchen."

Thanks for the subtle forewarning, Imelda!

Siena flung the cupboard door shut, catching it at the last second for a soft close. She hastened to return the chair to its spot at the table, then ducked around the corner and pressed her back against the wall of the service entrance just as the girlfriend's heels clicked onto the kitchen's travertine tile floor.

"Yeah, so like, he's totally disappeared," the girlfriend said. Siena identified only one set of footsteps and assumed she was overhearing a phone conversation. The girlfriend sounded as though she was in her mid-20s, even younger than Siena had been when she tricked Matthew into falling in love with her. The reason Matthew was attracted to young women was obvious, but why was this twenty-something wasting her time on Matthew? Why wasn't she enjoying the company of younger men with whom she had more in common?

Well now, Siena, don't you have a lot of nerve being so judgmental when you yourself married a man nearly twice your age.

"Yeah, so like," Girlfriend said, "I haven't seen Matthew since like Monday night."

Relying solely on her sense of hearing, Siena angled her ear closer to the doorway and focused on the clatter of Girlfriend's heels against the tile floor to track her movements.

"Yeah, so like, we had dinner at Milo's—I know like *where else*?—and then we came back to his apartment."

Siena detected the sound of the refrigerator door opening and glass bottles clanging against each other.

"Beats me. He was like really edgy, you know. Like,

he just couldn't like relax."

As Girlfriend chattered away, Siena detected the refrigerator door closing and the *pshh* sound of a carbonated beverage being opened.

"Yeah, so like, he didn't even want to have sex, so *you know* something was like *really* bothering him."

Siena began keeping tally of how many times the girl interjected *like* into her sentences.

"Yeah, so like, we had a big fight, and I got like pissed off and took a taxi back to my place."

The beverage bottle landed with a resounding thud on the countertop.

"Oh, like, come on! You and I both know he's like still seeing that low-life bitch." Whatever her friend had said caused Girlfriend's blood pressure to skyrocket. "No, like the one from that poker room he always goes to!"

Siena's eyebrows shot up. If she needed to explain to her friend which "bitch" she was referring to, just how many women did Girlfriend suspect Matthew was currently bedding?

"Yeah, so like, I think he wants us both. I flat out asked him if she's like that much better than me in bed."

Siena rolled her eyes. *Jesus.*

"Well, like, *of course* he said no, but like if he doesn't just want her for her body, then like why does he keep seeing her?"

If she could ignore the whining, Siena was tempted to place a sympathetic arm around the girl's shoulders and lend her a word of advice: *Honey, Matthew Kramer is not worth this much angst.*

"So, like, are you like kidding me, Josie? I've like told you about the crazy good sex we have. There's like no way she's better than me!…I know, right? Plus, she's like so old."

Chair legs scraped against the floor. Siena envisioned Girlfriend taking a seat in one of the high-backed bar chairs placed around the island.

"So, like, I don't know why Matthew can't keep his pants on when he's like around her… He like makes me all these promises about how he like loves me and wants me to disappear with him to, I don't know, like Fiji I think he said?…Shit. Beats me. Somewhere over by like Hawaii, maybe?"

Jesus, did neither of them even graduate high school?

"Yeah, so like, he said he's going to have all this money, like millions he told me, by like the end of the month."

Siena's back stiffened.

"So, like, I don't know! Somebody owes him like this huge payoff or something. You know how that kind of stuff bores me, so I was only like half listening…Yeah, so like, I think he's also got some expensive, I don't know, like jewelry and shit he wants to like sell. Plus, so like get this, he said he's like going to sell his business and everything he owns so we can like afford to live in this Fiji place and he won't need to like work…Yeah, so like, I don't know. I thought it might be fun for like a year, but now that he's like ghosting me…Yeah, so like, for all I know he like ran off to Fiji with Miss Bitch from the Poker Room instead. Well, like guess what?…I've decided that if he doesn't have the guts to be honest and just like break up with me, then he can like go screw himself. So, like, my brother says Matthew just wants me for like my money anyway."

Well, now, that's an interesting bit of information. Am I not the only person Matthew is swindling?

"Yeah, so like, I made the mistake of venting to my brother, and you know he probably told Daddy…No shit. You know Sal's like nothing but an overaged daddy's boy suck-up. I just hope he doesn't like spill his guts about the fifty thousand I borrowed from my trust fund and just like handed over to Matthew."

Siena lips formed a silent *Wow!* The list of people Matthew owed serious money to was growing by the day.

"So, like, *I know*, Josie. He promised he'd repay me when he like gets this payoff at the end of the month…So, like, do you think it's like my fault that he keeps coming up with excuses for why he like needs more time…So, like, listen to this, Miss *'I Told You So.'* Matthew like asked me the other day for like another fifty thousand and I refused to give him even one more dollar of my money. So there! So, like, don't you dare call me an idiot!"

A thud. Siena pictured Girlfriend slapping her hand against the marble countertop.

"Oh, God! Like, you don't really think Daddy would like do that, do you? Shit!" Her attitude suddenly shifted from fretful girlfriend to scorned lover. "Well, like, you know what? Since I've like called Matthew like a million times in the past like two days and he just keeps like ignoring me, I don't care if Daddy did have Matthew like beaten up and his guys left him in some ditch to like die."

The *likes* were all over the place now. Girlfriend was unraveling.

"No, I like really don't care what happens to him. Matthew and I are like through…No, I like really mean it this time. Like, I've already packed up all the stuff I have in his apartment and I'm like leaving. For good. Oh, shit! Look at the time!"

The chair legs again scraped against the tile after which Girlfriend's heels clattered across the floor.

"So, I'm like late for my meeting with that start-up cosmetic company I told you about. Yeah, so like, they're paying me big time to promote them on my platforms, so I can't be totally rude and just like blow them off."

With Girlfriend's voice fading as she stepped farther across the kitchen, Siena inched closer to the doorway to more clearly detect what she was saying.

"Oh! So, like, I forgot to tell you. I reached like twelve million followers this morning… Yeah, thanks! So, like, let's get together at Club Vinnie tonight and celebrate…Yeah, like for sure! Invite whoever you want."

Girlfriend's voice trailed off as she rushed to the opposite end of the apartment. Since gathering information about her life as an influencer was irrelevant to Siena's mission, she didn't worry about keeping within earshot. She stayed put for a few minutes, long enough to give Girlfriend time to exit the apartment for—if she held true to her promise—*like good.* Expecting the coast to be clear, she stepped gingerly into the kitchen at the same time Imelda entered from the opposite end of the room.

"Mr. Kramer's girlfriend is gone," Imelda informed Siena.

"Thanks, Imelda. I'll look around a while longer and then I'll be leaving, too."

Siena completed her inspection of the kitchen before

moving on to the dining room. So far, her hunt was proving to be a useless endeavor but she refused to give up hope. However, with the likelihood of Matthew walking in on her increasing by the second, she needed to *like* speed up the process.

Chapter 25

Siena

Stepping into Matthew's living room was akin to time traveling into the past. Visions of the con she'd played on him surrounded Siena in a kaleidoscope of alternating scenes. Matthew leering at her as they sat beside each other on the sofa. Matthew refilling her drink at the bar. Matthew running his grubby hands over her body as they embraced near the fireplace. Siena blinked away the images. Her dark memories didn't belong in such a pleasant space.

She was drawn to the built-in bookshelves on either side of the fireplace. The shelves on which Alva Kramer's priceless treasures had once been displayed now held nothing but a collection of dust. When she abandoned the apartment, Alva must have taken her artwork, her fine antiques, her first edition books and one-of-a-kind artisan figurines with her. Siena's eyes narrowed. In her haste to leave, had Alva noticed that a few of her pieces were missing?

Siena removed her cell phone from her crossbody purse and called Lou Biondi.

"Lou, how long would it take you to compile a list of all businesses in which Matthew Kramer has ownership, then a list of all properties owned by those businesses or by Kramer personally?"

"Geez, I don't know," Lou said. "A couple of hours, three at the most. Why?"

"Just do the research and meet me at four o'clock at Max's Deli on West 50th between 7th Avenue and Broadway. I'll explain then."

"Okay, boss," Lou chuckled. "See you at four."

Disconnecting the call, Siena dropped the phone back into her purse. She was done searching through drawers and peering into gravy boats. If the camera were anywhere in this apartment, she assumed Matthew had been wise enough to store it in a locked safe. The apartment, Siena recalled, had two safes—one in the main bedroom's dressing area where Alva had kept her most valuable jewelry and another in the home office which was the first room to the right of the foyer.

Unfortunately, Siena could not list safe-cracking as one of her many talents. For that, she needed Gus's expertise. Which he without a doubt would be willing to lend *if* she had a way to get inside the apartment a second time. And she would only re-enter this apartment *if* she were certain Matthew would be away from home for an extended period.

So, breaking into the safes was a great idea were it not for all those what-ifs.

Unless...

Siena speculated that Imelda would be interested in earning even more easy cash. Perhaps she'd prefer to take the rest of the afternoon off and return tomorrow to finish her chores. Then, while Siena invented a reason to lure Matthew away from the apartment, Imelda could admit Gus inside to work his magic.

Rushing from the living room, Siena detected a faint contralto voice coming from one of the bedrooms at the far end of the apartment. Imelda was singing along to a Latin bachata. Hit with a sudden wave of homesickness, Siena stopped short. The music flooded her with visions of Javier working in the garden or painting the wooden fence or making minor repairs around the house while being entertained by the melodies blasting from his earbuds. *Just a few more days, Siena. Then you'll be back home, and this awful craziness will be behind you.*

A ring of keys was sitting in a glass dish on a table in the foyer. At first, Siena assumed they were a spare set Matthew's girlfriend had dropped in the dish on her way out. She had, after all, vowed never to return. But the front door had only two locks and there were several keys strung on the ring. Keys that could not only open the locks to a man's apartment, but also doors to his business office...and possibly to his mother's house on Long Island.

A ring of keys.

Just sitting there.

Begging to be taken.

Or were they a warning that something was amiss? Although she hated to admit it, Siena was becoming concerned about Matthew's whereabouts. Why wasn't he answering his phone calls? Why hadn't he responded to the voicemails she'd left him? Why did he seem to be evading everyone, even his influencer girlfriend? If he'd gone somewhere, perhaps skipped town to ditch those to whom he owed money, why hadn't he taken his keys? And the biggest question of them all—Wherever Matthew was, had he taken the camera containing the incriminating video of Siena with him?

Siena snatched the key ring from the dish and dropped it into her purse. Finders, keepers—right?

She was wasting time. Before Matthew came strolling through the front door, she needed to speak to Imelda and be on her way. As she rounded the corner and entered the hallway, the house phone in Matthew's office began to ring. Siena grinned as she recalled Matthew saying he kept a landline for his mother's sake. She had to give him credit. He'd been a lousy boyfriend, husband, and all around horrible human being, but he was an exemplary son. By the time she reached the door to the office, the answering machine had clicked on. Siena overheard Matthew's recorded voice say, *"I can't take your call right now. Please leave a message."*

"Matthew," the woman's voice on the other end of the line said, "this is Shonda, the nurse at Elmwood. I'm calling about your mother."

Matthew's mother? Concerned that a serious situation had occurred at a time when no one could locate Matthew, Siena stood outside the doorway and listened to the entire message.

"It's nothing to be worried about," the nurse continued to explain, "but I wanted to let you know that Irene has been terribly agitated this morning. We've gotten her calmed down, but she's been searching all over her apartment for something she said you gave her the other day and now she can't find it. You know, with her dementia, we're not sure whether to take her seriously or if this might be an incident she's recalling from her past. But if there's truly something important that she needs to find, we'll keep searching for it. Anyway, could you call me back, so we know how to proceed? Thanks, Matthew. Oh, sorry, not sure if I already mentioned this but the item your mother said went missing is a camera."

Siena whipped around on her heels so fast, she nearly lost her balance. She rushed down the hall, skidded through the foyer, and bolted out the front door. While riding the elevator to the lobby, she yanked her cell phone from her purse and looked up the address and phone number for Elmwood Assisted Living Center in Hempstead, Long Island.

Chapter 26

Siena

At the whoosh of the double glass doors opening and closing, the woman behind the reception desk glanced up from her computer screen. "Hi, there. May I help you?"

"Good afternoon," Siena did a quick read of the woman's name tag, "Sheila. I'm Deborah Simmons. I called about an hour ago and said I would be stopping in to visit Irene Kramer. Was it you I spoke with?"

"Yes, I believe so. You said you were a friend of Irene's?"

Siena wrinkled her nose. "Well, in a roundabout way." She rested her elbows on the desk's high countertop along with a box of candy she'd purchased at Grand Central Station. "What I mean is, I've been friends with Matthew since middle school. I spent so much time at Matt's house when we were kids, I used to call Irene *Mom*. I haven't been to visit her since she moved here because my husband and I have been living abroad. We just last week returned to the States, and I told Don—that's my husband—that one of the first things I needed to do, now that we're back, is to visit Irene Kramer."

"And here you are!"

Siena raised her forearms and performed a mini version of jazz hands. "And here I am. I hope this is a good time."

"As a matter of fact, it is. The residents just finished lunch, so you'll find Irene either in her apartment or in the common area. Just sign our guest book, and you can go on through." Sheila slid the book across the counter and handed a pen to Siena. "Irene is in Apartment 112, down the hall and to your right."

"Got it." Siena checked the wall clock and recorded the time of her arrival, then completed the remainder of the requested information—Deborah Simmons as the name of the visitor and Irene Kramer's as the facility's resident.

"Here's a visitor sticker for you to wear while you're here, and please don't forget to sign out when you're ready to leave."

"Will do." Siena peeled off the backing and attached the sticker to her sweater. "Thanks, Sheila. It was good to meet you."

"You, too. Have a nice visit."

Playing the part of a 60-ish contemporary of Matthew Kramer, Siena strolled down the first-floor hallway in her sensible, low-heeled shoes. The disguise had been simple enough to piece together during a brief stop at her Manhattan apartment which was conveniently located between Matthew's co-op and Grand Central Station. She'd replaced the high-heeled boots that complemented her outfit with more age-appropriate flats. Next, she pinned up her hair and tugged on a dark brown wig styled in a short bob. In her makeup drawer, she'd found a darker shade of foundation which, when applied to the angles of her face, aged her appearance. A swipe of creamy mauve lipstick added the final touch. Within the hour, she was hailing a taxi to Grand Central and boarding the train to Long Island.

Siena rapped her knuckles on the door of Apartment 112. After a few seconds, she cocked her ear to the door. Had Irene invited her to enter? Unsure, she knocked a second time and listened more intently. Still, no voice called out in welcome. Perhaps, as Sheila had mentioned, Irene was with her friends in the common area—wherever that was. Siena decided to check inside the apartment before she went hunting.

With a twist of the knob, she cracked the door open a few inches. Poking her head into the apartment, she eyed a living room overcrowded with furniture and knickknacks. Slouched into the corner of a full-sized sofa was a diminutive gray-haired woman whose face was wrinkled with age. Although the temperature in the room bordered on tropical, she wore a heavy cardigan over her turtleneck sweater and her legs were kept toasty underneath a crocheted blanket. Her eyes were fixed on the television, but the TV screen was dark. The woman's mind appeared to be lost in another world.

Siena spoke gently, so as not to startle her. "Irene?" No reaction. "Irene," Siena said more forcefully.

"Oh, honey, you're gonna have to speak up louder than that for Miss Irene to hear you," the nurse's aide passing down the hall told Siena. "Here, let me help you." Siena stepped back and allowed the aide to open the door all the way. "Miss Irene," the aide nearly shouted as she burst into the apartment. "This nice lady has come to visit you."

Irene, her attention at last garnered, frowned as she gazed up at the aide. "What?"

"Miss Irene, did you remove your hearing aids again?" The aide picked up two devices from the table beside the sofa. "Here, let me put these in for you." As the aide inserted the devices into Irene's ears, she explained to Siena, "We go through this every afternoon. For some reason only she knows, Miss Irene takes these dang things out of her ears every day when she comes back to her apartment after lunch. I can't tell you how many times we've had to hunt for them because she can't remember where she set them down. And we really need to keep our eyes on her during our weekly lunch-and-shop outings, which reminds me is coming around again tomorrow afternoon. Tomorrow's Thursday already, isn't it? Dang, these weeks go by fast." She stood upright and placed her fists on her hips. "There now. All set. Isn't that better?"

"Oh, yes, yes," Irene said. "Thank you, dear."

"You're welcome, sweetie. Now, look here," the aide said, holding her arm out in Siena's direction. "You have a visitor."

"I do?" Irene swiveled her head and gazed at Siena. "Oh! Hello."

"Hi, Irene," Siena said, her smile bright as she stepped closer. "How are you?" She placed the box of candy on the table in front of the sofa. "I brought you a box of chocolate covered caramels, your favorites."

"Mm, mm," the aide said. "You make sure to save one of those for me, Miss Irene." She patted Siena's arm. "I'll check with you in a bit, see if you need any help." With that, she exited the room, closing the door behind her.

Irene stared at Siena with furrowed brows. "Do I know you?"

"No, Irene, you don't." Siena smiled as she slid into the chair adjacent to the sofa. "My name is Deborah and

I'm a friend of your son Matthew's." She tugged at the neckline of her sweater hoping to let in some cool air. *God, it's hot in this apartment.*

Irene nodded her head. "Is that so?" Without warning, her face pinched like a child's when told they can't go outside to play. "I'm mad at Matthew," she blurted out. "He hasn't come to see me in months, and he never calls. I'm his mother. A son should call his mother every day."

In Lou's surveillance report, he stated that he had followed Matthew to this assisted living facility every other day and that Matthew stayed each time for at least one hour. The truth was, Matthew visited his mother several times a week, but Irene had lost her concept of time. Siena's heart ached for her.

"That's so inconsiderate of Matthew. Would you like me to have a talk with him? Remind him to call you every day and to visit you more often?"

Irene's scowl disappeared as though Siena's offer to intervene had lifted a great weight off her shoulders. "Would you, please? Maybe he'll listen to you."

"I'd be happy to. As a matter of fact, I'll call this evening and remind him." Siena removed the clear wrapping from the candy box and opened the lid. "Now, how about we sample these caramels?" She held out the box and Irene helped herself to a piece. Siena's tense shoulders relaxed when Irene bit into the chocolate covered caramel and, mumbling a yummy sound, gave Siena a smile and a nod of approval. Siena had made a new friend.

"Speaking of Matthew," Siena said, taking advantage of a comment Joanie Osgood had made that morning, "he was telling me the other day about the delicious peanut butter cookies you used to bake."

"Oh, those were always Matthew's favorite." The smile on Irene's face stretched from ear to ear. "As soon as I took the cookie tray out of the oven, he'd grab a couple right away without waiting for them to cool off. I'd tell him, 'Matthew, you're going to burn your mouth', but he didn't care." She giggled. "If he ever did burn his mouth, he never let on."

Siena chuckled as though amused by the reminiscence. "That's why his friends nicknamed him *Mr. Impatient*," she said while dabbing the sleeve of her sweater against the moisture beading up on her forehead. Jesus. Had Matthew moved his mother into an apartment or a high-priced sauna?

She glanced at Irene and noticed her eyes had glazed over and she was staring into space. Attempting to keep her engaged, Siena vocalized the next thought that came to mind. "Matthew said you also made the most delicious fudge."

"Did I make fudge? I don't think so. But I did bake a lot of cakes. Matthew loved my mayonnaise cake."

"Well, you know what? I remember him raving about that as well." *I don't know what the hell a mayonnaise cake is, but it sounds awful.*

"I can give you the recipe, if you'd like." As Irene made this offer, a bewildered expression glazed over her face. She glanced around the room, as though she would like to locate her recipe for the mayonnaise cake if only she could remember where it might be. Siena guided the conversation to the blanket covering Irene's legs and asked if she'd crocheted it herself.

For the next fifteen minutes, Siena kept Irene conversing about her more youthful days, neighborhood block parties, and the time Matthew played an angel in his elementary school Christmas pageant. Most of the stories were repeated once, sometimes twice, but Siena reacted with renewed interest each time as if Irene were sharing a brand-new memory. She commented on the framed photos sitting on the side table next to the sofa and asked Irene to identify the people in the pictures and explain how she was related to each of them. If Irene's memory hit a snag, Siena was quick to move on to another topic of conversation.

Occasionally, Irene would stop and gaze at Siena as though trying to recall who she was, but her pride was strong. She never once admitted her confusion. Siena too often lowered her head, her eyes stinging with tears not only for the deterioration of this gentle woman's mind but also out of self-loathing. Instead of spending the afternoon with Irene out of kindness, Siena was there with a specific agenda in mind—an agenda which needed to be addressed sooner rather than later.

"Irene, I wanted to tell you that I'm planning a surprise party for Matthew's birthday."

Irene became agitated. "Oh, my goodness. Is it Matthew's birthday?" Her eyes grew wide as they darted back and forth. "Did I forget to buy him a gift?" With a sudden mood swing, her anger rose. "I hate this place," she snarled. "They took my car away from me, so now I can't go to the store whenever I need to."

Dammit, Siena. You should have anticipated her reaction and guided the conversation in a different direction.

Siena placed a calming hand on Irene's knee. "Irene, dear, don't fret. I'd be happy to take you shopping for a birthday gift." She made the offer assuming Irene would forget all about the promise of a shopping trip in a matter of minutes. "Would you like that?"

The scorn left Irene's face and hope appeared in her eyes. "Yes, but not today. Can we go tomorrow morning instead?"

"We can go whenever you'd like," Siena assured her. "Anyway, I wanted to get some photos of Matthew as a young boy to display at the party. I was hoping you might have some picture albums I could borrow."

"Oh, my. Photo albums?"

"Yes. Do you have any here in your apartment?"

Again, confusion descended on Irene. "Well, I don't know. I'd have to look." With considerable effort, she attempted to rise from her seat and got tangled in her blanket.

Siena jumped up to stop Irene before she fell. "Tell you what. You stay where you are and, if you don't mind, I'll have a look around and see if I can find the photo albums myself. Is that okay with you?"

Irene glared at her with suspicious eyes. "No! I don't know who you are, and I don't want you to go through my things. Oh, dear. Now I need to go to the bathroom. Bring my walker over here."

Worried that Irene wouldn't make it to the bathroom in time, Siena hurried to retrieve the walker from its place near the end of the sofa and positioned it in front of her. As Irene struggled to get to her feet, Siena offered her assistance. "Let me help you, Irene," she said, removing Irene's blanket from her lap and holding the frail woman's arms to support her as she stood. "Can you make it to the bathroom on your own?"

"Yes," Irene barked. "Just get out of my way." She glared at Siena. "I don't like you and I want you to leave."

Siena stepped aside as Irene, supported by her walker, squeezed between the coffee table and the chairs surrounding it, then down the short hallway to her bedroom and the attached bath. As soon as the bathroom door clicked in place, Siena began hunting through drawers and cupboards in search of the hidden camera. She lifted the furniture cushions and peaked underneath and behind the sofa and chairs.

With time running out, Siena conducted the same search in Irene's bedroom. The toilet flushed. Taking the huge risk of being caught, she opened Irene's closet and checked the pockets of her clothes. The kitchenette was her last hope, but even an inspection of the mini-refrigerator was a bust.

As the bathroom door swung open, Siena dashed through the living area. She opened the door to the hall just wide enough to slink out of the apartment undetected. Irene, she assumed, would return to the same warm spot in the corner of her sofa, help herself to another chocolate-covered caramel, and return to staring mindlessly at her TV screen without any memory of the stranger who'd stopped by that afternoon for a visit.

Chapter 27

Siena

"One pastrami on rye and one chicken noodle," the server at Max's Deli called out.

"That's mine!" Gus skirted around another customer and approached the pick-up counter. "I also had a soda and a coffee with skim milk."

The server checked the receipt. "Yep, got 'em right here." He snapped lids onto the to-go cups and added them to the tray of food. "Here you go, man. Have a good one."

"Thanks. You, too." After securing a drink straw and a handful of napkins from the service counter, Gus strolled to the last booth along the wall in the back section of the deli. He transferred the food and drinks onto the table and tossed the empty tray into the designated slot over the trash bin. "Any word from Lou?" he asked as he slid across the booth's red vinyl bench.

Siena dropped her phone into her purse. "I just got a text from him." She pried the lid off the coffee cup and relished the enticing aroma before downing a swallow. "He got somewhat lost, but he should be here in a few minutes." Touching a spoonful of the soup against her lips, she judged it hot but not too hot for consumption. The scone she'd eaten that morning had long since been digested and her stomach was grumbling. During the brief stop she'd made at her apartment to discard her wig and wash the heavy makeup from her face, she'd scoured through her old kitchen for something to eat, even a stale packet of crackers would do, but the cupboards were empty. No surprise there. In her haste to rush off to Europe with Jonathan five months ago, she couldn't have cared less about leaving her furniture and clothing behind. She had, however, taken the time to toss out the food. "Why isn't Marielle with you? Of all your favorite New York haunts, I imagined you wouldn't want her to miss out on Max's Deli."

Across the table, Gus was scarfing down what he'd been proclaiming was the most delicious sandwich ever invented for as far back as Siena could remember. "I asked her to join us," he said, shrugging his shoulders, "but Jacqueline is feeling under the weather and Marielle didn't want to leave her alone." His curious eyes gazed at Siena as he crunched into his dill pickle. "Tell me the truth, Sissy. Is Jacqueline pregnant?"

Siena continued to spoon soup into her mouth as though Gus had asked nothing more personal than if she thought they might expect more rain later that afternoon. She'd promised to keep the confidence—a promise she'd already broken by sharing the news with Jonathan—and was not about to let Gus worm a confession out of her.

"That's an odd question. Why do you ask?"

"Several things." Gus took a bite of his sandwich, gave it a couple of chews, then gulped it down. In an hour he'd be complaining of indigestion. Siena had learned to always carry a bottle of antacid tablets with her. "She's always tired, she looks green around the gills most of the day, and I've noticed how often she rushes to the bathroom."

Siena gave him a wary glance. "What does a confirmed bachelor like yourself know about a pregnant woman's symptoms? Maybe Jac is simply exhausted from traveling. Maybe she's stressed out over planning a wedding in record-breaking time."

"Yeah, maybe." Gus narrowed his eyes as he sipped his soda through the straw. "What the hell. You wouldn't tell me anyway, especially if Jacqueline asked you not to. You two always had that secretive twin thing going on."

Siena focused on eating her soup. Having never been comfortable lying to Gus, she avoided eye contact. "Well, if Jac is pregnant—"

"Aha! I knew it!"

"*If* she's pregnant," Siena continued, "and I'm not saying that she is, I would never take the pleasure of making that announcement away from her. Anyway, for whatever reason she's not feeling well, I'm glad Marielle chose to stay with her."

Gus grunted in agreement as he took another bite of his sandwich.

"I like Marielle a lot, Gus. I hope she's not going to be another of your love 'em and leave 'em girlfriends."

Gus gave Siena a sheepish grin. "No. I think Marielle and I are going to be together for a while."

Siena was about to ask Gus if his version of "a while" was measured in months, years, or decades when Lou set a pastry wrapper containing an oversized, fresh-out-of-the-oven chocolate chip cookie, a cup of coffee, and a stack of napkins onto the table. "Sorry I'm late," he said as he plopped down in the booth beside Siena. "This place is hard to find."

Siena scooted sideways, giving Lou more room. "Is that your lunch?" The delectable aromas of sugar, vanilla, and chocolate tempted her taste buds. Normally she stayed away from sweets, but a nibble of comfort food might be the remedy she needed to brighten up the horrendous day she was having.

"Nah," Lou replied. "I had lunch earlier. Some old-timer told me while I was waiting for my coffee that this deli makes the best chocolate chip cookies in Manhattan, so I had to try one." Popping a chunk of cookie into his mouth, he nodded and raised his eyebrows. "Mm...pretty damn good." He offered the cookie to Siena. "Want a taste? It's still warm."

Siena thought he'd never ask. "Thanks." She broke off a small piece, just enough to satisfy her craving. God, it was good! Maybe she'd buy a dozen on her way out...to share with everyone back at the hotel, of course.

"Gus?" Lou asked, extending his offer across the table. His cheeks bulging with pastrami and rye bread, Gus shook his head. "No?" Lou broke off another chunk and shoved it into his mouth. He licked his fingers—a gesture that made Siena cringe—before wiping them on a napkin. "Maybe later then." He chuckled, his lips smacking as he ate and spoke at the same time. "If there's any left, that is."

"Do you have anything to report?" Siena asked.

Lou washed down another bite of cookie with a gulp of coffee. "Yeah, so, I did some digging into Matthew Kramer like you asked, and I came up with this." Dipping one hand into his breast pocket, Lou retrieved a note pad which he opened and held out as far as his arm could stretch. "I think I need to get some readers," he muttered. Frowning and squinting his eyes, he flipped through the pages until he came to the one on which he'd scribbled down the information he wanted to share. "Ah, here it is. I found out our boy is the sole owner of Kramer Investments, LLC. Now, that's his legit business, but he also has a company called L.I. Enterprises Ltd. registered under his name which, if you ask me, is totally bogus."

Siena tilted the soup bowl and scooped up the last remaining spoonful of broth. "Why do you say that?"

"Because the articles of incorporation say the business purpose is to conduct property transfers, you know, like it's a real estate agency or something, but the only activity I could find was the transfer of the deed for a house out on Long Island. I think Kramer set this business up as a shell company for the sole purpose of hiding the fact that he owns that property."

Siena leaned her head forward and attempted to read Lou's scribbling. "Is that the address?"

"Yeah." Lou squinted and stretched again. "It's, uh…"

"Christ, Lou," Gus said. "Your arms aren't long enough. Give me the damned notebook. I'll read it for you."

"No, I got it. The house is in Malverne, 6211 Sussex Drive."

Siena's brow knitted with confusion. "What about his co-op on Central Park West? Kramer gave me the impression his ex-wife granted him the apartment as part of their pre-nup."

"Well, she may have agreed to let him continue living there, but she didn't transfer the ownership to him. I checked his current address and found out that property is deeded to…" Lou flipped to the next page of his note pad, "The Paulson Trust with the trustee being Olivia

Eden-Timms. With a name like that, I'm guessing this Olivia chick is English."

And I'm guessing Olivia is Alva's daughter and only child.

Siena bit her lip and stared at Lou, expecting more. Instead, Lou closed the notepad and slid it back into his breast pocket. "Is that all you found?" she asked.

"Yep. Two businesses, one property. No criminal record, no unpaid traffic tickets."

"Thanks, Lou," Siena said. "You may not have uncovered much, but you got what I need."

Gus crumpled up his empty paper sandwich wrapper. "Now the question is, what are you going to do with this information?"

"Yeah," Lou chimed in. "That's what I'm wondering."

Siena placed her forearms on the table and leaned in. "Kramer may not remember this," she said in a guarded voice, "but six years ago when I had him convinced that he and I were in a serious relationship, he shared a few secrets that are about to come back to haunt him. Lou, is your car parked nearby?"

"Yeah. It's in a garage ten blocks from here. Why?"

"In about an hour, when it starts to get dark, I need you to drive Gus and me to that address on Long Island."

"Why?" Lou asked. "Who lives there?"

"No one—*now*," Siena explained. "But I'm ninety-nine percent sure the house was Kramer's childhood home. Not long ago, he moved his mother to an assisted living facility and the house is currently vacant. At least that's my assumption."

"So, what's the big attraction?" Lou asked. "Why do you need me to drive you out to Long Island to visit an empty house?"

"Because there's something inside that house that I need to get my hands on." Siena leaned her back against the booth. "And that's as much as you need to know."

Siena was reluctant to disclose too much information. Lou had proved himself reliable since she'd enlisted his help, but she couldn't shake the memory of her brush with his seedy side. The one he'd been so eager to display during his attempt to enlist Siena's help in stealing the Duncan Cordray painting from Patrick Woodward's home two summers ago. If the cash and the jewelry Matthew had hidden inside the cubby hole in his childhood bedroom closet were still there, she didn't trust that Lou wouldn't knock her unconscious and disappear with the entire stash. For this reason, Siena wanted Gus there to act as a bodyguard of sorts.

"This sounds like a one-person job," Gus said. "I don't understand why you'd need me to tag along."

Siena hedged the truth. "I'm not sure what I'll find when we get into the house. I might need your safe-cracking skills, Gus. Just in case."

Gus nodded as if agreeable to offering his assistance. His eyes, however, held a look of what Siena interpreted as disapproval. Uncomfortable under his scrutiny, her eyes darted across the deli and focused on the server slicing thin slabs of lunchmeat behind the counter. She hated the fact that her behavior sometimes disappointed Gus.

Lou tossed the last piece of chocolate chip cookie into his mouth. "Okay, so I can either go get my car and drive back here to pick you guys up, or we can all walk over to the garage together. Whatever you want."

"We'll walk over with you," Gus replied. He

glanced at Siena. "Unless you object."

"No, I think that's actually the better plan."

Lou drained the rest of his coffee from the disposable cup. "Well, I for one need to hit the head before we start out on this excursion." He scooted across the seat and slid out of the booth. "Be back in a few." Tossing his empty cup and cookie wrapper in a nearby trash bin, he strolled into the shadows at the back of the deli.

"Now that we're alone," Gus said, "you and I need to have a serious discussion."

Siena shifted in her seat and sat up straighter. Something about the tone of Gus's voice made her uncomfortable. "What about?" she asked.

"Sissy, you're carrying this game of yours too far. I didn't mind going to see Ed Davis and doing some background research for you on this Kramer guy. I didn't even mind dragging Marielle into the ruse with me. But now you're talking about breaking into a home that, unless I'm mistaken, you're not even sure is Kramer's mother's house. This on top of you bribing his cleaning lady into letting you enter Kramer's apartment without his knowledge. I think you're blind as to how dangerous this plan of yours has become."

Siena shook her head. "You're wrong, Gus. I know the risk I'm taking, but I don't have any other choice."

"Yes, you do." Gus's troubled eyes bore into hers. "Come clean with Jonathan and all your problems will be solved."

Siena's heart sank as it did every time those lude images from Matthew's video flashed into her mind. "No," she snapped. "I can't."

Gus leaned forward and placed his hand over

Siena's. "Listen to me. During your visit to Santa Martina last week, I spent enough time with Jonathan to peg him as a man who's shrewd, protective, and picky about who he chooses to let into his world, but he's also compassionate and understanding and generously forgiving, especially where you're concerned. Whatever you think is so horrible about that video, I'd bet my life that Jonathan would be willing to overlook it. Please, trust me on this. Go home, have a heart-to-heart talk with your husband, and forget about this guy who's blackmailing you."

Siena gazed into Gus's eyes, the person who had been her rock for most of her adult life. Gus was the person whose shoulder she'd cried on when severe gunshot wounds had nearly ended her father's life. Gus was the glue who'd held the family together during that critical time and decided on their next best course of action. When Siena was considering getting into the business as a source of extra income to pay for her father's medical expenses, she'd sought Gus's counsel. He'd been her mentor and her partner in crime for over a decade, and he'd never steered her wrong. In normal circumstances she would have heeded his advice, but not this time.

He believes I've allowed my emotions to take control. I need to make him understand that I'm not overreacting, that I am making logical and reasonable decisions. "Gus," she said, sucking in a deep breath, "let me explain why—"

"There you two are!" a familiar voice called out from behind her. "Jacqueline told me I'd find you here."

At first, Siena assumed her ears were playing a trick on her. However, when Gus bolted upright and jerked his hand away from hers, the reality of the situation became clear. She snapped her head around, her eyes wide with disbelief.

"What a surprise," Gus said, coming to Siena's rescue as he'd done so often in the past. "Jonathan! What are you doing here?"

Chapter 28

Siena
Spring 2017

Siena hastened down the service alley to the back entrance of Gus's antique store, her senses on high alert. The evening shadows were deepening and, although Gus was reluctant to admit it, this Bronx neighborhood wasn't as safe as it had once been. She seldom visited the shop these days and never without first making a stop at home to swap her work attire for more practical clothing. Should she need to outdistance herself from who or what might be lurking behind a trash bin or inside a recessed doorway, straight skirts and heels weren't designed for speed. The leggings and running shoes she'd changed into, however, were.

She unlocked the service door with her key and dashed into the shop's dim, dank storage room. The area measured at most twenty by thirty feet and was empty save for a few boxes and crates stacked beneath a mesh, iron grate-covered window. Gus had never been concerned about keeping a storeroom filled with on-hand inventory. After all, selling antiques to walk-in customers wasn't the reason he maintained this business in the first place.

"Gus?" Siena called out, sliding the deadbolt closed behind her. "It's me."

"I'm in the office," Gus replied.

Siena headed toward the fluorescent light spilling from the doorway of the corner office. Inside, she found Gus at his desk sorting through invoices and receipts for purchases and sales that had never taken place. At least not legitimately. Gus, adverse to sending up red flags with the IRS regarding his money-laundering operation, had been devoting his time and attention over the last few days to making sure his personal and business tax returns were filed correctly and on time.

"You're having a party and didn't invite me?" she teased, bending down to give Gus a hug and a kiss on his cheek.

"Don't I wish." Gus swiveled around to face Siena and leaned back in his chair. "You're more than welcome to grab a pile of this paperwork and join in the fun. You'd be a hell of a lot better at figuring out incomes and deductions than I am."

Siena rolled her eyes. "You'll never give up trying, will you?"

This wasn't the first time Gus had attempted to enlist her help with his bookkeeping. With her degree in Finance, they both knew she would be much more astute at handling the paperwork, but their agreement was that she would scout out the jobs and run the cons while Gus crafted the forgeries and managed the backend of the business. Besides, she had enough on her mind right now without getting entangled in yet another discussion about tax exemptions and spreadsheets.

Shivering, Siena hunched her shoulders and took a seat in the chair beside Gus's desk. "It's freezing in here. Isn't the heat turned on?"

"I lower the thermostat when the front store is closed

for business. That's why I have this guy running." He cocked his thumb at the space heater plugged into the wall behind him. "He's much more cost-effective."

Siena grunted. "Huh. I've never known you to pinch pennies."

"Yeah, well, revenue is down at the moment."

Siena's brow knitted with concern. "Why?"

"A few of the crew decided they'd had enough of cold winters and moved to Vegas last month. So, I recruited this new guy, Roberto Lopez, fresh off the plane from Puerto Rico. Jobs will pick up once he's settled in and gets more familiar with Manhattan."

"Well," Siena said, clearing her throat, "not that I care to mention this again, but your safe could be filled with cash right now if I'd already wrapped up my Matthew Kramer job that, thanks to you, has been dragging on forever."

Gus crossed his legs and shot her the look he'd been giving her since she was eight years old. By now she was mature and wise enough to understand that, although he might be irritated with her smart remarks, she was still his favorite godchild, and he'd never raise his voice at her in reprimand. "I told you before, there have been extenuating circumstances."

Lowering her chin, Siena returned his glare. "Please don't bring up that 'I was sick with the flu' bullshit again. As I recall, your health has never stalled any of our jobs this badly in the past."

"Look, it wasn't just that I was laid up for a few days. I also had a hard time getting my hands on the right materials to make the forgeries."

Siena placed her forearm on Gus's desk and leaned closer. "Guess what? I don't care. I'm tired of making

Matthew Kramer believe I'm in love with him. If you don't have the forgeries ready for me to finish this job by tomorrow," she shrugged her shoulders and threw up her hands, "I'm calling off the job."

Gus chuckled. "Like my mother used to tell me, don't get your knickers in a knot." With a grunt, he rose from his chair and sauntered to the far end of the office. His knees cracked as he knelt and opened the door of his credenza, exposing the safe located inside.

Without warning, Siena's heart grew heavy. Gus's age was beginning to show and, instead of cherishing their relationship, here she was behaving like a spoiled brat making willful demands. Then again, wasn't Gus partly to blame for her snarky attitude? He'd played a major role in her upbringing, especially after her mother bailed out on the family. Whatever Siena had wanted from the moment she was born, Gus made sure she got it. She sighed and shook her head. Funny how she always managed to find a reason to justify her way out of a guilty conscience.

Gus rotated the dial on the safe to a set combination of numbers, yanked the handle downward, and wrenched the door open. From the top shelf, he removed a small, rectangular jewelry box. After relocking the safe, his knees reverse-cracked when he stood. "Here," he said, handing the box to Siena. "Take this and stop your whining."

Holding the jewelry box in her hands, Siena's face brimmed with satisfaction. As always, Gus had bent over backwards to give her what her heart desired. Raising the lid, her grin widened into a smile. The forgeries of Alva Kramer's earrings were magnificent.

"Holy shit, Gus! These are beautiful."

Gus plopped into his chair. He acted and sounded exhausted. "So, was the wait worth the while?"

"Without a doubt." She lifted one of the earrings from the case and held it at eye level. The stones swayed and sparkled as they caught the light. Siena stared at them as though hypnotized. In her mind she was visualizing the elaborate scam she had planned. "These will work perfectly."

Gus rocked back in his chair. "When will you complete the job?"

"Give me a minute," she said as she set the jewelry case on Gus's desk. From her purse, she withdrew the burner phone she'd purchased specifically for this job. Turning her back on Gus, she brought up Matthew Kramer's phone number. He answered on the first ring.

"Hello, darlin'," Siena said in her Ellen Randall voice. "How are you?…Well, I miss *you* more than you can imagine…Mm," she purred, "I'd love nothing more than to spend tonight with you, but work has me in a stranglehold. Looks like I'll be pulling another all-nighter…Oh, I know, darlin'. I know that's not what you want to hear, especially since this is our last night before your wife is due home. But the good news is, I'll be free tomorrow afternoon…Yes, I promise. My question is, can you leave your office early and meet me at your apartment, say around two o'clock?…No, I can't be there any earlier…Oh, now, I wanted this to be a surprise, but I need some time after I leave work to go shopping for new lingerie…If red and lacy is what you want, then red and lacy it will be." She forced a giggle. "Oh, my! Matty, you'd better get yourself behind a closed door. You'll give Margaret a heart attack if she walks in on you…Okay, darlin'. Enjoy yourself. I'll see you tomorrow at two."

"Damn," Gus said with a snicker. "That's a conversation I can't unhear." Siena swiveled around to find Gus holding the jewelry box and admiring his masterpieces. "My little Sissy," he joshed, "an alluring femme fatale."

Siena loved Gus with all her heart, but sometimes he tossed out remarks that made her want to throw her phone at him. She snatched the box from him and tossed it into her purse. "I've got to go."

"So soon? I was hoping we could grab dinner at Maestro."

"Not tonight," Siena said between clenched teeth as she slung her purse onto her shoulder. "I've got too much on my mind. I need to go home and focus on this job so that, when I walk into Kramer's apartment tomorrow afternoon, I'm confident nothing will go wrong. Dinner tomorrow night instead?"

"Sure." Appearing befuddled, Gus frowned and scrunched his chin. "But what's the big deal? It's not like you haven't brought dozens of jobs to a close before."

Siena shrugged her shoulders. "Nothing. I'm just more eager than usual to put this one behind me."

Before Gus had a chance to pry the details out of her, before he attempted to talk her out of proceeding, Siena rushed from his office. The scheme she had planned for Matthew Kramer was more sinister than merely swapping his wife's diamond earrings for Gus's forgeries. Gus would call her reckless, he'd call her crazy, but Siena didn't care. Matthew was a scumbag, and he deserved to be treated like one. And the sweet thing was, no one other than Siena would ever know the truth about exactly how vengeful she could be.

No one.
Ever.

Chapter 29

Siena
October 2023

"Sweetheart, you look like I'm holding a gun to your head. Aren't you happy to see me?"

You're sending up red flags, Siena. Breathe. Smile. Screech with excitement.

"Of course I am. I just can't believe you're here." Siena wrapped her arms around Jonathan's neck and kissed him. Although she'd been feeding him a steady diet of fibs recently, she was for once stating the truth. She'd ached for Jonathan every second of the day-and-a-half they'd been apart and could think of nothing she desired more than to press her mouth against his, to savor his musky scent, to catch that soft moan meant only for her ears. But his timing? This unexpected visit made her curious, anxious, and—*Don't you dare let your mind go there, Siena*—suspicious. Jonathan had blindsided her once before. Could she trust that he wasn't playing a similar trick on her a second time?

Jonathan placed his hand on the side of Siena's neck and ran his fingers upward into her hairline, caressing her scalp and sending tingles down Siena's spine. "Now, that's more like it." Jonathan pecked another kiss on her lips before breaking their embrace. He extended his hand across the table. "Gus. Nice to see you again."

Gus shook Jonathan's hand. "Same here."

Jonathan leaned back and trained his eyes on Siena. "I must admit, I was caught completely by surprise when Tyler and I showed up at the Baldwin and Marielle opened the door to your suite." He tilted his head in Gus's direction. "Siena didn't tell me that you two had accompanied Jacqueline to New York."

Gus held his own under Jonathan's scrutinous stare. "Yeah, well, our trip here was kind of a last-minute decision."

"And *you*," Siena teased, resting her hand on Jonathan's thigh and taking the heat off Gus. "Why didn't you tell me you were coming to New York when we spoke on the phone last night?"

"I would have, but I didn't know myself until Tyler called early this morning. He needed to fly to New York for an interview that his publicist scheduled at the last minute, and he suggested it would be fun if I also flew in and the two of us joined you and Jacqueline for a couple of days. Tyler has some new restaurants he wants to check out, and we talked about maybe seeing a show. Gus, of course you and Marielle are welcome to join us if you'd like."

"Yeah, sure," Gus replied. "We're game for anything."

Siena sat back and gave Jonathan and Gus the opportunity to get to know each other better. Although she recognized the fact that they would never become fast friends, she'd settle for at least a congenial relationship. While they conversed, Jonathan asking Gus what changes New York had undergone since he'd moved away and Gus asking Jonathan what he enjoyed most about his stay in Santa Martina, Siena glanced over

Jonathan's shoulder and noticed a man strolling across the deli toward their booth.

Oh, shit! Lou!

Her eyes wide with alarm, Siena gave Lou a slight shake of her head and a nod toward the exit. Lou, thank goodness, understood her message without question. He pulled a sharp about-face and scurried through the front door.

Jonathan glanced at the phone in Siena's hands. "Who are you texting?"

"Jacqueline," Siena lied as she messaged Lou that he should wait at the street corner until she figured out how to handle the situation. "I just remembered something I needed to tell her."

Lou, however, was only a small part of the much bigger issue Jonathan now posed. How could Siena continue to track down Kramer's incriminating video tape while she was romping around Manhattan with Jonathan? She would gladly pay Lou a higher fee to tackle this portion of the investigation on his own—if only she trusted him.

"Jonathan, do you mind letting me out of the booth? I need to use the restroom." What she truly needed was a few minutes alone to work through her dilemma.

"While I'm up," Jonathan said as he slid out of the booth, "I think I'll get a coffee. Gus, do you want anything?"

Gus shook his head. "No, thanks. I'm good."

"Sweetheart?"

Siena made her request while scooting across the vinyl bench seat. "Yes, would you please order a dozen chocolate chip cookies to go?"

Jonathan jerked his head back and grimaced.

"Chocolate chip cookies? You?"

"They're for Jacqueline," she said, laying her palm against his chest and grinning. "She's been craving sweets, but the entire dozen isn't all for her. I wanted to get enough to share with everyone."

"So, seven for Jacqueline and one a piece for the rest of us?"

Siena chuckled at his joke. "Something like that." She left Jonathan at the pastry counter and strolled to the far side of the restaurant and down the back hall. Inside the ladies' room, she leaned against the wall and brought up the search engine on her phone. In the browser window, she typed *Things to do in NYC tonight*. A long list of Broadway plays, concerts, small venue performances, and open mic events appeared on the screen—all activities a couple would do together. Ordinarily, she would have loved a relaxing dinner and a show, but tonight she needed to find a way to occupy Jonathan's time for a few hours while she drove to Irene Kramer's home on Long Island. Once her mission was completed, she'd give Jonathan her undivided attention.

Her thumb scrolled farther down the screen.

Comedy clubs.

No.

Skyscraper views of the city at sunset.

No.

Carriage rides through the park.

She wished, but no.

Professional basketball.

No.

Hold on...

She scrolled up and clicked on the last ad. Basketball season had started, and New York was hosting Boston at home that evening. Tyler was a native New Yorker and Jonathan hailed from Boston. The stars in Siena's universe couldn't have aligned more perfectly. Her thumbs tapped against the screen, selected two pricey seats, and added the order to her cart.

Siena bit her lip as she dug her credit card from her wallet. How many more expenditures like this could her dwindling bank account withstand? As she filled in the fields on the payment screen, her mind was busy inventing the tale she'd feed Jonathan to justify this impromptu gift. He'd be angry at first. He'd argue that she had ruined his and Tyler's intention of coming to New York to be with her and Jacqueline, but Jonathan would cool off as soon as the reality set in that he'd be attending the game with his favorite best-selling author seated by his side.

Her bigger concern was how best to break this news to Gus. Gus would be mad as hell that Siena wasn't also treating him with a ticket to the game, but tonight Siena needed Gus by her side more than Gus needed a boys' night out. Although Lou Biondi appeared to be on the up-and-up, Siena would never dream of turning her back on him.

Chapter 30

Siena

"Wait a second," Lou said as he steered his car east along the Long Island Expressway. "You're saying you gave your husband two center-court tickets to tonight's basketball game, and you expected him to put up a fight?"

"Sorry if you think that's odd but, yes, I did." Siena twisted her position for the third time but to no avail. Regardless of which way she sat, the cramped backseat of Lou's compact sedan was not designed with the comfort of long-legged people in mind. Having to share the seat with an assortment of ball caps, T-shirts, notepads, and unopened junk mail wasn't helping matters.

And all that garbage lining the floor behind the driver's seat was sickening. One's car wasn't meant to be used as a mobile trash bin, although Lou seemed to believe otherwise. Her nose crinkled with disgust when she spotted a rotting apple core peeking out from the corner of a soiled napkin. Jacqueline would be horrified. Using the toe of her boot, she shoved aside a pile of paper bags filled with empty fast-food wrappers. Had those grease-soaked carry-out bags previously occupied the upholstery on which she was now sitting? If so, she would be deducting the cost to replace her slacks from

Lou's final invoice.

Siena dragged her attention away from the garbage dump beside her and focused her gaze on the back of Lou's head. "Wouldn't you be suspicious if you came to New York to be with your wife and she seemed hellbent on finding something for you to do that *didn't* include her?"

Lou checked his mirrors before changing lanes. "I don't mean to sound like I'm coming on to you," he said, "but, I mean, let's face it—you're hot as hell. Your husband's probably thinking he'll only be at the game for a few hours. Then he'll meet you back at your hotel suite and you guys will have the whole rest of the night to…" He raised an eyebrow and grinned at Siena in the rearview mirror. "…you know."

Siena tsked and rolled her eyes. "Jesus, Lou. Do you treat all your clients with such a high level of professionalism?"

"Hey, I just call 'em like I see 'em."

"You're right, Sissy," Gus chimed in from the front passenger seat. "If I was Jonathan, I'd have at least questioned why you didn't buy tickets for our entire group. And if he noticed any holes in that lame excuse you handed him, he sure didn't let on."

"No," Siena muttered in response, "he didn't."

Let on? Hell, he didn't so much as shoot me a sideways glance. And that was the crux of why she'd developed an aching throb in the center of her forehead. Jonathan's blind acceptance of her tall tale—that she'd made an impulsive purchase at the suggestion of a random stranger with whom she'd struck up a conversation in the restroom of a midtown deli—was completely out of character. Which left Siena questioning whether someone—*but who?*—had made Jonathan aware of the plan she had on her agenda for that evening, and if he was purposely giving her enough rope to hang herself.

Her headache stretched its tentacles deeper into her brain.

"Okay, Gus, this is our exit." Lou flipped on the right turn signal. "What's my next move?"

Gus consulted the directions on his cell phone. "At the stop light, make a right onto Pearson Avenue."

"Yes, sir. Right at the light."

Gus swiveled his head toward the backseat. "So, where did you tell Jonathan we'd meet him and Tyler for dinner after the game?"

"I didn't," Siena replied while fishing through her handbag for a bottle of anything to relieve the ache in her head. "He's going to call me when the game ends."

Gus stifled a burp. "You wouldn't happen to have any antacid tablets in that bag of yours, would you?"

Siena couldn't resist jabbing him. "What's wrong, Gus? That pastrami sandwich you basically inhaled not digesting well?" She located the bottle and handed it to Gus. "Here you go."

Lou made a right turn on red. "Okay. I'm on Pearson. Now what?"

"Stay on this road for about two miles," Gus instructed, "then turn left onto Sussex."

"Got it." Lou kept his eyes on Siena in the rearview mirror while she dry-swallowed two pain killers. "Tell me again why you dragged us out here."

Good question.

Siena stared out the window at the passing scenery. Darkness had fallen and people were returning to the comfort of their homes. Cars were pulling into driveways, interior lights were flicking on, dinner was being prepared inside cozy kitchens. She would love to be with Jonathan in their kitchen right now, him sliding a tray of biscuits into the oven while a pot of stew simmered on the stove, her opening a bottle of wine and chatting about the day's events. Instead, she was squeezed into the backseat of a car belonging to a private investigator whom she'd once set up as the patsy in one of her most devious schemes and to whom she was now paying a hefty fee to drive her out to a home on Long Island that was owned by a person who was blackmailing her. All because six years ago she'd allowed her vengeful streak to careen out of control.

I couldn't have screwed up my life any worse if I'd tried.

Massaging the back of her neck, Siena responded to Lou's query. "I'm hoping to get my hands on some valuable assets that I can use as leverage."

"This is the second time you've involved me in a B and E," Lou reminded her. "The first time didn't go so well for me. I'm not walking into another trap, am I?" Braking at a four-way stop, he glanced up and met Siena's steely gaze in the rearview mirror.

"Stop worrying, Lou," Siena said to his reflection. "Tonight, you're simply my driver."

Lou redirected his attention to the road before him. "Gus, am I getting close to Sussex yet?"

Gus leaned forward. "It should be the next street." His squinted eyes darted back and forth between the cell phone in his hand and the upcoming street signs. "Damn if I'm not having a hard time seeing in the dark lately. Seems like everything went to shit right after I turned sixty."

Lou snorted. "That's what you get for making fun of me at the deli when I couldn't read my own notes."

Gus glanced sideways at Lou. "You hit sixty yet?"

"Nope," Lou grumbled. "But it's coming up on me faster than I'd like. Is this Sussex?"

Gus consulted his phone. "Yes. The map says to turn left here."

Lou waited for the traffic to clear, then made the turn. "This is the street, right?"

"Yep," Gus assured him. "We're looking for 6211. Go down a couple of blocks and the house will be on the left."

Siena sat up straighter and leaned forward. Angling her head between the driver and passenger seats, she helped Lou and Gus scout the street for the correct address.

"How about Leon's Steakhouse?" Gus asked Siena, getting back to their dinner plans. "It's only a couple of blocks from our hotel."

"Tyler is a vegetarian."

"Oh, right." Angling closer to Lou, Gus gazed out the driver's side window. "Slow down, Lou. Looks like it's that house with the white picket fence."

"Park here in this open spot," Siena instructed Lou. "Gus and I will walk the rest of the way." She slung her crossbody purse over her shoulder while Lou steered the car along the curb, across the street and two houses down from Kramer's. "Wait for us here. This shouldn't take long." She tapped Gus on his shoulder. "Let's go."

Streetlamps were stretched out in even intervals along the road, illuminating the neighborhood under a moonless sky and casting shadows beneath mature oaks which hadn't yet lost their leaves to the season. Siena and Gus exited the car, closing the doors softly to avoid attracting the attention of nosey neighbors. Stopping near the front fender of Lou's car, they waited for a motorcycle to pass before dashing across the street.

"This way," Gus said, guiding Siena beneath a tall oak in the front yard of the house next to Kramer's. Anyone gazing out a window would be hard pressed to notice their neighborhood had been invaded by two strangers intent on breaking into the empty house where Irene Kramer had once lived.

Dogs, on the other hand, miss nothing. Siena heard the Doberman's bark a second before his face appeared on the inside of the picture window just a few feet from where she was passing. Regardless of the forewarning, she nearly jumped out of her skin. From inside the living room, the owner's muted voice could be heard shouting, "Roscoe! Get down!" Siena and Gus took off in a sprint.

"Do you think that woman saw us?" Gus asked, his voice low.

"No," Siena responded, although she was just as concerned as Gus. "I doubt she even got out of her recliner."

Kramer's home was a small cape cod with a front and rear entrance and a detached garage at the back of the property. Coach lights illuminated the front door. At the rear of the house, a security light mounted near the roofline brightened the entire backyard. Fortunately, the house featured a covered patio. Anyone entering the house at night through the backdoor would be hard to detect.

"You have the keys?" Gus asked as he swung open the aluminum screen door.

"Right here." Siena held out her hand to show him the ring of keys she'd lifted from Matthew Kramer's foyer. She removed a small flashlight from her purse, flicked it on, and handed it to Gus. "Hold this for me so I can see what I'm doing." Selecting a key at random, she attempted to fit it first into the door lock and second into the deadbolt. "Let's hope one of these keys works."

"And if none of them does?"

"Do you remember the night you posed as Stanley Bartlemay and we went to Kramer's apartment at the Hudson?"

"Yeah."

"Do you also remember the call he got from his mother while we were there?" Gus frowned and shook his head. "She couldn't find her key to get into the house and Matthew reminded her that a spare key was kept in a fake rock in the flower bed next to the back patio."

"Christ, do you ever forget anything?"

"No." Siena glanced sideways at the disheveled mound of dirt and dead leaves beside them. "However, if that area used to be the flower garden, finding the fake rock might not be as easy as I anticipated." On her third try, one of the keys fit the deadbolt. The next key on the ring fit snugly into the door lock. "But, lucky for us, now we don't need to worry about it."

Siena turned the knob, opened the door just a few inches, and held her breath while waiting for an alarm to sound. When the house remained silent after ten seconds, she pocketed the key ring and glanced at Gus. "Can you believe it was that easy?"

"No." The smooth entry didn't appear to sit well with Gus. "There might be a silent alarm."

"Precisely. Hand me the flashlight." Siena shined

the light along the door frame, her hand trailing behind the beam. In the dim light, she might not spot a small sensor, but she'd certainly feel one. "Nothing. And I don't see a keypad on any of the walls. We're clear." From her crossbody purse, she removed two pairs of thin cotton gloves and two pairs of disposable booties to cover their shoes. She handed one pair of each to Gus. "Doesn't surprise me. Kramer seems to spend his money on things that give him pleasure rather than on what's important."

Gus's brow was heavy with concern. "Sissy, are you sure you want to go through with this? It's not too late to turn around—"

"My mind's made up, Gus," she said, her words sharp, her eyes determined. "Don't ask me again."

Siena gently swung the door open, being cautious of rusty and therefore squeaky hinges.

She poked her head into the house and scanned the area with her flashlight, getting an idea of the layout before entering. Gus followed her in, closing the doors behind him.

"This obviously is the kitchen," she commented. "The window blinds are all closed, which is good."

"Yeah, but that dog next door is still barking. Let's get this job done fast before the neighbors decide to make their way over here and start poking around."

Gus remained a few steps behind Siena as she explored the first floor. A hallway, they discovered, divided the downstairs floor plan in half. The back of the house consisted of the kitchen and one bedroom with a full bath wedged between them. Across from the kitchen, in the front of the house, was a dining room. Lastly, they entered the living room. A dull glare from the streetlamps filtered in around the edges of the curtain-clad windows, shedding enough light to outline the larger pieces of furniture.

"This is creepy," Siena whispered.

"What is?"

"All the furniture is still here, and the decorations are still on the walls and shelves." She lifted a magazine from the coffee table and examined the date.

"Are you sure no one lives here? Maybe Kramer's renting the place out."

"Doubtful. This magazine is four years old." Dropping the periodical onto the table, she focused the flashlight on a framed photo sitting on the end table. "And that's a fairly recent picture of Matthew and his mother. Jesus, this house is like a freaking museum. Why doesn't Kramer sell it? It's not like his mother is ever coming back here to live."

Gus shrugged his shoulders. "Don't know and don't care. Let's just finish the job and leave."

Keeping the flashlight beam directed at the floor, Siena took measured steps as she maneuvered around the furniture and found the staircase to the second floor situated between the living and dining rooms. Standing at the foot of the stairs, Siena gazed up into the cavernous darkness. When she directed the beam of her flashlight up the stairs, she half-expected bats to swoop down toward her.

"I'm guessing the downstairs bedroom with all its frilly lace was used by Kramer's mother," she said. "What I came here to get should be upstairs in Kramer's childhood bedroom."

"Should be? You mean to tell me we came out here on a wild goose chase?"

"Maybe, maybe not. Like I said, I'm basing my assumption on secrets Kramer shared with me six years ago." She placed her foot on the first step and grasped the handrail with her free hand. "From what I overheard his girlfriend say this morning, though, his stash should still be here."

Gus mounted the staircase behind Siena, the carpeted steps creaking under their weight. "And what do you expect to find?"

"Cash and jewelry he pilfered from his ex-wife—his dead ex-wife—while they were still married."

"Jesus, doll, you sure know how to pick them."

"Don't I, though?"

They'd reached the landing at the top of the stairs. Siena scanned the flashlight's beam over the area and exposed three closed doors: one to their right, one to their left, and one directly in front of them.

"Two bedrooms and a bath?" Siena speculated.

"That'd be my guess." Gus chuckled. "Hey, can I trade my watch for what's behind door number three?"

"Your watch?" Siena scrunched her face into a question mark. "What are you talking about?"

"You know," Gus said, raising his eyebrows, "like the game show."

"What game show?"

Gus's voice rose an octave. "The one on TV for Chrissake! I forget what it's called. Something about making a deal."

Siena shook her head as she approached the door to their right. "Sorry. Don't know it."

"Christ," Gus muttered under his breath. "I swear to God your grandmother raised you girls like you were living in a convent. Forget that. Even nuns watch TV."

Siena opened the door and shined her flashlight into the bedroom. "Looks like Irene Kramer was into crafting. There's a sewing machine by the window and a basket filled with yarns and knitting needles on the floor beside it. However, that's not to say this wasn't originally Matthew's bedroom." She stepped into the room and opened the bifold closet doors.

"Well?" Gus asked.

"Just some stacks of material and a four-drawer cart on wheels. No built-in shelving unit like the one Matthew described." Siena slid the closet doors closed. "On to the next room," she said, making sure to shut the bedroom door as well, leaving everything in the house as if they hadn't been there.

Siena opened the door to the room that faced the back of the house and ran the flashlight beam across the fixtures inside. "A bathroom, as expected." While closing the door, she pointed with her chin toward their final choice. "Two down, one to go."

Gus swiveled around and twisted the knob, but the door was unyielding. "Hm…" he grunted.

"Is the door locked?"

"No, the knob turns." He gave the door another shove. "But the door seems to be stuck."

"Gus, stop!" Siena edged closer and directed the flashlight beam along the door frame. "The rest of the house isn't protected by an alarm system, but if Matthew has millions in cash and jewelry stored in this room, he may have installed an alarm on just this door." She expanded her inspection to include the walls surrounding the door.

"What do you suggest?"

"There should be a keypad—"

Suddenly, the muted crash of shattering glass resounded from somewhere on the first floor, as if a cloth-covered fist had broken through a window.

"Gus," Siena whispered, "did you hear that?"

"Yeah. Sounds like we have company."

Siena clicked off her flashlight and trained her ear toward the stairwell. Glass crunched under footsteps. Two, maybe three, intruders barked short commands at each other as they plodded through the rooms below. Their muffled voices grew louder, an indication that they were approaching the front of the house.

Gus stole the flashlight from Siena's hand and grabbed her arm. "Quick. In here."

Chapter 31

Siena

Gus gently inched the bathroom door open, stopping short when a pin scraped against the knuckle on one of the hinges and sounded a mild complaint. Flicking on the flashlight and directing the beam to the floor, he squeezed through the opening. Siena followed, quietly closing the door behind her.

"Whatever those guys downstairs came here to steal," he whispered, "they won't expect to find anything of value in the bathtub."

Nodding her head in agreement, Siena stepped into the tub. The protective shoe booties dulled the thud of her heels as they struck against the porcelain. Gus fitted himself into the space beside her and switched off the flashlight. Slivers of the backyard security light streamed into the room between the slats of the window shutters, providing enough light for Siena to work by as she tugged the vinyl shower curtain across the full length of the tub, carefully lifting the metal hooks to keep them from scraping against the shower rod.

Siena stood as still as a statue while in the rooms below cupboards were slammed open, furniture was overturned, and dishes were smashed against the kitchen floor. Who were these men and what were they after? Was this a random break-in, or was it somehow related to the incident Gus and Marielle had witnessed yesterday in Eddie Davis's poker room? Then again, considering the one-sided conversation Siena had overheard in Matthew's apartment that morning, certain members of his girlfriend's family seemed capable of ordering a violent attack on Matthew. Wouldn't the break-in and destruction of his family home also be within their realm?

"Christ, they're tearing the place apart," Gus muttered, his hand brushing against Siena's.

Siena instinctively grasped Gus's hand. Whatever happened in Irene Kramer's house tonight, they were in this situation together. Maybe this break-in would turn out to be as innocuous as the night the three goons burst into Gus's basement workshop at the antique store, imposters she later learned were former gang members posing as thugs who'd been hired by Jonathan—

Oh, dear God.

Siena's breaths came in rapid succession as her eyes darted back and forth in the semi-darkness. Was Jonathan behind this home invasion? Had the P.I. firm he'd employed in the past been following her around Manhattan? If they'd informed Jonathan of her involvement with Matthew Kramer, Jonathan may have ordered them to thwart her every attempt to find Matthew's damaging video. Maybe Jonathan's unexpected appearance at Max's Deli was part of this plan. Which would explain why he so willingly agreed to attend tonight's basketball game—to give her the freedom to proceed with her scheme. Maybe—

Gus squeezed Siena's hand. The intruders were standing at the bottom of the stairs, their voices loud enough to carry up the stairwell.

"Check the second floor," one of them said with an inflection that reminded Siena of the Bronx accent Gus had been working for years to lose.

"You kiddin' me?" Another New Yorker, probably from the same neighborhood. "It's dark as hell up there."

"So, turn on a light, idiot. Who's gonna see?"

Footsteps stomped up the stairs. When the intruder reached the landing, he stopped as if deciding which door to open first. He chose the one directly in front of him.

Siena bit her lower lip, convinced the man on the other side of the shower curtain could hear her heart pounding out of her chest.

Don't move. Don't breathe. Don't so much as blink an eye.

The intruder flipped on the overhead light and proceeded to yank open the vanity drawers in rapid succession. Judging by the hollowness of the clatter, Siena guessed each one was empty. The door to the medicine cabinet opened and closed. He was in and out in thirty seconds, leaving the light on and the bathroom door wide open.

Siena glanced sideways at Gus. He was staring at the back of the shower curtain, his head lowered. Gus must have sensed her eyes on him. He angled his head in her direction and nodded as if to say he'd been right about the bathtub being a safe haven. Siena squeezed his hand even tighter. At that moment, she couldn't imagine wanting anyone else by her side.

The intruder swung left when he exited the bathroom. From the sound of things, he was tossing the contents of Irene Kramer's sewing room. Based on the choice curse words spewing from his mouth, he hadn't found what he'd come looking for among her supply of dress patterns and skeins of yarn.

He stomped across the hall to his third and final choice. The door resisted opening just as it had for Gus. This guy, however, wasn't taking no for an answer. Siena couldn't distinguish whether he was slamming the door with his shoulder or kicking it with his foot, but he succeeded in busting the door open on his fourth try.

Siena's breath caught. She expected the piercing blare of an alarm to be set off but, to her surprise, nothing happened. Perhaps the door had merely been bolted shut. Or maybe the room was secured by an alarm—a silent one—and the authorities had been alerted without the intruder realizing. Siena's internal clock started ticking. If these unknown assailants didn't make their escape soon, they'd be trapped inside a police barricade.

And so would she and Gus.

The contents of room number three were evidently not worth the burglar's time. In seconds, his feet were thumping down the staircase. He shouted to his partner that the second floor was clean.

"Same down here," the other guy responded. "Shit. This was the easiest money we ever made. Let's finish the job and get outta here."

More conversation followed, although too muffled for Siena to discern. She picked up on some unidentifiable scuffling noises, then what sounded like the back door being slammed shut. She and Gus waited and listened. Siena counted to twenty.

"I think they're gone," she said, remaining cautious and keeping her voice low.

"Sounds like it." Gus yanked the shower curtain across the rod and stepped onto the bathroom floor. "He sure had a hard time breaking down that last door." Gus held Siena's hand as she lifted her legs over the edge of the bathtub.

"Yes, and I'm worried that he may have set off a silent alarm. The police could be arriving in a few minutes."

"Great." Gus headed for the stairs. "Let's get the hell out of here."

"Not yet," Siena said, rushing across the hall. "I want to check out this other room first."

"What is wrong with you?" Gus followed Siena into what was once Matthew Kramer's childhood bedroom. "Didn't you just tell me the cops might be on their way?"

"*Might* being the operative word." Siena stole the flashlight from Gus's hand, flipped it on, and scanned the space before her. The room was bare save for a twin bed, a chest of drawers, and a child's desk and chair. "And, if they are, I have at least a couple of minutes. I am not leaving without searching for Kramer's stash."

"You're crazy. I'm telling you right now, the second I hear sirens, I'm leaving. With you or without you."

"Stop taunting me with idle threats," Siena snapped. She hurried toward the open closet door and aimed the beam of her flashlight inside. There, precisely as Matthew had described to her six years earlier, was the dual-purpose shelving unit his father had installed. Siena knelt before the built-in, hoping that the opening latch would be easy to find and simple to operate. Craning her head to the side, she discovered a three-inch gap between the shelf and the wall. "Shit."

"What's wrong?"

Siena tugged the shelving unit open all the way and directed her flashlight inside the cubby hole. The space the young Matthew had used to store his prized rock collection and which the adult Matthew had used to hide his heiress wife's money and jewels appeared just as Matthew had described—with one exception. The shelves inside Matthew's secret hiding place were empty.

"I'm too late," Siena said, her voice raised in anger. "Someone got here before me." She smacked the palm of her hand against the wall. "*Dammit!*"

"Tough luck. So, what do you think? That guy who was just in here emptied it out?"

Siena shook her head. "No way. He wasn't in this room long enough to figure out how to open the latch and remove all the money and jewelry Matthew supposedly had stored in here."

Siena's anger stewed as she stared into the empty space. Plan A—her attempt to confiscate the video camera and Matthew's cell phone—had proved worthless. And without the cash and jewelry she'd expected to find in this closet, she could also toss out her Plan B. Now what was she going to do? She'd hardly had a second to ponder her next option when Gus, still standing in the doorway behind her, raised his nose and sniffed at the air.

"Sissy," he said with an apprehension that sent shivers through Siena's body, "do you smell gasoline?"

Chapter 32

Siena

Glass shattered somewhere in the front of the house followed by a loud whooshing sound. Siena jumped to her feet. "What the hell?"

"We need to leave," Gus said, clutching her arm. "*Now!*"

Gus shoved Siena toward the staircase. As she started to descend, her foot slipped on the carpeting. She bounced down several steps, her arms flailing.

Shouting Siena's name, Gus rushed down the stairs after her. With his arms outstretched and his hands grasping for Siena but failing to catch her, he lost his footing and careened forward. Midway down the staircase, Siena, acting on pure instinct, gripped the handrail and stopped them both from sliding farther down the steps.

Her heart racing, Siena said, "Get rid of these damned booties before they get us killed!"

The few seconds Siena and Gus stole to rip the booties off their shoes proved to be a critical hindrance to their escape. Spreading rapidly through the first floor, the fire had created an impassable barrier between the stairwell and the front door. Siena and Gus stared in horror as the flames licked up the steps toward them.

Siena swiveled around. For one terrifying moment,

she and Gus gazed at one another, their eyes filled with dread. Siena's mind raced to reimagine the second story floor plan. At once, the solution came to her. "Gus! The bedroom window!"

Coughing and choking on the billowing smoke, she and Gus scrambled up the stairs and into Kramer's childhood bedroom. As Gus slammed the bedroom door closed, Siena wrenched up the blind on the sash window facing the back of the house. A glance out the window confirmed what she'd hoped. "Gus, look! We can get out through this window and onto the patio roof."

Gus stepped in front of Siena, unlocked the latch, and attempted to raise the window but it wouldn't budge. After an unsuccessful second try, he leaned closer and inspected the frame. "Shit! It's nailed shut. I'll have to break the glass." He shrugged off his jacket and draped it over his head and his left arm. "Cover yourself," he warned as he swung his elbow toward the window.

"Stop!" Siena stilled Gus's arm with one hand while pointing at Matthew Kramer's study desk with her other. "Gus, use that chair instead."

Gus dropped his jacket to the floor and rushed over to the desk. Lifting the chair with both hands, he hurried back to the window and swung the chair like a baseball bat, thrusting it forward with all his strength. The chair crashed through the window, splintering the glass into hundreds of tiny shards. Siena pivoted toward the wall and shielded her head and face with her arms as Gus spun face forward against the adjacent wall. The chair clattered down the patio roof, plunged to the ground, and splintered into pieces.

The flames had reached the top of the stairs and were spreading through the second floor at a threatening pace.

Smoke snaked underneath the closed bedroom door as Gus kicked away the jagged glass still clinging to the window frame. He held his hand out to Siena. "Let's go! You first!"

Facing Gus and clasping his arms for support, Siena lifted one leg over the window ledge and fixed her foot against the vinyl siding on the back of the house. She craned her neck and glanced downward, judging how far of a drop she needed to negotiate. By her estimation, the patio roof was attached to the house no more than five feet below the window ledge. When she jerked her head forward to face Gus, Siena caught a glimpse of the disastrous scene taking place behind him. Tremors of fear shook her body.

Although the bedroom door was keeping the flames in the upstairs hall at bay, the angry fire had burned through the floorboards and was inching its way toward them. Within seconds, the bedroom was scorching hot and filled with smoke. Siena needed to kick her ass into high gear and clear their only escape route for Gus.

Her feet touched the patio roof as the distant wail of sirens announced the first responders were on their way. "I'm okay," Siena told Gus. "Let go."

She dropped onto her hands and knees which, she determined, was not her best position. As she twisted her body around, she began to slide. The low pitch of the roof wasn't a problem, but its moss-covered corrugated metal was. Having nothing for her hands to grab on to, she set her feet flat to the surface and slowed the skidding. She glanced up as Gus, engulfed in smoke and coughing hard, cleared the window and touched his feet onto the roof. He shouted as if in pain and let go of his grip on the window ledge. Stumbling, he lost his footing and rolled sideways.

Siena's heart leapt into her throat. "Gus!" She stretched her arm out toward him in an effort to clench his shirt, his hand, anything she could get hold of, but he was too far away. Still scrambling to get his bearings, Gus rolled off the side of the roof and disappeared from her sight.

"Gus!" Siena screamed even louder as she slid her butt at full speed toward the edge of the roof. Swinging her legs over the gutters, she pushed off the roof and dropped down, hitting the ground feet first and toppling onto her side. She wasted no time getting herself upright, but when she attempted to run toward Gus she stumbled and fell. The heel of her left boot had broken off in the fall.

Flames exploded through the kitchen window, spraying glass into the backyard. Above the roar of the fire, shouts of "Jesus Christ!" drifted her way, followed by a variety of other vulgarities. Back on her feet and tottering with each step, Siena rounded the corner of the patio and found Gus holding his bent knee and writhing in pain. Although he missed falling into the prickly bushes planted against the back of the house, he'd evidently sustained an injury. She rushed toward him.

"Gus! Where are you hurt?"

Gus extended his arm to Siena. "It's nothing. Just help me up."

As the sirens grew louder, Siena hauled Gus to his feet. She wrapped her right arm around his back as Gus placed his left arm across her shoulders. With Siena hobbling on her one good heel and Gus leaning on her for support, they headed toward the driveway.

"Don't bullshit me," Siena growled. "You wouldn't

be limping if nothing was wrong."

The dog in the house next door had worked himself into a barking frenzy. Neighbors were poking their heads outside their front doors. A few could be heard exclaiming to whoever was within earshot that Irene Kramer's house was on fire.

Gus winced. "I landed on my knee. It hurts like hell."

Halfway down the driveway, Siena glanced to her left. The lights of the emergency vehicles were flashing in the darkness three, maybe four blocks away. She and Gus would never make it to Lou's car before being surrounded by fire trucks and police cars. Her anxiety spiked.

"Gus, can you walk any faster?"

"Don't you think I'm trying?" he grumbled.

As they neared the sidewalk, Lou's car appeared as if out of nowhere, spun into a U-turn, and came to a screeching halt at the foot of the driveway. Siena opened the front passenger door and helped Gus into his seat. Swinging open the back passenger door, she hopped in behind him.

"Go!" she screamed. Lou pressed his foot to the accelerator as Siena yanked her door closed.

A mile down the road, Lou slammed his hand against the steering wheel and cursed. "Goddamnit! I nearly had a heart attack when I noticed flames pouring out of that house. I thought you guys were dead." Siena cocked her head. Was that a crack in Lou's voice? "Then, when I saw you running down the driveway…" He sniffled and swiped the back of his hand under his nose.

"That was hardly what I'd call running," Gus groaned while rubbing his knee.

Lou stopped at a four-way and glanced over at Gus. "What'd you do to your knee?"

"I fell on it." Gus was clearly not in the mood for a chat.

Lou craned his neck around to the backseat. "Are you hurt, Siena?"

"I'm fine. Just rattled." Nervously kneading her hands against her knees, Siena's finger poked through a rip in her slacks. When the hell did that happen? She poked her fingers through the hole and checked her leg. No cuts, no bleeding. She did a quick scan over the rest of her body. In the darkness and with little room to move in the cramped back seat she couldn't be positive, but she seemed not to have acquired any wounds. Bruising was a whole other matter.

Staring out the side window, Siena fought to hold back the tears. She suspected someone had challenged her to a wicked game of chess and the odds of her winning were not looking good. But worse than losing the game was her growing suspicion that the person she was competing against was Jonathan.

"What happened in there? Shit, you guys didn't start that fire, did you? How'd you manage to get out?"

"Lou," Siena said with pursed lips, her nerves about to snap, "we'll tell you the whole story some other time. For right now, can you just stop talking and get us back to the hotel?"

Lou let out a slow whistle. "Yes, ma'am." Spying on Siena in the rearview mirror, he sucked in his breath and went for it. "Can I ask one more question? Did you at least find what you were after?"

Gus snickered. "That's the irony of this damned useless excursion. The treasure she expected to find was already gone when she got there."

Lou took one hand off the steering wheel and ran his fingers through his hair. "Damn," he mumbled under his breath.

Exactly.

Chapter 33

Siena

Siena hadn't intended to dig herself any deeper into her lies, but she did.

"I'm sorry," Jonathan said through his cell phone. "There's a noisy crowd of people around us and I don't think I understood you." His voice turned testy. "Why did you say you can't meet us for dinner?"

Siena pinched her eyes shut. Somehow, doing so made the fib easier to tell.

"Gus was mugged," she repeated, speaking louder this time. "We were walking on Broadway when two teen-aged boys knocked Gus down and stole his cell phone. He hit the pavement hard, and his knee has swelled up. He can barely put weight on it." When Jonathan failed to respond with the anticipated *"That's terrible!"* and *"Please tell me you weren't hurt"*, Siena was convinced he knew she was hiding the truth from him.

At least the tale she fed Jonathan was partially true. Gus had lost his cell phone, but only because it was in the pocket of the jacket he'd discarded in Matthew Kramer's childhood bedroom. In their frantic haste to escape the fire, neither Gus nor Siena had given thought to retrieving the jacket or the phone while they were scrambling through the bedroom window to safety. The realization that he'd sacrificed his cell phone *and* his brand-new jacket dawned on Gus about the same time Lou was merging onto the Long Island Expressway. He'd been bitching non-stop about it since.

Jacqueline had examined his knee. She didn't think it was fractured, but she encouraged Gus to go to urgent care and have an X-ray taken. Gus had refused. He was currently reclining on the couch with an icebag straddling his knee and a tall glass of scotch in his hand while Nurse Jacqueline and her assistant Marielle tended to the minor cuts he'd sustained. He'd told Siena to get out of his face—only with a lot less diplomacy.

That nasty headache Siena had gotten rid of earlier in the evening was back for an encore performance. She'd downed two painkillers before going into her bedroom, closing the door, and calling Jonathan to inform him of their change in plans. She was lying on the bed massaging her forehead while on the other end of the call Jonathan was relaying the situation to Tyler. Siena overheard Tyler say, *"My God! That's horrible!"*

Suddenly, Jonathan was much more compassionate. "Sweetheart, Tyler and I feel awful about what happened to Gus. What can we do? Get some carry-out and bring it back to the room?"

"Don't bother. Marielle ordered room service."

"Oh. Okay. Well, then, Tyler and I will get a taxi and come straight back to the hotel. We're both starving, so save some food for us."

Siena ended the call and lay motionless on the bed. If she kept her head still, her brain didn't ache quite as badly. She was just beginning to relax when a light rap on the bedroom door gave her a jolt. The door opened, and Jacqueline stepped into the room.

"Sissy, are you okay?"

Siena blinked away the tears. "Gus and I just narrowly escaped from a burning house. What do you think?" She elbowed her way into a sitting position and leaned back on the pillows stacked against the headboard. "Plus, I've got a killer headache."

"Mind if I turn on a light?" Jacqueline switched on the bedside lamp without waiting for Siena to grant her permission. "Did you take anything for your headache?"

"I swallowed a double dose of painkillers while you were examining Gus's knee. So far, they haven't kicked in."

Jacqueline perched herself on the edge of the bed next to Siena. "That's because you need to eat something. Go into the living room and make yourself a plate of food."

Siena wrinkled her nose. "I'll think about it."

Jacqueline huffed. "I know you, and I know you *won't* think about it. So, I'm ordering you to put some food into your stomach."

"Jacqueline, you're sweet for having my best interests at heart, but now is not the time to get bossy with me. I'll eat when I feel like it." Siena ran her fingers through her hair. What she wouldn't give for a head massage right now. "Which reminds me. When I spoke with Jonathan, he and Tyler were just leaving the game. They're coming straight back to the hotel."

"I know. Tyler called." Jacqueline sucked in a deep breath. "Listen, I packed up my stuff. Tyler and I are going to spend tonight at his apartment, and right after his interview tomorrow we're flying back to Santa Martina. You should know that Gus just booked a morning flight out for him and Marielle."

"He's not going to wait until his knee gets better?"

"No. I told him they could stay at Tyler's place for a few days, but he refused the offer. He wants to get home as soon as possible." Jacqueline hesitated. "You know, he's really angry with you."

"Well, that's obvious. Even though I insisted on buying him a new jacket and replacing his phone."

Jacqueline rolled her eyes. "Sissy, I can't believe you."

"Why?" Siena frowned and painted a befuddled look on her face. She knew what the source of Gus's fury was; she just didn't want to admit it.

Jacqueline tsked. "Don't act clueless with *me*. This whole scheme you're trying to pull off behind Jonathan's back—Gus has been opposed to it from the beginning, but since you're his favorite he can't say no to you. And I don't need to tell you again how *I* feel about it. Why can't you let it go? Tell Jonathan what's been going on and let him help you deal with it."

Siena shifted her gaze and stared out the window. "You're right, Jac. I'll talk with him tonight."

Jacqueline crossed her arms and raised her chin. "Tell me that straight to my face."

Siena's defiant eyes darted sideways, her head following more deliberately, as she stared down her sister's authoritative air.

"Fine," Jacqueline snapped. "Do what you want. Tomorrow, at least *I'll* be flying home with a clear conscience." She rose from the bed and scrutinized Siena's appearance. "By the way, you might want to change clothes and clean yourself up before Jonathan gets here. You look like you just fought your way out of hell." She stomped out of the room and slammed the door closed behind her.

A growl rooted itself in Siena's chest. Sometimes Jacqueline's mannerisms and her voice—minus the French accent—too closely resembled their mother's. A childhood memory surfaced of the afternoon she and Jacqueline were in their parents' bathroom playing with the contents of their mother's makeup drawer. Jac, born with what Siena was convinced was OCD, had been fascinated by the variety of cosmetics and was busy examining and organizing each item by product type and color. Meanwhile, the more adventurous and daring Siena had smeared the darkest eye shadow, blush, and lipstick of the lot onto her face.

When Yvette strolled into the bathroom and caught her eight-year-old twins red-handed, she was furious. Seizing Jacqueline by the arm, she'd yelled in French, *"How many times do I need to tell you girls you are forbidden to touch my things?"* Yvette had ordered the sobbing and obedient Jac to return all her cosmetics to the drawer along with the threat that each piece had better be placed precisely where Jacqueline had found it. She then trained her wrath on Siena.

Yvette wet a washcloth and, gripping Siena's face by the chin, scrubbed away the makeup with the ferocity of a medieval scullery maid scouring the evening's charred cookware. Although the cleansing hurt like hell and left her sensitive young skin raw for several days following, Siena refused to bare even a hint of vulnerability, nor did she shed one single tear. That afternoon marked the first time Siena witnessed their mother's increasingly frequent mood swings. That was also the day she added several unsavory words to her French vocabulary.

Merci beaucoup, Jacqueline! I have plenty enough problems to deal with right now without you dredging up hurtful confrontations with our neurotic mother.

In a fit of anger, Siena grabbed one of the bed pillows and, targeting the door as though it were Jacqueline's back, flung the pillow across the room. The outburst didn't change matters, but it did wonders for Siena's mood.

Siena dragged herself off the bed and sauntered into the bathroom. Flipping on the light, she glanced at her reflection in the mirror and—*Holy shit!* Jac wasn't kidding. Her mascara was smudged, she had a bruise on her chin, and her hair was a mess. She stood back from the vanity and assessed her clothing. Her sweater and slacks were filthy and torn and—she raised her elbow to her nose and sniffed—reeked of smoke. And here she'd presumed all those people they'd passed while hobbling through the hotel lobby were gawking solely at Gus.

Well, isn't this nice? I've ruined a brand-new outfit. That I really liked. And that was incredibly expensive. And that I need to dispose of before Jonathan arrives.

Siena stomped into the bedroom and retrieved an empty plastic shopping bag Jacqueline had pitched into the waste can. Stripping down to her underwear, she stuffed her sweater and slacks into the bag. Her broken boots would fit in the bag as well, if only she could remember where she'd left them. Damn if this headache wasn't making her brain foggy. She closed her eyes and massaged her temples.

Retrace your steps, Siena. After Lou dropped us off at the hotel entrance, Gus and I crossed the lobby and called for the elevator. While riding up to our floor, I removed the boots and trekked down the hall to our suite in my bare feet. I tolerated Jac's and Marielle's indignation and answered all their questions, after which I came into the bedroom to call Jonathan. I plopped onto the bed and—

"There you are," she said to the boot with the broken heel as she rounded the foot of the bed. Kneeling, she lifted the bed skirt and found that its mate had been kicked underneath the mattress. The fit was tight, but she stuffed both boots in with her clothes and buried the bag inside her suitcase. As soon as she returned home, and definitely before Anita got to her suitcase first, she would pitch her beautiful new outfit into the trash.

Siena stripped off her bra and panties and strolled into the bathroom. Choosing a hot shower over a soak in the suite's whirlpool tub, she stepped into the stall and snapped the glass door closed behind her. When the water temp was cranked up to a degree just shy of scalding, she piled her hair onto the top of her head and allowed the therapeutic hot water to pummel her shoulders and the back of her neck. She closed her eyes and cleared her mind of all thoughts. A low moan resonated in her throat—*Jesus, this feels good*—as the tension drained from her muscles. Plus, the meds she'd gulped down had finally reached her brain.

But her mind didn't stay free of worry for long. Try as she might, she couldn't erase the memory of Gus hoisting her through that busted out bedroom window, of him holding onto her arms, making sure she was safe before attempting his own escape as the white-hot flames behind him drew steadily closer. Her stomach roiled. They'd come within inches of dying.

Dammit, Siena, how much bigger of a wakeup call do you need?

This charade of hers had to end. She'd discovered the hard way that Matthew Kramer was dallying on the wrong side of some extremely dodgy characters. Whether the men who set fire to his mother's home were associated with Eddie Davis's gang of thugs, or they'd been sent by Matthew's girlfriend's family, or they'd been paid by Matthew himself so he could collect on the homeowner's insurance policy, Siena couldn't afford to take any more risks like this last one that came way too close to getting Gus and her killed. She would wait to hear back from Matthew and hope to negotiate her way into a settlement other than the $5 million he was demanding.

The big "but" was, how would she find the time to meet with Matthew now that Jonathan was in town? *Jonathan.* A frown furrowed across her brow. *How, for one second, could I have blamed the torching of the Kramer home on Jonathan? Brushing that close against danger, I wasn't thinking straight. Even if Jonathan had seen right through the tales I've been feeding him, even if he'd hired his investigators to follow me around town, he isn't capable of—*

The shower door clicked open, jarring Siena back to reality.

"Mind if I join you?" Jonathan asked.

Siena's insides tingled at the sight of him. "Please do." Letting her hair tumble to her shoulders, she held out her arms and welcomed Jonathan into her embrace. They kissed under the spray of the showerhead as glistening streams of hot water trailed down their skin. *This* was her Jonathan, the man who adored her, who would do anything to please her and keep her safe. She'd been crazy to imagine anything less of him.

"Where's Jac?" Siena asked when the kiss ended.

Jonathan nuzzled her neck. "She left with Tyler."

"And Gus and Marielle?" Her voice quivered as Jonathan's hands caressed the curves of her body.

"In their bedroom." His lips brushed Siena's cheek as they traveled to that spot under her ear that always sent her passion soaring. "Too far away to hear us."

"Mm…" she purred, turning her back on Jonathan and squirting shower gel onto a loofah.

"Who won the game?"

Jonathan wrapped his arms around her. "Boston," he said between the kisses he was planting on her shoulder.

"Oh?" Siena lathered the loofah. "How did Tyler take the loss?"

"Not well. Pouting doesn't become him." Jonathan's lips slid up her neck. He buried his face in her hair. "Why does your hair smell like smoke? Like you were inside a burning building?"

Siena's hands stilled. *Is this Jonathan's subtle way of letting me know he* did *pay his investigators to follow me? That he has a written report of every place I've gone and every person I've spoken to over the last two days? That he knows my story about Gus's mugging is a big, fat fib? Is he taunting me, trying to get me to admit the truth? Well, guess what, Jonathan? That trick may have fooled Marie Lacroix, but it isn't going to work a second time.*

She automatically slipped into her femme fatale persona and created a diversion she'd used so often during her con artist years. She swiveled around and draped her arms around Jonathan's neck. "You need to stop talking," she whispered as she parted her lips and pressed her mouth against his.

****

They lay side by side under the sheets, their legs intertwined. Siena would normally fall into rhythm with Jonathan's steady, shallow breaths and soon be lulled into her own dream state. This evening, however, relaxation eluded her. Something was niggling in the back of her mind, something she couldn't quite put to rest.

With all that had happened in the past two days, she couldn't get Matthew Kramer off her mind. She found it odd that, after persistently hounding her he was now giving her the silent treatment. Would a man so desperate to obtain $5 million allow so much time to pass without responding to her voicemail messages? Especially when she gave him the impression that she'd come to town with a bagful of cash earmarked with his name. Her guess was no.

Or maybe Matthew had returned her call. The last twelve hours had been hectic, and she hadn't taken the time to check the burner phone for messages. Although she hated to leave the coziness of Jonathan's warm body, perhaps giving the phone a quick check would put her mind at rest.

Untangling her body from Jonathan's, Siena slid out of bed and swiped her purse off the dresser. She entered the bathroom, closed the door, and flicked on the light. Her purse was compact, just large enough to carry the essentials, all of which she located inside the bag. All except for the burner phone. *Really?* Siena emptied the purse of all its contents and double-checked. No phone.

That's odd. I had made a habit of keeping the burner phone in this purse to make sure it was always with me. So, if it isn't in this bag, then where the hell—

Oh, no. Oh, God!!

Suddenly, she had the clear memory of being in the lobby of the Hudson that morning and deciding to remove the burner from her purse and place it in the pocket of the cape she was wearing. The cape she'd deemed too heavy for such a warm autumn day. The cape she'd removed and thrown over a hook in the service entrance of Matthew's apartment. Where it was hanging at this exact moment.

That is, unless Matthew had returned home from wherever he'd been the last couple days.

And had attempted to contact her using the burner.

And had tracked down the phone he noticed ringing at the far side of his kitchen.

And was right now holding the evidence in his hand that she'd been snooping around his apartment without his consent.

Shit, shit, SHIT!!

Chapter 34

Siena

Siena returned to bed, but what little sleep she managed to grab came with a price. She had a nightmare about being trapped in a fire. Jonathan was with her, guiding her to safety, then he simply vanished. Surrounded by flames, Siena was alone, unable to escape and terrified. With her heart racing and on the verge of screaming, she startled awake.

The glaring red digits on the bedside clock reported the time was an unforgiving 3:17. She groaned and rolled toward Jonathan. Her esteemed husband, his soul free of guilt and worry, was resting undisturbed.

Exhaling a weary sigh, Siena rolled onto her back. Her thoughts wandered to Gus. Had the mixture of pain killers and scotch settled him into a restful sleep? Or, like Siena, was Gus staring into the darkness unable to stop his mind from replaying the evening's horrific events?

If wishes could come true, she would travel twelve hours back in time and purchase not two but three tickets to last night's basketball game. She'd kiss Gus on the cheek and send him off to have a fun night with Jonathan and Tyler. She would take a leap of faith that Lou would not attempt to double-cross her when they arrived at the Kramer house together. The outcome wouldn't have changed for her, but at least she would have kept Gus out of harm's way.

Gus was her godfather, and Siena didn't doubt that he'd love her regardless of what dangerous schemes she concocted. However, had Siena not dragged him out to Long Island, he wouldn't be facing the strong possibility of needing corrective knee surgery and the potential of having to deal with chronic pain for the rest of his life. Gus held her responsible for his injuries, and rightly so. Gus was also known to hold a grudge, and Siena worried he would shut her out of his life for longer than she could stomach.

And then there was Jacqueline who had expressed her sentiments on the current situation by slamming the bedroom door in Siena's face. But Jac was her twin, and like Gus she would stand by Siena's side no matter what. Jac also had an enormously soft heart, and *un*like Gus had probably already forgiven Siena for her wrongdoings.

With all these frustrations weighing on her mind, Siena spent the next few hours curled up in a ball, exhausted and drowned in self-loathing. Six years ago, avarice and vengeance had led her down a path she never should have followed. Rather than learning from that experience and righting her course, she'd been emboldened by her success. In the intervening years, she'd compromised the reputations of several other men in the sake of furthering her own self-serving goals. When Jonathan whisked her away from New York, she truly believed fate was offering her a fresh start, a way to leave all her regrets behind. That fantasy had been wonderful, but she should have presumed it wouldn't last.

What troubled Siena the most was not knowing how

many other Matthew Kramers had figured out they'd been the target of one of her cons and were also searching for her face in the crowd.

Shortly after daybreak, Siena hauled herself out of bed and into a cold shower which was torture, but exactly what she needed. She opened the shower door to the surprise of Jonathan leaning against the vanity counter. Siena smiled a good morning and thanked him as he handed her a fresh towel.

"How much longer do you expect to stay in New York?" he asked.

Siena kept the left side of her face angled away from Jonathan while she fastened the towel around her. She didn't want him to notice the bruise near her jawline which had morphed overnight from a faint red to a purplish blue. "I'm not sure. Maybe another day or two."

Depending on how much trouble I've gotten myself into by leaving behind evidence that I illegally entered the home of the man who's blackmailing me. I was a professional con artist for most of my adult life. How could I have made such an amateurish mistake?

"Well, as much as I would love to stay in town with you, I just got a notice from the president of Burgess University. An emergency board meeting has been set for four o'clock this afternoon. It's mandatory that I attend."

"Huh."

The good news is, after devoting several hours to fretting over this predicament, I'm ninety-nine percent positive that I had muted the volume on the burner phone. So, the chances of Matthew discovering the phone inside the pocket of my cape are slim to none.

She glanced in the mirror at Jonathan's reflection.

He appeared to be waiting for a response. "I'm sorry, Jonathan. When is your board meeting?"

"Four o'clock. This afternoon, in case you were too preoccupied and missed that part as well."

"Uh-huh."

Plus, there's a high probability Matthew has not yet returned to his apartment. If that's the case, and since I have the keys to his apartment, I can easily get inside and retrieve my cape and the phone without Matthew being any the wiser. I just need to figure out how to get past the security guard.

Siena flipped open the cap on her bottle of facial moisturizer and squirted a dab onto her fingers. "So, what are you saying?"

"That I need to fly back to Burgess by early afternoon. I called Brenda while you were in the shower and asked her to charter a plane for me." He stood close against Siena's back and, placing his hands on her shoulders, kissed the side of her neck. "I don't want you to stay in New York. Come home with me."

Maybe I can bribe the guard. How much should I offer? A hundred? Two? There slides even more of my hard-earned money down the drain.

Siena snapped the lid back onto her deodorant stick. "Jonathan, nothing would make me happier than to go home with you." She gazed at his reflection in the bathroom mirror while she applied body lotion to her arms. "But I'd like to clear out the rest of my apartment while I'm here. It would save me from making another trip to New York. Doesn't that make more sense?"

Jonathan gave up more readily than she would have imagined. "You're right." He rested his chin on Siena's shoulder and squeezed his arms around her waist. "But don't forget we have that charity luncheon to attend on Sunday. Promise me you'll be home by then."

Siena smiled at his reflection as she unzipped her makeup bag. "I promise."

What if the guard becomes indignant, refuses my bribe, and orders me off the premises? Then how will I wheedle my way up to Matthew's apartment? Well, there's always...

"Did I tell you I bumped into Joanie Osgood yesterday morning?"

Jonathan leaned against the vanity and faced Siena while she applied her makeup, a heavy layer to the bruise on her chin before moving on to the rest of her face. "You didn't, but Joanie sent me a text that she'd had you up to their apartment."

Siena nodded. "Yes, and she was disappointed you weren't with me. So, I was thinking…Joanie mentioned that Gaylor rarely goes into the office on Thursdays, and since you have a few hours before your flight, why don't we use the time to pay them a visit? Joanie's favorite bakery, Domani's, is just down the street from the Hudson. We could stop by and pick up some croissants."

"That's an excellent idea. While you're getting yourself together, I'll give them a call." Jonathan tilted his head ever so slightly. "But first, I've been waiting since last night for you to tell me how you got that bruise on your chin."

Siena grimaced. Did she honestly imagine her battered chin would escape Jonathan's scrutiny? "Oh, this?" she asked, faking bewilderment as she touched the bruise with her fingertips. "I'm not sure. I vaguely remember one of Gus's muggers bumping into me when he knocked Gus down. He must have hit me hard enough to cause this bruise."

Jonathan grunted. "Maybe you need to escape New York before you get yourself into some real trouble."

Siena lowered her hand and gazed into Jonathan's eyes. He hadn't glared at her this way since the time they faced off in the early morning hours at his son Patrick's home. Then, he was hinting at his knowledge of her scheme to steal his Somerset Necklace and both Singing Bird Pistols. What hidden message was he sending her this time?

"I'll go make that phone call." He turned his back to Siena and strolled away, closing the bathroom door behind him.

****

Joanie Osgood flung open the door of her co-op at the Hudson and rushed at Siena with outstretched arms. "Siena! Two days in a row! Why, if you lived nearby, I swear I'd insist we start off every day by meeting for breakfast."

Siena chuckled and returned the hug. "I'd certainly be up for that."

"Oh, my!" Joanie held Siena at arm's length. "Siena, what happened to your chin?"

Shit. Even the most expensive makeup on the market won't disguise this nasty bruise.

Before she could respond, Jonathan spoke up. "Siena and her friend were the victims of a mugging yesterday."

Joanie gasped. "Oh, dear heaven, no!

Siena nodded and touched her chin without thinking that—*Ow!*—the bruise was still sore. "Yes. The good news is, we're both okay. Only my friend's cell phone was stolen."

"Well," Joanie said, breathing a sigh of relief, "thank goodness for that."

"Yes, they were both quite lucky. Anyway, good morning, Joanie." Jonathan closed the apartment door and held up a box of baked goods. "Siena insisted we stop at Domani's on our way over to pick up a variety of croissants," he raised his other hand in which he was carrying a paper bag, "plus some fruits and cheeses from the market."

"Jonathan," Joanie cooed, pronouncing his name as though she'd just bitten off a chunk of the world's silkiest, most delectable chocolate. "Dear friend." She placed her hands on either side of Jonathan's face and pecked a kiss that lingered a beat too long on his lips.

Siena raised an eyebrow. *So...seems as though that co-ed torch Joanie carried for Jonathan is still burning strong. What's next? Is Joanie gutsy enough to glance over her shoulder and ask if I wouldn't mind giving them the room?*

Her face still within inches of Jonathan's, Joanie asked, "Are fruits and cheeses your secret to appearing at least ten years younger than the rest of us? Do tell, *please*. At this age, Gaylor and I could use all the advice we can get."

Jonathan grinned. "Sorry, Joanie. I have no special formula, just good genes."

Joanie sighed as she rested her hands on Jonathan's shoulders. "You're right. Your mother, God rest her soul, was the most youthful woman I've ever known. And talk about elegance! Oh my, there I go again. The older I get, the more I tend to reminisce about the past." She wrapped an arm around Jonathan's, then Siena's, and guided them into the apartment. "Where are my manners? Please come in. Let's get those pastries and such on a plate and brew a pot of coffee. How did you know I woke up this morning with a craving for a chocolate croissant from Domani's?"

"Where's Gaylor?" Jonathan asked. "He didn't skip out on us, did he?"

"Oh my, no," Joanie chuckled. "He's in the office with the door closed. The last few years, he's been working from home on Thursdays but only as needed. And, as luck would have it, this morning he was asked to join a conference call at the last minute. I expect it will be over soon, though, and then we'll have him all to ourselves. Now, I'll take that bakery box off your hands while you two have a seat." Joanie rambled on as she set the box on the kitchen island and removed two serving platters from an overhead cupboard. "Tell me, do you prefer coffee or tea? Or should we celebrate this impromptu get-together with mimosas and Bloody Marys? Wouldn't that be fun?"

"Let's start with coffee," Siena interjected the second Joanie paused to take a breath. She flipped open the lid of the pastry box and offered her assistance. "I'll set out the food while you make the coffee."

"Oh, yes, thank you. You're a love for helping." Joanie sauntered over to the coffee maker, detached the water reservoir, and refilled it from the tap. "Now, just the other day I purchased the most delectable Ethiopian blend. However, if you don't like dark roast, we also have—Oh, here's Gaylor. Darling, is your call finished then?"

"Yes, it is." Gaylor stepped up behind Siena and placed his hands on her shoulders. As Siena was, in her heels, an inch or so taller than him, Gaylor rose up on his tiptoes and planted a light kiss on her cheek. "Siena, so good to see you."

"You as well, Gaylor. Thank you for letting us barge in on you like this."

"It's our pleasure." Gaylor smiled broadly as he strolled over to Jonathan with his hand extended. "Romeo, you're looking well. I'd say married life is agreeing with you."

Jonathan shook Gaylor's hand as they man hugged. "Jazz, how are you? And you're right. Married life is wonderful. Siena makes me happier than I've ever been."

Siena cocked her head in bewilderment. "What did you two call each other? Jazz and Romeo?"

"Old college nicknames, dear," Joanie explained. "Pay them no attention and they'll stop. Eventually."

"Fat chance of that happening," Gaylor chided. "Joan, were you thinking of serving coffee in the living room?"

Joanie's head shot up with a start, as though Gaylor had informed her the King of England was about to join them. "Oh!" she blurted out, her eyes wide. "Well, yes, I suppose that would be more comfortable than chatting here in the kitchen. You and Jonathan go on through. Siena and I will be along in a few."

Siena waited for the men to leave the kitchen before steering the conversation in a direction that benefited her. "I love seeing this side of Jonathan's personality."

"What side is that, dear?" Joanie asked while focusing on which buttons to press on the coffee maker.

"The way he behaves around his friends from college. I love hearing about their parties and their frat house pranks. The stories give me insight to what Jonathan was like in his youth."

Joanie opened the cupboard door above her head and withdrew four coffee mugs and small plates. "Yes, I see what you mean. But here's a word of advice from someone who was an eyewitness to most of their antics: Don't take all their stories as the God's truth." She continued to speak while selecting a serving tray from one of the lower cabinets and placing it on the countertop. "Many of the tales they regale us with have been greatly embellished over the years." While arranging the serving pieces on the tray, she asked a favor. "Siena, would you mind rummaging through the fridge for the coffee cream?"

"Be happy to."

"Oh, dear, there I go thinking only of myself and Gaylor and not asking how you and Jonathan prefer your coffee."

Siena chuckled as she swung open the refrigerator door and scanned the shelves. "You're fine. Jonathan drinks his coffee black, and cream is fine with me. Ah, here it is." She closed the door, opened the container, and poured the liquid into the silver creamer situated on the serving tray. Before Joanie launched into another of her lengthy, one-sided conversations, Siena took advantage of being away from the men to bring up the topic that had been weighing heavily on her mind since last evening. "Speaking of the Harvard frat brothers, did you ask the other gentleman who lives in the building to join us this morning? You know, the one you tried calling yesterday while I was here. What was his name again?"

Joanie frowned as she arranged the fruit and cheese on a serving plate. "His name is Matthew. And, no, I didn't invite him. I wouldn't dream of forcing him and Jonathan to be in the same room together."

Siena's back stiffened. "You wouldn't? Why not?"

"Dear girl, you must have noticed by now that Jonathan speaks fondly of all the frat boys, but has he ever once mentioned Matthew Kramer to you?"

Siena dared not respond. She didn't want to appear to be overly interested in Jonathan's relationship with Matthew. Instead, she scrunched her chin and waited for Joanie to continue.

"I thought not." Joanie shot a furtive glance at the doorway leading to the hall, as though concerned Gaylor might walk in and catch her gossiping. "Those two are polar opposites. Jonathan was born with a silver spoon in his mouth; Matthew comes from a blue-collar family. Whereas success has always come so naturally to Jonathan, Matthew's life has been one big struggle. And don't even get me started on their sex lives. You've never met Matthew, so I'll tell you—he's a handsome man with a great physique, even as he's entered his sixties. Now, don't get the wrong idea. I only know this because I've seen him in a swimsuit when we've gone sailing in the Hamptons. Still, the dear man has lost every woman he's ever set his sights on to Jonathan." She rolled her eyes. "Is it any wonder? Two seconds with Jonathan and any fool would understand why. Anyway, all things considered, Matthew has always resented Jonathan, even though Jonathan has bent over backwards to help Matthew. Until a few years ago, that is."

Siena didn't imagine her interest could pique any higher, but she found herself hanging on Joanie's every word. "Why? What happened a few years ago?"

The coffee had finished brewing. Joanie flicked off the coffee maker and poured the fresh brew into a carafe which she placed on the serving tray. "Well, let me ask you this: do you know who Alva Paulson was?"

Siena played dumb. "I think so. Wasn't she the heiress to Paulson Industries?"

"That she was. And such a lovely woman. Sadly, she had a rare illness that did her in at too young an age. Now, I only mention Alva because Matthew was married to her for a few years. They divorced just before she passed because Matthew couldn't, well, keep his eye from wandering to put it nicely. Anyway, the important part of this story is that Matthew would never have met Alva if it hadn't been for Jonathan."

Siena attempted to swallow, but her mouth had gone dry. "Please, don't stop there. How did Jonathan introduce them?"

"Oh, it was quite accidental. Jonathan and Alva grew up together. Their families had been close for years. Someone in the Woodward family was married to one of the Paulsons. I've forgotten the connection, but that's neither here nor there. Anyway, one evening, Jonathan was in town for whatever reason. He and Alva were having dinner out and who did they come across but Matthew. Jonathan was, of course, a gentleman and invited Matthew to join them. When Matthew learned Alva had just come out of her second bad marriage, he turned on the charm and moved right in. Theirs was a whirlwind courtship, as they say, and I don't think Alva was aware that Matthew was cheating on her from the minute they said their *I do's* until he literally got caught with his pants down. That in itself is quite a sordid story for another day."

Siena's face reddened. *How would Joanie react if I informed her that I was the woman who literally pulled Matthew's pants off him?*

"So," Joanie said, "what say we take these trays to our boys before the coffee gets cold."

"I suppose we should." Siena lifted the plates of food while Joanie carried the coffee tray. "I am curious, though. How did Jonathan react to Matthew and Alva's divorce?"

After only a few steps, Joanie set the tray down again on the countertop. "Oh, Jonathan was furious. Matthew made himself out to be the victim, which is so typical of him, but we all knew better. The men pretended to rally around him—you know how fraternity brothers are there for each other through thick and thin." She sighed and shook her head. "Some could forgive and forget, but I don't think Jonathan has seen or spoken to Matthew since Alva's funeral."

The words had barely passed Joanie's lips when Gaylor appeared in the kitchen doorway.

"What's keeping you two? Isn't the coffee brewed by now?"

"Oh, Gaylor, don't be such a fussbudget," Joanie said, again lifting the serving tray but making no attempt to move forward. "We'll be along shortly." She waited for Gaylor to saunter out of earshot before sharing one more morsel of news with Siena. "I must tell you, though. I am worried about Matthew."

Siena's eyes widened. "Why?"

"He hasn't yet returned my call from yesterday morning, the doorman hasn't seen him, and no one in his office has spoken to him since Tuesday. I know because I called there." Her expression took on a frown of concern. "It's as if Matthew has vanished into thin air."

Chapter 35

Siena

"Do you need to leave so soon?" Joanie pouted.

"Sorry, Joanie." Jonathan rose from the sofa and strolled her way. "You know Siena and I would love to stay and gab with you and Gaylor all day, but the driver texted that he's waiting outside to take me to Teterboro." Jonathan leaned down and pecked a kiss on Joanie's cheek.

"Well, you're a treasure for spending your morning with us." Joanie raised her right hand and placed it against the side of Jonathan's neck, keeping his cheek pressed against hers for a few extra seconds.

The gesture was subtle, but not slight enough to escape Siena's notice. Based on the comments Joanie had been dropping, Siena surmised that in her youth Joanie's attempts to win over her favorite frat boy's heart had been in vain, and that for the past forty-five years she'd clung to even the most fleeting of intimate moments with Jonathan—such as this scene playing out right before her eyes. Siena glanced at Gaylor just as he averted his gaze, choosing instead to stare out the window. As he stood beside Joanie on the altar all those years ago, had Gaylor been aware that he was her second choice, the man she had settled for? Was ignoring his wife's displays of affection toward Jonathan his way of coping with Joanie's secret desires? Siena's heart was stung by the pathos.

Siena set her coffee cup on the serving tray. "And since I have a ton of things to take care of, I'll be going as well. Joanie, may I use the facilities before we leave?"

"Of course, dear. You know where the half bath is located, don't you?"

"Yes, I do." Siena placed her hand on Jonathan's arm. "I'll only be a minute. Wait for me, and I'll walk out with you."

****

Inside the elevator, Jonathan punched the button for the lobby. "You and Joanie seem to get along well."

"We do. She's an interesting person. I enjoy talking with her."

Jonathan snickered. "You mean, if you manage to squeeze a word into the conversation."

"Well," Siena said with a grin, "there is that. Do you think she talks to herself when she's alone?"

"I wouldn't doubt it." Jonathan placed his palms on the handrail behind him and leaned back. "I do have a confession to make, though. When we first met, I was attracted to Joanie."

"You were?" Siena hadn't seen that one coming.

Jonathan nodded his head. "Yes. I considered dating her, but after hanging out together a few times I knew, even at that young age, that I could never have serious intentions for a woman who couldn't stop talking long enough for me to kiss her."

Poor Joanie. She might have had a shot at her "Romeo" if only she'd known her proclivity for long-winded chatter was what prevented Jonathan from inviting her up to his room. But I suppose I should be grateful. Her loss was my gain.

"Speaking of kisses…" Jonathan grasped Siena's arm and drew her into an embrace.

"What was that about?" she asked when the kiss ended.

"Nothing. I just had a sudden urge to kiss the woman I did choose to spend the rest of my life with." His wistful eyes danced across Siena's face, as though reminding himself of all the reasons he'd fallen in love with her. Brushing a lock of hair behind her shoulder, he straightened his stance and enveloped Siena in his arms. His next kiss was longer and more ardent. Ending the kiss, he rested his forehead against hers. "Please take this flight home with me," he whispered.

"Jonathan, I…" Siena lowered her head. She didn't care to see the disappointment in his eyes. "I can't."

Releasing her from his arms, Jonathan stepped back. "Fine," he said, his response clipped. "Your flight home tomorrow then is all arranged. In case your plans change, do you have the number to call the charter service?"

"I'm sure I do but let me double-check." The elevator bell dinged, the car stopped, and the doors opened onto the lobby. Siena rummaged through her purse as they exited the elevator. "What the…Where is my phone?" Faking a befuddled expression, she snapped her head up. "Oh!" she said, pretending the light bulb had just gone off. "Jonathan, I think I left my cell phone in the Osgoods' apartment."

"Are you certain it's not in your purse?" The tone in Jonathan's voice gave Siena the impression that he wasn't buying her act. Regardless, she soldiered on.

"I remember now. While I was using their half bath, I got a text from Jac." *Liar.* "After I replied, I'm positive

I set the phone on the vanity while I washed my hands. I must have walked out of the bathroom without it."

Or, I may have left my phone in their half bath on purpose.

Jonathan removed his cell from the inside pocket of his jacket. "I'll call Joanie and ask her to look for it."

Siena placed her hand on his forearm. "No, Jonathan. You've kept your driver waiting long enough. Let's say our good-byes now. Then I'll go back up to their apartment and take care of the matter myself." She placed her hands on Jonathan's cheeks and gave him a light kiss. "I love you. I'll see you when I get home tomorrow afternoon." She pressed the *Up* button, triggering open the doors to the elevator they'd seconds ago vacated.

"I love you, too," Jonathan said as Siena entered the car. "I'll call you after the board meeting. And I'll keep my fingers crossed that you change your mind about this business you need to take care of here in New York."

Siena's brow wrinkled. *This business I need to take care of in New York? That's an odd way of saying "cleaning out your apartment." Could Jonathan be hiding from me the fact that he's aware I'm hiding from him my real reason for being here?* As the elevator doors closed, she caught the sullen expression on Jonathan's face. Siena's frown deepened. That niggle of suspicion had awakened again in the back of her mind. She didn't want to distrust Jonathan, but the sting of the trap he'd set for her once before was still fresh in her mind. The question she dared not answer was whether she believed he was capable of orchestrating the same trick on her a second time.

In case Jonathan was lingering in the lobby and

keeping his eye on which floor the elevator stopped, Siena punched the button for the seventh floor to indicate she was indeed headed to the Osgoods' apartment. However, once on seven she hastened down the hallway to the stairwell and climbed the steps to the twelfth floor. She hadn't told Jonathan a fib; she did intend to return to the Osgoods' to retrieve her phone. She simply needed to salvage a different cell phone from another of the building's residences first.

Siena rushed down the twelfth-floor hall and rang the doorbell to Apartment 1201. While fishing her cotton gloves from her purse, she angled her ear to the door and paid heed to any indication of movement inside the apartment. She waited a minute and rang the bell again. Another minute passed with no response. Convinced she was safe to enter, Siena slid the gloves onto her hands. Unzippering the side pocket of her purse, she yanked out the set of keys she'd snatched from Matthew's foyer yesterday morning. Through a process of trial and error, she hit on the winning combination of keys to locks and gained entry to the apartment.

Ever so gently, in case Matthew or his cheeky girlfriend had merely taken their good old time getting around to responding to the doorbell, Siena opened the front door just far enough to peer inside. She perked up her ears but detected no footsteps, no voices, no music, no television. The apartment was as still as a morgue. Remaining cautious—after all, finding Matthew asleep in bed or behind a closed bathroom door wasn't out of the realm of possibilities—she tiptoed into the foyer and, making barely a sound, closed the door behind her.

Before going any farther, Siena removed her shoes and chucked them into her oversized shoulder bag. With much trepidation, she stepped barefooted across Matthew's foyer and glanced into the living room and down the hallway. The entire apartment was dark, eerily tranquil, and seemingly unoccupied. Her fear of being caught in a home she'd, in essence, broken into subsided as she traveled down the main hall and crossed through the kitchen.

Siena held her breath as she entered the back entrance service area. "Oh, thank God!" There, draped over a hook near the back door right where she'd left it, was her black and gray plaid cape. She shoved her hand into the pockets, first the right, which was empty, then the left, and breathed easily again when her fingers brushed against the burner phone Matthew had given her. Removing the phone from the pocket, she anxiously flipped it open and checked for recent activity. To her bewilderment, rather than finding a series of missed calls and messages from a perturbed Matthew asking where she was and demanding to meet with her asap, the phone's history indicated zero calls had been received. She stared at the screen as if the data she expected would be downloaded at any moment, but nothing happened. She bit her lip as she flipped the cover closed.

Matthew hasn't made one attempt to get in touch with me for two days. So, where the hell is he? And more to the point, what has he done with that damned video?

Her chances of beating Matthew at his own game were growing slimmer by the minute. Although Siena wasn't sure what tactic to follow next, she was certain of one thing: Just because Matthew had been MIA for several days did not guarantee that he wouldn't come cruising through the front door while she was dallying inside his apartment. She tossed the burner phone into her purse, draped the cape over her arm, and headed back toward the foyer.

As she stepped from the kitchen and hastened down the main hallway, Siena detected a faint, intermittent chiming noise. The muscles in her neck tightened. She stopped and glanced over her shoulder toward the apartment's private quarters. Had someone set an alarm clock? Someone who was sleeping in one of the bedrooms and had just awakened? *Shit!* Siena was about to make her quietest, most fleeting dash to the front door when the chiming ended.

Her breath caught. Fearing she was about to encounter the late sleeper who may or may not be Matthew, she dashed into the nearest room, the dining room, and pressed her back against the wall next to the doorway. With her heart hammering inside her chest, she waited several seconds for the sound of a yawn or the padding of bare feet against the carpet runner, but the apartment remained silent. A minute later, when the faint chiming resumed, Siena nearly jumped out of her skin.

She poked her head closer to the doorway and listened intently. After a few seconds, she came to her senses. The chime wasn't coming from an alarm clock but from a cell phone receiving an incoming call. The question was, where was the phone's owner?

Not in this apartment, Siena reasoned, or the call would have been answered by now. And if that phone belonged to Matthew, what better chance would she have to confiscate his cell and destroy the copy of the video it contained? Taking one step at a time, Siena treaded down the hallway. She peered into the rooms she passed, finding each as vacant as the one before it. After more than six years, she was amazed that the layout of this apartment was still so familiar.

The ringing, which Siena was convinced had come from Matthew's bedroom at the end of the hallway, once again stopped. She moved a few steps closer to his bedroom doorway. One glimpse inside the room and Siena was hit with a rush of memories she had no desire to recall yet found impossible to forget.

The chiming resumed. Whoever was calling that cell phone was determined to contact its owner. Siena tiptoed closer to the doorway. She stopped and waited for any sound of a person plodding around the bedroom, opening a drawer, even simply clearing their throat. Believing she was safe, she poked her head through the doorway. The coast appeared to be clear.

The chiming stopped, but not before Siena located the source. She entered the bedroom and trudged directly toward the suit coat laying strewn across the foot of the bed. Patting the coat, she found the cell phone tucked into the inside breast pocket. Siena removed the phone and tapped it, bringing the screen to life. Little good that did her. Without the password or facial recognition, the phone was useless. Still, running with the assumption that this was Matthew's primary cell and that the video of her was stored on this device, the phone Siena held in her fist was worth more to her than gold.

She glanced down at Matthew's suitcoat. Why had he flung his jacket onto the bed as though he'd been in too big a rush to properly hang it? The Matthew Kramer she'd known had many faults, but he'd been fastidious about his appearance. If he'd come into the bedroom to change clothes, he would have hung his suitcoat in the closet, not leave it tossed on the bed to wrinkle. Had he been interrupted? Unexpectedly called away? What could have been so urgent that he'd dash out of the apartment without his jacket or his cell phone?

Unless he'd been forced to leave against his will.

A dreadful chill made her shiver. *Get a grip, Siena. Whatever happened to Matthew isn't your concern. The only thing you need to focus on right now is getting the hell out of this apartment.* She dropped the phone into her purse, intent on exiting the bedroom.

Swinging around on her heels, Siena found herself standing before the infamous mirror hanging above Alva Kramer's dresser. She recalled Matthew telling her that he'd talked Alva into installing a mirror with an intricate design. Leaning over the dresser, her eyes narrowed as she ran her gloved fingers over the frame in search of the hidden camera. Damn! There it was, hiding in plain sight. She'd been such an idiot not to suspect a degenerate like Matthew of wanting to capture his exploits on film.

She swiveled her head around, her discriminating eyes viewing the scene from the hidden lens's perspective. Although the furniture was the same, the bedding was different. Matthew had replaced the lace and ruffles with a masculine design, and throw pillows no longer consumed half the bed. Her gaze traveled upward to the headboard as a vision of herself handcuffing Matthew's wrist to one of the wooden slats sent her mind reeling six years into the past.

Chapter 36

Siena
Spring 2017

Siena gazed through the taxi's rain splattered window and caught sight of the Hudson as it came into view. Her pulse quickened with anticipation. She'd gone over every detail of the devious act she was about to commit inside the historic building's walls at least a dozen times—and had talked herself out of changing her mind at least twice as many.

The driver pulled up alongside a line of parked cars at the building's entrance. Siena paid for the ride and exited the cab, her umbrella shielding her against the wind and the rain. How she envied her sister who was right now lathering her skin with sunscreen and basking in the Caribbean sunshine. *Only a few more years*, Siena promised herself, *and I'll be lying on a beach in Santa Martina beside Jacqueline*. A few years that at the moment seemed more like an eternity. She slammed the taxi door closed and dashed toward the Hudson's canopied entrance.

"Good afternoon, miss," the doorman said. "This sure turned into a nasty day, didn't it?"

Siena switched on the charm as she collapsed her umbrella. "It sure did," she said in her Ellen Randall voice. "Don't y'all hate this cold rain, Russell? Makes me homesick for Virginia."

"I hear you." Russell opened the door for her. "Let's get you inside where it's warm and dry."

"Hey there, Clark," she said to the security guard at the front desk. Ellen Randall had visited Matthew's co-op so often—too often for Siena's liking—that she'd gotten to know the staff by name. For their part, the doormen and guards kept her name, as well as any assumptions they made regarding her frequent visits to Apartment 1201, to themselves. In exchange for their discretion, Matthew tipped them handsomely.

"'Afternoon, ma'am," Clark responded, flashing Siena a smile that flaunted his perfectly straight, ultra white teeth. "How are you today?"

Siena dropped her wet umbrella into the copper stand beside the guard's desk. "I'm well, but I sure could do without this rain."

"Welcome to springtime in New York City," Clark said, his smile fixed firmly in place. "Go on up. Mr. Kramer phoned down to say he's expecting you."

"Thank you."

Siena's heels clacked against the mosaic tile floor as she sauntered across the deserted lobby. Supposedly having traveled straight from her office to the Hudson, she was outfitted in a short skirt over which she had shrugged on a lightweight coat. She didn't need to glance over her shoulder to know that Clark's eyes were following her, admiring the toned muscles of her bare legs. Siena's natural beauty had been attracting the desirous eyes of most men, and the jealous stares of most women, since the day she said good-bye to puberty.

While riding the elevator to the twelfth floor, she reviewed her game plan one last time. In a short while, she'd make the swap—Alva Kramer's $300,000 diamond earrings for Gus's forgeries—without Matthew being any the wiser. Siena bent her head toward one shoulder then the other, her neck cracking against the tension. Only one more hour and Matthew Kramer would be nothing more than another name on her list of successfully completed jobs. Still, Siena was impatient. The next hour couldn't pass quickly enough.

Stepping off the elevator on the twelfth floor, she ambled down the hall to Matthew's apartment. She sucked in a deep breath and rang the bell. Her finger had barely released the buzzer when the door was flung open. There Siena stood, face-to-face with her prey.

In addition to his lascivious grin, Matthew was wearing an easy-to-remove T-shirt and lounge pants. He was evidently ready for the fun to begin. "You're right on time. Come on in, babe."

Siena swore her jaw clenched tighter with each successive time Matthew called her *babe*. Nonetheless, she gave him an enticing smile as she strolled into the apartment. "I've always had this thing about being punctual," she said, tossing her coat and handbag onto the Louis XIV chair Alva utilized as a decorative piece for the foyer. Matthew was instantly at Siena's back, his arms cinched around her.

"Mm…You smell wonderful." He nuzzled his face against her neck and pecked a series of kisses upward toward her ear. He obviously didn't want to waste any time, which was fine with Siena. The faster she got this job done the sooner Matthew would be out of her life forever.

"Matthew, I'm hardly through the door," she giggled. Ellen Randall was such a flirt.

"Babe, you know as well as I do," he said as he spun her around to face him, "today, time is of the essence." Placing his hand on the back of her head, he parted his lips and planted his mouth over hers.

****

Siena sauntered out of Alva Kramer's bathroom and found Matthew standing by the windows on the opposite side of the bedroom. Positioned in front of the windows were two matching easy chairs between which sat an antique wooden trunk that doubled as a table. Placed on the trunk was a silver tray holding a bottle of chilled wine and two crystal glasses. At Ellen Randall's request, Matthew had opened a vintage bottle from Alva's wine collection.

He lifted a remote-control device from the window ledge and lowered the shades. Siena lips formed a mischievous grin. *A darkened room is all the better to trick you with, my dear.*

Matthew's eyes burned with desire as Siena padded barefoot across the carpeted floor. He tossed the remote control onto one of the chairs. "Babe, you look so damned hot in red silk." He drew her into his arms. "Did you borrow one of Alva's robes from her closet?"

Is he serious? Does he honestly believe that I, the woman he's having an extramarital affair with, would have the audacity to seduce him in his wife's lingerie? Of all the men I've conned, Matthew wins the prize for being the most shameless.

"No, Matty," she giggled. "This is my robe." She rested her arms on his shoulders and wiggled up against him. "I was thinking of you when I bought it."

"Is that so? Well, I'm more interested in seeing you in the red bra and panties you promised to buy especially for me." He tugged one end of the robe's sash, but Siena slapped his hand away.

"Matty, slow down," she teased while retying the bow and ignoring Matthew's scowling face. "Let's take it easy and savor the afternoon." She planted a kiss on his lips before glancing over at his makeshift bar. "Has the wine had enough time to breathe?"

He shrugged his shoulder and grunted. "Probably."

"Well…" Siena slinked a finger across his cheek and down the cleft in his chin. "Are you going to be a gentleman and pour me a glass?"

Matthew snickered. "You Southern belles." He sauntered toward the windows and lifted the wine bottle from the ice bucket.

"Oh, now," Siena said, pleased that she'd honey-talked her way back into his good graces, "if you think I'm high maintenance, you should meet some of my girlfriends from back home."

As Matthew filled their glasses, he raised a suggestive eyebrow. "If they're as sexy as you, please invite them to visit. My bed can accommodate more than just you and me—assuming that's what you have in mind."

And I thought he couldn't be any more nauseating.

Matthew returned to Siena's side and handed her one of the wine glasses. "Matty," she said, "don't think for one red hot minute that I'd ever share you with another woman." She sipped her wine sparingly. The ruse she was about to execute required her to be stone-cold sober.

He downed a generous gulp from his own glass and inched closer. "Well, if you ever change your mind, just say the word." He kissed the side of Siena's neck as his fingers trailed down her spine. When he palmed her ass, Siena's instinctive reaction was to run for the door as fast as her feet could take her. *Stay in the game, Siena. Don't blow your opportunity.* She seized a fistful of Matthew's T-shirt and backstepped across the room, drawing him closer to the bed.

"I'll keep that in mind." She set her wine glass on the dresser top and addressed Matthew's reflection in the mirror. "Speaking of doing kinky things, I watched a movie once about a man who had this fetish. Whenever he was with his girlfriend, he couldn't get turned on unless she was wearing a certain piece of jewelry."

Matthew set his glass next to Siena's. "Oh, yeah?" Standing behind her, he placed his hands on her waist and slid them forward. "And when have I ever needed anything but your body to get me excited?" Grasping the sash, he made another attempt to untie her robe. Siena again slapped his hands away.

"Matty," she chided, placing her arms over his and holding them in place. "I said to slow down. You know how I like to be romanced. Come on, let's spice things up! Let's pretend I'm a model and you're my photographer and we're doing a shoot for one of those adult magazines. Every time you adorn me with a piece of diamond jewelry, I'll remove one piece of clothing and strike a pose while you pretend to take my picture."

Matthew placed his chin on her shoulder and pouted. "All right. If you insist."

"Oh, now, it'll be fun. I promise." Siena bit her lower lip and wrinkled her brow. "The only problem is, since I didn't plan this game in advance, I didn't bring any of my own jewelry." She pivoted around and gazed at Matthew with pleading eyes. "Do you think we could borrow some pieces from your wife's collection?"

Matthew smirked. "I guess what Alva doesn't know won't hurt her." He planted a kiss on the side of Siena's neck. "Speaking of jewelry, I have a surprise for you." He crossed over to the nightstand on the right side of the bed.

Siena kept her eyes glued to Matthew, wary of what he might be planning to spring on her. "What kind of surprise?" she asked, forcing herself to sound tickled with excitement.

Matthew plucked a box off the nightstand and strolled back toward her. "I was going to give you this present later on, but now that you want to play this game…" He handed Siena a long, thin jewelry box. "Here's a nice something I found that I thought would look perfect on you."

A flush of guilt ignited in Siena's neck and spread to her face. Why did Matthew wait until now to turn into a nice guy? Not that his gift could persuade her to change her mind about finishing the job. Among the many skillful traits Siena possessed was the ability to ignore her conscience.

"Matthew, what is this?" Siena forced her jaw to drop as she pulled off an expression of delight but when she lifted the lid her reaction turned genuine. Contained inside the box was a pendant of diamonds attached to a silver necklace. The diamonds were arranged in a swirled geometrical design. A solitary ruby that appeared to be half a carat larger than the diamonds was inserted along the upper left curve. Her breath caught. For reasons she couldn't explain, Siena developed an immediate connection with this necklace, as though the designer had a window into her soul and had created the piece with her in mind.

"Oh, my goodness!" Taking the necklace into her hand, Siena set the empty jewelry box on the dresser. She gazed into the mirror, draped the piece around her neck, and fastened the clasp. "This is beautiful," she said, her voice breathy as she ran her fingertips over the jewels.

"Do you like it?" Matthew asked. He pressed up against her back and placed his hands on her shoulders.

"I don't just like it. I love it." She met his gaze in the mirror. "Thank you so much, Matty."

"You're welcome. Now, if I'm not mistaken," his fingers once again grasped the sash to her robe, "I believe you owe me one article of clothing."

****

Siena halted Matthew's hands as they slid up her back to the hook of her bra.

"Oh, no you don't," she reprimanded. "Nothing else comes off until I adorn myself with another piece of jewelry."

"Mm…" Matthew grunted. Having decreed that he would also remove an article of clothing each time Siena did, he was now shirtless. His hands snaked down her backside as he gazed into her eyes. "What do you want? A ring? A bracelet?" He nodded his head toward the walk-in wardrobe area that separated the bedroom and the bath. "Help yourself to Alva's jewelry collection. She has plenty of rings and bracelets to choose from."

"We-l-l-l…" Siena drew out the word as though stretching back the rubber band on a slingshot. She twirled a lock of Matthew's hair around her finger. "I sure did fall in love with those earrings I arranged to have appraised for you." She held her breath as she waited for Matthew's response. Since she was holding a wild afternoon of passion over his head, she expected he'd be cooperative. However, if need be, she was willing to grovel.

To Siena's dismay, Matthew hesitated. He knitted his brow and shook his head. "Oh, babe, I don't know. Those earrings…" Suddenly, a sly grin took over his face. "You know what?" Matthew narrowed his eyes. "Alva would be so pissed if she knew a hot babe like you was wearing a pair of earrings her father had given her. Excuse me, a *naked* hot babe like you." To seal the deal, Siena clenched her hand around the nape of Matthew's neck and gave him a kiss he wouldn't soon forget. "Give me a minute to get her earrings from the safe. I'll be right back." He kissed her again and hastened toward Alva's dressing room.

Siena waited until Matthew had disappeared around the corner. Her heart was in her throat as she rushed to her robe which lay at the foot of the bed where Matthew had tossed it. From the pocket, she withdrew a small plastic vial.

In her apartment that morning, Siena had crushed two sleep aid tablets into a powder form, then poured the powder into the vial. While in Alva's bathroom, she'd transferred the vial from her handbag to the pocket of her robe. Acting as fast as her fingers would work, she unscrewed the vial's cap while hustling over to the wine glasses sitting atop the dresser. She emptied the vial into Matthew's wine glass and dissolved the powder by giving the liquid a swirl with her index finger. Scurrying back to the bed, she returned the vial to the pocket of her robe. When Matthew reentered the bedroom, she was calmly standing before the mirror admiring the necklace he'd given her.

"Here you go, babe." He placed the open earring box on the dresser before her. "Your wish is my command." He leaned his backside against the dresser and trailed his finger down Siena's arm. "But do we really need to keep playing this silly game?"

Siena sulked like a child upset at not getting her way. "Yes, Matty. We agreed. One piece of jewelry," she said as she attached a diamond earring to her right earlobe and positioned herself between Matthew's legs, "one piece of clothing. Then we drink some wine," she lifted Matthew's wine glass to his lips and made sure he took a healthy gulp, "and play around some more before finishing the game." She placed her cheek against his and whispered into his ear, "It's called foreplay," while mentally crossing her fingers that the sedative would kick in before she got around to inserting the second earring into her other earlobe.

"Okay." Matthew wrapped his arms around Siena, his fingers going straight for the hook on her bra. "But first, you owe me another piece of clothing."

****

Siena cajoled Matthew into swigging down all the wine in his glass. She poured him another glass and, pretending to be hungry, sent him to the kitchen in search of cheese and crackers. As thunder rolled in the distance, she ran to the window and faked being interested in which direction the storm was heading. She teased and continued to play her game of hard-to-get, employing every stall tactic possible to avoid intimacy. She was biding her time, all the while keeping a keen eye on Matthew. Fifteen minutes had passed. At any moment, she was certain his eyelids would begin to droop.

****

Five minutes later, Matthew lifted Siena into a fireman's carry and announced they were done playing games. Stretched across the bed and pinned under his weight, Siena barely detected Matthew's moans and whispered endearments over the noise of her own voice screaming inside her head.

Why the hell didn't I grind three *pills into that vial this morning?*

Chapter 37

Siena
Spring 2017

The drug hit Matthew with the force of a wrecking ball. One moment he was making an inane joke—"Babe, you'd make a damned sexy pirate with this shirtless, one-earring look you've got going on!"—and the next, he was speaking nonsense and slurring his words. Siena propped herself up on her elbow and savored his tumble into dreamland with a cockeyed grin on her face.

Matthew appeared to be out cold, but Siena wanted proof. She poked him in the ribs and shouted into his ear but received no more response than a snort and a grumble. Even when a flash of lightning lit up the room and was chased by a crack of thunder that shook the entire building, Matthew didn't budge. Siena was confident he wasn't going to wake any time soon. At the least, he'd be comatose long enough for her to carry out the remainder of her plan and vanish into anonymity.

Rain pelted hard against the windows. The raging storm had created a chill in the room, making Siena acutely aware of her state of undress. She shivered and wrapped her arms across her chest as she gathered up her bra from the floor beside the bed and her panties from one of the easy chairs across the room. While slipping on her undergarments, she scurried into the bathroom, retrieved her handbag, and dug to the bottom for a pair of jeans and a long-sleeved knit shirt. The warm clothing immediately chased the goosebumps off her flesh.

Siena carried her bag into the bedroom, dropped it on the dresser top, and fished out all the articles essential to completing the job. She began as always by sliding on a pair of cotton gloves, a staple in every handbag she owned, and set about tackling the most important task first. Tossing a pair of handcuffs from one hand to the other, she strolled over to the bed and tickled Matthew's foot, testing his responsiveness. When he merely grunted and flexed his ankle, she was confident she had the green light to proceed.

Climbing onto the bed, she dropped the handcuffs and anchored herself on the mattress. Firmly gripping Matthew by his armpits, she yanked his body clockwise, grunting and groaning with the effort and grabbing the headboard several times to catch her balance. A mattress that adjusts to your every movement is wonderful while you're sleeping, but a nuisance when struggling to maneuver a grown man's deadweight body. By the time she'd gotten Matthew centered on the bed, the sheets were in disarray, the pillows had been tossed about, and the handcuffs were nowhere to be found.

"Dammit," Siena cursed through gritted teeth. She couldn't afford to waste even one second of time. "Where the hell…" She patted the bedding, lifted the sheets, and at last found the cuffs hiding under one of the over-sized bed pillows.

She snapped one of the cuffs around Matthew's right wrist and, dragging his arm over his head, attached the other cuff to one of the slats on the wooden headboard. Siena sat back on her haunches and studied

Matthew for any indication of consciousness. When he began to snore lightly, she grinned and laid her hand on his chest. "Thanks for being such a good sport, Matty."

Bounding off the bed, she rushed into Alva's wardrobe area and collected her shoes and the skirt and blouse she'd been wearing when she entered the apartment. Back in the bedroom, Siena reversed her handbag to show the black lining on the outside. She pitched the shoes into the bottom of her bag, then stuffed in her rolled-up skirt and blouse beside the shoes. Lifting her robe off the carpet at the foot of the bed, she folded and tossed it into the bag as well.

Next, she needed to stage the scene. Siena unzipped one of the compartments in her handbag and withdrew a small pair of scissors. She snipped the price tags off a lacey black bra and matching panties, dropped the scissors and the tags into her purse, then flung the undergarments haphazardly onto the bed as though they'd been discarded in the heat of passion.

On to the wine goblets. She carried both glasses to the bathroom and washed their contents down the sink's drain. She rinsed the glasses, wiped them dry, and carried them back to the bedroom. Using a tube of red lipstick, she swiped a stain resembling a woman's lower lip on the rim of one goblet. To give the impression Matthew's rendezvous with his lady friend had gone on for a while, she poured the remaining wine into the glasses, more in hers than in Matthew's, and glanced around the room. *Where would I like Matthew's wife to find her elegant tulip-shaped crystal wine goblets?* The nightstand, Siena decided, was the ideal place.

A thorough wipe of every surface in the bedroom with a soft cloth ensured that she left no fingerprints behind. The rest of the apartment didn't concern her. Siena had been careful not to touch any doorknobs or pieces of furniture before entering the bedroom. Besides, Matthew had told her Alva employed a cleaning woman who vacuumed and dusted the entire apartment every morning. Therefore, any evidence she'd left behind during her previous visits had already been erased.

She had one last order of business to attend to—altering her appearance. As of that second, Ellen Randall no longer existed. Siena stood before the dresser mirror and removed first the pins that held Ellen's short chestnut hair in place, then the wig itself. All items were placed in a plastic bag and added to the paraphernalia inside Siena's oversized purse. She wiped off all her makeup and fluffed her blonde hair with her fingers. Then, erring on the side of caution, she popped in her blue Marie Lacroix contact lenses. Once Siena exited the Hudson and journeyed along the streets of Manhattan, she ran the risk of bumping into someone who might recognize her from her legitimate career, which meant she needed to look the part. Siena Ricci may be many things, but she wasn't a woman who made foolish mistakes.

"And, finally, Matthew," Siena said to his motionless reflection in the mirror as she unfastened his wife's diamond earring from her right earlobe, "I get to take care of the reason I cozied up to you in the first place." After placing the earring next to its mate in Alva's jewelry box, she flipped open the case she'd removed from her handbag and swapped Gus's forgeries for the genuine pair. She admired the sparkling jewels one last time—why were diamonds so mesmerizing?—before tucking the case inside the zippered compartment of her handbag.

Siena breathed a sigh of relief. The exchange had been made, and tonight she and Gus would celebrate her success over dinner. Setting Matthew up for this con ranked as one of the most unpleasant jobs she'd ever pulled off, but the outcome was worth every irritating second of every miserable minute she'd spent with him. Her biggest consolation was in knowing that, once she was gone from this apartment, she and Matthew Kramer would never cross paths again.

As if sensing he was in Siena's thoughts, Matthew grunted and kicked his leg. Siena gasped. Were the meds wearing off already? She twisted her torso around, expecting to meet his eyes staring back at her. What she witnessed instead was Matthew, still in a deep sleep, making a futile attempt to roll into a different position.

"Sorry, Matthew," she said, her pulse slowing. "I'm afraid you won't be going anywhere for a while." Matthew whimpered and settled back into his corpse-like state.

Okay, Siena. That brief interruption was a warning to wrap up this job and get your ass the hell out of here.

She grabbed the last weapon in her arsenal off the dresser and bounced it in the palm of her hand. This little item would be the *coup de grâce* that, when Matthew came to, would drive him out of his mind. She sauntered over to the nightstand and draped a chain holding the key to the handcuffs over the rim of his wine glass. Oh, the names Matthew would call her as he contorted his body, grunting and groaning and grousing, as the key (she prided herself on the pun) to his salvation taunted him just inches out of his reach.

If vengeance isn't meant to be this gratifying, then

why am I smiling?

The time had come to pack up and leave. Siena rubbed one gloved hand across the top of the dresser, wiping it clean, and positioned the open jewelry box containing the bogus earrings front and center. The earrings stared at Matthew as though they were a pair of accusatory eyes intent on judging his integrity. *Matthew,* they seemed to imply, *this is the treatment you deserve for being a lying, greedy, and above all, disloyal husband.*

Siena had one last issue to deal with—what to do about the necklace Matthew had given her. She glanced at her reflection in the mirror, her index finger tracing the swirl of diamonds and stopping on the single ruby. She bit her lower lip and fought with her conscience. "I adore this necklace, Matthew, and even though my gut tells me it came straight out of your wife's jewelry safe, I'm going to choose to believe you were telling the truth when you inferred that you'd purchased it for me." She unhooked the necklace, secured it in its box, and dropped the box into her purse. "So, thanks again for your generous gift. I'd like to say I'll think of you fondly each time I wear it, but I don't want to pile another lie on top of all the others I've been feeding you."

Siena slung her handbag over her shoulder and padded across the bedroom carpet. She paused in the doorway and performed one last scan of the room, ensuring everything was in its proper place and that she was leaving no trace of her identity behind. Also, she couldn't leave without saying farewell to Matthew.

"Well, Matthew, after today I hope you'll think twice about picking up strange women in bars." Turning away, she had an afterthought. "Oh, and in case you haven't figured this out yourself, Ellen Randall isn't my real name so don't waste your time trying to track me down. You'll never in a million years find me." With her lips curled into a sardonic grin, Siena blew a good-bye kiss. "So long, Matty. Have fun weaseling your way out of this one."

Siena sauntered down the hallway that led to the foyer, her focus shifting to Gus. Oftentimes, after the con was completed, she'd use a runner to transport the acquired goods from a predesignated location to Gus's hands, but tonight she'd make the delivery herself. Siena had been concerned for Gus since he'd confided that his revenues were down, and she wanted to present him with a surprise in addition to the diamond earrings. Something to help him get out of his slump.

Gus had a buyer who collected Italian majolica pottery and Siena had noticed an exquisite eighteenth-century vase of that style in the Kramers' living room. She identified the artist by his signature marking on the underside of the base and had consulted with the experts in majolica pottery at Willow's. The piece, Siena's colleagues informed her, was valued at $20,000.

Siena grasped the vase with both hands and lifted it off the living room shelf. She stole a moment to admire the intricate design and multitude of colors that, due to the unique firing and glazing technique, were as vibrant today as they were three hundred years ago. Gus's client would be delighted to add this piece to his collection, but not nearly as pleased as Gus would be when Siena, refusing to take her standard cut, insisted that Gus keep the entire profit for himself. She unzipped her handbag and removed a pair of flat-heeled shoes. The vase fit snugly in their place.

A framed portrait of Alva Kramer hung on the wall adjacent to the bookshelves. Siena spent a moment admiring how skillfully the artist had captured her essence. As part of her research for this job, Siena had delved deeply into Alva Kramer's background. Every article she unearthed had portrayed Alva as a woman held in high esteem, a benevolent and generous person of considerable influence who threw her weight behind a select number of organizations focused on eradicating poverty and bringing clean, potable water to underdeveloped countries. Now, tragically, her life was being cut short by an illness even the world's most renowned medical experts could not cure. And who was she leaning on for love and support through her final days? Her louse of a husband.

Alva Kramer was a remarkable woman who deserved better. Perhaps, Siena surmised, Alva had relatives and close friends who were on to Matthew's game. Perhaps they'd whispered the cold truth in her ear, and perhaps Alva had chosen to dismiss their warnings as idle gossip. Such speculation shouldn't have been Siena's concern, and admittedly she'd overstepped her bounds, but if that were the case—if Alva wasn't inclined to accept what she heard—perhaps she'd believe what she saw. And nothing, Siena was certain, would convince Alva of her husband's true colors more than the scene Siena had created for her to walk in on when she returned home that evening.

The mantel clock chimed, announcing the hour and reminding Siena that she was wasting precious time. She was about to exit the living room when she stopped short and did a double take. Why had she never noticed the piece hanging on the wall near the doorway to the foyer?

The painting was small, maybe fourteen by eighteen inches, and depicted a simple yet captivating geometrical design in monochromatic shades with a singular crimson dot in the upper curve. The intriguing aspect, and the reason Siena was captivated by the piece, was that the design in the painting was an exact replica of the necklace Matthew had given her.

She examined the bottom corner for the artist's signature, expecting to find the signing of Picasso or O'Keefe or Warhol. Instead, the painting was that of an unfamiliar artist, *P. A. Woodward.* Maybe Alva had purchased the piece at a gallery in SoHo, a work she took a liking to by a struggling painter she wanted to support. Still, Siena's curiosity was piqued. Had the same artist crafted the necklace as well? Siena shrugged her shoulders. She could do the research but, in the end, what did it matter?

Siena snatched up the coat she'd tossed onto Alva's Louis IV chair in the foyer. At the front door, she slipped on her shoes and allowed herself one last glance at the apartment. Matthew was right. She would enjoy calling such an opulent residence her home, but only if she could share it with the ideal man who would one day enter her life and utterly capture her heart. Siena heaved a sigh. Too bad her perfect man would drop her in a hot second when he learned of her tainted past.

Oh, well. A girl can dream.

She opened the door and exited the apartment, making certain the lock clicked in place as she yanked the door closed behind her.

Chapter 38

Siena
October 2023

Siena recalled how regret had begun creeping into her bones the moment she'd closed the door on the Kramers' apartment that afternoon, although she was never sure what bothered her more—her reckless behavior or how pleased she was with the outcome. Over the years, she kept reminding herself that she'd committed such a heinous act as a favor to Matthew's wife, but that mantra was merely a ploy to ease her guilt. Now, six years later, she believed that having to deal with the consequences was a justifiable punishment.

Karma could be such a bitch.

Regardless, she hadn't broken into Matthew's residence to waste time staring at his bed's headboard and ruminating over the past. She locked up the incident in her memory bank where it belonged and trod out of the bedroom. She would return Matthew's keys to the bowl in the foyer from which she'd "borrowed" them and exit the apartment for the absolute last time.

As she scurried down the hall, Siena glimpsed into the multitude of sparsely furnished and, she speculated, rarely used rooms she passed along the way. What sort of deal had Matthew struck with the Paulson estate that granted him the privilege of continuing to reside in this grand apartment? She couldn't imagine why he'd even want to live there. The place was far too spacious for one person, not to mention the huge drain the upkeep must have on his income. But then, Matthew had always been overly concerned with appearances. For the chance to drop a *Me? Oh, I have an apartment in the Hudson, twelfth floor* into every conversation—well, she imagined Matthew would happily hand over his last dime to purchase those bragging rights.

Siena slowed her pace as she approached the farthest doorway on the left, the one which led to Matthew's office. When she passed this room a scant ten minutes ago, she hadn't noticed that the door was semi-closed, nor that the room was in partial darkness. A chill ran up her spine. She glanced over her shoulder. Was someone else in the residence? Someone who'd slinked into the office and shuttered the windows against the bright sunlight while she was daydreaming at the far end of the hall? Someone who was waiting to pounce on her as she strolled by, unsuspecting? She took a cautious step closer and peered into the room.

What in the hell?

Now fearing she had stumbled upon a crime scene, Siena extended her arm through the doorway and slid her hand along the wall until her fingers touched a light switch. She flicked on the ceiling light and swung the door open farther while her eyes swept over the disheveled mess before her. An armchair had been tossed onto its side. The desk lamp was knocked over, its shade broken. Every drawer in Matthew's desk was laid open and the contents were strewn across the top of the desk and on the surrounding floor. Siena slowly exhaled the breath she'd been holding. The room was a mess, but at least she hadn't stumbled across Matthew's dead body splayed out across the plush Oriental rug in a pool of his own blood.

Behind the desk, a painting that was used to conceal the wall safe had been swung open and was hanging by a hinge. The safe had been opened—or broken into, judging by the condition of the room. Apparently, whoever did this damage had not been concerned about covering up the fact that they had plundered the room in search of anything worth pilfering.

Siena's jaw dropped. When did this happen? She'd stood outside the office door yesterday morning as the nurse at Irene Kramer's facility left a voice message for Matthew, but she'd had no reason to enter the room or even glance inside. Other than herself, the only people whom Siena was certain had been in the apartment in the last two days were Matthew's influencer girlfriend and Imelda, his housekeeper. Girlfriend was too wrapped up in her own drama to have noticed if something in the apartment was amiss. Imelda could have stumbled upon this mess, but Siena doubted she'd have registered her finding with the building manager for fear of falling under suspicion and, depending on her immigration status, facing possible deportation.

She stood in the doorway, fists on hips, and pondered several perplexing questions. Had the office been in this state of disarray yesterday, or did this invasion happen between the time Imelda finished her cleaning duties and this morning? Had Matthew, in a fit of rage, done this damage himself, or was this evidence of a home burglary? That conjecture led her to question how a robber could have gotten past the security guard in the lobby. She supposed the guard could have been in on the crime. Or the burglar could have bribed the guard into letting him enter the residential floors. *Or,* and this she deemed the most likely scenario, the intruder had strolled into the building as Matthew's guest—the same method she'd used six years ago to gain access to this apartment and Alva Kramer's jewelry.

If the latter were the case, what might have happened to Matthew after the thief successfully completed the heist? Was he lying unresponsive in an alley somewhere in the bowels of Manhattan? According to the phone conversation on which Siena had eavesdropped yesterday morning, Girlfriend's family seemed capable of such brutality. But then, based on Gus and Marielle's observations of the goings-on in Eddie Davis's poker room, Eddie's thugs may have performed some unthinkable deeds and disposed of Matthew's body in a place never to be discovered. The best-case scenario was that Matthew, under threat and terrified, had taken whatever cash he had on hand and left town voluntarily before any of the people to whom he owed money could get to him. Siena wanted to believe that right now he was enjoying a cocktail at a beach bar in the South Pacific—with or without his influencer girlfriend by his side.

She eyed the gaping door to the safe and hoped with all her heart that, whoever the violators of this room were, they had strictly been interested in looting Matthew's cash and jewelry and had left all the safe's other contents behind—such as a particular camera they may have come across. After all, how much resale value does a small digital camera have these days?

Tiptoeing around the debris covering the floor, Siena dropped her purse and cape on top of the desk and approached the safe. Her heart was racing as she grasped the edge of the safe's door and pried it fully open. Inside, she uncovered a stack of tri-folded documents which she rifled through—Matthew's will, a couple of life insurance policies, legal paperwork pertaining to his business. Shoved toward the back was a little leaguer's baseball glove and an album containing photos from Matthew and Alva's wedding.

So, Matthew has a sentimental side. Who'd have thought?

After emptying the safe of all its contents, Siena ran her gloved hand along the inside to ensure she hadn't overlooked any items that might be taped to a wall or notches in the surface that could be maneuvered to gain passage into a hidden compartment. Discovering nothing, she tossed the contents she'd removed back into the safe and pounded her fist against the wall.

"Dammit!"

She swiveled around. Refusing to give up hope, Siena surveyed the room in search of anything she may have overlooked. The desk, with its drawers flung open and emptied, was worthy of deeper inspection. Unlike Jonathan's antique library desk with its many hidey-holes, Matthew's desk was a sleek, modern design. Still, she smoothed her hand over and underneath every surface. Again, she found nothing. Her narrowed eyes scanned the room. Where else would Matthew conceal an item that he didn't want anyone to find?

Nowhere. At least not in this room. No bookshelves lined the walls, no artwork veiled a second wall safe, and no furniture aside from the overturned armchair filled the empty spaces. She was wasting her time. Huffing, Siena lifted her shoulder bag and cape and was stepping away from the desk when her foot kicked the answering machine connected to Matthew's home phone. She glanced down and noticed the message light was blinking. Her conscience warned her not to do it, but since she'd already crossed the invasion of privacy line…

Dropping her purse and cape back onto the desktop, Siena knelt next to the recorder and pressed the playback button. The electronic voice announced *You have five messages*. The first was the message the nurse at Irene Kramer's assisted living facility had left yesterday morning. The next two were from charities seeking donations. The fourth message was from Irene herself.

"Matthew," Irene spat out, "this is your mother. Where have you been? I haven't heard from you in two months. Don't you know a son is supposed to call his mother every day? Shame on you!" A lengthy pause followed during which Siena detected sounds of the phone being jostled around. Then, Irene issued a reminder. "Matthew, this is your mother. Call me." Several beeps sounded, as if Irene had punched random buttons on her phone in search of the one that would end the call. "Oh, now, which one is it?" she muttered. More beeping followed until the call finally ended.

The fifth and last message was a second call from the nurse at Elmwood.

"Hi, Matthew," the overly pleasant voice said. "This is Shonda from Elmwood again. I didn't see that we received a call from you regarding the message I left on your machine yesterday, so I hope all is well. Anyway, I just wanted to follow up on my previous message. Turns out there's no need to worry about that camera your mom was in a fuss about yesterday. One of our aides told me she was present in the room when Irene gave the camera to one of her visitors. Looks like the camera isn't missing after all, and Irene is back to being her normal, happy self again. I think she's forgotten the incident altogether, so there's no need for you to call me back unless you feel you need to. I'll also leave this same message on your cell phone just in case you're not checking calls on this number any longer. Thanks, Matthew. Have a great day."

The machine beeped. The electronic voice said *End of messages.*

Siena chewed on the inside of her cheek. Although this new bit of information was quite enlightening, the notion that another person was now in possession of Matthew's camera complicated the situation. She needed to make an immediate trip to Elmwood Assisted Living Facility to investigate who beside herself had paid Irene Kramer a recent visit.

While listening to the messages, Siena had been staring at the wall behind the desk, the wall directly beneath the safe. She scrunched her chin. Something about the wainscoting was off. In the bottom left corner of the panel, the trim didn't meet to form a 90-degree angle. She duckwalked to the wall for a closer look and discovered a hole in the paneling just large enough to accommodate a pinky finger. Her pulse quickened as she recalled the latch to the secure hiding place in the bedroom closet of Matthew's now smoldering-in-ashes childhood home. Siena inserted a gloved finger and located a notch. With a tug and a snap of the latch, the wall panel popped open.

The space, having been built into an outside wall, was wide but less than a foot deep, just large enough to conceal a brown leather travel bag. A bag that appeared disturbingly identical to the tote Bill had loaded into the back of the SUV when he drove her and Jonathan to Manhattan earlier that week. *Hmm...* She took a deep breath and grasped the handles.

Siena was no weakling but when she attempted to lift the bag, its contents proved heavier than she'd expected. Standing to give herself better leverage, she dragged the satchel onto the floor and rolled it onto its side. There, stamped into the smooth brown leather, were the initials *JCW*—the monogram of Jonathan Collier Woodward.

The hairs on Siena's arms stood on end. Why the hell was a travel bag that belonged to Jonathan hidden inside a covert panel in Matthew's apartment? And what was weighing it down? In one impulsive move, she tugged the zipper across the top and thrust the sides open. All the air seemed to escape the room as she stared into a tote brimming with bound stacks of $100 bills. Dozens of them. Siena collapsed onto her knees. She lifted one of the packs and fanned the edge with her fingers. By rough count, each stack contained fifty bills. She was staring at, ballpark, half a million dollars.

All this time I've been fretting over the secrets I've kept from Jonathan when he's been conducting his own shady business behind my back! Is this what Jonathan's impromptu visit to his friend Mack, a name he'd never mentioned before this past Monday, was all about? Jonathan did seem awfully eager to change the subject when I asked him about his visit with Mack during our phone conversation the other night. So, if Mack is truly Matthew Kramer, then does this money have anything to do with the voice mail message left by Irene Kramer's nurse?

Matthew's cell phone rang. Anxious to discover

who had been attempting so persistently to contact Matthew, Siena jumped up and rushed to her handbag. Desperate to locate the phone before the ringing stopped, she rummaged through her purse in a frenzy. Digging the phone from the bottom of her bag, she stood behind the desk and gazed with unbelieving eyes at the caller ID. What were the chances Matthew had more than one person in his contact list who went by the name *Romeo*?

Siena hit the green phone icon and connected with the caller. "Yeah?" she grunted in as deep a voice as she could muster.

"Matthew!" Jonathan's voice bellowed from the speaker. Siena sunk into the desk chair, her stomach roiling. "I've been trying to get in touch with you for the last two days. Why are you ignoring my calls? Have you listened to any of my voicemail messages?"

Siena rested her head against her free hand and massaged her forehead. The headache she'd been plagued with yesterday was making a vicious comeback.

"Are you there? Matthew!" The longer he went without receiving a response, the more agitated Jonathan's voice grew. "I thought you'd at least be man enough to call and explain why you ditched me the other day. Or are you too spineless to offer me an apology?" He paused, as if waiting for a reaction, then let out a disgruntled snort. "You'll never change, will you? As many times as I've bent over backwards to help you, all you can do is take advantage of me. Well, now I've gotten what I needed from you, so we're even."

Siena glanced at the bag of cash sitting at her feet. *Thank you, Jonathan, for confirming my theory. Excuse me for hanging up on you, but I need to get out to Irene Kramer's facility and gather the evidence—*

"Matthew?" Something about the skepticism in Jonathan's voice stopped Siena cold. "Your lack of response makes me question whether I'm speaking to Matthew…or if it's you, Siena, on the other end of this call."

Siena did a slow rise from the chair. The last time she'd been this unnerved, this *trapped*, was the morning Jonathan tossed the forgeries of the Somerset Necklace and Singing Bird Pistols into her suitcase and disclosed that he'd been aware of the con she was playing on him all along. Siena didn't appreciate being played for a fool twice.

"Your intuition serves you well, Jonathan," Siena said matter-of-factly.

"Siena." No one had ever sullied her name with such disappointment. "Sweetheart, what are you doing?"

"What am I doing? Why don't you ask the investigators you hired to trail me around Manhattan this week. I'm sure they can give you a full report. Oh, and by the way, I found your bag of cash in Matthew's apartment, so I now know the reason *you* came to New York earlier this week."

Jonathan took a moment to respond. "Siena, I don't know what you *think* you know or what you're accusing me of, but you need to come home. Now. We need to talk."

God, how I hate when he speaks to me in that superior tone, as if I were a child.

"You're right, Jonathan. You and I have a lot to talk about. I will be home, but first I need to take care of some unfinished business." She ended the call without saying goodbye.

Siena zippered the travel bag, shoved it back into the

cubbyhole, and clicked the panel door closed. She dared not leave any trace of her intrusion for Matthew to discover when he returned to the apartment. Grabbing her purse and her cape, she scurried out of the residence and rode the elevator to the seventh floor.

****

Joanie Osgood was holding Siena's cell phone in her hand when she flung open her apartment door. "Why, Siena dear, where have you been? Jonathan called a while ago to say you were coming back for your phone. Here, I found it in the powder room just where you left it. Do you want to come in? Gaylor and I are about to have lunch. You're welcome to join us."

Siena's grip tightened around the straps of her shoulder bag as she tossed in her cell phone. *Jonathan called Joanie? The nerve! What was he doing, following up to make sure I'd truly forgotten my phone in the Osgoods' apartment? That I wasn't making an excuse to stay in the building so I could rendezvous with another of the residents? Like Matthew Kramer, for instance.*

Siena kept her voice even so as not to betray her mounting anger. "Sorry if I kept you waiting. Someone I used to work with got into the elevator on one of the lower floors and we got to talking and, well, you know how it is."

"How coincidental! I know everyone who lives in the building. Who is she? Or he? I supposed I shouldn't presume your friend is a woman."

"Oh, she's not a resident. She was here visiting someone, but she didn't say who."

"Well, how nice that you had a chance to catch up. Anyway, would you like to join us for lunch?"

"Thank you, Joanie. I'd love to, but I have several

things I need to take care of before the day gets away from me."

"Then we'll plan for lunch the next time you're in town. I do so enjoy your company."

"Yes, absolutely. Please say good-bye to Gaylor again for me." Stepping through the doorway, Siena pretended a thought had right that second sprung into her head. "Oh, I meant to ask earlier when we were talking about the frat brothers' nicknames but then the conversation turned around and, well, anyway, I remember Jonathan mentioning someone named Mack. Was he one of the fraternity brothers?"

Joanie appeared to be taken aback. "Really?" she asked, her voice skeptical. "Jonathan was talking to you about Matthew?"

Siena's left eye twitched. Which was worse—having confirmation that Mack and Matthew were the same person or discovering that Jonathan had purposely hidden "Mack's" identity from her? Her day was going downhill faster than a thunderous avalanche.

"Matthew?" Siena asked, her eyes wide with faked innocence. "Isn't he the man who lives in the apartment upstairs?"

"Yes. You see, there were two Matthews in the fraternity. To eliminate confusion, Matthew Burton was nicknamed *Ballsy*. Don't ask why. Trust me, you're better off not knowing. The other Matthew, Matthew Kramer—now he's the man who lives here in this building—was nicknamed Mack because his initials are MAK. If I'm not mistaken, his middle name is Allen." Joanie cocked her head. "As I said before, Jonathan and Matthew haven't spoken in years. Well, at least not as far as I know. I'm surprised Jonathan would mention

Matthew Kramer to you at all, and I'm especially surprised that he'd refer to him as *Mack*. The fellows only use those nicknames these days as a sort of term of endearment."

Or when one of them doesn't want his clueless wife to know who he's traveling to New York to meet, and to whom he's handing over a bag stuffed with half a million dollars in cash.

Chapter 39

Siena

Lou steered his car onto the Long Island Expressway exit ramp. "You've been awfully quiet. Is everything okay?"

No.

"Everything's fine. I just have a lot to think about."

Such as, why my loving and adoring husband is playing head games with me. Again. Everything that's happened in the last two weeks is too reminiscent of the way Jonathan tricked me when I attempted to steal his and Patrick's Singing Bird Pistols. Did he honestly think his smooth savvy and dazzling charm would blindside me a second time?

"Sorry. I don't mean to bug you, but which way am I going?"

Siena consulted her phone for directions. "At the next traffic light, turn right. The facility is about five miles south of here."

"Got it." He checked over his shoulder for traffic before changing lanes.

How could I have been so naive when the clues were there all along—Jonathan's subtle innuendos, his accusatory stares, his appearing out of nowhere at the most inopportune times. If only I'd figured this out sooner, I would have been on the lookout for his investigators. Wouldn't they have been stunned if I'd strolled right up to them and said, "Excuse me. I couldn't help but notice that you've been following me. May I ask why?"

Lou glanced over at her. "How long do you think you'll be in there?"

"A few minutes at most." Siena stared out the passenger window at the scenery. "Just long enough to confirm one of my suspicions."

"Then we're heading back to Boston?" Lou flipped on his turn signal and made the righthand turn.

"Yes. After this stop, we're going home." Having no reason to remain in Manhattan any longer, Siena cancelled her charter flight home in favor of driving back to Boston a day earlier with Lou. "Stay in the left lane. You'll see the sign for the drive leading into Elmwood as we get closer."

"What about everybody else? Gus and Marielle? Your sister?"

"They've gone home as well. They all flew out this morning."

Siena's stomach knotted every time she thought of her last conversations with Gus and Jacqueline. She needed to speak with them, to apologize and ask what she could do to make things right, but without his phone she had no way of getting in touch with Gus and all the calls she'd made to Jac that morning had gone straight to voice mail, which was understandable. Jac's phone was set on airplane mode, or at least that was the assumption Siena preferred over the alternative—that Jac was intentionally ignoring her. Then again, perhaps not speaking with Gus and Jac for a few days was a good thing. Maybe they all needed to step back from the week's unforeseen outcome and take a breath.

"What about that Kramer guy you had me tailing? He sure seemed to have disappeared all of a sudden."

Siena raised an eyebrow. "That's one way of putting it."

Lou braked for a stop light. Angling his upper body toward Siena, he placed his right hand on the top of her headrest. "So, what's up with you?"

Siena gave Lou a sideways glance. "What do you mean?"

"These short responses. Your sullen mood. Seems like that fire you were caught in last night knocked the wind out of you."

Siena shrugged her shoulder. "I don't know."

The light changed. With both hands back on the steering wheel, Lou guided the car forward. "We've got a long ride back to Boston. If you want to talk about what's bothering you, I'm all ears."

No way! The last person I'd even dream of unburdening my soul to is you.

"Do you see the sign for Elmwood Assisted Living Center? Right after this strip mall?"

"Yep. And, conveniently, there's a gas station on the next corner. I'll stop there to fill up before we get on the road."

Lou made the left turn and navigated the car along the short driveway that led to Elmwood's main entrance. This being the middle of a Thursday afternoon, he had no trouble finding a parking space close to the front door.

"Like I said," Siena told him while unbuckling her seat belt, "I should only be a few minutes."

"Take your time." Lou switched off the car's engine and, closing his eyes, reclined his seat. "This is still part of my billable hours, and I got nowhere else to be."

Thanks for the reminder of how much this fruitless escapade is costing me.

Siena strolled into Elmwood's lobby on a gamble. To save time, she hadn't donned the disguise she'd worn to the facility yesterday but instead took the chance that someone other than Sheila would be manning the front desk. When a younger woman with bright red hair glanced up from the novel she was reading and greeted her, Siena interpreted her luck as a good omen.

"Hello," the receptionist said. "Are you here to visit one of our residents?"

"Well, not quite," Siena replied with a smile and a shake of her head. "You see, I was here yesterday to visit Irene Kramer, and I'm pretty sure I left my jacket in her apartment. I'm just going to bop in for a second to say hello and get my jacket."

Siena was also rolling the dice on a comment the nurses' aides mentioned while they were both in Irene's apartment yesterday. The residents, the aide had said, would be leaving the facility today for an afternoon of lunch and shopping. The aide indicated that Irene typically participated in this weekly excursion.

"Gosh, I wish I could let you go through," the receptionist said as she perused a print-out of names attached to a clipboard, "but I think Irene's...oh, yep, there's her name." She raised her head and gazed at Siena with apologetic eyes. "Sorry, but Irene has gone out and won't be back until later this afternoon. Our policy is to not allow visitors into the residents' apartments when they're away."

So far, my luck is holding out.

Siena faked a wince. "Well, darn. That's the

warmest jacket I have and with the weather turning colder this weekend, I could really use it. I don't know where else it could be. I've looked everywhere."

"Tell you what. Why don't you describe what your jacket looks like, and I'll check Irene's apartment for you."

And my good fortune continues.

"Oh, my gosh! Would you please? You have no idea how much I appreciate you doing that for me. So," Siena gazed at the ceiling as she conjured up a description, "it's a short, black zip-up jacket. Wool, not leather. Oh, and it has gold buttons on the sleeves."

The receptionist rose from her chair. "That should be easy enough to find. Have a seat and I'll go take a look." She slid the guest sign-in book forward on the countertop. "If you wouldn't mind doing me a favor in return, while I'm gone can you please remind anyone who comes in to sign our visitor book?"

"Will do." Siena plopped down on an upholstered chair in the waiting area. "Again, thank you so much."

"Sure, no problem. I'll be right back."

Siena waited until the woman had disappeared down the hall before springing off the chair and scurrying back to the reception counter. Starting with the current day, she flipped the pages of the sign-in book backwards through the week. As her fingers coursed down the columns of names in search of Jonathan's familiar signature, she formed an image in her mind of Jonathan turning on the charm as he sat beside Irene on the sofa in her apartment. Had Irene remembered Jonathan as one of her son's college friends and willingly relinquished Matthew's camera to him, or had Jonathan flashed Irene that disarming smile of his and sweet-talked the camera out of her gnarled grasp?

Having flipped back several pages without finding Jonathan's name written in the book, Siena was beginning to have doubts. Had the stress she'd been under the last several days taken its toll? Her insistence that Jonathan had been conspiring behind her back and intentionally setting her up for a fall was proving to be nothing but a paranoid notion she'd allowed to run rampant in her imagination.

Siena raised her head and stared blankly at the wall behind the reception desk. Why hadn't she talked sense into herself *before* blurting out those baseless accusations she'd hurled at Jonathan over the phone? A heaviness weighed on her chest. She had an urgent desire to return home as quickly as Lou could get her there. She needed to apologize to Jonathan for her rash behavior and share with him every detail of what she'd been through over the last two weeks. Jonathan would understand. After all, he'd begged her to come home. He'd said they needed to talk.

Suddenly, a truly disturbing thought niggled its way forward. If Jonathan hadn't taken the video from Irene Kramer, who among her other visitors had? And what were they planning to do with it?

Siena lowered her head and resumed her search. Halfway down Tuesday's page of signatures, her index finger came to an abrupt halt. Two people had signed in that afternoon as Irene Kramer's visitors. The first name was Olivia Eden-Timms, Alva Kramer's daughter and only child. The second name, the person who'd signed the guest book as having arrived and departed at the same time as Olivia, was Veronica Lambert.

The heat of anger crept up Siena's neck as she

thudded her index finger against Jonathan's daughter's signature.

Sonofabitch.

Chapter 40

Siena

"Hello, Siena. I wondered when you'd get around to calling."

A gust of brisk autumn wind whipped a strand of Siena's hair across her face. She shivered and wrapped her cape tighter around her thin frame. Edging closer to the perimeter of the service station's parking lot, she lowered her head and pondered which, out of all the questions rambling around in her mind, she needed the answer to first.

"Veronica, what did you do with the camera you took from Irene Kramer's apartment?"

"So, you finally tracked it down. You know, I assumed a woman with your level of expertise would have gotten to that camera long before Olivia and I did."

"What do you mean, a woman with my level of expertise?"

Veronica let out a sarcastic grunt. "Huh! Don't even try to play dumb with me, Siena. It took a while, but I finally found out exactly who you are and what you used to be."

Siena raised an eyebrow. Under normal circumstances, this bombshell would have devastated her. Tonight, however, matters of much greater importance demanded her attention. Still, the question begged to be asked.

"Okay, let's hear it. What did you find out? What *exactly* did I used to be?"

"Oh, there are so many terms I could use to describe the kind of person you were when you lived in Manhattan. A lowlife criminal. A conniving thief. A shrewd con artist. Which do you prefer to be called, Siena?"

Chuckling to herself, Siena shook her head. "Sticks and stones, Veronica. I'm not that person any longer, so I honestly don't care. But I've *got* to know—since you're so good at manipulating your Daddy into giving you everything your heart desires, what did you do? Pester Jonathan during your weekly father-daughter dinners until he caved in and told you every detail about me and my tarnished past?"

"Don't you dare drag my father into this conversation!" Siena sensed Veronica's blood boiling on the other end of the line, a small victory that made her stand a little taller. "Daddy, FYI, hasn't told me a thing about you. Lou Biondi, on the other hand…" Veronica's voice assumed an unmistakable tone of self-delight, as if she were this close to taunting Siena with, *I know something you don't know*. "Well, it's amazing what five thousand dollars will buy you."

Siena's head jerked sideways, her eyes darting toward the filling station. Lou was leaning against his car's back bumper as the nozzle hose pumped fuel into its gas tank. He grinned and gave her a wave of his hand. Siena glared back. Of all the private investigators who would have welcomed her business, why the hell had she placed her trust in Lou Biondi?

Siena drew in a deep breath and moved on. She'd

deal with Lou later. "Next question—How did you find out about the camera in the first place?"

Veronica snickered. "Now, that bit of luck was pure coincidence. You didn't know this, but I needed to drop off some paperwork at Daddy's house—oops, forgive me, at *your* house—the morning after your wedding celebration and I overheard you talking with Matthew Kramer in the great room as I was leaving. Well, my curiosity got the better of me. I mean, who could pass up the chance to eavesdrop on such a provocative confrontation? While you lured Matthew onto the terrace to have what you assumed would be an intimate *tête-à-tête*, I snuck into the first-floor bedroom and cracked open the adjacent bathroom window just wide enough to listen in on your conversation."

"Let me guess," Siena interrupted. "Rather than keeping such a private matter to yourself, you couldn't wait to share that scandalous gossip with Jonathan."

"O-o-o-oh, is that what you think? Oh, no, no, no. I never breathed a word of what I'd overheard to Daddy, although I'm sure he would love to have been there to witness for himself how masterfully you handled Matthew. Just how did you cultivate that badass swagger of yours, Siena?" Veronica tittered. "That was a silly question, wasn't it? I imagine you had a lot of practice standing up to overbearing men in your former line of business. And I'm *not* referring to your job at Willow's."

"Get to the point, Veronica."

"Fine," Veronica said with a tsk. "Anyway, for a few seconds I did consider driving straight home and forcing myself to forget everything I'd overheard. But I simply couldn't in good conscience not phone Olivia immediately from my car and share my news with her. I knew she'd be positively livid when she learned Matthew was attempting to blackmail you."

"You're talking about Olivia Eden-Timms, Matthew's former stepdaughter?"

"Well, yes, I suppose that is how she's related to Matthew, although I think of her strictly as Alva Paulson's daughter."

"And your relationship with Olivia is…?"

"Has Daddy never told you? Olivia and I have been best friends since birth. In fact, we were born just two days apart. We grew up together and were even roommates at prep school and college. Olivia detested Matthew from the moment he tricked her mother into marrying him. She could see what Alva couldn't, that Matthew didn't love Alva. He was only interested in his own financial gain. Olivia was thrilled when her mother discovered what a two-timing loser Matthew was and divorced him. Isn't it coincidental that we have *you* to thank for their breakup? Anyway, since Alva's death, Olivia has taken advantage of any situation that presents itself to seek revenge on her mother's behalf."

Siena frowned. "So, by confiscating the video he has of me, Olivia would be getting back at Matthew…how?"

"Siena," Veronica said in that condescending tone Siena abhorred, "are you seriously that naive? Matthew's world is collapsing. Without those millions he's trying to squeeze out of you, he'll be penniless." Veronica breathed an exasperated sigh. "Oh, I'm sorry. I often forget you're an outsider and don't know him as well as we do. But you must have realized by now that Matthew Kramer is a compulsive liar. He loves to give the impression that he's ultra wealthy and that he owns the apartment he lives in at the Hudson, but the truth is the apartment belongs to Olivia. Matthew only lives there because Alva had an enormously soft heart. That and the fact that the apartment held too many bad memories for her, and she couldn't wait to be rid of it.

"As part of their divorce settlement, and against Olivia's wishes, Alva agreed to let Matthew stay in the apartment rent-free for five years during which time he had the option to either buy the place or move. That deadline passed a while ago. Matthew wants to stay in the apartment for obvious reasons, but he keeps stalling, keeps telling Olivia he needs more time to secure a loan. I mean, honestly! What lender will extend credit to a man who's flat broke and has neither the funds to front the loan nor sufficient income to pay down the mortgage? So, you see, Olivia will do anything to ensure Matthew remains insolvent, including confiscating his reason for blackmailing you out of five million dollars."

"What about his income from the brokerage company he owns?" Siena knew better. From the first night she met Matthew she presumed his business wasn't nearly as successful as he let on. She merely wanted Veronica to confirm her suspicion.

"Ohmygod, Siena! Are you serious?" Veronica loved to gossip, even when she was sharing her drivel with the person who she spent most of her time backstabbing. "His business is about to go under. I'll let you in on a secret if you promise to keep it to yourself. Earlier this year, Olivia got wind that Matthew has been embezzling his client's accounts so, in a roundabout way, she notified the FBI. The company's been under investigation, and we expect they'll raid his office any day now. Olivia can't wait."

Siena kicked a stone into the grass. *And I thought I*

had a lethal vengeful streak. Olivia Eden-Timms was clearly a woman with a long arm and endless resources. Before now, Siena had tossed around the possibility that either Eddie Davis or the men in Influencer Girlfriend's family had something to do with Matthew's disappearance. With this latest revelation, the notion struck Siena that Olivia, if not one of the clients from whom Matthew had been skimming funds, should be at the top of her list of suspects. "Veronica, are you aware that Matthew hasn't been seen or heard from in the last two days?"

Siena anticipated a response that would shed light onto what might have become of Matthew. Instead, Veronica abruptly changed the subject, giving Siena the strong impression she was purposely nixing any further discussion regarding Matthew's disappearance.

"To answer your initial question," Veronica said, "I left the camera on the desk in Daddy's library."

Siena's heart leapt into her throat. "When?"

"About an hour ago. Don't worry. No one was in the house to get their hands on it. Both Brenda and Anita had already gone home for the day."

"What about Jonathan?"

"He went straight from the airport to his board meeting after which he has plans for an early dinner at the club. So, Siena, it's a race as to who gets home and finds the camera first, you or Daddy."

"You surprise me, Veronica. Since you eavesdropped through the bathroom window, you must have a good idea of what's on that video. I would think you'd want to place the camera in your father's hands and personally hit the play button for him yourself. Make sure Jonathan got an eyeful of the kind of sordid deeds I performed when I was *the person I used to be*. Isn't this what you've been waiting for—the perfect reason to get rid of me so you can once again have Jonathan all to yourself?"

Veronica was silent for so long, Siena checked her phone to make sure the call hadn't been dropped. "I'll be honest, Siena. Until a few weeks ago, I would have wanted nothing more than to have you permanently removed from our lives. But on the night of your party, I recognized for the first time how Daddy's eyes sparkle when he looks at you and the way your face glows when he touches you. My mother used to gaze at Daddy that way." Siena could have sworn Veronica's voice cracked. As hard as it was to believe, the witch might have a heart after all. Veronica cleared her throat and continued. "So, although I hate to admit it, you two truly do love each other."

Siena uttered three words she never imagined she'd have the occasion to say. "Thank you, Veronica."

"I suggest you get home the fastest way possible. If Daddy beats you there and finds that camera before you do, I claim no responsibility for what might happen. You made this mess, Siena. You deal with the consequences."

Siena glanced at the time. If she got to the airport in the next thirty minutes and chartered a plane, she had a solid chance of beating Jonathan to their front door.

"I have one last question. Did you and Olivia watch the video?"

"Ohmygod! Why would either of us watch what amounts to a porn film starring Matthew Kramer?" Veronica made a guttural sound that expressed her disgust. "Now, if you're really asking if Olivia watched the portion in which you were caught on camera stealing her mother's jewelry, you don't need to worry. Olivia doesn't care about what you did that day or why you did it. She's just happy your scheme brought an end to Alva and Matthew's marriage."

Siena could only hope that Jonathan would be as forgiving.

****

Siena stomped across the parking lot, her face flushed with anger. "What the hell, Lou?" she spat out. "Do you not know the meaning of 'conflict of interest?' Because I'm pretty sure I read a clause pertaining to client confidentiality before I signed your contract."

"I'm lost." Lou screwed on the cap to his car's gas tank and flipped the cover door closed. "Where is this coming from?"

"From the call I just had with Veronica Lambert."

Lou rolled his eyes. "Ah, shit." He rotated his head, first to the right then to the left, as if wanting to kick himself for trusting that Veronica and her loose lips were capable of keeping a secret.

Siena waved her hand at the car. "Open the trunk."

"Wait." Lou took a hesitant step toward her. "At least give me a chance to explain."

"Nope. Don't want to hear it. Open the trunk so I can get my suitcase. The driver I ordered will be here any minute."

"I thought we were driving back to Boston together. Why are you wasting your money on another driver?"

Siena thrust her fists onto her hips. "Don't you get it? You and I are done. Now, in case you didn't hear me the first two times, *open this goddamn trunk!*"

Lou rounded the back fender and stood face-to-face with Siena. "We're done? What does that mean?"

Siena folded her arms across her chest and let out a short, sarcastic laugh. "You can't possibly be that stupid. Oh, wait! I forgot who I'm talking to—the man I hired to perform a confidential service who then turned around and disclosed what service he was providing to an uninvolved third party. Which, since you don't seem to understand, is the very definition of 'conflict of interest.' So, what *we're done* means is this—you're not getting a dime more out of me than the amount I've already paid. And, if you have an issue with that, you can take me to small claims court. I'm pretty sure the judge will rule in my favor."

"Listen," Lou said, standing his ground, "I wasn't lying when I told you I hadn't contacted Veronica Lambert in over a year."

"Is that so? Then how did she know why I came to Manhattan and what I was after?"

"Because that other lady, Veronica's friend, hired her own P.I. to follow Kramer. He noticed that I seemed to be everywhere he was, and he got suspicious."

Siena's jaw dropped. "But you didn't pick up on *him* being everywhere *you* were?"

"Well," Smartass Lou replied with sarcasm, "I guess I didn't. Anyway, he snapped a photo of me and showed it to Veronica's friend who showed it to Veronica who recognized me. So, I didn't contact Veronica. *She* called *me* and…asked a few questions."

Siena's eyes narrowed. "Like what?"

"Like what I was doing hanging around Matthew Kramer's apartment building. To which I answered it was none of her business. To which she said she didn't care. What I was doing in New York didn't matter to her anyway." Convinced he'd only given her half the story,

Siena waited patiently for him to cough up the rest. Cowering under her glare, Lou took a deep breath and continued. "Then she asked me what I knew about you. What you were involved in when you lived in Manhattan. You know, before you hooked up with her father."

Again, Siena remained silent while she waited for Lou to continue. "I told her I didn't know anything." Siena raised her chin and one eyebrow. Lou fidgeted and glanced away. "So, then Veronica said she didn't believe me. She remembered the accusations I'd thrown out about you the night you and I tried to steal that painting from her brother's house. When I shut my trap tighter, she threw some money at me."

Siena scowled. "Jesus, Lou."

"Hey," Lou said in self-defense, "business has been slow lately and the bills are piling up. I needed the money. So, I told her what I found out about you which isn't much, basically assumptions I've made based on stuff I've observed and overheard and the information I dug up about that antique store I followed you going to last year in the Bronx." Lou hesitated and glanced away. "Then she offered me even more money." He lowered his head. "So, I told her why you hired me and what I've been helping you with in New York."

Siena shook her head and glowered at Lou. "If I thought it was worth my time, I'd sue your ass off." A sedan matching the description of the model Siena was expecting drove into the parking lot. She waved her hand and caught the driver's attention. "Here's my car. Now, open this trunk so I can get my bag."

Lou, his face a mixture of dejection and just plain pissed off, popped the lid and yanked out her suitcase. "I don't know what else to say except—I'm sorry."

Siena grasped the luggage handle and headed toward the idling sedan. "Yeah, well, considering our previous experience, I should have thought a lot harder before hiring you in the first place."

Chapter 41

Siena

The afternoon sun was beginning to dip behind the treetops as the driver eased her car into the Woodwards' circular drive. From her position in the back seat, Siena craned her neck and glimpsed out the windows. Jonathan's sedan was nowhere in sight which, although a good sign, was no guarantee that he hadn't arrived home before her and parked his car in one of the garage bays, believing he was settled in for the night. Or that, while pouring himself a glass of Chardonnay, he hadn't received a call from Veronica who, deciding she'd made a huge mistake by giving Siena the advantage, warned Daddy of the "gift" she left him on his antique mahogany desk. Or that Jonathan wasn't right now in his library, camera in hand, playing back the images of the regrettable deeds Siena had performed one fateful afternoon in what seemed like a lifetime ago.

The driver brought the car to a stop and shifted into *Park*. "That credit machine's been running slow today," she said, glancing over her shoulder at Siena. "I hope you don't have a problem."

"It's fine." Siena had already slipped her card into the mobile device, added a tip, and was gnawing on her lower lip while waiting for the payment to be processed.

"Great. While you're doing that, I'll get your bag."

Siena tapped her fingers against the machine. *Come on, come on, come ON! You're wasting my time. Process the damned payment!* When the ding sounded, Siena yanked her card from the slot a split second before the screen instructed her to do so. Grabbing her shoulder bag, she swung open the back door and scrambled out of the car.

"Thanks," she said as the driver handed off her suitcase.

"Thank *you*. Have a good evening."

Fat chance of that happening.

"You, too," Siena said, barely managing a smile.

Siena climbed the two fieldstone steps and stood under her home's porticoed entryway as the electric vehicle hummed out of the drive behind her. During her chartered flight home, she had prepared herself for the confrontation with Jonathan that would undoubtedly take place before the evening ended. In the aftermath of the unfounded allegations she'd slung at him over the phone, he was bound to have a lot of questions. And Siena had a lot of explaining to do.

Sucking in a deep breath, she unlocked and opened the front door.

The faint strains of a Mozart sonata greeted Siena as she entered the foyer. Jonathan was in the den lost in his daily therapeutic hour of music and meditation. He had arrived home before her, but the question weighing on Siena's mind was whether he'd gone straight to the den and his piano or if he made a stop in their library first. As she wheeled her suitcase across the threshold and closed the front door behind her, she noticed Jonathan had tossed his coat and attaché onto the hall bench at the foot of the stairs. Chances were, he hadn't yet gone into the library to plug in his laptop for a recharge. All hope was not lost. Not yet anyway.

The lilting melody abruptly ended, pitching the house into an unnerving silence. Siena dropped her shoulder bag on the floor beside her suitcase and shrugged off her cape. Night was falling and, as she hastened down the hall, the deepening shadows seemed to drape around her like a burial shroud. A shiver rocked her shoulders as she approached the library. What fate awaited her behind its closed door?

With a twist of the knob, she thrust the paneled door open and flipped the light switch. The wall sconces at once flooded the room with their warm glow. Siena's eyes shot straight to the desktop where she found the camera, exactly as Veronica had promised.

Or—Siena was stricken out of the blue with this alarming possibility—was the camera a decoy? Matthew, with his penchant for toying with her, may have removed the memory card and left nothing more than an empty case in his mother's care. Her anger spiked as she pictured Matthew proudly patting himself on the back for inventing such a cunning maneuver.

She rushed to the desk and snatched up the camera. On its underside, Siena found the tiny compartment where, she confirmed with a sigh of relief, the SD card was snugly inserted. She pressed the power button. The screen came to life with a frozen image of the Kramers' bedroom. She hit the *Play* button and, a second later, viewed herself sauntering across the bedroom while off-screen Matthew's voice rang out with, *"Babe, you look so damned hot in red silk."*

Siena smiled from ear to ear. *Yes! I got it!* Reveling in her victory, she didn't notice that Jonathan had entered the room and was standing in the doorway behind her.

"I see you decided to come home tonight after all," he said, his tone more acerbic than welcoming.

Siena's gasp was loud enough to be embarrassing. She quickly switched off the camera and concealed her hands behind her back as she spun around and faced him. "Jonathan, hi!" She attempted to play it cool even as her heart was pounding out of her chest. "I didn't think you'd heard me come in."

Jonathan stepped closer. "I hadn't, but the app on my phone sent an alert that the front door had been opened. When I found your bags sitting in the foyer, I knew you were in the house somewhere."

Ah, yes, the app. Damn that new security system.

"I thought you were having dinner at the club." Siena longed for his welcome home hugs and kisses. Normally, Jonathan would have enveloped her in his arms and slinked his hand underneath her sweater by now.

"That was my intent, but I changed my mind. After our phone conversation, I was hoping you'd decide to come home tonight, and I wanted to be here when you arrived." Jonathan's brow wrinkled. He glanced away, as if her comment had just sunken in and given him pause. His eyes shifted back to Siena. "How did you know about my dinner plans?"

Oops!

"Veronica told me."

"*You* spoke with Veronica? When?"

"This afternoon. I called her with a question I knew she'd be able to answer. Your dinner plans somehow came up in the conversation."

Half the truth is better than none, right?

"I see." Jonathan's eyes narrowed. "Siena, what are you hiding behind your back?"

So much for trying to be discreet, and for being foolish enough to hope Jonathan hadn't picked up the voices in the video playback as clearly as she had. Still, he couldn't have overheard much, and Siena refused to relinquish for naught all the effort and time and money she'd poured into finding and destroying the video before Jonathan discovered it even existed. She brought her arm forward, held out her hand, and opened her fist.

"Only this old digital camera I found when I was cleaning out my apartment." Yet another lie, but a necessary one. "I can't believe I still have it."

Jonathan glanced at the camera. His lips tightened and his jaw clenched. "Then explain why I heard Matthew Kramer's voice on the video you were playing just now."

Siena opened her mouth to respond. However, no contrived yet reasonable explanation was forthcoming. Her brain and her conscience were locked in a battle. The latter was urging her to come clean and tell Jonathan everything while the former was spewing out justifications to continue the charade.

Jonathan chastised Siena as if she were one of his grad students feeding him a bogus reason for cancelling that morning's Intro to American Lit class. "You and I both know that camera didn't come from your apartment, Siena. As I said on the phone, we need to talk."

He was standing close—too close—and Siena didn't like being made to feel as though she were caged in. She wanted to cross the room, put some distance between them, but she didn't trust her unsteady legs to take her there. Instead, she rested her hip on the edge of the desk and stole a moment to regain her bravado. "Okay," she said, going on the offensive. "Go ahead. Talk."

Jonathan massaged the back of his neck as he ambled toward the wall of built-in bookshelves. "Your recent behavior has me so befuddled, I'm not sure where to begin." He swiveled around to face Siena. "First, I'd like to know what you were doing in New York." He raised his hand to stop her before she spoke. "I know your story was that you and Jacqueline were gown shopping for her wedding. What I want to know is what you were *really* doing in New York, and how your escapades led to you being on the other end of the phone call I made to Matthew Kramer this afternoon."

Siena sneered. "Oh, come on, Jonathan. Don't pretend you don't have a written report of every move I made while I was in Manhattan. How else would you have known it was me who answered Matthew's cell phone?"

"This is the second time you've thrown that accusation at me," Jonathan said, resting his hands on his hips, "and I still don't know what you're talking about."

Siena rolled her eyes. Did he honestly expect his dumb act to work on her? "The private investigation firm you used to vet me last year. I know you hired them to follow me while I was in Manhattan."

A deep crease formed between Jonathan's brows. "What makes you think I was having you followed?"

"I can read between the lines, Jonathan." Siena's voice rose a notch as she leaned forward. "How many times did you ask if I had something I wanted to tell you? How often did you refer to the 'business' I was tending to in New York? And when I answered, you glared at me as if you knew I were lying."

"Were you?"

"No," she reluctantly admitted, "I wasn't lying. I just wasn't giving you the whole story."

"Huh," Jonathan grunted. "I'm not sure I see the difference."

"Regardless, that wasn't my only clue." Siena's adrenaline kicked in as she paced the floor. "You showed up yesterday at Max's Deli, *unannounced*, a blatant move on your part to throw a wrench into my plans. So, what did I do? I spontaneously purchased tickets to a basketball game for *only* you and Tyler when you, just moments before, had suggested we all attend a Broadway show together. Did you not think that was odd, or did someone give you a heads-up that I needed you out of my hair for the next few hours? Or maybe you'd read about my plans in the report your investigators provided to you."

Interlocking his fingers behind his head and lifting his face to the ceiling, Jonathan crossed to the opposite side of the room. "Siena," he said through gritted teeth, "stop insisting that I paid someone to follow you." Lowering his arms, he turned to face her. "Sorry to disappoint you, but I'm not in the habit of hiring my investigators to track your every move. However, since you seem so awfully worried that I *was* having you followed, I'm beginning to think that perhaps my trust in you is misplaced. And that leads me back to my original question—What were you doing in New York, Siena?"

Jonathan's exasperation and the disenchantment in his eyes finally shook Siena out of her delusion. What a fool she'd been the past two weeks, reading imaginary insinuations into their conversations, inventing doubts that didn't exist. But then, when you've told as many tall tales as she had, you tend to assume others are responding in kind. Siena recalled the sentiment she'd shared with Gus during their visit to Santa Martina, that she was failing miserably at her marriage. If ever she needed to unburden her soul and regain Jonathan's faith in her, that time was now.

"Okay," she said, fastening her eyes on Jonathan's. "The truth is, I did go to Manhattan to shop for gowns with Jacqueline, but I also took advantage of being in the city to meet with Matthew Kramer." She imagined that making this admission would be a cleansing experience, but the truth left a sour taste in her mouth. As a con artist, her unwavering guile had been the key to her success, but Jonathan had proved to be her kryptonite. She was no longer on top of her game, and Siena Ricci wasn't accustomed to being a loser.

"All right." Jonathan shrugged his shoulder. "Why?"

"Why do you think?" His interrogation was beginning to annoy her. Siena grabbed the camera from the desktop and held it up, as though presenting Exhibit A to a trial judge. "To get this."

"I see."

Dammit! Why doesn't Jonathan ever lose his temper? Doesn't even my planning a clandestine meeting with his detested fraternity brother get under his skin?

"Aren't you the least bit curious about how I know Matthew, the one fraternity brother you've not only never introduced me to, but whose name you've never even uttered in my presence?" Jonathan didn't need words to reply. Siena read the answer in his eyes. "Jesus! You've known all along, haven't you?" She held out the camera in her clenched hand. "You recognized me from the pieces of this video Mathew sent in those group texts."

Jonathan raised his eyebrows. "How could I *not* know that was you in those videos? Do you think I haven't memorized the way you move, the tone of your voice, every curve of your body? While all the others were speculating about who Matthew's mystery woman might be, I didn't need to see your face to identify you. Besides, that video confirmed what I've known in my heart since the day you dropped your Marie Lacroix act and confessed to being a criminal—that you were indeed the *other woman* who served as the catalyst for Matthew and Alva's divorce."

"What?" Siena choked on the question. "How—?"

"Isn't it obvious? Matthew has been whining for years about the woman who ruined his marriage and helped herself to Alva's jewelry. So, when you attempted to pull a scam on me, I compared Matthew's experience to my own. The similarities, I'm sad to say, were uncanny."

"This may come as a news flash to you, Jonathan, but I wasn't the only con artist working the streets of Manhattan six years ago."

Jonathan nodded his head. "True. But how many of them were in their late-20s and drop-dead gorgeous with long, shapely legs that don't quit and a body a guy can't keep his hands off?"

Good point. Siena turned her head and gazed out the window.

"That, by the way, was Matthew's crude description of you. Not mine." Jonathan inhaled a deep breath and ran his fingers through his hair. "You and I had agreed to keep the specifics of your former life in the past, so even though I had my suspicions I never asked if Matthew had been one of your many victims. To be honest, I didn't want to know. After suffering through Matthew's boasting and the many graphic details he'd shared about their sexual encounters, the last thing I wanted was confirmation that you and the woman Matthew had an extramarital affair with were the same person. I'd all but erased your possible connection to him from my mind—until you sauntered down the staircase wearing Alva's necklace on the evening of our party."

Siena's eyes darted around the room as her brain scrambled to connect the dots. "How could you possibly have known that necklace once belonged to Alva?"

Jonathan's stare had gone cold. "Because, Siena, I'm the person who gave that necklace to Alva in the first place."

Siena could hardly find the breath to blurt out, "What?"

Jonathan lowered himself onto the ottoman by his reading chair and leaned his elbows on his knees. "I never mentioned this to you—I guess the subject was simply never relevant—but Alva's parents and mine were old friends. She and I, being close in age, spent a lot of time together when we were young, and we formed a lifelong friendship. For her fiftieth birthday, I had a jeweler design a necklace that replicated Alva's favorite painting. A piece, I might add, that was painted by my late wife, Patricia, and given to Alva when her daughter, Olivia, was born. Only two days earlier, Patricia and I had welcomed Veronica into the world, and Trish meant the design to symbolize the eternal connection she and Alva, as new mothers, would always have with their daughters."

Siena's eyes glazed over as her mind was transported six years into the past. She may as well have been standing in Alva's living room. "I admired that painting when I noticed it hanging on the living room wall in her apartment at the Hudson. I remember reading the artist's signature but not recognizing the name." The irony made the hair on the back of Siena's neck stand on end.

"No, you wouldn't have. Trish painted for pleasure rather than fame. Still, when you told me Willow's had offered the necklace as part of an estate sale, I wanted to believe you. Many of us frat brothers suspected Matthew was selling off pieces of Alva's jewelry and keeping the profits for himself. I figured he could have put the necklace on consignment at Willow's, and you might have, as you inferred, legitimately purchased it. However, you had a wariness in your voice when I asked about the necklace and, considering your history, I was convinced you'd obtained it illegally. That video provided the proof that, in fact, Matthew gave you the necklace—a gesture that doesn't at all surprise me. He hated that necklace for the simple reason that it was a gift to Alva from me. Alva was so ill by then she probably never noticed it was missing."

The flush rose from Siena's chest and spread to her neck. "You didn't? You watched the video? All of it?"

Jonathan shook his head. "Only the last part starting with you handcuffing Matthew to the bed. And only because Matthew insisted that I get a good look at the repulsive acts the woman I married is capable of performing."

"But...when? When did you see it?"

"This past Tuesday, right after we arrived in New York. While you met Jacqueline at the hotel, I went to Matthew's apartment." Jonathan sighed. "I didn't find it necessary to bother you with this, but Matthew contacted me a few weeks ago and begged me to help him out of yet another dire financial situation. He rarely speaks to me otherwise, but when he's in trouble I seem to be the first person he crawls to for help. He likes to play the 'You were my Big Brother at the fraternity' card when it's to his advantage. Even though he's always managed to pay me back, this time I refused to help. The next day, he began texting pieces of that video. After his third text, I consented to give him the money—I even told him to forget about repaying me—but only if he stopped sending the texts and surrendered all copies of that video to me."

"That's why I found your travel bag filled with money in Matthew's office."

Jonathan nodded. "Yes. In exchange, Matthew deleted the video file from his cell phone and flushed the SD card from his camera down the toilet. Since I don't trust him, I stood over his shoulder and watched as he did both. By then, it was early afternoon and Matthew insisted on treating me to lunch. We were leaving the restaurant and…well, that's when Matthew showed the degenerate side of his personality. He informed me there was a duplicate copy of the video that he had hidden in a secure location outside of his apartment, and he wanted another half million to destroy the copy. After calling him a liar and a few other choice names, I agreed but only if he did so immediately.

"When we returned to the Hudson, Matthew told me to wait in the lobby while he went to his apartment to get his car fob and then we'd drive to the place where he had the video hidden. However, he never returned. At first, I thought he'd skipped out on me, but Matthew wouldn't have done something so rash when he stood to gain another half million dollars. By the next afternoon, I was convinced Matthew had a medical emergency with no one around to help him. I called Joanie, thinking she may have been in touch with him, but she said not to worry. His housekeeper had been in that day, and she would have contacted the building manager if she'd walked in on Matthew's dead body.

"I continued phoning him every few hours, but still no response. So, while I was on my way to the airport this afternoon, I contacted Alva's daughter, Olivia. Since she owns the apartment, and if something tragic did happen, I thought she should be involved. She agreed to go over to the apartment and said she'd get back to me but in the meantime, she asked if I were aware of the blackmail scheme Matthew was running on my wife."

"And that," Siena said, nodding her head, "is how you knew I was the person who answered Matthew's cell phone."

"I'd call it more of an educated guess. So, now that you know why *I* went to New York, can you please answer my question? What were you doing in New York, Siena? And this time, the real story. No half-truths."

Siena drew in a deep breath. "I guess the best place to start is the night of our party. Do you remember, towards the end of the evening, I told you I'd stepped outside for some fresh air?"

"Yes."

"Well, the truth is, I noticed a man glaring at me from the back of the crowd who I could have sworn was

Matthew. One minute he was there and the next he was gone. I searched everywhere for him, including the parking lot, but when I couldn't find him, I figured I'd had too much champagne, that my imagination had gotten carried away. The next morning, however, Matthew showed up on our doorstep."

Beginning with Matthew's blackmail threat, Siena detailed her pursuits over the past several days—from her hiring of Lou Biondi to enlisting Gus's help and being trapped in a house fire with him to her phone call with Veronica earlier that afternoon which prompted her hasty return home. Jonathan remained stoic through it all, giving Siena the latitude to share her account without interruption. When she finished, Jonathan rose from his seat and stood before the bank of windows overlooking the garden. Siena granted him as much time as he needed to process the information she'd dumped on him.

"My God, Siena. You could have died in that fire."

"Yes. I don't need to be reminded of how lucky we were."

Jonathan shook his head as though in disbelief. "Why did you keep all this from me?"

"I didn't want you to know. Not about the money, not about the reason I knew Matthew, and especially," she held up the camera, "not about this video. I'd rather die than let you witness the depths to which I lowered myself, all in the name of *getting the job done*."

The muscles in Jonathan's neck tightened. "I'm not naive, Siena," he said, keeping his back to her. "Since you fell so easily into my bed, I assumed you'd done the same many times over with the men you scammed before me. I could live with your indiscretions because all those men were faceless. But the idea of you having been with

Matthew—"

"Do you understand now why I was trying to stop him? If he disclosed any more of that video, you and all your friends would eventually see my face. I had to prevent your reputation from being ruined. More importantly, I had to stop the damage this video would do to our marriage."

Jonathan spoke to Siena over his shoulder. "And how would destroying the video have made things any better? What was your long-term plan, Siena? That you and Matthew would share this secret behind my back for the rest of our lives? You must have imagined that one day he'd use the seedy relationship you'd had with him against me."

"What would you have preferred? That, one night over dinner, I say, 'Oh, by the way, Jonathan, you should know that I once drugged and handcuffed one of your fraternity brothers to his bed while I stole his wife's jewelry'?"

"If only you'd been honest with me, we could have worked this out together."

"No, Jonathan. I couldn't risk that entire video going out to all your friends."

Jonathan swung around to face her. "Siena, you're not listening to me. It never would have. I know how to handle Matthew. I could have made this whole issue go away."

"No! This wasn't your mess to clean up." The veins in Siena's neck strained against her skin as she struck her palm against her chest with each self-admonition. "I'm the one who ran the con on Matthew. I'm the one who set him up for a fall. I'm the one who didn't think to check his bedroom for a hidden camera lens. If not for me and my rookie mistake, Matthew would have never discovered who I was."

Jonathan drew in a deep breath. "I disagree. Perhaps this incident is part of a bigger issue you and I were destined to face at some point in time."

Siena's heart jumped into her throat. "What are you saying?"

"Are you happy here, Siena? I mean, truly happy?"

"Jonathan, why would you ask me that?" *Dare I confess how irritated I get when he speaks to me as though I've been a naughty child? How I'll scream if he starts one more conversation about starting a family? How my dream of a peaceful life in the suburbs has turned out to be one huge bore?*

"Do you know what I see when I look at you, Siena?"

"No, but please, tell me." Siena folded her arms across her chest and strolled toward the garden windows. "What do you see, Jonathan?"

"I see a woman who's trying to be someone she isn't."

Siena's head snapped around, as though Jonathan had slapped her across the face. "What is that supposed to mean?"

"When you said yes to leaving New York and marrying me, I think you got wrapped up in a fairy tale. While we were in Europe over the summer, you imagined yourself a princess traveling around with her knight in shining armor. To be honest, I had fun playing into that fantasy myself. But once we returned home to the real world, I noticed you growing more disillusioned every day. Getting involved in our quiet community couldn't compete with the excitement of the big city and the danger and intrigue you thrived on in your previous life. So, you can say Matthew was your personal problem to fix all you want, but deep down you know as well as I do that you didn't tell me about your history with Matthew because his blackmail attempt gave you permission to resurrect your old habits. You may not be willing to admit it, but I can see right through your façade. The thrill you get from organizing a scheme is one of the few things that genuinely makes you tick."

Siena gazed out the windows as the last rays of sunlight fell below the horizon. She hated facing the truth, but Jonathan was right. Since moving into his home, she'd been forcing herself to squeeze into a lifestyle that wasn't designed to fit her skin, and she was tired of pretending.

"I'll give you credit, Jonathan. In just a few months, you've gotten to know me better than I know myself."

Jonathan grunted. "Maybe there's a reason you're still holding onto your apartment in Manhattan."

Siena couldn't face him, couldn't show the tears stinging her eyes, couldn't let Jonathan read the admission that was written on her face: *Guilty as charged.*

"You know, from the first day Matthew started texting pieces of that video, I gave you so many opportunities to confide in me—chances you mistook as hints that I was plotting a sinister trick behind your back. Several times I asked if there was something you wanted to tell me, or questioned what you were doing in New York. I so badly wanted you to be honest with me, but each time you skirted the truth. And each time you disappointed me just a little more." Jonathan's voice wavered. He let a moment pass before continuing.

"When I asked you to marry me, I sincerely thought you had changed. I can see now how I've allowed my obsession with you to cloud my judgment."

Jonathan paused, as if giving Siena an opening to convince him that he was wrong about her, that she *was* the woman he fell in love with, that this incident was nothing more than a hiccup every couple faces now and again. But she was done telling fibs. Besides, her throat was so tight she couldn't have spoken if she'd tried. When he sniffled and cleared his throat, Siena lowered her head. If Jonathan were to step in front of her right now and she witnessed the tears she sensed were welling in his eyes, her heart would shatter.

"Our marriage doesn't have a chance of surviving, Siena, if we can't trust each other."

Siena closed her eyes and held her breath. How else could she fight back the tears?

"I need some fresh air," Jonathan said. "I'm going for a drive. Hopefully by the time I return you'll have decided which version of yourself you want to be—the woman who was serious about leaving her past behind or the adrenaline junkie who isn't happy unless she's feeding her addiction."

Jonathan's footsteps grew fainter as he plodded from the library and down the hallway. Siena stood before the windows, unwilling to move and barely able to breathe. She should have gone after him, stopped him, pleaded with him to stay, but she didn't. Like his friend Alva, Jonathan deserved to share his life with someone who was worthy of him. Although Siena loved Jonathan with a passion that permeated every cell of her being, she had to face the fact that the woman Jonathan should spend the rest of his life with wasn't her.

If you truly love him, Siena, you'll let him go.

Glancing down at the camera clasped in her hand, Siena's anger seethed. She stormed out of the library, determined to remove Matthew Kramer from her life forever. Making a brief stop in the foyer, she retrieved Matthew's cell phone from her handbag. She crossed the great room, unlocked the terrace doors, and stepped into the brisk evening air.

With no regard for the darkness and the falling temperature, she rushed through the garden. Her feet gained speed as she sprinted across the damp lawn to the spot where their yard met the lake. With all her strength, she pitched Matthew's cell phone into the air. The camera followed. Both devices plunked, one after the other, into the dark water. Only then, alone and desolate, could Siena drop to her knees, bury her face in her hands, and sob.

****

The driver popped open the hatch of her car and lifted Siena's suitcase into the storage compartment. "Didn't I drop you off at this house something like an hour ago?"

"You did." Siena opened the car door and slid onto the back seat. "Turns out my plans changed."

The driver closed her door and punched their destination into her GPS. "So, we're going to South Station in Boston, right?"

"Yes, and hurry, please. I have just enough time to catch the last train out."

The driver eased the car away from the house and onto the street. "Traffic shouldn't be too bad this time of night, but I can't make any promises."

As the car cruised down the road, Siena gazed out

the back window and committed to memory the image of what she called, until this evening, her forever home. The car wound around the curve in the road and in one split second her home, along with her dreams and desires, vanished. She faced forward in her seat and swiped the tears from her cheeks.

Jonathan. Where had he gone when he left the house? Where was he now? If he were still driving, trying to get as far away from her as possible, he wouldn't have checked his phone when the security app alerted him of the activity taking place at his doorstep. He wouldn't have spied on Siena through the video cam as she climbed into the taxi and drove away.

Or maybe he'd had second thoughts and was rushing home right now to make amends. As the driver steered them onto the main road, Siena ignored the cars passing in the opposite direction. She didn't want to spot Jonathan's sedan and be tempted to tell the driver to turn around.

Siena had packed her suitcase with only those items that belonged to her—some clothing, a few pairs of shoes, and a meager amount of cash. Everything else, everything that had been purchased with Woodward money, she'd left behind. Jonathan had no way of getting in touch with her. She'd left her cell phone, along with her engagement and wedding rings, on his nightstand. By the time Jonathan arranged for his investigators to find her, she'd have taken what she needed from her Manhattan apartment and would be secluded in a location only one other person beside herself knew existed.

Chapter 42

Siena

Siena could have waited until noon when the antique store opened for business, but she was determined to get the next phase of her life rolling as soon as possible. Having blown through most of her savings while hunting down Matthew Kramer, she needed a source of income to replenish her funds. She'd been up since 5:00 pacing the floor, mulling over her options, and overdosing on caffeine. By 8:00, she was en route to the one employer she was certain wouldn't ask her for a comprehensive resume.

With the transfer of the antique store's ownership from Gus to Christopher, Siena expected to find new security installed on the shop's back entrance. When her keys slipped easily into the lock and deadbolt, she was pleasantly surprised. Her hand shook as she rotated the doorknob, the upshot of anxiety and too much coffee. She stepped inside and relocked the door behind her.

Nothing had changed since Siena's last visit. Still the same nearly empty storage room, the same cramped office, the same musty smell of a building nearing its one hundredth birthday. The fluorescent lights were turned on which meant that Christopher, like Gus before him, began his day in the calmer, more productive early hours of the morning. She inhaled the scent of freshly brewed coffee as she descended the staircase to what had been and, in her mind, always would be Gus's basement workshop.

The wooden stairs creaked under the weight of her footsteps. Christopher glanced up from the forgery he was in the process of soldering and removed his safety goggles. "Well, well, well," he said, swiveling his chair in her direction. "Siena Ricci. You're about the last person I ever expected to see walking down that staircase again."

"Good morning, Christopher. How are you?"

"I can't complain. You're looking good, as always. What are you doing here? I thought Gus said you moved to Boston."

"I did. However, things didn't work out for me there, so I'm back."

"Sorry to hear that. About Boston, I mean. So, what can I do for you?"

"I'm eager to get back into the game. Can you use a person with my experience on any of your upcoming jobs?"

"Are you kidding? You're like a godsend! Tell you what—I just brewed a pot of coffee. Pour yourself a cup and have a seat. Let's talk."

Epilogue

The headline caught Siena's eye.

Body of Manhattan Investment Broker Found
by Frederick Wellman, Staff Reporter

Police discovered the body of Manhattan investment broker Matthew Allen Kramer in a Lower East Side alley at approximately 2:00a.m. on Thursday, October 26, 2023. Cause of death is under investigation.

Kramer, 61, was the third ex-husband of deceased socialite Alva Paulson, heiress to Paulson Industries. He was also the owner of Kramer Investments, LLC which is currently under FBI inquiry for fraud and embezzlement.

The incident is being probed by Manhattan Homicide Detectives. Anyone with information regarding the death is asked to call (212) 555-1712.

A word about the author...

Award-winning author Rosemary Kubli was born and raised in Northeast Ohio where she and her husband currently reside. She enjoys travelling, on land to visit family and friends and on sea to any destination a cruise ship will take her. When not creating digital photo books of her adventures or researching her family ancestry, she can be found curled up in her favorite easy chair with her nose in a book or obsessing over the latest binge-worthy TV series. Learn more about Rosemary by visiting her website at www.rosemarykubli.com.